Star Lake Saloon
and
Housekeeping Cottages

STAR LAKE SALOON
&
HOUSEKEEPING COTTAGES

* * * * * * * * * * * * * * * * * * * *

We offer a clean, modern Housekeeping Resort
on Star Lake, part of the beautiful 1000 acre
Celestial Chain of lakes: Sundog Lake, Lake
Sickle Moon, and the Lost Arrow River, with
miles of unsurpassed wilderness shorelines.

Enjoy our rustic beer bar and game room. We
serve hamburgers, pizza and snacks. Special
Weekly Pot Luck Supper on Mondays. Open May
through October for your fishing pleasure:

MUSKY
WALLEYE
SMALL & LARGEMOUTH BASS
CRAPPIE
and those little bait catchers
PERCH   BLUE GILL   SUNFISH

With each cottage we furnish:
* Private Pier
* 1 Aluminum Boat
* Modern Kitchen Facilities
* Cooking and Eating Utensils
* Automatic Gas Heater
* Weber Grill

All the necessary housekeeping items and
fresh bed linens weekly are provided.
Bring your own towels, dish towels and soap.

Check in time is 2:00 p.m. Saturday.
Check out time is 9:00 a.m. Saturday.

A $_____ Deposit is required for each
week of your reservation. Thank You!

All our cottages have lakefront locations
with screened porches and private pier. All
cottages have hot and cold running water,
showers and toilets. Except for Castor and
Pollux, which have twin beds, all cottages
have double beds and some have Hide-a-beds
for additional persons.

For your convenience we offer fishing
licenses, guide service, tackle, night
crawlers, minnows, gas and oil, fish cleaning
house and freezer space to keep your catch.
Motors may be rented.

Between Memorial Day and Labor Day, join our
Tuesday morning fishing contest and Monday
Pot Luck Supper. It's lots of fun.

STAR LAKE SALOON
*
HOUSEKEEPING COTTAGES

Harold A. Larkin, Prop.
Antler, WI 54561
(715) 266-8347

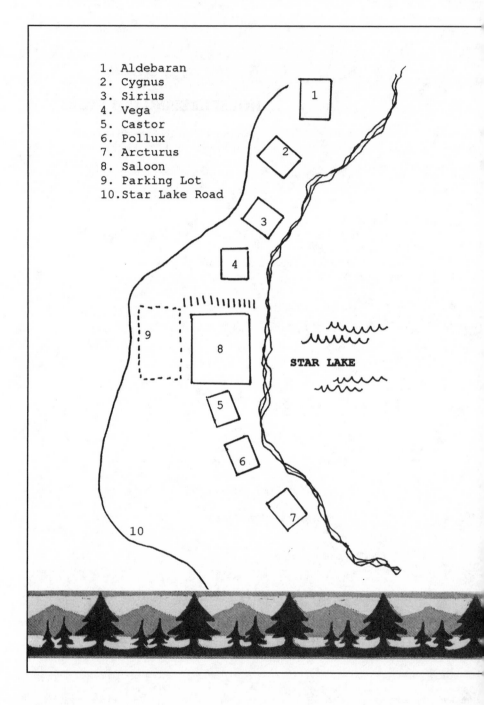

1. Aldebaran
2. Cygnus
3. Sirius
4. Vega
5. Castor
6. Pollux
7. Arcturus
8. Saloon
9. Parking Lot
10. Star Lake Road

STAR LAKE

STAR LAKE SALOON
&
HOUSEKEEPING COTTAGES

Directions: Take Highway 50 to Antler.
Turn East on County Tr. "J." for approx.
4 miles, then left on C. Tr. "H" and follow
signs to STAR LAKE SALOON after
turning right on Star Lake Road.

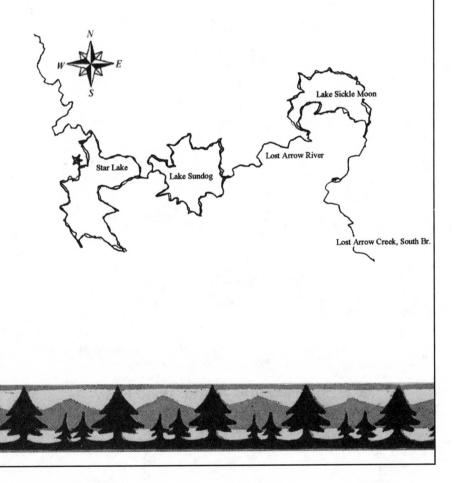

Lake Sickle Moon

Lost Arrow River

Star Lake

Lake Sundog

Lost Arrow Creek, South Br.

Terrace Books, a division of the University of Wisconsin Press, takes its name
from the Memorial Union Terrace, located at the University of Wisconsin–Madison.
Since its inception in 1907, the Wisconsin Union has provided a venue for students,
faculty, staff, and alumni to debate art, music, politics, and the issues of the day.
It is a place where theater, music, drama, dance, outdoor activities, and
major speakers are made available to the campus and the community.
To learn more about the Union, visit www.union.wisc.edu.

Star Lake Saloon
and
Housekeeping Cottages

A Novel

Sara Rath

THE UNIVERSITY OF WISCONSIN PRESS
TERRACE BOOKS

The University of Wisconsin Press
1930 Monroe Street
Madison, Wisconsin 53711

www.wisc.edu/wisconsinpress/

3 Henrietta Street
London WC2E 8LU, England

5   4

Printed in the United States of America

Library of Congress Cataloging-in-Publication Data
Rath, Sara.
Star Lake Saloon and Housekeeping Cottages: a novel / Sara Rath.
p.   cm.—(Library of American fiction)
ISBN 0-299-21520-2 (hardcover: alk. paper)
ISBN 0-299-21524-5 (pbk.: alk. paper)
1. Wisconsin—Fiction.   I. Title.   II. Series.
PS3568.A718S73   2005
813′.54—dc22   2005008263

FOR
MAGGIE LAMONT
(1991–2003)
OUR OWN SWEET "BABE"

The secret of stars is distance, their splendid isolation,
as anyone's secret is the unrevealed motive,
the hidden relation of self to another and another and the world.

August Derleth

Acknowledgments

Years ago I purchased a T-shirt at the Star Lake General Store with the slogan *Star Lake, The Ultimate Retreat*. I am indebted to the Wisconsin Arts Board for a generous grant that encouraged me to create my own (imaginary) safe-haven.

I could not have told this story without the help of Joyce Melville and Al Gedicks, both active in the anti-mine movement in northern Wisconsin. The folks at Island View Lodge on Fisher Lake near Mercer warmly welcomed my inquiries about running a summer resort, as did Rich and Sandy Huffman at Hideaway Bay where we shared many pizzas and beers with Manawa pals Jim and Jackie Roland. Jack Rath offered needed advice on Wisconsin probate and real estate, and dear friend Ludmilla Bollow followed each chapter along with my long-suffering *Byliners* gang. Thanks also to James Gollata at UW–Richland and Diane Kostecke at Wisconsin Public Television.

My brother and sister, Art and Marsha, share my passion for the northwoods and for Lindsay Lodge, the rustic cabin built by our grandfather on Catherine Lake, where our family continues to seek solitude, healing, and renewal.

To my children, Jay Rath and Laura Rath Beausire—I appreciate your patience with an unconventional mom.

And to my husband, Del Lamont, I offer my most heartfelt gratitude. You made it possible for me to seek the sanctuary of my imaginary retreat and your love and reassurance continue to be a source of abiding strength.

Author's Note

Star Lake, Wisconsin, bears little resemblance to its legendary past as a booming northwoods logging town at the end of the nineteenth century when nearly two billion board feet of pine was logged from the area. These days, summer residents outnumber the regulars. The Star Lake General Store has a couple gas pumps out in front and post office boxes can be found inside next to shelves of beer, bait, and souvenirs.

But the lake and resort imagined in this novel are just that, pretend places in a make-believe setting, and the characters who inhabit "Antler" are not based on anyone in particular. Ingold Mining is not real either, although northern Wisconsin *is* currently threatened by at least a dozen mining operations. Nicolet Minerals, for example, a subsidiary of London-based Billiton PLC, recently spent more than ten years and over $70 million seeking state and federal permits to remove fifty-five million tons of zinc and copper ore from a mine near the Mole Lake Indian Reservation south of Crandon, at the headwaters of the Wolf River.

The old-fashioned summer resort is rapidly disappearing, too. Wisconsin's Turtle Flambeau-Flowage, a protected wilderness encompassing 18,900 acres of water, once had eighteen family-owned resorts secluded along 212 miles of winding shoreline. Now only four resorts remain; the rest have been sold, divided into condominiums.

Star Lake Saloon
and
Housekeeping Cottages

Here and There

Hannah's name was a palindrome. That fact had always given her a secret satisfaction; the magical pattern of letters establishing a sense of order early in her life, as if the synchrony of her name ensured a steady balance no matter what.

Today, however, she found her equilibrium severely challenged. She had noted the warmth in the bartender's smile when she walked into Buck's Bar and chose a stool at the far end of the room, but then she removed her sunglasses and found herself surrounded by a swarm of twiggy deer horns and flyers advertising church suppers, motorcycle rallies, euchre contests, fisheries: this was a foreign land.

"If your name's Hannah Swann, then I've got something for you from Ginger Kovalcik." Buck placed a pink envelope before her. "And a drink on the house. Your uncle was a good buddy of mine."

"Thanks," Hannah replied weakly, squinting to read the menu on the wall. A Diet Pepsi would be safe. Better a Diet Pepsi and a cheeseburger than a Loon Fart, the house drink. She didn't even want to ask what that was.

It had taken her five hours to drive the length of the state and arrive in Antler on time for a meeting with Uncle Hal's lawyer. Five hours to make a two o'clock appointment that she'd hastily arranged after Ginger's call, yesterday afternoon. But now Attorney Windsor was out, according to his secretary, due to an emergency. He left word that he'd like to meet her for dinner tonight instead.

A couple men at the other end of the bar glanced back down at their beers when she happened to look over their way. They began remarking on the late frost last night.

The weather was definitely cooler in Antler than it had been in Madison that morning where the advance of spring was at least two weeks ahead. But those guys over there (to whom she *was* giving a cold shoulder) would probably say Madison always figured it was ahead of the rest of Wisconsin, anyway. The Milwaukee paper wise-cracked that the capital city suffered from being "terminally hip," and Governor Dawson campaigned outstate by claiming that Madison was "sixty-nine square miles surrounded by reality" because of its Mad City reputation as bleeding-heart, knee-jerk liberal, and slightly zany.

Buck set her Pepsi on the bar. Hannah found a pill case in her purse and removed two capsules, hoping to avert a migraine she felt emerging beneath the curve of her left eyebrow like a narrow pulse of blue lightning. Then she placed a faded snapshot on the bar for Buck to see.

"My dad said Hal was about ten when this was taken."

Buck studied it carefully. "Nice old Packard, must be a '37, '38?"

She had searched the attic for the photo last night, to refresh a childhood memory. The dog in the faded picture had once captured her heart, the black dog her uncle, seated on the running board, had his arm hung so casually around. "Babe." Her father's voice always got soft when he explained, "That damn retriever was my brother's pride and joy. The two of 'em hunted together, swam in the Mill-pond, slept in the same bed and I swear Hal probably ate Friskies for all I know."

Daddy got so sad whenever Hannah dragged out the album and she anticipated the stern warning that inevitably followed:

"Put this away. Don't mention it to Grandpa Larkin and don't mention Hal, neither. For him that boy might just as well have been

4

killed in the war, though the candy-ass couldn't put up a fight to save his life. If the mosquitoes aren't eating him alive up in the goddamn wilderness he'll get his ass froze when snowdrifts are twenty feet high and it's forty below. Dad used to talk about the Larkin's logging camps. Hal should of known."

Like an old friend, the snapshot had accompanied her on today's long drive propped up by an Evian bottle on the passenger seat. Chloe hadn't noticed it when Hannah stopped impulsively just for a moment to seize a bit of reassurance. She'd remembered her daughter was planning to demonstrate on the Capitol Square and that's where she found her, leaning against a placard that read "Mines Not Worth the Cost." Chloe wore a pair of black jeans, a faded blue sweatshirt of her boyfriend's with sleeves torn off just below the elbows, and a pair of black boots more appropriate for a telephone lineman. Her dark brown hair was shorn closer than ever to her scalp.

"Pro-choice rally?"

"Wilderness mining, Mom." Chloe rolled her eyes. "I told you yesterday, remember? The Guv's having breakfast with a bunch of execs from Ingold Mining and we're waiting for vans to take us out to the mansion in Maple Bluff."

Hannah shoved in the clutch. "Mining played a big part in Wisconsin's early history. . . ."

Her irritation over the necessity for this impromptu trip was seeping out.

"Thanks for reminding me, Mom. I learned that in fourth grade: we're *the Badger State* because lead miners dug caves in the side of the hills, like badgers. Did you take your Valium? Are you freaking out over this?

"No I'm not, and yes I did."

Chloe quickly checked to see if her friends might overhear.

"You're obviously not very well informed on current environmental issues, Mom. International mining corporations are threatening the whole northwoods ecosystem! And you don't even care!"

Of course she cared. She cared about every protest rally her daughter took part in but it was hard to keep track of the *demonstra-tion de jour*. And of course she was unnerved about making such a long drive into the wilderness all by herself. Her daughter, as usual, wasn't far off target. But a little compassion would have been appreciated. Anyone would be upset if they had to suddenly give up a whole weekend and spend it up in the sticks because some ancient relative they'd never even known and thought was already stone-cold dead finally *died*, for God's sake.

"Don't feel obligated to check on the cat," Hannah called out as she pulled away from the curb. "I'll be back on Monday. Ratso will be fine."

Chloe thrust a leaflet through the window of the Toyota as Hannah turned onto the street.

"Get *with it*, Mom."

In the barbaric gloom of Buck's Bar, the anti-mining tract was all she had to read while she ate her cheeseburger.

Get with *what*? She still ran three miles a day, when she found time, and carried only a hundred and twenty pounds on a five-foot-two-inch frame. But this April she had turned forty-seven. Hannah glanced at her reflection in the mirror behind the bar for reassurance. How long had it been since she'd been mistaken as Chloe's sister? They used to enjoy the duplicity; their coloring was similar and sometimes Hannah wore her daughter's cast-off clothes.

Today, for a change, everything she was wearing was her own. She'd expected to meet with a lawyer, so that involved pantyhose that had been killing her for the last two hundred miles, a pair of red suede pumps (ditto), and a light wool cashmere suit, also deep red. Also egregiously out of place in Buck's Bar, Hannah grimaced.

To her right, a couple of doors were decorated with chunks of bark that serendipitously reproduced male and female genitals. Hannah chose the vagina-bark door and discovered she was starting her period. A week early. It figured. The migraine, too. Why hadn't she thought to tuck a tampon in her purse? Too rushed, too distracted.

Sometimes restrooms had vending machines that dispensed sanitary napkins; this one had a machine that sold condoms.

Buck placed the cheeseburger on the bar as she emerged but she said she had to run across the street. All three men had watched her come out of the restroom, flustered. Of course they must know why she had to run to the IGA. Not too slick, Hannah Swann. The second time she emerged from the restroom she glistened with perspiration. Her face was burning hot.

Then one of the other men burst out of the men's room and called to his buddy, "You know, Buck's selling real estate in the can!"

"No shit."

"Yeah, I saw an ad for condominiums on the wall."

"You must'a had your brains in your hands while you were in there."

Hannah cringed. This redneck routine was all for her benefit. She was a long, long way from Mad City, no doubt in the world about that.

I

Laugh and the world laughs with you;
Weep, and you weep alone,
For the sad old earth must borrow its mirth,
But has trouble enough of its own.

Ella Wheeler Wilcox

1

Thank Your Lucky Stars

This is It!

The hand-lettered sign was tacked to the trunk of a charred maple that appeared to have been struck by lightning. Below it another sign suggested, *Thank Your Lucky Stars!*

Surely this was not the home of her recently deceased uncle, Hannah must have made a wrong turn. In dismal spring rain, log buildings at the end of the road appeared ramshackle and neglected. She pulled into a parking space behind the largest structure, took off her glasses, and rubbed her eyes.

"Terrific," Hannah muttered in disgust. "*This is it.* This is a dump."

Deer hunters found the partially decomposed body believed to be that of Hannah Swann, noted Madison writer and authority on nineteenth-century feminist poets, who was reported missing in early May when she failed to arrive for the funeral of her late uncle. According to her daughter, Ms. Swann had seemed uneasy about her journey and was seriously out of touch with current environmental issues.

Hannah changed the imaginary scenario to an opening for a documentary video, under the credits. Only her heroine would drive through the forest and come upon a resort like this as it was, back in the 1800s. She had selected similar locales from nineteenth-century iconography to illustrate the lives of the poets she wrote about for educational videos, women poets who were sometimes so romantic and sentimental that she privately referred to them as her Bad Women Poets, or BWPs. They would call this gargantuan log building a *Lodge,* where genteel city folk could doze in bent-willow rocking chairs on broad verandahs while seeking a "place of resort."

Usually such dreamscapes amused her, but Hannah wasn't laughing now. Okay, so maybe her trip up here *was* more mercenary than familial: If Uncle Hal was eccentric enough to write his own memorial service, she presumed he owned a place in the woods, or on a lake. How could she turn down the gift of a hideaway where she could write and relax. Buy a new car. Pay off Chloe's student loan.

A cherry pie sat in a grocery bag on the passenger seat: it was "Piearama Day" at the Antler IGA. Hannah fished a plastic spoon from the bottom of the glove compartment and wiped it with a corner of her red cashmere jacket. What the hell.

Joe Mickelson, producer of her educational video series, was usually pretty understanding. Two of her scripts (on Mable Bigelow Bodden and Sadie Reese Sheridan) were already in production. The Ella Wheeler Wilcox script was in the treatment phase and Hannah needed a solid two weeks of writing and revision before she'd have something for Joe. When she left Madison this morning Hannah told Joe's voice mail that he would have the script on his desk by her deadline. The inevitable freelancer's lie.

The pie was not great, but eating took her mind off the ominous two-story building of dark logs that tilted toward what must be a lake. If no one came to greet her, she'd have to see if someone was inside. Nervously, Hannah scanned the radio dial. Between polkas and country twang a station in Upper Michigan repeatedly referred to "Gogebic Country," which made this place seem even more foreign and inhospitable because she had no idea what that meant.

Since no one was around to notice, Hannah dug even more greedily into the pie. The neon red cherries and oozing syrup were so sweet her teeth ached, but she couldn't stop.

Ella Wheeler Wilcox would have raised an eyebrow at such indelicacy. But the outlandish poet would also have scorned the pillow Hannah saw in a Christmas catalog embroidered "Laugh and the world laughs with you; Snore and you sleep alone." Then there was the bumper sticker still on her Toyota that Chloe's boyfriend had slapped on as a joke: "Laugh alone and the world thinks you're crazy." That was sweet of Eric, she thought, even though the phrase seemed to echo Chloe's contention that her mother was neurotic and self-absorbed.

A wedge roughly the size of a respectable slice of pie appeared at the bottom of the aluminum pie plate. Hannah kept nibbling at the edge of the triangle, evening it out.

I will peacefully approach one thing at a time

Breathe, Hannah told herself.

I am love, health, happiness, success . . .

Before Wilcox sailed to France in 1916 to attempt a psychic reunion with her dead husband, she advised American women to repeat, twenty times a day: "I am love, health, happiness, success, opulence, and all I want or desire is mine." Hannah had secretly adopted that affirmation but omitted "opulence," because she didn't know how it would apply.

Breathe.

I am hungry.

By the time she had finished whittling away at the edges, the entire cherry pie was gone and the rain had thinned to a fine drizzle. Chagrined, Hannah stuffed the sticky container back into its plastic bag and shoved it under the front seat. It was definitely not like her, to let things get so out of control.

She opened the driver's side window to allow a fresh, damp breeze, practically green with the scent of pine, to wash over her. Deep breaths, three deep, Yogic breaths: Inhale. Exhale.

Fir trees meshed in a thick overhead canopy and a syncopated drip onto a thick carpet of brown needles and pinecones was the only sound to emerge from a ponderous and eerie silence.

Now Hannah recognized the silvery-gray surface of a lake beyond the wooded slope. She stepped out of the car. The heels of her red suede pumps sunk into the soggy ground.

A narrow path led toward the water, and worn railroad ties set into the bank provided a mossy and irregular stairway along the side of the log building to a wide, screened porch below.

"Hello? Anybody here?"

The torn screen in the door flapped impatiently as she entered. Just inside, a deer head with a massive rack of antlers glowered out at the lake with glass eyes. At least a dozen more of these ubiquitous trophies projected further on down the wall above a series of French doors set into the wall of varnished logs.

Pushed against the wall on the right, beneath the series of antlers, Hannah noticed a large metal glider heaped with faded pillows, an assortment of wicker rocking chairs and an old chaise lounge. She paused to peer through one of the windows and made out a pool table inside the building, and perhaps a fieldstone fireplace. But the French doors were cloudy with grime and torn yellowed curtains obscured the view.

Toward the lake, opposite the deer, the outside wall was cluttered with an unmatched bunch of chrome dinette sets. At the far end of the porch, beside a sturdier door, a hand-lettered sign said, simply, BAR.

Maybe the place didn't open until evening, Hannah speculated. The proprietors had gone into town for groceries. Anxiety was not the cause of her nausea, it was the cherry pie. She was not going to throw up. Swallow, hard. Now, swallow again. She tried another Yogic breath.

Except for the sibilant raindrops through the pines, the hush was almost like a vacuum. Everything was much too still, as if all the sounds of civilization had been sucked away.

Where had she read the line—"the roar which lies on the other side of silence?" Some addled nineteenth-century woman poet, no doubt. Well, this was like that roar. With the back of her wrist she wiped sweat from her upper lip.

"Please don't let this work," she prayed, then fit the key Buck had given her into the old-fashioned lock. The tumblers turned with a practiced click. The heavy door swung open to release a cloud of musty tavern odors, stale beer and sour grease, fried onions and cigarette smoke from years of accumulation that made her gag.

Hannah pulled the door shut quickly and locked it again. If she left now, no one would know she had been here. Except for her tracks.

A growl emerged from somewhere on the porch, back near the screen door.

Beneath a bed of blankets and pillows on the glider, a shadowy form stirred.

The growl sounded again: slow, menacing.

"Good doggie," Hannah crooned, timidly. If dogs could smell fear, she was really in deep shit.

"Good dog. Nice dog," she said, forcing her voice lower. "It's okay, I'm your friend."

If dogs could sense lies, she was in even deeper. Then, it was only a hunch.

"Babe?"

From beneath the awning-striped pillows a young black Labrador retriever emerged, tail wagging wildly.

"Babe? Are you another Babe?"

It could not have been more than a year old, she guessed, but Hannah had never owned a dog.

She squatted as the puppy, wiggling, approached. It sniffed her outstretched hand, licked her palm.

"Okay, that's enough," Hannah said finally, standing up. The knees of her pantyhose sagged. "Now go away. Be a good girl and let me alone."

The old glider squeaked in complaint as Hannah sat down wearily and massaged her forehead.

The expanse of slate gray water before her was ringed with a shadowy forest of birch and pine. A vast and empty, discouraging space. Not the "limpid lakes" and "salubrious atmosphere" that

Mabel Bigelow Bodden, famed BWP, romanticized. Where in hell were the "azure waters that mirror skies of wondrous blue; where Nature smiles, and beautiful wood dryads beckon all who will to follow." Hannah was willing to bet there wasn't a *wood dryad* to be found for miles, and the lake, like the weather, mirrored her emotions, not azure skies.

The pup nuzzled Hannah's elbow with a cold, wet nose.

"Get lost, okay?" Hannah shoved it roughly aside with her knee. Again, the dog poked at her arm and placed something wet in her lap.

"Let me alone!" She brushed a damp sock onto the floor.

The dog retrieved it and sat before her with questioning brown eyes, tail tapping with rhythmic anticipation.

"This is the only good outfit I brought along," Hannah complained, "I don't want to smell like a wet dog when I meet with Hal's lawyer."

The pup leaped up and curled beside her on the swing. It put its head in her lap, and Hannah's quivering sigh caught in her throat with a painful throb.

The dog's head was warm and smooth and shiny. The pup's ears felt like velvet between her fingers.

Hannah and Babe sat in the glider for a long time that afternoon. The two of them shared, Hannah finally realized, a strangely symbiotic sense of sorrow. She watched the pewter surface of the lake assume a silvery sheen, then tarnish black as lead as the sky lowered once again. Wind swept through the branches overhead, waves scrubbed the rickety pier and bumped the boats tied there as another thunderstorm crescendoed over the water. Shivering, Hannah draped a blanket from the dog's bed around her shoulders while she and Babe rocked back and forth. Rain splashed under the eaves and sifted through the screens. Back and forth. The spring storm moved on.

There was a good chance that Uncle Hal had actually bequeathed this place to someone else. Hannah's obligation might merely involve signing some papers. It could be a simple matter. Over and done, quickly. Wait to worry, as her mother would say.

She was beginning to feel queasy from her worsening headache and the movement of the glider.

"C'mon dog, let's go for a walk."

Seven cottages faced the lake: four on the upper lakeshore north of the big log building and three along the lower shore, to the south. Each was constructed of logs and had its own screened porch. But the place had obviously suffered quite a bit of neglect. Broken limbs were strewn everywhere and two of the lower three cottages needed serious repair. One had been practically flattened by a large branch that still rested on its roof.

The buildings along the upper shore were in better shape. None of the doors was locked, and inside each porch was a varnished plaque with the name of the cottage. The largest, "Aldebaran," was named for a double star in the constellation Taurus, Hannah knew. The name had been neatly printed onto a slice of tree trunk with a wood-burning tool, and the constellation Taurus was recreated with brass upholstery tacks . . . several of which were missing. Another cottage was called "Sirius," for the brightest star. Next to that was "Cygnus," or The Swan, for a constellation in the northern hemisphere. Hannah's childhood interest in astronomy had been nurtured by Grandpa Larkin who had taught her what he knew of the mysteries of the night sky.

Except for Aldebaran, each of the cabins had one small bedroom with a sagging double bed, a bathroom with toilet and metal shower, and a dingy living room/kitchen paneled in knotty pine. The wall of kitchen facilities incorporated a Kelvinator refrigerator, Universal gas stove, metal sink, and two metal cupboards. Wooden tables had, if lucky, four matching chairs with plastic seats that were not cracked. On top of each stove was a tin can labeled "Grease." Only "Vega," the smallest of the seven cabins, had twin beds and lacked a kitchen.

Aldebaran seemed to have been built earlier, around the same time as the main lodge. The larger cottage hid behind tall pines on the far end and had two bedrooms, a fairly nice kitchen, a bathroom with a combination tub and shower, and a big fieldstone fireplace in the living room between two small, high windows.

None of the facilities possessed even common amenities—no telephones or televisions, not even a radio. This seedy resort was definitely for steadfast Fin, Fur, and Feather fans.

A narrow dock led to the water from each cabin. A larger pier served the main lodge, where dented metal rowboats rode rough waves and soggy flotation devices (Hannah was sure there must be another name for those square lifesaving pillows) sloshed around in oily water beneath the seats. Thwarts? She knew nothing about boats.

On the lawn between the lodge and the pier various boat motors were clamped onto a board between two posts. Red gas cans were scattered beneath the porch. Nearby, a dinner bell hung upon a wooden pillar, perhaps a remnant of bygone days when guests were summoned from their wilderness pursuits three times a day to a sit-down dining room meal.

More than the shock of this wreck of a place, more than anything, Hannah felt overwhelmed by the hush. The brutal silence was so engulfing it actually made her head hurt more than ever. Soggy pine boughs released captured raindrops with a whoosh when a breeze swept by, but, other than that, complete and utter quiet prevailed.

From where she stood, Hannah could not make out another cabin, house, or resort, only a dense border of trees on the opposite shore and a couple flocks of fishing boats here and there. Near a raft of lily pads in front of Aldebaran she identified a pair of loons.

The large pier spread into a wide T-shape at the end where two crude benches faced the vista. Hannah turned around to look back at the lodge.

"Star Lake Resort," a well-aged sign on the front of the porch greeted boaters and fishermen, "Beer Bait Food Boats Games." She guessed that covered it all.

Imagine, people actually paid for such merciless isolation.

"Yoo-Hoo! Hannah! You left your car window open! Your seat's sopping wet!"

Babe gave a quick bark and lurched past Hannah, nearly knocking her into the lake. An older woman with frizzy pumpkin hair carefully made her way down the crude stairs next to the lodge. She was tiny and wore baggy jeans with a hooded gray sweatshirt.

"Hello, Baby," the woman greeted the dog warmly, then opened the screen door to the porch and called again. "C'mon inside, Hannah! Get in here out of the damp, for goodness sake!"

"We've been having a look around," Hannah offered, entering the porch. "You must be Ginger."

"Sure am," the woman extended her hand. "Ginger Kovalcik. Kinda wet for exploring, isn't it?"

Hannah looked down at her ruined shoes and picked at the black fur that clung to her red cashmere suit.

"Didn't Buck give you that key?"

Hannah handed it over.

"Well then, let's have a look," Ginger replied, unlocking the door to the bar. She flipped all the switches on the wall just inside. The stale air rolled out again, and Hannah flinched. Beer signs flickered into flashy neon action and the jukebox jumped into anticipatory mode.

A dozen barstools stood before a long counter, and four old chrome tables, each with chrome kitchen chairs, took up the corners. Taxidermy reigned: a multitude of fish, including several disgusting muskellunge that even Hannah could identify by the fierce teeth jutting from ugly jaws, swam in flipping, flapping poses around the room's perimeter. Mingling with the peaceable piscine were a fox, a bobcat, and the head of a small, brown bear.

"This here's my hangout," Ginger said, proudly. "I been tending bar for Hal since 1950, give or take a few weeks once in a great while."

The room had served as the central dining room for the original lodge, Hannah was certain. A makeshift wall divided the bar from a game room, where she found the pool table, assorted video games, and even a few pinball machines. An imposing fieldstone fireplace, similar to that in Aldebaran but much larger, had been sealed off with a warped piece of plywood to conserve heat in winter, she surmised. Ginger chatted on while Hannah poked around. Resorts like this, Hannah knew, had often been fashioned from logging camps in the late nineteenth century when the timber harvest declined. Travel was accomplished via railroads that had been built to serve the lumber trade.

"I did all these mounts myself." Ginger was pointing at the assortment of animal trophies. "Pretty proud of 'em, too, if I do say so myself. Learned by correspondence. Best twenty bucks I ever spent. Still tinker at it. Fish are the hardest, you got to really know your fish."

Hannah tried to seem impressed, and hoped her anguish was aptly disguised.

Behind the bar, snapshots were taped to the wall near a swinging door—fishermen brandishing prize catches. Printed on the edge of each snapshot was the date, the size of the fish, and the name of the fisherman. Or fisherwoman. Fisher*person*. Jesus, you're not in P.C. Madison now!

Beyond the swinging door Hannah glimpsed a commercial kitchen.

"This is really something," Hannah admitted, trying hard to respond with an upbeat tone.

"Let's go on upstairs," Ginger crossed to a door where a "PRIVATE" warning in metallic stick-on letters led to a once-grand, open stairway now enclosed with cheap paneling and dimly lit. Babe bounded up ahead of them, but Ginger's progress was made with some difficulty. Hannah paused on the landing to allow both of them more time.

"Now, this here is Polaris, that's what Hal called his living quarters." Ginger reached the second floor of the lodge. "The North Star. He used to say there wasn't a better view in the whole State of Wisconsin than he had from up here."

Heavy, old-fashioned furniture cluttered the apartment: an ornate library table, a worn burgundy horsehair sofa and two overstuffed chairs with crocheted antimacassars. Recent magazines overflowed the coffee table, and there was an old Motorola television that Hannah knew must be black and white. She noticed a sleeping porch beyond another set of French doors. It was not as large or as grand as

20

the verandah off the Saloon below but offered an even more expansive northwoods vista.

"I hardly know what to say," Hannah acknowledged, truthfully.

She had a feeling that the sitting room originally divided the second floor—kind of a lobby—with bedrooms opening off a central corridor on either side. Babe was conducting a restless investigation, as if searching for a trail.

"The folks that owned it before Hal and Miriam, they shut off the south end, there over the game room. Where the fireplace is downstairs. And they turned this end," Ginger indicated two rooms across the interior hall, "where the plumbing was put in, into a couple bedrooms and a kitchen. The bathroom's over there, by the way. Maybe you want to freshen up."

Judging by the pull-chain toilet in its own separate closet and the ornate tub perched on eagle claws, the bathroom was also from a much earlier era.

Hannah found a clean washcloth in a cabinet. She looked like a raccoon in her reflection; tears had smeared her mascara. A fat dribble of cherry pie ran down the front of her white silk blouse, but that was minor. All she really wanted was to curl up somewhere dark with an ice pack to quell the throbbing pain of her migraine and make the rest of this awful nightmare disappear.

Ginger waited in the kitchen. A pot of coffee percolated on the stove.

"You're looking kind of peaked," Ginger said. "Seems longer ago than yesterday when I first called you, doesn't it? Like I said, Hal told me, 'Get ahold of Hannah,' and that's why I called. It was one of the last things I heard Hal say."

Hannah sat down, obediently, in the chair that was offered.

"I like to sit here, too," Ginger said. "You can see all the way down to the far end of Star where it joins up with Sundog. This is as good a place as any for us to get acquainted, don't you think?"

Ginger swept an assortment of letters and envelopes, flyers and catalogs off to one side of the table with her forearm, then set down two mugs of thick coffee.

"I'd offer you a cookie, but Hal never was much of a one for keeping sweets."

"That's all right," Hannah replied, pointing to the stain on her blouse, "I had some cherry pie not long ago."

"Hope it was tasty," Ginger chuckled.

"Not really," Hannah admitted. "In fact, I'm not feeling very well. I have a terrible headache."

"I *bet* you have a headache," Ginger blew over the surface of her coffee to cool it. "I'd have one too, if I was you. The shock and all."

Hannah took a deep breath, then sighed.

"I'm sorry—It's been a tremendous surprise, really. I had no idea . . ."

"No idea, what?"

Hannah thought she heard an edge to Ginger's voice. "No idea that my Uncle Hal was still here. Around. Alive, really. All of this . . ."

"Hadn't seen him for some time, that what you mean?"

"No, I hadn't. Yes."

"Ummm." Ginger took a tentative sip. "You talk to Denny Windsor?"

"He wants to see me later."

"George Windsor, Denny's dad, he's the one who wrote up Hal's will, you know. Denny tell you that?"

Hannah nodded, and lifted her mug.

Ginger chuckled again and shook her head.

"You are a sorry sight. You want some aspirin, you just say so, okay? I think there's some in the bathroom. Anyway, your uncle would be glad to know you came up here when I called."

Hannah stared into the steaming liquid, black and bitter.

"Let me tell you something about your uncle. Refresh your memory," Ginger said. "He and Miriam, they were married around 1940, I think. I know it was before you were born, that's for sure. But I guess you probably know all about his history, being that you're 'family.'"

Hannah was startled at Ginger's sudden gibe. What was the point?

"I don't know anything about my uncle," she confessed, coolly. "And even less about his wife."

Ginger bit her bottom lip and gazed out the window for a while.

"Oh, I know that, Honey. I shouldn't be so hard on you. It must be a heck of a surprise, me giving you a call out of the blue and then all this falling in your lap. No wonder you're all upset. No wonder at all."

Ginger reached across the table to clasp Hannah's hand. After an uneasy moment, Hannah pulled hers away.

"Any*hoo,*" Ginger sighed after a pause, then continued, "What's done is done and I'm going to tell you a few things, like it or not. It was 1945, I think, Hal and Miriam were driving around one Sunday when they saw a 'For Sale' sign. So they came on down the road and found this lodge, the one we're sitting in right now, with three hundred feet of lake frontage on Star Lake. A few years later they bought another four hundred feet and it's a blessing they did because you couldn't touch it for anywhere near what they paid, today. That's a fact."

"They fixed up the lodge, I suppose," Hannah said.

"Fixed it up, remodeled it practically, from the ground floor to the top. Except for what was done to it before, like I told you. That big cabin down there on the far north end, Aldebaran, was already built. They rented out the cabin and rooms upstairs here to begin with, but then Hal built the other cottages. One at a time he worked on 'em and before they knew it they had themselves a summer resort business. My job's always been in the bar. Give folks a smile or a beer or a shoulder to cry on, listen to their fish stories and whatever else they got to brag on. Like grandkids. Don't have any of my own yet. I keep telling my son to get to work. You got any kids?"

Hannah nodded, thinking of Chloe's haughty attitude that morning.

"Hal, he was the one who fussed with the bills. And outdoors, the boats, motors, handyman chores—he was one to putter. Sometimes I'd give him a Honey-do list but I never got very far. He only fixed what he wanted to anyways."

23

"Honeydew?"

"Honey do this, Honey do that," Ginger explained. "The toilet in Pollux, that little cabin right over there?" She pointed south, "I don't know how many times I told Hal to tighten it up because the damn thing wobbles like a bucking bronco."

The two women drank their coffee and Hannah glanced out toward the far end of the lake where a fishing boat rocked on gray waves. The wind had come up again.

"Did Hal make the signs for the cottages? The star-signs?"

"No, that was Miriam. She was an artist. It was her idea, naming the cabins after stars and such. Such a sweet girl. Not near strong enough for the kind of life we had back then. Nothing much in the way of what you'd call modern conveniences, but Miriam didn't complain."

Ginger was lost in thought. "Wait a second," she said suddenly, pushing back her chair and rising with a grunt. "Hold your horses."

Hannah could hear Ginger opening and closing drawers in another room. Raindrops began to splatter the kitchen window. Her stomach was growing even more rocky from the black coffee and her migraine raged.

When Ginger resumed her seat across the table, she held a Christmas card with a black and white picture of a chubby Hannah clad only in diapers, about eight months old, on a hobbyhorse.

Merry Christmas from Lily, Fred and Hannah

"Look familiar?" Ginger asked. "Hal showed me this once upon a time. Said when it came in the mail Miriam fell in love with this baby named Hannah and told him she wanted a little girl of her own. She was already in her thirties, I think. Not a year later, Miriam passed away in childbirth. The little baby died, too. It was a little girl. Hal never recovered from it. The doctor had told them she never should have children, and for a long time afterward, maybe forever, Hal blamed himself."

A shiver passed through Hannah as she touched the card. Was it a sign of some kind, that she and her uncle knew each other only through photographs? She was tempted to run out to her car and bring in her picture of Hal and the dog.

"So, anyway, I came out here this afternoon to welcome you in place of your Uncle Hal."

Ginger got up and dumped the rest of her coffee in the sink. Then she came over to put her arm around Hannah's shoulders and kissed her cheek.

"Welcome to Star Lake, Honey. Wish I could stick around and chat but I've got to run. One robin doesn't make a spring."

"What?"

Hannah was not sure she'd heard correctly.

"I shut your car window, but if I was you I'd take along something dry to sit on or you'll sop it all up with your keister."

Ginger exited through a back door in the living room, next to the stairway. It opened at ground level behind the building where Hannah had parked.

I *don't* care, and I *won't* care, Hannah told herself. She filled the dog's water dish and scooped dog food into a bowl from a bag of dry kibble on the kitchen counter. Babe had disappeared and that was fine with her.

She swallowed another capsule for her headache. It was too soon after the others but she was desperate. This was becoming a really bad migraine and she hated feeling helpless when she was alone. If only Chloe were with her. Chloe might even have agreed to come, if Hannah had asked. Her daughter was so pragmatic. She never seemed to get rattled like Hannah did.

The door to Hal's bedroom was open now—Ginger must have been in there, rummaging. It was dark inside, cool and welcoming. In the dim light, Hannah noticed the worn patchwork quilt on Hal's bed had been pulled back. Near the pillow, Babe was curled in a fetal position. The dog's eyes followed Hannah, but the animal did not move.

Hannah, exhausted, pried off her shoes. With a deep sob of anguish, she lay back down on the bed and wept. When she woke, maybe an hour later, Babe was licking the dried tears from her cheek. That made her cry all over again until she noticed the teeth.

A pair of dentures still soaked in a glass of water on the nightstand next to the bed. How could Hal's *teeth* have been overlooked?

The telephone rang six times before she managed to find it under all the junk mail and catalogs on the floor beneath the library table.

"Charlie Jenkins. Undertaker. Denny Windsor tell you to call me?"

"He may have forgotten . . ."

"Ah. Well, I heard you got into town okay, and I wondered how you were coming along out there. I told Denny I'll be needing some items. Hal's clothes, that is, and such."

He explained that Hal wished to be cremated and had paid for everything in advance, but there would be a visitation and could Hannah find Hal's good suit.

"I'll see what I can do," she said. "I guess it's getting kind of late."

"I was thinking," Charlie Jenkins continued. "If you got plans to be out at the lake tomorrow afternoon, say about two o'clock or so, I could stop by. It'd save you the extra trip. I'll be in the vicinity."

"Sure," Hannah replied without enthusiasm. Where else would she be?

"I . . . also have his teeth," she said.

"His *teeth?*" The mortician seemed astonished. "By golly. I spent an hour out there yesterday. Turned the place upside down, looking for Hal's dentures. Where'd you come across 'em?"

"On the nightstand, next to his bed."

"Well, I'll be darned," Charlie Jenkins exclaimed after a lengthy pause. "I could of sworn I looked there. Next to the bed, huh? I'll be darned."

Without much difficulty, Hannah found her uncle's one suit, dark gray with wide lapels, in a closet that reeked of mothballs. A new white shirt still in cellophane wrapping lay on top of the dresser. Had Ginger left it there? Hannah pulled a necktie from the top dresser drawer and placed all the clothes over the foot of the bed while Babe watched intently. The dentures were taken into the bathroom where she poured the water out of the glass and caught the teeth in a clean washcloth.

A strong wave of nausea brought Hannah to her knees before the toilet. She went through this with the climax of every migraine; it was part of the routine. Finally, tired of waiting for the inevitable, Hannah stuck a finger down her throat until the gagging reflex brought up the cherry pie.

2
The Yank 'Em Inn

Hannah's dreams were thick with herds of deer, soft-eyed gentle beings that wandered everywhere, like sheep. Over snowdrifts, through lush grass, pausing on the shoulders of the road, speckled fawns encroached upon the margins of her life while does watched from the periphery of her vision.

As she rose slowly to the surface of consciousness, Chloe was a baby again, warm in rumpled flannel pajamas, still damp and smelling of sleep. The child climbed in bed with a moist hug to fold herself between Hannah and Robert. Even when she realized the illusion was dissolving, Hannah tried to continue the dream. It was already eight-thirty. It was Sunday. She was still in Antler. She needed more sleep.

She lingered beneath the thin blankets, transfixed by watery patterns that flickered on the pale wall. Without her glasses the blurred effect resembled mesmerizing mandalas from the period when she had tried Yoga meditation.

Among other things, Chloe accused her of inventing things to worry about. There was a modicum of wisdom in her daughter's assertion, although there had been sufficient worries through the years without those of her own creation. Take her marriage to Chloe's father, for instance. No, not now; she didn't want to think about Robert this morning. And especially not Tyler—he and Dawn were at a "Marriage Enhancement" workshop this weekend. She didn't want to think about Uncle Hal, either, but she couldn't escape his intrusion and fell back into lethargy.

Dennis Windsor had called for her at the Yank 'Em Inn last evening. Hannah's still-rocky stomach rebelled at the thought of a supper club menu, but a shower and another tranquilizer improved her outlook and her appetite. In taupe silk pants with matching silk sweater, her mirror image, at least, seemed to suggest that whatever her uncle's Last Will and Testament revealed, she would deal with it.

The attorney surprised her by driving a silver Porsche. "Hannah!" As he held the car door open, he greeted her like an old friend. "Did you keep your nose out of trouble this afternoon?"

She was amused by his display of familiarity. Over the phone she'd visualized a chunky, small-town lawyer, not this tall, suave, silver-haired gentleman who looked like he'd just come from the yacht club in his navy blazer and tan linen slacks.

"I apologize for the change in plans," he said, pulling out of the motel parking lot with a smooth burst of acceleration. "I hope I can make it up to you."

"Was your emergency resolved?"

"Bunch of tree-huggers. We skirmish now and then."

Hannah was about to mention Chloe's activism, but he continued, "Opening day of fishing season's, tomorrow. Do you fish?"

"No," Hannah had to laugh, "I don't."

"Better watch out, that's a crime around here! But I don't fish either. We've got a terrific little country club—Lofty Pines—where I try to sneak in a quick eighteen holes whenever I can. Do you golf?"

"Not really," Hannah admitted.

"Then what *do* you do for fun, down in Madison?" Windsor teased. "I'm a Badger myself, you know. Class of '61. Still hold a block of season tickets for Badger football."

He came back to Antler to practice law with his father following graduation. Now his dad was retired and Dennis and his wife had a five-bedroom house on a lake near Cedar Springs, the Lakeland county seat (and a silver Porsche that looked more than a little out of place among the local pickups and SUVs, Hannah wanted to add). They discussed their mutual affection for favorite campus haunts and by the time they reached Manitowish Waters, Hannah felt almost comfortable with him.

In a sylvan sort of way, the entrance to the supper club was impressive: three massive concrete stumps on either side framed a long drive bordered with rows of towering white pines that led to a lodge built of logs aged to a rich dark patina.

"You know the story of this place?" he asked, as the hostess led them to their table on the back porch.

"I saw a sign in the lobby about a *Dillinger* exhibit . . ."

Hannah had learned all about Little Bohemia as a child. Grandpa Larkin loved to tell stories about the lumber camps and Prohibition, when northern Wisconsin served as a convenient hideaway for Chicago hoodlums. But now, for some quixotic reason, she decided to let Windsor tell his tale.

They were seated near a window by the lake. Another window, another picturesque lake. She was thinking back to her visit with Ginger, half-heartedly monitoring Windsor's version of the escape of John Dillinger and Baby Face Nelson from Little Bohemia one night in 1934. The FBI, hot on their heels, mistook a car filled with locals for the gang members and killed one of them, instead. The sound of gunfire alerted the gangsters just in time for their getaway.

Windsor was pointing down toward the shore, describing "missing loot" and "gun-molls."

"You've got to have a look at the relics in the other room. People come here just to see them. The guy who owns this place calls them 'bullet-holers' because they're fascinated by the bullet holes, but he's got the ammunition bag in there, and a tear gas shell that was fired at the lodge."

Hannah smiled. Windsor was a "bullet-holer," himself.

"I'm surprised your uncle never told you about Dillinger and Baby Face Nelson. Al Capone's brother had a bar near here, too."

"I didn't actually know my Uncle Hal," she began, then, noting the quick concern in Dennis Windsor's eyes, added, "very well."

"Came up to the lake when you were a kid though, I'll bet," he said, with certainty.

"Of course," she lied with confidence, "every summer. I have such fond memories of those times."

The waitress interrupted and took their order for drinks.

"I suppose we'd better talk business," Windsor said somberly as soon as the waitress was out of earshot. "Charlie Jenkins get in touch with you?"

"We're all set for Monday morning," Hannah said.

"I know I don't have to tell you how eccentric your uncle was, but it's a peculiar setup, if you ask me, when he's going to be cremated anyway. Typical of Hal Larkin, though, to want something unconventional like that."

The waitress served Hannah her glass of wine and set a martini before Windsor.

"To Star Lake Saloon and Housekeeping Cottages," he said, raising his glass with a hand that revealed a slight tremor.

"To Uncle Hal," Hannah responded, taking a sip of her wine.

Windsor slipped an envelope from an inside pocket of his jacket. "Your uncle's will, Hannah. I'll go over it with you, and explain it as we proceed. As I told you yesterday over the phone, Dad drew it for him. Had to move my father out to Northern Lights a few months ago. He and Hal were fishing buddies. Matter of fact, I think you can find a picture of him out at the lake with a good-sized musky."

Windsor removed the olive from his martini glass with the cocktail pick and rolled it around on his tongue. Then he stared, ruminatively, at the shallow glass and moved it in a circle on the tablecloth.

Hannah saw that he was flirting, teasing her, and she laughed, "All right, I'm ready to hear about my rather incredible inheritance."

He gazed up at Hannah and narrowed his eyes ever so slightly, but not so subtly that Hannah didn't notice.

"I suppose you're wondering what to do."

"Well, yes, I am."

The conversation grew serious, but his explanation made it all seem very simple: If she cleared out Hal's personal possessions from the resort this weekend, Windsor would put her in touch with a real estate agent to get the whole place on the market, furnishings and all, ASAP.

"Then, if nothing unusual turns up, and I don't anticipate that it will, we'll have a personal representative named on Tuesday. Hal named my dad as executor, but I assume you'll want me to take over."

"That does make the most sense," Hannah conceded, "but will I have to stay until then?"

"Until Tuesday, at least," Windsor explained apologetically. "Tuesday's our day for probate, here in Lakeland County. We'll ask for an immediate hearing, instead of waiting the usual weeks. You'll have to testify in court to the fact that you're the sole heir, and so forth. But then once we get that out of the way, the P. R.'s appointed—we used to call it executor, but now we just say P. R.— then you're free to return to Madison with total confidence. Your uncle's property will be in safe hands."

"I'm so relieved! That sounds almost too good to be true," Hannah confessed.

"Of course, whatever you realize from the sale will be subject to any creditors who might come forward once the notice runs in the local paper. Then, about six months from now I'll be able to write you a check for the proceeds. Minus expenses, fees, and so forth."

Windsor would send a realtor out to Star Lake this afternoon to give her a tentative estimate.

"We'll have to get a more official appraisal for actual probate purposes," he added. "But I want you to have a rough approximation of what you might be able to realize when the whole thing's said and done."

After the tension and worry she'd experienced, the attorney's clarification was wonderful news. The sudden release prompted her to agree when he suggested they share a bottle of wine. Later, over coffee as the long day wound down, Windsor again urged that the resort be sold right away.

"I hear it's in a pretty sorry state of disrepair," he said. "You and I both know it's never a good idea to throw good money after bad, so I wouldn't hire a bunch of handymen to fix up the place. Quite frankly, that would take up a lot of your time and cut into your proceeds. We see Chicago buyers all the time who are on the lookout for old resorts. They clear the land or divide everything into condos. To tell you the truth, you can get more for the land than for those old buildings."

His smile was warm and reassuring, Hannah noticed. By the time he pulled up in front of the Yank 'Em Inn and said goodnight, Hannah felt she'd met a dependable ally who had nothing but her best interests at heart.

"Thank you," Hannah said with sincerity, placing her hand on Windsor's where it rested upon the gearshift. He lifted her hand and brought it tenderly to his lips.

"Hannah . . . ," he began, and held her glance with his.

She thought of Tyler with his wife at their Marriage Enhancement, and leaned toward him. It was a careless move, she knew, but casual, and by that time she felt relaxed and at ease.

He pulled her close, murmured in her ear. "I want you to take it easy, Hannah, get a good night's rest. This will all be over very soon. And remember, you're not alone—I'll be right here with you every step of the way."

His arms were comforting, and she turned away reluctantly.

"I am awfully tired."

"I'm glad our appointment didn't work out this afternoon," Windsor said softly.

His gaze had been so direct, so soothing and genuine, Hannah was certain she could trust this man. Sure, she was stuck at the Yank 'Em Inn through Tuesday, maybe Wednesday at the latest, but then this entire miserable episode would be pretty well wrapped up. Wasn't it fortunate, she thought, that she could leave all the details to Dennis Windsor's capable supervision.

Chloe's birthday gift to Hannah this year was a T-shirt with a quote from Gandhi, "There is more to life than increasing its speed." She'd brought it along, although she was sensitive about displaying a slogan she could not whole-heartedly endorse. Maybe she would wear it today, when she found the energy to get out of bed.

For Christmas, Chloe signed her up for an evening class in watercolor painting because she thought Hannah wasn't getting out enough. Hannah was touched by her daughter's thoughtful effort, so she gave it a resolute try. But the key to success with watercolor, she quickly learned, was the serendipitous adaptation of random splashes and dribbles. Hannah tried to control the paint and ended with pages of brown puddles that dried into muddy blotches. The class made her nervous. Afterward, when Chloe asked to see what her mother had painted, all she had to show for six weeks of deliberate effort was a painting of a rock, a single rock that happened by accident during three unusually dry brush strokes. She had hoped to capture some wildflowers, anemones, like those that would be blooming in Grandpa's woods right now.

This time of year Hannah felt a deep and lonesome tug for the small, rural village in central Wisconsin where she had been raised. Between her backyard and the Little Wolf River, Grandpa Larkin's woods had been a place to hide and make-believe. She'd always thought of it as his woods, not just because he owned the land but because he was the first to take her there. Grandpa pointed out secret paths and hidden places where delicate trilliums grew, sad white stars strewn idly in the shade. There were pale violets, too, and golden cowslips that bloomed in the marsh. She was fascinated by the stain that bloodroots left on her palm.

As with most places that one cherished as a child, the secret paths lost their magic through the years and Hannah found herself wandering down there before her father's funeral years ago, wishing mysteries still colored every shadow and life could be filled with radiant promise.

There would be wildflowers at Durward's Glen, where Tyler and Dawn were experiencing Day 3 of their marital revival. In one of her newspaper columns for Hearst, Ella Wheeler Wilcox referred to a woman like Hannah—one who loved another woman's husband—as the kind who "likes to see how far she can lean over the roof of the house without falling off."

Hannah was aware of the risks involved with loving Tyler, and of course she had longings that went unfulfilled. With Chloe all but moved out of their home and Tyler currently wrapped up in his marital stress there were times (like this) when Hannah felt very lonely, almost.

Chloe, still in graduate school, met Eric last year at a nonviolence workshop. Hannah hoped that Chloe really felt a true commitment to the issues she was supporting and was not allowing herself to be exploited, even arrested and jailed, because of her infatuation with him. In February, Hannah agreed to go along when Chloe and others picketed local Planned Parenthood clinics targeted by "rescuers," but since then Chloe had campaigned *for* Indian treaty rights, *against* the nuclear command facility Project ELF, and espoused the left-wing approach to whatever topic happened to be current, popular, environmentally and/or politically correct. Hannah happened to agree with most of her daughter's positions but preferred a quieter way of supporting them: a check, a bumper sticker; nothing controversial or revolutionary. But then, Hannah wasn't in love with someone like Eric: he had a masters in philosophy but chose to work as a carpenter. For her birthday he had given Hannah a jewelry box fashioned out of cherry with mother-of-pearl inlay. And Eric was pleasant to have around; he could even cook, which was more than Hannah could say for her daughter whose culinary expertise ran the gamut from tofu pizza to a deli soup-of-the-day, preferably vegan. But besides his carpentry and his political activism, Eric didn't seem to have much direction. Chloe lacked goal orientation too. She seemed content to follow Eric, putter along in school and work as an office temp whenever her funds got low. At least they never mentioned getting married (what *did* that diamond stud in her nostril mean, by the way?).

Hannah certainly had no desire to marry again. She valued the independence she had earned, enjoyed her lifestyle too much to give it up for any man. So Tyler was a safe choice, in many ways. He was a generous lover, monogamous (in his own fashion) with very little risk that he'd dump his wife for her (and if he did, Hannah realized long ago, the mystique of the attraction would dissolve incredibly fast).

When they met for the first time in Birge Hall she was aware that tall, bald, Tyler Cole, PhD, was a legend on campus. "Remember, he's a respected malacologist, and our only National Medal of Science winner," Joe Mickelson warned her. "He's got government research money coming out of his old wazoo."

Hannah saw intense eyes that scrutinized her darkly and a neatly trimmed black beard that made him look, oddly, like Lenin. He had nice hands. Sensitive hands. She always noticed men's hands. First their eyes, then their buttocks, and then their hands. His touch was soft though his grip was firm. He also wore great cologne.

Malacologist sounded sinister but that only meant someone who was involved in the scientific study of mollusks. Frankly, Hannah was surprised that he would bother with their little educational video based on his research, *Imperilled Pelecypoda: Threatened Mollusks of North America.*

After the first month of meetings, however, the subject of mollusks consumed less and less of their time. The welcoming handshake became a kiss on the cheek that turned into an embrace and eventually more ardent expressions of affection took place right there in his Birge Hall office where he left word with the department secretary not to be disturbed.

He had telephoned her from Durward's Glen the other night while she was packing her bags for Antler, dialed the minute his wife's flip-flops echoed down the hall to the shared bathroom in the dormitory for a shower. Hannah hated when he did that. It demeaned him. And at home, when Dawn ran out for groceries and he rushed to call her, Hannah would envision him standing guard behind the draperies, the telephone cord trailing behind his ass like the tail of a rat. Which he was, she had to admit.

More and more often, Tyler's actions were irritating her. Why should he presume, for instance, that she was sitting around with nothing better to do whenever he found an opportunity for clandestine conversation?

Surely Tyler had some kind of sexual encounter with Dawn last night. It was probably required for the final evening of their "Enhancement." Maybe they had to report on it at a group discussion the next day, give each other a score. ("I'll give him a 95 for effort.")

Hannah hoped he'd been able to get it up.

All right, that was cruel.

When he experienced erectile dysfunction with Hannah, it took a lot of coaxing and some direct persuasion on her part for the little guy she jokingly referred to as Uncle Wiggily to stand straight for a moment or two so they could approximate a missionary position or a variation thereof. But occasionally, almost as quickly as the miracle happened his penis would slide down again, becoming an amorphous puddle of flesh that no amount of teasing or tickling or licking would inspire to rise again.

One book said some men got an erection if you bit them softly on the buttocks. The effect was close, but no cigar.

He refused to try the new, helpful medications, because of threatened side effects. An implanted pump was out of the question.

Hannah shifted her position and plumped up her pillow. She switched her thoughts to Uncle Hal's teeth, to replace the image of Tyler and Dawn.

It had occurred to Hannah, just before falling asleep after midnight, that maybe Uncle Hal's teeth had made their appearance after his body had been removed. What if Uncle Hal had not died in his own bed but somewhere else?

Occasionally she'd had a fleeting worry about what might happen if Tyler expired above her, or below her, in *her* bed or even in his office, in a position of disgrace so that she would need to dispose of the body in a more suitable, less difficult-to-explain location. Try this scenario: Uncle Hal experiences his heart attack while with a woman (maybe Ginger!), in her bed. Then his body is transported back to his own, inadvertently minus his teeth which are delivered later with the hope that by being placed so obviously in that glass on the nightstand anyone who comes upon them will rush them to their rightful owner—assuming, of course, that he is still above ground and able to open his mouth to receive them.

That was a spellbinding hypothesis, but it was easier to accept Hal's demise while sound asleep in his own bed. Why would he take his teeth out to make love? That didn't seem very romantic.

Tyler claimed the danger posed by their illicit lovemaking added to his ardor. Maybe that's why Tyler's plumbing problem (as Dawn reportedly referred to it) had not been apparent to her in the beginning.

Three years ago in April they'd driven out to Indian Lake, a county park with a steep hill overlooking a small body of water once prized by the Winnebago tribe. Climbing the rugged trail they had to stop to catch their breath a couple times and fell into a sweaty embrace, enjoying the exhilaration of their adventure and the knowledge that they really were all alone.

At the top of the hill, Hannah showed him a crude little stone chapel built by a farmer in the mid-1800s when his family had been spared from an epidemic of diphtheria. Inside was a tiny space no larger than a child's playhouse. Worn linoleum covered the floor and damp rock walls were still frosty with winter's chill. A simple altar with a vase of plastic flowers and statue of the Blessed Virgin stood beneath a wooden crucifix opposite the door. Hannah paused for a moment, grateful for the joy nearly bursting her heart even as she knew she should be begging forgiveness.

Tyler found a sheltered spot to spread their blanket on a grassy space between rocky boulders. The early sunshine infused her with a sense of renewal, as if the primal source of summer itself were warming her through to the bones. She glowed with gladness from within, her face already flushed, radiant from the climb.

Hannah ate her yogurt, then gave Tyler part of an orange. He shared half of his sandwich and the ubiquitous carrots and celery Dawn always prepared.

Until that afternoon their expressions of affection had consisted of soulful kisses and some brief but enthusiastic rubbing together of fully-clothed bodies in Tyler's office. The April sun willed them to lie back on the blanket and Tyler reached over to nip Hannah's neck beneath her ear. Clumsy in his eagerness, he fumbled with the buttonholes on her blouse. Hannah lay quietly, her hands behind her head, watching him, amused. He caught her smile and returned it, then folded back the edges of her shirt, bending to kiss her before placing his face between her breasts. Unhurried. Lazy. Warm.

When she couldn't lie still any longer, she ran her fingers through his hair, urged him on.

Tyler unzipped her jeans. He knelt beside her and pulled them from her legs, then removed her flowered underpants, too, opening her thighs to the sun.

"Did I ever tell you that you have a beautiful little ass?" he said, his palms cupping her buttocks. "I love these cheeks! They're lovely cheeks, *sweet* cheeks."

She marveled at her lack of embarrassment, her body fully revealed in front of this man and beneath an azure ceiling free of clouds. It did not seem at all incongruous that she was completely naked while Tyler remained fully clothed.

He decorated her legs with kisses, moving up to tease the smooth, inner softness of her thighs with a flickering tongue. Her mouth shaped words, a silent scream, a sob. Then she lay on the blanket in the grass among sun-warmed boulders and damp leaves left over from autumn, their rotting humus a pungent perfume, musky and dark.

When she could move again, she reached for Tyler, who lay on his side, watching her. She placed her palm on the crotch of his jeans and felt a firm bulge. But when she tried to unbuckle his belt he drew her hand away, said they needed to get back, he had a class. He derived pleasure just from pleasing her, he told her, and from that afternoon on he would think of her as his very own Sweetcheeks. So she hadn't a clue that anything was less than wonderful.

The experience lingered in their shared memory. "Remember that day at Indian Lake?" one of them would say, and they would be back on top of the glacial moraine in thin April sun, at the beginning of a new season, the beginning of their love. But they never returned there in reality, recognizing the futility of trying to recapture the rapture of that moment or the excitement of that fresh passion.

Mrs. Swann?"

Hannah was drawn from her reverie by a knock at the door of her room.

Nine-thirty.

"Just a moment," she muttered, grabbing her glasses. "I'm coming."

Hannah stumbled out of bed and pulled on her robe.

"You got a telephone call . . . ," a man's voice shouted.

As Hannah opened the door, the manager of the Yank 'Em Inn handed her a portable phone.

Perhaps it was Dennis Windsor, suggesting they meet for breakfast.

"Cheeks," Tyler said tenderly, "I only have time for a quick hello but I wanted to take a chance. You arrived safely? All is well?"

"Tyler, this is so strange. I was just thinking about *Indian Lake*."

"How was your meeting with the lawyer?"

"Um, that's hard to say," Hannah felt herself blush, standing in the doorway. She hoped he would understand her cryptic response. The manager wandered a few paces away but hovered, awaiting the return of his phone. Hannah turned her back.

"It's not what I expected," she whispered, feeling tears well up. Her throat constricted, making it hard for her to speak.

"You sound like you need a hug, my Darling Hannah." Tyler's voice was caring, and she realized how badly she needed his words of tender endearment.

The manager cleared his throat. Nearby she could see the headquarters of the Antler Chamber of Commerce, a little log cabin adjacent to the motel parking lot. In front of the cabin a family of gigantic fiberglass deer grazed, welcoming visitors to Antler, Wisconsin, "The Deerest Place on Earth."

"There's so much I need to tell you, but I can't explain it right now," Hannah said. "It's a lot more complicated. This might take a few more days than I thought." She really wanted to wait and tell him in person about her unexpected inheritance. "How are *you* holding up?"

God, she was sorry she'd said that! But Tyler didn't seem to notice her double entendre.

"Okay, I guess. Dawn's been going through some tough stuff, though. We had this assignment for last night . . ." Hannah *knew* it! They'd been ordered to make love. "to fill out this questionnaire," he continued, "make a list of reasons we want to keep our marriage intact. It's not easy to describe if you haven't been to one of these, but there's some harebrained homework. I need to talk to you, Cheeks. Do you think you might be back by Tuesday?"

"Tuesday night. Wednesday at the latest, I'll have to see. It depends," Hannah replied.

"I know you have responsibilities up there," Tyler said, soberly. "So, you know, I understand."

Understand? Understand what?

"What do you understand, Tyler?" Hannah turned back around to face the manager of the Yank 'Em Inn who was blatantly eavesdropping.

"That you're not able to be here to help me out, right now. I know you would be, if you could."

"Right," she replied.

"What?"

"Right. Yes. Sure, I'd rather be there than here. Help you out . . ."

He had no idea what *she* was going through. "This place is really up in the goddamn boonies," she said, suddenly hostile, glancing up to see if Mr. Big Ears had caught her less-than-flattering reference. But he was waving at somebody coming out of the bait shop across the street.

"Gotta run," Tyler said, cutting her off.

"I'll try to call you Monday afternoon," she added quickly. "I might be still tied up with funeral stuff but I'll try to get to a phone if I can."

She started to add that her cell phone probably wouldn't work, so far from civilization, but Tyler interrupted.

"Talk to you later."

"I love you, Tyler."

"Love you, too, Cheeks," he whispered.

Hannah took a deep, shaky breath but before she could say goodbye, he was gone.

I love you, *too.*

As she twirled the faucet inside the shower, Michael Caine encroached upon her thoughts. Michael Caine? In her shower? Standing under the thin stream of hot water Hannah recalled a line of his from an old late night TV movie she'd caught last week: "My tailor asked me, 'If your wife and your mistress were drowning, which one would you save?' And I said, 'My wife, because my mistress would understand.'"

3

Zing, Creak, Bang

Charlie Jenkins was waiting for Hannah when she arrived at Star Lake Sunday afternoon. The funeral director was a wiry little man in a dark suit and tie, not given to much conversation. She handed over Uncle Hal's things and, after a few additional exclamations about the dentures, he was off. She heard the screen door on the porch open and close: *zing*, as the rusty spring stretched, *creak*, when the hinges squeaked, and *bang*, the door slammed against the jamb.

Hannah realized how desperately she needed companionship when she found herself wishing Mr. Jenkins had hung around longer. She couldn't even find the dog, though she called for Babe and looked everywhere.

The entire resort looked more forlorn in sunshine than it had during rain. Just inside the door of the Saloon were coat hooks she'd missed the day before, made of severed deer legs bent at right angles, hooves up. More of Ginger's artistry? Procrastinating, Hannah helped herself to a can of Diet Pepsi from the cooler behind the bar. Then she took a couple bags of salted peanuts and, to quell her anxious stomach, swallowed a Valium with the soda. This was lunch.

A sunbeam glancing through the window near the bygone fireplace illuminated the claret jukebox as if it were a honky-tonk jewel.

It took only a nickel to play one of the 75 rpm polkas. She emptied an ashtray and wiped it clean with the bar rag to the familiar strains of "Beer Barrel Polka."

Fishermen smiled out of their snapshots with grins of triumph, such enormous pride! Polaroids. Mostly men, only a handful of women: *Toots Henderson, 40″ musky, released. Swede Johnson, 42″ musky, released. Ollie Hug, 29″ walleye, 9½ lbs. Gertie Hoezer, 51″ musky, 30 lbs.* And there was Denny's father, *Geo. Windsor, 45″ musky, 6/30/86.*

She tried to picture the bar bouncing with activity, Ollie and Swede and their buddies (and their wives) bobbing in time to the jukebox, drinking beer, playing sheepshead. The Milwaukee Brewers might be playing on TV, or the Green Bay Packers. A hamburger slapped on the grill would sizzle out from the kitchen and more people would think they were hungry. Pretty soon the whole place would pulse with accordion music and laughter and the spit of hot grease would mingle with cigarette smoke and spilled beer and we'd be having fun. We'd be having fun, you bet!

Of course Ginger would be lost without her hangout, but if the new owners wanted to keep the Saloon going maybe they'd let her stay on. Seeing everything razed, all those vacation memories going back to who-knows-when disappearing in a puff of dust and rubble—well, Hannah wouldn't have to stick around to watch.

Her conscience was beginning to prickle. Should she pay for the Pepsi and the peanuts? To be safe, she dug some change out of her purse and pressed the buttons on the cash register. She was still standing behind the bar when she heard the screen door on the porch open and close.

"Hi, there," a friendly voice observed. "Can an old goat still get a cold beer in this here establishment?"

Hannah had to smile at the jovial greeting. A heavy-set man in a blaze orange windbreaker flipped up a pair of clip-on sunglasses. His red cap advertised "Our land is dirt cheap."

Sure, she'd serve him a beer, she replied with a smile, grateful for the friendly face. At the same time she made a mental note to check on the regulations of the liquor license or bartender's license or whatever was involved, and find out whether or not such transactions were lawful.

"Gus Schultz," he said, offering her a pudgy hand, his voice a shade more serious. "Denny Windsor sent me out here to give you a ball-park figure, though the place ain't seen a lick of work. Not for a long time, anyways."

Hannah opened a Miller with a bottle opener that was fastened to the counter with a length of string.

"I'd appreciate a general estimate to give me something to think about. It's kind of hard to absorb the extent of all of this," Hannah was indicating her uncle's death, the barroom, the resort, the no man's land beyond, with an impatient sweep of her hands.

Gus took a long swig of his beer, then belched. He grinned.

"You know, I got an eye for a good lookin' woman, but I don't remember seeing you before, up here in our neck of the woods."

"I haven't been here lately," Hannah lied. "I didn't . . . didn't know my uncle was ill."

"Hah! Harold Larkin's biggest problem was being such a stubborn-ass son of a bitch." Schultz took another long swallow of his beer. "Forgive me for saying so, Miss Swann—or is it Mrs.?—I guess now's not the time, ain't that so. I shouldn't be disrespectful."

"It's Mrs.," Hannah replied, but she declined to reveal any more of her personal background even when Schultz asked, "Any more family come with you? Hubby? Kids?"

"I drove up yesterday."

"All the way from Madison, Denny says."

"That's right."

"Don't see many Madison folks up here. Milwaukee, maybe. Illinois, mostly. Lots of Illinois buyers looking for land, winterized cottages, condos, you name it." Schultz pronounced the "s" in Illinois so the name of the state rhymed with *noise*.

She was trying to figure out how to encourage Schultz to move along when she heard the happy clatter of Babe's paws on the porch. The screen door opened with a zing and a smack, once again.

"Gus, how're you doing?"

Schultz looked over his shoulder at the man in faded jeans, T-shirt, and worn tweed sportcoat who entered.

"Kerry." The realtor's flat greeting was indifferent. "You met Mrs. Hannah Swann yet? She's the lucky gal who Hal left this trash heap to." His laugh ended with a snort.

Hannah greeted the newcomer, extending her hand across the bar, "I'm Hal Larkin's niece."

"Dan Kerry," he responded. The blue eyes behind wire rim glasses were cool and direct, analytical. Hannah glanced nervously away.

"Well, gotta get to work, no rest for the wicked." Schultz drained the last of the beer from his bottle, smacked it down on the counter with a bold wink at Hannah, and walked out.

"Excuse me . . ." Hannah called after him, "Mr. Schultz?" But the screen door banged shut and he was gone. She wondered about the etiquette of asking Schultz to pay for his drink. He may have assumed she was just being hospitable. He was out here to do her a favor, though it would be to his advantage if she listed the resort with his firm. She knew nothing about the real estate business *or* barroom protocol.

"Would *you* like a beer?" she asked Kerry, hoping the offer would disguise her discomfort. Why hadn't she taken the time to put on some makeup this morning. Just a touch of blush and mascara would have made her feel a lot better right now.

Kerry's blue gaze could be described as icy, almost, Hannah thought.

"I wouldn't mind a cup of coffee."

"Coffee." Hannah repeated, dully. "I know there's a percolator upstairs . . ."

Kerry brushed past her and went through the swinging door into the commercial kitchen behind the bar. She hadn't even looked in that kitchen, yet. A massive rolltop desk stood at one end, opposite the black gas range. An old, beat-up refrigerator (she resisted the morbid impulse to peer inside) had recipes for beer-battered fish, grocery coupons, and faded newspaper clippings taped to the doors. A clip-on magnet held descriptions of the cottages and their rates.

Hannah leaned against the chopping block table in the center of the room while Kerry rinsed out a coffeepot and found a can of ground coffee without any trouble.

"You've obviously done this before," Hannah offered, trying to lighten the solemnity.

"More than once," Kerry replied.

"Were you a close friend of my uncle's?"

"I was."

Hannah took a deep breath, a deep Yogic breath. *I will peacefully approach one thing at a time,* she repeated to herself.

"I'll bet this place has quite a history. Do you know much about it?"

"Some," Kerry replied. "Ginger's the one you should ask."

The coffee was brewing now. Hannah left the kitchen and returned to the bar. She could hear Babe crunching the dog food in the bowl she had brought down to the porch.

"I looked all over for the dog when I got here today but couldn't find her anywhere," she called to Kerry, eventually.

"Picked her up last night," Kerry said. He brought two mugs of coffee from the kitchen and placed them both on the counter. "She's just a pup."

"Let me show you something," Hannah pulled the wrinkled snapshot of her father and Hal from her purse. "My father told me this was Uncle Hal's first dog. The picture was in a box of mementos from my father's side of the family and I had to search all over for it before I came up here. Anyway, it worked. 'Babe,' I mean. The name. Lucky I remembered. I always wanted a dog."

At the sound of "Babe," the dog stopped eating and gave a soft woof, then resumed crunching her dry food.

Hannah knew she was babbling, but Dan Kerry was so indifferent! She'd had her fill of human companionship now and wished he'd finish his coffee and leave. The realtor, too. Babe could stay.

Kerry took the snapshot from Hannah and flattened it on the surface of the bar. He was silent for a long time.

"You didn't know your uncle very well." This was not a question. She took a moment to consider her response.

"I didn't know my uncle at all." It seemed important to tell this man the truth although she had passed off an easy lie to the inquisitive Schultz.

"If you'd known Hal," Kerry said, studying the snapshot, "you'd have known that he called *all* his dogs 'Babe,' after this retriever."

It was Hannah's turn to be silent. Kerry handed the photo back to her and she searched it again before placing it carefully back in her purse.

"Well, he never called it by the wrong name, then," she quipped. Hoping to smooth the resulting awkward silence she added, "That Packard was my dad's first car."

Kerry sipped his coffee. "You ask Schultz to come out here?" he asked abruptly. "Or did he show up on his own?"

"I asked him to. Or, I assume Mr. Windsor did. The attorney that's handling the estate. Dennis Windsor. You probably know him, right? I mean, Antler's a pretty small town. His father drew up my Uncle Hal's will. Mr. Windsor's, I mean, not Mr. Schultz's." Her face grew warm. "Dennis Windsor said I should get a ballpark idea what the place is worth." My God, she sounded like a raving idiot. "What I can get for it. Because, apparently, my uncle left the place to me."

There was another uncomfortable pause.

"Why do you ask?"

"Because Hal shook off realtors like woodticks. They could never understand that he wasn't interested in selling."

The edge of irritation in Kerry's voice caused a sudden surge of anger in Hannah. Enough of this friendly facade.

"And you don't think I should sell it, either?"

"I'd advise you not to give that damn fool Schultz the time of day."

"Seems to me, Mr. Kerry," Hannah responded archly, "if my

48

uncle felt you should be the one making these decisions, *it seems to me* he would have bequeathed the property to you."

Kerry took another swallow of his coffee.

Hannah came out from behind the bar to sit near him, accepting his unspoken challenge but leaving a vacant barstool between them.

"Okay, so I didn't know my uncle. I can't see why that's such a big deal. Nobody ever mentioned him anymore. Not even my mother. So I suppose I thought he was already dead, if I thought of him at all. Which I did not."

"You've made that clear," Kerry said. He tightened the laces on his sneakers with hands, Hannah noticed, that appeared well-shaped and nicely cared for. He smelled good, too, and gray curls fell over a forehead that was already tan.

"I have no idea how he even knew I existed, either, except for an old Christmas card my mother sent him when I was a baby. Ginger dug it out of that mess upstairs. Believe me, I'm not thrilled about inheriting this nightmare. I don't appreciate the aggravation, and I don't need a guilty conscience besides, thank you very much."

She took her glasses off to rub her eyes, then put them back on because she could feel the sting of tears forming there.

"This isn't easy . . . I don't . . . I've been having a difficult time."

"I realize that," Kerry mumbled, "I shouldn't have said anything."

"Yesterday . . . yesterday when I got here it was raining, and I ate a whole cherry pie. Out in the parking lot. In my car. I've never done anything like that in my life, it's really not like me at all."

Why did she have to admit *that,* she wondered, wiping her nose with the back of her hand.

Kerry swiveled on the barstool and turned his back to Hannah so, she assumed, she could pull herself together. Then he grabbed his coffee and walked out onto the porch.

Yes, he had a nice ass, too. Tyler didn't even look that good in jeans. How old was this guy? Fifty-five, fifty-six?

Hannah sighed and slid her fingers through her hair to fluff it up. She found a napkin behind the bar, blew her nose, and followed him.

Kerry was seated on the glider and Babe lay, content, at his feet.

She could see Gus Schultz walking on the footpath along the shore north of the lodge between the cottages and the lake, pausing every now and then to peer through a window. Hannah wondered what he could see through the grime. She watched him try the door of Aldebaran, the two-bedroom cabin set back from the others. He disappeared inside.

Dan Kerry was watching Schultz, too.

"Those cabins would be filled today, if Hal hadn't closed down because of the damage. We had a bad windstorm a week ago. He found vacancies for his May reservations with friends at other resorts, but Hal was sure he'd be back in business by Memorial Day."

Three more weeks, Hannah noted mentally.

"Ginger told me he died of a heart attack, due to the storm, probably. The work he'd had to do. To clean up, clearing the downed trees." She couldn't form a complete sentence to save her life. Pull out a chair from the nearest table, she ordered herself, and take another Yogic breath. Where was her Valium? "It really is a peaceful spot," Hannah offered. "Very peaceful."

Dan Kerry looked over at her sharply, as if he could read her mind.

"You think so?"

"Well, I can see why it would appeal to . . . to some people. People who want to get away from it all." There, she was doing better. She took another deep breath. "The fresh air is really quite refreshing."

He was still watching her and had hardly touched his coffee. She was itchy and restless; there was a lot of work ahead, and she wished he'd go.

"What do you do up here, Mr. Kerry?"

"I fish," he said, clearing his throat. "I make a living, fishing. I'm a guide."

"A guide?"

"A fishing guide."

Hannah had no idea what he was talking about.

"Ordinarily I'd be booked this weekend, too. But your uncle gave me a hand when I needed it, years ago."

There was an awkward pause while Hannah wondered what to say next. His less-than-friendly attitude could be blamed on deep grief.

"I'm sorry I kind of lost it in the bar," she apologized. "This is all new to me. Only three days ago my biggest worry was meeting a writing deadline, and now . . ."

Kerry nodded. "Three days ago Hal and I were going to clean up those downed trees south of the Saloon. The insurance adjuster finally got out here to give Hal an estimate so we were ready to go ahead. But Hal's old chain saw—he wasn't real big on maintenance. You might have noticed that."

A weak smile. Kerry reached down to fondle Babe's head, then cleared his throat.

"Hal called, to ask if I'd bring my chain saw over. But I was out and didn't get his message right away. In the meantime he took out his axe and got to work. By the time I got here he'd pretty much decimated a dead pine and hauled a pile of brush over to the clearing by the entrance. I found him upstairs. He was already gone. The EMS guys—the volunteer fire department's emergency medical squad—were just leaving; they said he was unconscious when they arrived."

Hal hadn't died in bed with Ginger, after all. She decided not to mention the confusion about his dentures.

"My father died of a heart attack. So did Grandpa Larkin."

"Hal never said a thing about his health, and almost nothing about his family." There was still a chill in Kerry's ice-blue gaze, Hannah noticed, but now his shoulders slumped.

Schultz emerged from the Aldebaran cottage, trudged closer to the lodge and when he saw them on the porch, waved goodbye.

"I'll be in touch, Mrs. Swann," he said.

"Thanks," Hannah waved back.

"For what it's worth," she told Dan Kerry softly, "my attorney assures me I can trust that man."

Kerry leaned forward, elbows on his knees, and seemed to be choosing his words carefully. He held her gaze with a cold blue intensity.

51

"For what it's worth, Hannah Swann," he warned, "Dennis Windsor's opinions are questionable and Gus Schultz is a dangerous fool."

Hannah turned away to face the lake, pretending to study the far shore, the rim of dark trees against the cloudless sky. This guy gave fishing lessons; what did he know about administering probate? Dennis had assured her last night that all the legal and real estate work would be competently looked after. She recalled how comfortable she had felt in his presence. Dennis *could* be trusted, she was confident of that.

Kerry was saying something about the "grassroots environmental roads leading to Hal Larkin," but it was a cheap ploy, Hannah decided, an emotional tweak, a comment made to appeal to her liberal, Madison origins.

Staring at the water certainly had a mesmerizing effect. She tried to picture the first tourists who visited this resort, intrepid travelers who slept on pillows and mattresses stuffed with balsam. She knew all about Wisconsin's history, environmental and otherwise, and she didn't want to hear any more about "grassroots issues" from her daughter or this guy, either. Finally, Kerry's voice faded away.

When Chloe came home with a peace sign tattooed on one shoulder blade Hannah viewed the symbol with amusement. After all, Hannah had begged for her own parents' permission to leave Little Wolf and enroll at the University of Wisconsin, a school with a "pinko" reputation in the early 1960s. But when Chloe had her left nostril pierced, Hannah saw that as something entirely different. Two weeks ago Chloe arrived for dinner with a diamond post sparkling there in place of the gold ring. "Does this mean you're engaged?" Hannah remarked sarcastically while Eric cleared the table.

Hannah had stayed in Madison after graduation, content with the work she found and the way the city reflected her new persona: intellectual, inclusive, idealistic, and culturally informed. How dare her daughter accuse her of not being up to date on certain issues? The rebuke still stung like a slap in the face.

Silent now, Kerry must have realized at last that she wasn't listening.

Hannah squinted and tried to spy the elusive loons she had seen the day before. If she saw them again, maybe it would be a good omen.

"I hope you don't think my uncle's death was your fault," she offered.

Kerry was peering across the lake, interested in something on the opposite shore. "I was in a hurry last week. Had other things on my mind. I didn't take the time to think about his health. Now, all of a sudden Hal's gone."

Hannah had no idea how to respond to this man. She was aware of Kerry's struggle to contain his emotions. She jumped when the chilling tremolo of a loon broke the uneasy silence and echoed eerily across the water.

A shiver rippled across her shoulders and shimmied down her back. If that was the sign she was waiting for, what did it mean?

"We all have things that happen in our lives, things that, in retrospect, we wish we could change," Hannah said, and realized she was thinking of Tyler.

Kerry told her, "See that loon?"

The loon was diving for fish about twenty yards off the end of the pier. Hannah watched, and tried to guess where it would emerge after it disappeared. It stayed below the surface for an uncomfortably long time.

"What about it?"

"They're the most primitive birds we have, in North America. Loons have been around for about a hundred and ten million years. That one comes back to Star Lake every spring, as soon as the ice is out."

"How can you tell it's the same one?"

"Loons always return to the same territory to nest, year after year. They mate for life."

"I find that hard to believe," Hannah replied.

"Well, don't believe me then," Kerry said simply with a shrug of his shoulders. He was in no mood to be challenged, either. "Ask Victor Redhawk, our Loon Ranger. He runs the Star Lake General Store."

"Don't you mean Lone Ranger?" Hannah joked. What in the hell was a *Loon Ranger?* She bet even Chloe hadn't heard of that one.

"Victor leads the Loon Watch every spring. He takes a loon count on the lakes in our area. Keeps track of all the nests, the number of eggs, ascertains the reasons for nest failure, when that happens. On this lake, for example, they nest on that island right down there beyond Aldebaran, on that low, marshy ground next to the water. Victor will be out here one of these days when the eggs hatch to make sure everything's all right."

"So . . . ," Hannah tried to change the subject. She'd already learned enough about loons to last a lifetime. "Hal planned to re-open by Memorial Day?"

This seemed to pull Kerry out of his funk, and he straightened up, realized he was holding a mug of cold coffee in his hands, went to the door, and dumped it outside.

"Memorial Day. Hal keeps the notebook with the reservations in the kitchen. Rolltop desk. Want me to show you where it is?"

Finally, she was accomplishing something.

"Why don't you," Hannah suggested. She'd copy the names and addresses, notify every person who'd reserved a cottage and refund their deposits right away.

Kerry walked briskly through the bar into the kitchen with Hannah and Babe trailing behind. He pulled a worn, spiral-bound notebook out from under a Polaroid camera on the rolltop desk—the camera used to capture exploits of champion fishermen, Hannah surmised. Then he leafed through the notebook to a page headed "May," in what must have been her uncle's handwriting because it so closely resembled her dad's.

Hannah estimated that at least a hundred names and addresses had been entered, along with cabins, boats and motors reserved, and deposits paid. Amounts ranged from $175 to $275 per reservation, per week, from the first of May to the last week in October.

"Hal depended on repeat customers," Kerry explained. "People loved Hal and they love this place."

Hannah nodded, but she was devising a plan.

"A man works in a factory in Milwaukee or on an assembly line in Rockford, he can't wait to go fishing up north. Get some of this 'fresh air' you find so invigorating."

"I said 'refreshing,' not 'invigorating,'" Hannah snapped, annoyed. Something feisty inside her was beginning to rise like yeast and needed punching down.

"No matter how romantic you try to make it sound, Mr. Kerry," she said testily, "I'll have to prick a few dream-vacation balloons. No way am I going to hang around here all summer, scrub toilets and wash dirty sheets and listen to barroom baloney."

"You might want to wait a week or so," Kerry suggested calmly with a narrow glance. "See what happens. Get a better feel for what's going on."

"I don't owe these people anything," Hannah interrupted, pointing at the names in the notebook. "Or you, or even my Uncle Hal, for that matter."

"I think he meant . . ."

"How do you know what he meant?" Hannah asked, irritated. "Tell me what he meant! I really would like to know just what in the hell my crazy uncle had in mind for me in this *neck of the goddamn woods!*"

But Kerry was silent.

"Maybe it's news to you, Mr. Kerry, but your northwoods isn't some kind of dazzling Shangri-la. My father would have another fatal heart attack if he knew what I'd inherited."

"I just thought—" Kerry began.

But Hannah interrupted. "I happen to have a life of my own that does not coincide with salvaging this dump. Can't you figure it out? I really don't give a damn!"

Hannah coolly dropped the notebook of reservations at his feet.

This time Kerry didn't contradict her, he merely turned and left the kitchen, walked out of the bar and slammed the screen door on the porch. *Zing, creak,* and *bang.*

Babe scooted after him, merrily wagging her tail.

4

Choose a Star

When she thought about it afterward, Hannah would recall the Monday of Hal's funeral or memorial service or however he intended the event to be remembered, as one of the strangest days of her life.

After Kerry left the resort on Sunday, she tried to call Dennis Windsor but his home number was unlisted. Since she would probably see Windsor at Hal's funeral the next day, she decided she could wait to ask if he'd check with the bank for her and find out if the deposits for the summer season were kept in a special account.

Then, just in case her quirky uncle had been somewhat more casual about business matters, hid the checks in his refrigerator for example, or under his mattress waiting to cash them later, she searched every imaginable hiding place. Nothing.

A number of handmade brochures had spilled out of the spiral notebook that still lay on the Saloon's kitchen floor. Each displayed a carefully drawn map of the resort, indicating the names of the cottages and facilities supplied. On the back was a diagram of the Celestial Chain, showing Star Lake, Lake Sundog, the Lost Arrow River, and Lake Sickle Moon.

Babe was back in the porch swing, asleep. "Shoo," Hannah said, and she slapped the dog with the notebook. Babe crawled off meekly, then retrieved a slab of chewy rawhide in an attempt to appease Hannah's mystifying displeasure.

Except for the first half of May and the last half of October, the place was nearly booked for the entire season, twenty-two weeks. Only Aldebaran, the two-bedroom cottage, and Vega, the tiniest, were still vacant for any appreciable amount of time. Rental for boats and motors was extra. Quickly adding the numbers in the deposit column, Hannah came up with roughly sixteen thousand dollars. Okay, that was the dollar amount she would have to refund.

Time for a break, to digest this information.

While Babe chased sticks and a worn tennis ball that she threw when the dog pestered her, Hannah snapped pictures of Star Lake with the Polaroid for Tyler. She captured the grungier aspects of the resort, the damaged cottages, dented boats, and the battered red pickup in the parking lot. With that out of her system she took some scenic shots, as well: A loon swimming close to the lily pads. The vista from the sleeping porch above the Saloon. And one of Babe waiting patiently on the pier, inviting Hannah to toss the tennis ball into the lake so the dog could splash over the edge and retrieve it, again and again.

Monday morning Hannah arrived at the funeral home early. She was mostly concerned about facing Dan Kerry and his disdain, so she was not prepared for the shock of recognition when Mr. Jenkins led her into the carpeted room where a simple pine coffin was surrounded with floral arrangements. The person lying inside could have been her grandfather.

"I'll leave you be," Mr. Jenkins whispered, "and keep the doors closed for a while so's you're not disturbed until you're good and ready."

Hannah stared at the neatly combed white hair, the familiar chin.

"Oh, Uncle Hal . . . ," she repeated silently, over and over to the motionless body in the gray suit and new shirt and tie that she'd found. "Oh, Uncle Hal . . ."

In his presence she was washed by a flood of forgotten emotions. Her father's death, a few years ago, had not been easy, but her grandfather died when Hannah was ten and the sorrow she'd felt over that intractable loss had never dissipated. She had been an only child and Grandpa had been her best friend. Now that childhood grief was resurrected with a more complex response.

She had spent a night with her grandparents about a year before Grandpa Larkin died, and was helping him fix a surprise breakfast for Grandma on the wood-burning cookstove he refused to discard.

"Here, peel this baked potato," Grandpa handed her a leftover from supper the night before. "Then I'll show you how to chop it up with a baking powder can like we did in the lumber camps."

Hannah wanted to please him and struggled with the cold, shriveled potato peel by trying to remove every blemish and discoloration. The paring knife was slippery and awkward in her small hand.

"The spots won't show after they're cooked," Grandpa explained, patiently. He placed the potato on a cutting board where he sliced it in half. "Now, just chop it up in little pieces like this. Be careful, the edge of this can is mighty sharp."

After she nicked the tip of her little finger, blood spilled onto the cutting board and Grandpa threw the potato into the cookstove.

"There, don't carry on so, Hannah. I never saw anybody cry so many tears."

"Not even when the dog got run over?"

"What dog, Hannah?" He asked with what seemed like confusion.

"Uncle Hal's dog."

Nothing could equal such a tragedy, she thought, if she'd been able to have a dog of her own and it got killed.

"Daddy told me Uncle Hal's heart was broke when his dog got hit by a car."

"Yes, he cried," Grandpa's voice seemed different as he wrapped her finger in soft gauze and sealed it with adhesive tape.

"Did you cry, too? Did you cry when Hal ran away?" The pain of her cut finger caused her to forget her promise never to mention his name. When Grandpa didn't answer, she asked him again because he was getting deaf.

"Grandpa?"

"Yes, I cried, Hannah. And Grandma cried, too," he said, softly. "Let's make cinnamon toast."

Her grandfather had been a gentle and sensitive man. What could Hal have done to hurt him so? Or, was it possibly the other way around? She tried to imagine the circumstances: Hal got a girl pregnant and refused to marry her. Hal stole something of her grandfather's. Whatever it was, it left a wound in her family that never healed.

"What's your secret, Uncle Hal?" she whispered. "And why have you involved me in your death when you barely acknowledged me while you were alive?"

Hannah sat quietly. She wanted say something about the pain he caused her family in the past. She wished she could express her resentment for upsetting the comfortable rhythms of her life right now.

Ten minutes passed.

She wandered from one floral display to another, wondering how she would manage enough chirpy small talk to carry her through the rest of the morning. Here was the arrangement of purple iris and painted daisies from her and Chloe, and a spray of calla lilies from her mother, Lily Larkin, who often sent a "signature" bouquet. Spring blossoms from Dan Kerry spilled gaily from a delicate hand thrown vase. Pussy willows, sprigs of plum blossoms forced into bloom, held a card signed by someone into New Age jargon: Celestial Summer. And then there were wreaths from local organizations like the Lakeland County Board, the Sportsman's Club, and the Lakeland County Citizens' Action Group. There was also an odd and distinctly Hawaiian display of black and red feathery flowers with juniper berries, ginger blossoms, and two birds of paradise that seemed garish and out of place. The accompanying card read, "With all my love, Ginger, Until we meet again."

Voices in the outer hall signaled the beginning of her official duty. Hannah realized she was melodramatically wringing her hands.

Mourners crowded the small funeral home. Grieving neighbors walked slowly past Hal's body. Some touched his shoulder and said farewell.

Hannah slipped off to one side in a futile attempt to dissolve into a corner, but her identity seemed to be common knowledge. The mourners' greetings were warm and their handshakes seemed heartfelt. "Your uncle was a really nice guy," she must have heard at least fifty times.

Although she scanned the crowd anxiously, Dennis Windsor was not there. Neither was Gus Schultz.

The responsibility for leading the service fell to Dan Kerry, who seemed more composed and relaxed with this group than he had been with Hannah yesterday. In his dark gray suit and tie he looked appropriate in that role. Hannah watched people draw to him and lean in close to hear what he had to say. Not once did he glance in her direction, so she presumed—with some relief—that she was not the subject of their conversation, nor, with a tinge of regret, did her current discomfort rank very high in his immediate concerns.

A pale young couple, Lyle and Lynne, in their mid-thirties with identical blond ponytails, played mournful tunes on their fiddles. Then a blond boy of about eleven joined them in singing a song about loss and love that Hannah could not follow.

There were readings by individuals who had earlier introduced themselves to her but whose last names she had not bothered to retain. A rather elderly man named Walt read, appropriately, a poem by Walt Whitman. Ben, a balding young man with freckles stroked a ragged red beard as he read a page from Aldo Leopold's *Sand County Almanac*.

Victor Redhawk (the Loon Ranger, Hannah wouldn't forget that), a Chippewa with a long braid down the back of his red plaid flannel shirt, explained that Hal shared Native Americans' concepts of the essential relationships of human existence. "Hal understood that everything needs to be measured in its effects upon the next seven generations." Victor then recited Chief Seattle's famous quote: "This we know: All things are connected. Whatever befalls the Earth befalls the sons of the Earth. Man did not weave the web of life, he is merely a strand in it. Whatever he does to the web, he does to himself."

Hannah was next. Kerry introduced her by saying she was Hal's only surviving family member, the daughter of Hal's brother, Fred, and sister-in-law, Lily Larkin, and she had "traveled from her home in Madison to be with us on this sad occasion."

Now at the lectern and facing a pensive audience, Hannah raised her eyes to read the typed poem that Charlie Jenkins had given her just that morning.

> "When death arrives and my soul is set free
> To dwell amidst the vast celestial sphere,
> Choose a star and name it after me;
> A symbol of my love forever near.
> For you, my dearest, enlumined my own heart,
> With lustre of your promised radiance.
> When, then, forevermore our lives must part
> The spark within my soul bears evidence
> Of this: I never shall abandon you . . ."

Hadn't she accused her uncle, only a little while ago, of appearing to her at the same time he abandoned her? She nervously cleared her throat and continued.

> "In times of joy or hours of solemn night.
> If haunting dreams seem horrible and true,
> Above dark clouds is everlasting light.
> Though I am gone I have not fled afar,
> My love is constant as the Northern Star."

She resumed her seat, head down. The sonnet was embarrassing. Worthy of one of her eminent BWPs.

Dan Kerry was introducing Ginger Kovalcik, "Hal's special friend," who chose to speak beside the spectacular Hawaiian bouquet. Ginger had arrived too late for Hannah to greet prior to the beginning of the service, and with her purple and green flowered dress she displayed a fresh carrot rinse and tightly spun permanent wave.

Presumably, Hannah decided, in a place like Antler the definition of "special friend" was the same as "lady friend" but carried a less unseemly connotation.

Ginger's offering was the last in the brief service. She dabbed at her nose with a tissue, then clasped her hands in front of her bosom and took a deep breath.

"Hal never would have wanted a eulogy, but I thought somebody ought to say a little something more about Hal Larkin and what he meant to all of us here in Antler and out at the lake."

Ginger told of Hal's generosity, his love of nature and echoed previous statements about his strong commitment to the land. "He never said if he was Republican or Democrat, he said he was a conservationist first and he meant it. That was enough to get him elected to the County Board for twenty years, anyway, back when it meant something to be on the Lakeland County Board."

There was laughter at this comment, and a few people applauded softly before Ginger went on.

"Hal had his rules of life, as he called them, and he was always a good man and a kind man and I'll always remember that. He had a sense of humor, too. He was like a little child when it came to some things, being so curious and such, and he had a real enjoyment for living. Star Lake just won't be the same without you, Hal."

Ginger's voice got higher and threatened to break.

There was polite applause from the crowd when Ginger sat down, and more noses were blown.

In closing, Dan Kerry read the time-worn lines from Thoreau, about living in the woods because he "wished to live deliberately, to front only the essential facts of life." Kerry said that concept was one with which he and Hal had found a common bond. Then Kerry issued an invitation to the nearby Sportsman's Club, where coffee and a light lunch would be served. That was unsettling news to Hannah, who had hoped to be relieved of her responsibilities as soon as possible.

She lingered near the casket as the crowd filed out the door and the only other person left was Dan Kerry. He remained seated in the back of the room, bent forward with his face hidden in his hands. The man was involved with his own private sorrow. She respected that.

The impact of the past few days and the tension she'd felt all morning were causing a provocative mix of reactions and resentment. She focused on her uncle, a man who physically resembled her grandfather, and whose genetic composition and blood were similar to her own. She wished Dennis Windsor had been present; she needed his confident smile, maybe even a reassuring hug. As eager as she might have been to return to Madison, events would be transacted in court the next day that would drastically change the local landscape. A gnawing guilt, a peculiar responsibility toward her inheritance, was conspiring to demolish her resolve. It wasn't just the physical landscape; that had already been altered with Uncle Hal's death. But the psychological landscape of Star Lake—that was also about to sustain a big transition.

If Hannah canceled the summer reservations, if the cottages were torn down and the resort closed up tight, the balance of man and nature that Hal and Miriam, and Ginger, too, had established out there through the years would be destroyed. A certain equilibrium was necessary to enjoy the environment without exploitation. A synchrony had to be reached.

"I'm sorry I can't keep your dream alive as you'd hoped I would," she found herself telling her uncle quietly. "There's just no way."

Hannah paused to blow her nose.

She noticed that he still wore a thin gold band on his left hand.

"I can understand why you and Miriam fell in love with Star Lake, and I hope you won't think I'm not grateful that you entrusted the place to me. But expecting me to live up here and run a fishing resort, the burden of owning such a place, that's *way* beyond my capabilities, Uncle Hal. If you'd known me at all, you'd have been aware that I'm not strong enough, or wise enough for that."

It was inane, she knew, rambling aloud to a corpse, and the tears did not make sense, either. But what she did next was instinctive and sincere, and encompassed her heartfelt sense of loss.

"I brought you something to take along on your travels, Uncle Hal. She misses you so much."

Hannah held the Polaroid snapshot she'd taken of Babe waiting on the end of the pier. She slipped it into the pocket of Uncle Hal's new shirt, the pocket that rested upon his heart.

5
Wetlands

"You're still looking peaked, Honey," Ginger said with concern, plopping down two slices of pie and pulling a folding chair up to the card table where Hannah sat.

Last Friday night's fish fry could still be detected in the rancid ambiance of the Sportsman's Club. Beneath more dusty specimens of wilderness wildlife on the walls above her, Hannah was introduced to a buffet with slices of boiled tongue, three kinds of cheese, bowls of German potato salad, dill pickles, and white rolls. The mere sight of cherry goop spreading over the paper plate Ginger slid before her was more than she could handle right now.

"Oh, I gotta take a load off my feet." Ginger landed with a deep sigh, "These damn high heels! I always say, if my feet were any wider they'd be round."

With some effort, Ginger reached down and shucked the purple shoes. "I sure liked that poetry, Hannah. I could never get head nor tail of poems as such but the one you read today got me thinking of that old Christmas card. Don't have the foggiest, but it did."

"It was a nice service."

"Plenty of flowers, too," Ginger continued. "I had my son ship the Hawaiian bouquet. He's stationed over on Maui. Anthuriums, though, they give me the creeps. I'm not crazy about those shiny red saucers with their yellow peckers dangling out."

"I noticed some ginger in that bouquet."

Ginger's smile grew watery. She put down her coffee cup and placed her hand on Hannah's arm. "There probably isn't another soul in this room that knows there was ginger in that arrangement besides you and me, and Charlie Jenkins. I asked him if he'd throw one of them in the fire along with Hal and he said he would."

Hannah agreed that would be a meaningful gesture, but decided not to mention the Polaroid snapshot of Babe.

"Now," Ginger said with renewed gusto, attacking her pie, "I'll bet you're having a dilly of a time out there, trying to set things to rights."

Hannah nodded, picked up a fork and pretended to be interested. Obviously Kerry hadn't informed Ginger of their confrontation the day before.

"I've been thinking," Ginger said. "Why don't you just move your things to Star Lake. Save all that driving back and forth."

Hannah protested, "I'd be out there all alone . . ."

"You'd have Babe," Ginger said. "She's a great little watchdog. And Aldebaran, that big two-bedroom cabin isn't too messy, I ran a dust rag around it the other day. You could be comfy there, don't you think?"

"I'm going home in just a few days," Hannah argued.

"You'd save a little money," Ginger suggested, helpfully. "Aldebaran's even got its own kitchen, and how often do you get the free use of a cottage on a beautiful northern Wisconsin lake?"

Over the weekend a flush of spring seemed to have caught up with Star Lake, and feathery green softened the branches of the white birch. Tyler didn't answer when she called his office so Hannah left the number of the Saloon with his department secretary who would be thrown off by the 715 area code. Then she tried calling Chloe to let her know she'd be staying at the resort for a few days, but her daughter wasn't at Eric's. When she called her own number Hannah retrieved three messages: two from Joe Mickelson wondering how the Wilcox script was coming along and a third offering his condolences.

She finally found someone to talk to when Lily answered, down in Tampa: "I'm certain Miriam wrote that lovely poem," her mother said. "We knew she had an artistic nature." Hannah described the homemade star signs next to each cottage door. She wanted to salvage the poignant pieces of folk-art, even if they were falling apart. The star-sign for Aldebaran dangled precipitously from a rusty nail.

"Why didn't you tell me Uncle Hal was still alive?" Hannah complained, "I really feel put-upon. I shouldn't have to be the one in charge!"

"I was the executor of Daddy's estate, Hannah, and that wasn't easy for me, either . . ."

"You were *married* to Daddy, Mother. I never even knew Uncle Hal!"

She realized she was whining. "What's the big deep mystery, anyway," Hannah demanded. "Why did Hal run away from home?"

"Dear, don't get so keyed up that you bring on a migraine," her mother cautioned. "It's all in the past."

"It's screwing up my present!"

There was silence on her mother's end of the line.

"Daddy and Hal had words. I don't remember over what."

"But how can you *not* remember! It must have been something big, something momentous, for Hal to run off like he did!"

"My memory's not what it used to be. Maybe it was because of a remark Hal made to Grandpa Larkin."

"God, Mom . . ." Hannah realized she sounded remarkably like Chloe.

"Hannah, I don't remember the details. It was many, many years ago. Before you were born. You can't expect me to remember that far back!"

"Elderly people are supposed to remember the past better than yesterday," Hannah replied, irritably.

"Daddy might have tried to get Hal mad. Goaded him to fight. But Hal wouldn't do it."

"Did Daddy hit him?"

"Just a little. He might have. Yes. A little bit."

"Jesus."

"Hannah, I don't like it when you swear. It isn't ladylike."

"Fuck 'ladylike,' Mother! I'm going nuts up here, telling so many lies! People ask if we stayed at Star Lake when I was a kid and I tell them sure, every summer. Everybody wants to know if I realize what a good guy Hal was and I have to say of course!"

"I begged Daddy to apologize," Lily said. "I sent Christmas cards to Hal and Miriam and never told your father. And I did suggest once that we visit Star Lake, but Daddy said it would be disloyal to Grandpa Larkin."

Babe romped along while Hannah dragged her suitcase down the footpath to the largest cottage. She plugged in the refrigerator and took bags of groceries from her car. Aldebaran would do for a couple days, if she didn't lose her mind from the isolation. Turning on the water was simple enough, but the gas was another matter and Hannah hoped someone might show up who knew what to do about that because the hot water heater wouldn't work without gas and neither would the stove.

At least there was the dog. Babe had found her old tennis ball and tried to convince Hannah it was time to play. Hannah sat on the steps of the cottage and idly tossed it to Babe who raced to bring it back, placing the ball carefully at Hannah's feet. Then Babe pranced backward, muscles tensed, waiting for the ball to be tossed in her direction again.

In Madison students would be sprawled on the grass on Bascom Hill, cramming for final exams. If Hannah were there today she would be sharing lunch with Tyler on Muir Knoll, enduring nauseating details of his rekindled marriage. Was that really preferable to this?

Finally tired of playing, Babe lay in a patch of sun near the cottage and chewed on a stick while Hannah changed into a pair of shorts.

An entire afternoon going to waste, when she could have been working on the Ella Wheeler Wilcox script. Why didn't she think to bring her laptop along? Why hadn't she made excuses when Ginger called last Friday to ask if she could drive north the next day? Why hadn't she quickly thought to say, "Oh, *that* Hannah Swann! She doesn't live in Madison anymore." She slipped a sweatshirt over her T-shirt and walked out onto the pier.

A loon floated serenely in the center of the lake.

Hannah could feel the smooth water beckoning. All those empty rowboats, waiting, and all this free time going to waste. Babe leaped into the boat tied to the end of the pier and sat on the front seat. The dog placed the soggy tennis ball carefully at her side and woofed as if to say, "What're you waiting for? Let's go!"

If they explored the lake there would be less time to sort out Polaris, Uncle Hal's apartment. She dreaded going through the personal residue of someone else's life. The act had a voyeuristic quality that seemed disgusting and repugnant.

Taking just a few minutes to look around the lake would be a spontaneous move and usually that wasn't her style. But right now she needed to do something physical to work off a smoldering rage that was building toward her father, mother, Uncle Hal, and especially Dan Kerry.

She could do what she damn well pleased; it was her boat now, her resort.

Her albatross.

There was a motor already clamped onto the stern but she decided to row for a while. The boat did not progress far from the pier, however, before Hannah took another look at the motor.

It must start much like the motor of a lawnmower, she presumed. She pulled out the choke, drew the rope toward her two or three times quickly, pushed the choke back in and drew the rope again. The little motor began to sputter. What a surprise! A brief period of experimentation with the handle of the motor and she knew how to speed up or slow down. Hannah was embarrassed at her elation.

Babe's nose was high in the air, sniffing a breeze that must carry the scent of beaver and bear, otter and skunk and deer. Hannah breathed deeply, too. She inhaled the fishy water-smell, the damp pungency of spring mixed with a faint essence of gasoline.

Over near the opposite shore an occasional cottage was revealed where boats were tied to docks and woodsmoke trickled up above the trees.

The scent of woodsmoke piqued her euphoria with a thread of melancholy. It must be a primeval response, she reasoned; the woodsy fragrance made her feel wistful, almost. *Wistful,* she spoke the word aloud, trying it on her tongue. *Wistful.* It was a BWP word.

Their wake feathered out and folded over, leaving a slowly settling trail. According to the map of the Celestial Chain in Hal's brochure, Hannah was headed for Lake Sundog which was connected to Lake Sickle Moon by the Lost Arrow River. She couldn't see how to get over to Sundog though, and only when another boat emerged from behind a bog of cattails and reeds did she realize the entrance was hidden.

Behind the bog, a large culvert acted as a bridge for the road overhead. The tunnel inside the culvert connected the two lakes. Hannah aimed for the semi-circle above the water and held her breath. She slowed the motor to a crawl. They rumbled through, emerging into an open area surrounded by water lilies and ferny-looking weeds. A great blue heron standing near the shore flapped its wings and took off, overhead. This was probably a good place for fishing, but she didn't need to know.

Dan Kerry would, though. She could understand that he had not been able to say hello at the funeral, he was busy and sad and had a lot of responsibilities. But he had ignored her at the Sportsman's Club, afterward. If he had seemed the slightest bit sociable she'd planned to ask that he keep her decision to sell to himself.

A cluster of fishermen gathered in the middle of Sundog waved from their boats as she passed. Hannah responded with thumbs-up and a grin.

At the end of Sundog, a marshy area marked the entrance to the Lost Arrow River, framed with tall, dead trees and an enormous osprey nest perched at the top of one of the most grotesque. Narrow and twisted, the river's grassy banks closed in almost at once and black roots encroached like knobby knees, bark peeling, grasping large boulders close to the bank. It took all Hannah's concentration to guide the boat between sunken stumps and fallen logs, maneuvering to miss the huge rocks that she could see just below the surface. She was spooked by the darkness, and felt chilled. At one turn the boat rocked against the bleached carcass of a deer: white ribs poked out of the water in a graceful arch.

"What am I trying to prove?" she asked Babe with a shudder. "I should be sorting Uncle Hal's socks and underwear."

Immediately, there was a clunk and the motor raced crazily. She thought they might have collided with an underwater rock. The boat slowed even as the motor whirred. They floated backward with the current while Hannah struggled with the motor, trying to figure out what went wrong.

Finally, she grabbed an overhanging pine bough and managed to turn the boat around. Again and again she tried to maneuver the knobs and buttons. Apparently May was not too early for biting flies—she slapped them from her arms and angrily brushed them away from her face.

"Goddamm it, Babe! Look what I've done!"

Hannah turned off the motor. Then she changed to the middle seat, turned around, slipped the oars into the oarlocks and began to pull. She checked her watch. They had already been out for over an hour and rowing back against the wind would take a lot longer than that.

She rowed, unable to see where she was heading. They collided with stumps, rocks, and once (Hannah *knew* this had been a sign; why hadn't she realized?) the hideous skeleton of the deer. She screamed and Babe, frightened, barked, which scared her even more.

Why hadn't she thought to bring along some food? An apple would have been a good idea. A picnic lunch would have been better.

72

Even the cherry pie she'd left on her plate at the Sportsman's Club would be welcome right now.

She was also getting warm. Impatient and angry, Hannah propped the oars up on the side of the boat for a moment while she pulled her sweatshirt up over her head. Her sunglasses popped off with the sweatshirt and flew over the side of the boat. Luckily, they landed upon a clump of lily pads.

Hannah quickly tried to retrieve the glasses, tipping the boat so it nearly capsized. At the same time she dislodged an oar, which fell free and floated away in the rapid current. The dog leaped into the water to get the tennis ball that rolled off the seat and bounced over the side.

"Goddammit! Get back in this boat *right now!*" Hannah yelled, exasperated.

Babe swam over to the boat, paddling with difficulty in the weeds. She snorted water, shook her head, the yellow ball securely clenched in her jaws. Hannah could swear the dog was grinning. Babe was having a great time, sleek and shiny as a seal. But how could Hannah get her back over the side of the boat without flipping everyone and everything?

It took a while. There were many false starts, but finally Hannah found that if she hugged Babe backward to her chest under the dog's front legs and propped her own right foot against a tree branch to counterbalance the weight, she could boost the slippery, dripping dog up over the edge and down, onto her lap.

Now Hannah was dripping, too, and sweating from the exertion of lifting a slick and slimy dog. Babe wriggled out of her grasp, licked Hannah's face, then shook herself in a gigantic shiver that began with the whiskers on her nose and ended at the tip of a tail that wagged like a crazy whip. At least one of them was happy.

"I can't believe I'm so fucking stupid," Hannah's voice caught with a ragged sob.

Her purse was in the cottage, which wasn't locked, and her Valium was there, too.

"Son of a bitch! What in the hell is happening to my life?"

A mother duck and her ducklings swam placidly past their boat: organized, focused, synchronized. Hannah's hair was pasted to her face and her T-shirt and her shorts were glued to her body. Gnats swarmed around her head. She slapped at the buzzing fat black flies. Her sweatshirt was in the bottom of the boat sopping up a mixture of oily dark water and questionable residue probably composed of fish guts, last year's nightcrawlers, and reconstituted bait.

The boat was hung up on a submerged log.

Hannah grabbed the one remaining oar and with some difficulty managed to free the boat from its obstinate trap to push it back out into the current. She devised a plan: There was no sign of the lost oar, so she would paddle with just one, as if the rowboat were a canoe. Then they would sort of drift with the current back into Sundog, where she could alert the friendly fishermen who would certainly come to her aid.

The process was exhausting. Blisters formed on her hands within minutes, and the heavy oar got heavier with each clumsy swing from one side of the boat to the other. But the end of the river was in sight. Hopefully, the fishermen were still there. Anticipating a change in luck, Hannah took off her sunglasses for a moment and pulled the filthy sweatshirt on to cover her clinging clothes. She still had *some* pride, after all.

But she hadn't bargained on the rain.

A curtain of white, it advanced from the far end of Sundog when she and Babe emerged from the swampy entrance to the river. The squall line already masked the culvert that led back to Star Lake, and there wasn't a chivalrous fisherman in sight.

Whitecaps whipped ahead of the advancing sheet. Hannah knew they would be in the thick of the storm within a few minutes.

"Hannah!"

Compared to the wind, the motor on the boat approaching the rear of her own made so little noise that she hadn't heard it coming.

It was Victor, the Loon Ranger. "You've got to watch out for rocks in there this time of year. Did you shear a pin?"

"How the hell would I know?" Hannah replied with a quivering voice.

Victor tossed a rope to Hannah and turned his boat around.

Concentrating on locating the entrance to the river, she had not noticed the dock or the log house tucked into the hidden bay. Now at least a half-dozen people watched from that dock as Hannah and Babe were towed to safety, including Dan Kerry.

She tried to imagine some humor in the humiliating situation. How could she relate this to Tyler? Surely he'd find it hilarious. Everything pointed to the fact that she did not belong here, didn't fit *at all*.

The storm arrived just as the boats bumped into the dock, and Kerry offered her a helping hand with a hint of a smile that, to Hannah, looked more like a mocking leer. Ginger bustled her to the front door of the sprawling log house, and, once inside, wrapped her in a bath towel.

"We saw you going upriver and then when you didn't come back for a long time I told them something must be wrong."

Everyone in the small group had been a part of Hal's funeral only a few hours before—the fiddling duo, the red bearded young man, Walt Whitman, even the kid.

"You take a hot shower, Honey," Ginger said, hurrying Hannah toward the bathroom. "You'll feel lots better afterward. I'll fix you up some hot chocolate. And a sandwich, too. I'll even scare up some dry clothes. Can I get you anything else?"

"Could you scare up a tampon, while you're at it? I'd even settle for a pad," Hannah whispered.

That's it! The ultimate end, zip, zero, *finis*. How much more humiliation could one woman cause for herself, Hannah wondered, how much mortification could she endure?

Dejected and defeated, Hannah peeled off her wet clothes and let them drop, sopping, onto the bathroom floor. The crowd must be having a hearty laugh at her expense.

Ginger had insisted on starting the shower for her and the hot water felt really good. But even hot water and a lot of shampoo could not wash away Hannah's disgrace.

If everyone who took part in the funeral was getting together later, wouldn't it have been courteous to see that she was invited too? Maybe Kerry was divulging her plans to sell the resort.

Ginger removed the wet clothes from the bathroom floor while Hannah was in the shower, and replaced them with a pair of soft jeans (much too big, but clean and dry), a man's plaid flannel shirt (ditto), and some thick socks, folded and placed upon the sink. Lynne, the female fiddler, had donated a tampon, Ginger said.

Babe was lying in front of a crackling fire and there was an empty rocking chair on one side of the fireplace to which Hannah was directed when she emerged, dry and dressed. The others were gathered in quiet discussion around the kitchen table.

"You relax here and warm yourself up for a few minutes, then one of us will take you home," Ginger said. "We're almost done with our meeting."

Home? Not likely.

The muted voices in the kitchen were mildly intriguing, but soft jazz in the background and rain spattering the windows in windy gusts made it impossible for Hannah to overhear.

Seeing herself bobbing ridiculously out in the storm with only one oar, she rocked and sipped the hot chocolate, rocked and sipped.

She ate all but one bite of the ham and cheese sandwich on dark homemade rye and shared that last bite with Babe.

The natural log walls of the home's interior were oiled and glowed with a warm satin sheen, reflecting the Navajo rug above the stone fireplace and the muted shades of red, black, and gray wool repeated in similar rugs on the wide, pine plank floor. Since Victor Redhawk had come to her rescue, she assumed the spacious home was his.

Hannah would have welcomed a nap, but when she caught herself nodding she sat up straighter and rubbed her eyes. She could not allow herself to get comfortable; had to stay alert, ready to head back. But the snapping blaze at her side felt luxuriously comforting.

Keep your mind busy. Where's Mrs. Redhawk? Among a cluster of photographs on the mantel, Hannah spotted a photograph of three kids, Dan Kerry, and a woman. Oh, shit. This wasn't Victor's home.

And these weren't Victor's clothes that she was wearing, either.

Now Hannah was wide awake.

Dan Kerry was outspoken and patronizing, and she resented his insolent attitude. The way he'd assumed she'd naturally carry out her uncle's wishes which had *nothing* to do with who she was and presumed a whole lot of erroneous . . . well, presumptions. And he didn't get along with Dennis Windsor. Who, on the other hand, seemed to appreciate her need for a more civilized lifestyle. Her attorney understood why she had to get home. Home to Madison, where she belonged. Where she had never felt as helpless and disheartened as she did right now.

Without a car—or a boat—there was no way she could escape. If she pretended to doze, she at least would be exempt from making awkward goodbyes with the gang in the kitchen. Hannah gave herself permission to relax.

She was vaguely aware when the group broke up, and heard someone ask, "Is she a goner?"

Voices hushed. Farewells were whispered and the last voice Hannah recognized was Ginger's.

"You be patient with her, Dan, you hear me? She's put in one heck of a hard day. Just look at her. Poor thing's worn to a frazzle."

She slept for almost an hour.

Few words passed between Hannah and Kerry before they got in his truck. She knew she should thank him for coming to her aid (she couldn't bring herself to say "rescue") and for the loan of his clothes, but his aloofness held her back. In the cab of his Chevy Blazer she leaned as far away as possible. Babe, alert and delighted to go for a ride, sat in between, eyes on the road.

The storm had passed over and the evening sky was bright with stars. With no city lights to dilute them, they blazed like hot sparks from a bonfire.

"I didn't know you lived on Lake Sundog," Hannah said in a meager attempt to fill the void.

"You never asked."

She tried again, wishing as she spoke that she could shut up and keep still. But she yearned to provoke him, somehow.

"What were you talking about in the kitchen? Did I interrupt an important meeting?"

"You might say that."

"Was it about my Uncle Hal?"

"His name was mentioned once or twice."

She had gone this far, there was no way she would quit.

"Is it something I'm not supposed to know about?"

Kerry stopped at an arterial, then turned right onto familiar gravel—Star Lake Road. This would get her to the resort in about five minutes, the way he drove. Enough stupid questions. She could tolerate five minutes of silence.

But he never shifted into full speed. Instead, Kerry slowed again and turned left. In the beam from the headlights Hannah saw a narrow gravel path.

"Where are we going?"

They drove for a few more minutes, negotiating sharp turns and deep ruts around trees, over marshy hummocks. Then Kerry came to a "No Trespassing" sign. He stopped the Blazer and shut off the motor, switched off the lights. The stars over the dark woods that surrounded them seemed to settle in the branches of the trees.

From behind the seat he pulled out a battery-powered lantern.

"Let me guess," Hannah said nervously. "We're at the town landfill and you're going to show me some bears."

"I wish it were as simple as that, Hannah," Kerry said. "If you had shoes on we'd go for a little walk."

A little walk! Suddenly, Hannah was scared.

She rolled down the window on her side of the truck. If she had to scream, no one would hear. If she ran she'd get lost before she had gone a hundred yards.

Then Kerry chuckled, as if he knew what she was thinking.

"I'm not going to make a pass at you, Hannah Swann."

He needn't have made it sound like it was such an absurd idea; crime statistics said that rapists almost always knew their victims.

But his voice lost its cold edge with the impulse of his laugh. "You asked what we were talking about. It has to do with those orange cylinders out there. Can you see them?"

Kerry reached around the dog to aim the flashlight out Hannah's open window. She could see a grouping of slender orange tubes, maybe four or five feet tall, sticking out of dried grass. There were perhaps ten of them, perhaps more, beyond the lantern's beam.

"Where are we?"

"About a hundred and fifty yards from the shore of Star Lake, where the road passes over the culvert. Remember when you took the boat through there, earlier today?"

Hannah thought back to her sense of exhilaration and the great blue heron she and Babe had scared into flight.

"Know what this is?" Kerry illuminated the orange cylinder closest to her door.

"I haven't the slightest idea," Hannah admitted.

"It's drilled for taking core samples."

"Samples of what?"

"Copper and zinc. We're parked on top of one of the largest copper deposits in North America."

"On this very spot?"

"Bingo."

"How do you know that?"

"Hundreds of studies, besides the coreholes. Aerial magnetic surveys and other research. You ever hear of Ingold Metals Limited, down there in Madison? Do your newspapers ever mention Ingold/American and what's happening in northern Wisconsin?"

Hannah vaguely recalled something about Ingold, maybe in Chloe's anti-mining flyer.

"I guess I haven't been paying much attention," she admitted.

"Ingold's a Swiss consortium, one of twenty-five mining corporations—international mining corporations. They've been leasing or buying up hundreds of thousands of acres of land here in northern Wisconsin. I tried to tell you about this yesterday, but you didn't seem to be paying attention then, either."

Hannah was sure he was exaggerating. Hundreds of thousands of acres: that was an incredible amount of land.

"A mine's going in *here*?"

"Ingold's been trying to locate an open-pit mine on this property for the last five or six years."

"But it's so close to the lake! The state must have regulations about doing something like that. I'll bet the Department of Natural Resources has pretty stiff requirements."

Kerry switched off the flashlight and the cab of the Blazer was dark. The leftover rind of last week's full moon weakly illuminated his profile as he spoke.

"When your governor's pro-mining, there's not much anyone can do. We've gone around and around with the DNR the last few years to try and get Ingold out of here with every legal angle we could think of. At one of our annual town meetings we passed zoning laws to restrict mining, and then Antler's esteemed mayor, Gus Schultz— you remember Gus?—he claimed he was speaking for the Town of Tamarack. Gus got the DNR to drop their plans to designate the Celestial Flowage as an 'outstanding' waterway because that would've barred mining and other projects that might degrade water quality. After that, township officials ignored the zoning laws and went ahead and signed with Ingold."

"*Our land is dirt cheap,*" Hannah said. "I suppose his real estate firm would benefit from a mining boom."

"A lot of folks see nothing but a big rosy future. Even with an outcry from our side, Lakeland County's pretty well divided on whether mining's a good idea or not. The economy up here has been depressed for a long time. People get excited when they hear 'jobs.' Schultz agreed to a public forum on the mining issue, on the condition that only so-called experts in water biology and forestry could participate. When Hal tried to speak out against the mine, he was ruled out of order and Schultz told him to sit down."

Hannah picked up the flashlight and illuminated the orange cylinders again.

"So what are you going to do?"

"We're holding a rally against the mine this coming Saturday. The final plans were put in place this afternoon."

Hannah had to laugh. "A rally? That's the best you can come up with? A protest rally isn't worth a damn unless you get the press involved," Hannah sniffed. "And nobody's going to cover a little demonstration way up here."

"You got any better ideas, I'm listening . . ."

"You'll have to set off a bomb or something. Make it newsworthy. Otherwise, who's going to give a damn. Who's going to show up for your 'rally' except a few local radicals?"

Chloe and Eric would love this, Hannah thought, if they could hear her telling Dan Kerry how to organize a protest. She couldn't wait to get back home with news of a mining controversy at Star Lake. Out of touch with current environmental issues? Chloe, your mother's not such a dud after all.

"Ginger, too?" Hannah asked. "Is she involved?"

"Ginger, all of us. Your uncle was an important member of our group, and you can see why; almost his entire life was devoted to preserving this wilderness."

"We're arguing over my selling the resort again, aren't we?"

"Star Lake is worthless, if Ingold goes ahead. No one's going to want to buy a resort across the lake from a mine. Except the mine."

Hannah bit her lip. The possibility had not occurred to her.

"Then why is Schultz so eager for me to list with his firm?"

Kerry sighed. "Ingold doesn't give a good goddamn about the place as a resort, Hannah. But they've been trying to get their hands on the property ever since they decided to go ahead with the mine. For one thing, the more geography they control, the more feasible their operation will be. Your land stands in their way."

"Okay. This might be a little more complex than I thought," Hannah conceded. "I appreciate that you brought me here to see these core-things. But I really don't feel I can get involved with your movement."

"You already are involved, whether you want to be or not," he said. "Whether you realize it or not."

Kerry started the motor and turned the truck around, heading back out toward Star Lake Road.

"Hal left his property in your hands. We'd have a lot more leverage if you kept the resort open this summer."

Hannah said nothing.

"Buck claims you left an anti-mining flyer in his bar, last Saturday. He thought you might have left it there on purpose."

"Actually, that was given to me by . . . an activist, when I was leaving Madison. You know how Madison is, full of knee-jerk liberals and all kinds of weirdos. Protest rallies every weekend . . ." She tried to make him laugh again, but apparently it didn't strike him as funny as it had Dennis Windsor.

"Buck's on our side, but it's a good idea to keep your ideas to yourself unless you want to make a lot of enemies. Your lawyer, for example."

"Dennis isn't my enemy!"

"He's been handling some issues for Ingold. Helped ram through an agreement between them and the DNR to change mining guidelines. Ginger says he's so crooked that when he dies they'll have to screw him into the ground."

Hannah squirmed. She recalled the way the Windsor had charmed her the other night, the reassurance of his embrace.

"My uncle drew up his will with Dennis's father."

"*George* Windsor was against mining. Maybe still is, but Denny just put George in a nursing home."

"I'm meeting Dennis tomorrow, in Cedar Springs. He's going to begin probate of Hal's estate."

"I'd keep a close eye on him, Hannah, if I were you."

"His dad was named executor, but Dennis wants to do it."

"*That's* no surprise."

"Well, he lives up here, he knows what's going on."

"Damn right, he knows what's going on. Why can't *you* be the executor?"

"They call it personal representative now, not *executor.*"

"Whatever it's called, you should do it yourself."

"I don't have time. And I wouldn't know the first thing about what to do."

"Can't be too hard, I'll bet even you could figure it out."

Hannah was stung by his sarcasm. "I'd have to care, first."

"Why do you want to go through all this bullshit and get swindled in the end?"

"We've been through all this, haven't we? Look, Dennis offered to take care of everything, and I don't want be stuck up here, or running back and forth . . ."

"You want to let Denny manipulate your inheritance for his own benefit?"

Of course Hannah didn't want that, and she was sure Uncle Hal didn't intend for that to happen, either. But she resented Kerry trying to order her around.

"You ought to know, Hannah, there used to be seven family-owned resorts on these lakes. Yours is the only one left," Kerry said. "Due to the threat of the mine you'd never get a thousand dollars per foot of lake frontage like the others did. Family-owned resorts like yours are disappearing fast."

"I should've said something to Dennis on Saturday if I wanted to get involved. Now it's too late—he'll have the papers all ready to sign."

They were back at Star Lake. Hannah reached for the door of the truck before Kerry shut off the motor.

"You told me yesterday to butt out, Hannah, and that's your prerogative. I even understand that I might have a loyalty to your uncle that you can't ever feel, because you didn't know the man."

Kerry sounded drained, and Hannah was at a loss for a caustic response. Instead, she found herself trying to repress a kind of self-pitying grief.

"All those years," she finally began, "if I'd had any idea that he was still alive or cared about getting to know me, I might have visited him. Or brought my daughter. I'll bet Chloe would love this place."

"Then tell Denny you've reconsidered and you want to be the P. R. You're the logical choice and Homer Twichell, our county judge, hates Denny. He'll agree."

Babe climbed over her lap to get to the door. Hannah let her out.

"Ginger says you need the gas turned on in Aldebaran. Want me to light the pilot lights in there, too?"

The gas. Hannah didn't want to check back into the motel tonight, and spending the dark night in the bed where Uncle Hal died was not an inviting thought. But accepting Kerry's help in getting the cottage ready for her use seemed to involve more baggage than she could handle, right now.

"Tell you what," he said, "I'll show you how it's done, how to turn on the gas and light the pilots for the water heater and the space heater. Then—don't get all agitated—you'll know how to get the other cottages ready for summer, if you find you're eventually so inclined."

With that kind of rationalization her indebtedness was reduced, she had to agree. Kerry led the way down the footpath toward Aldebaran. Star Lake was as smooth as a mirror in the stillness.

The silence that made her anxious during the day had dissolved into skittering squeaks and rustles of woodland nightlife.

Hannah stopped on the path to admire the brilliance of the stars' reflections on the water, making it, literally, a magical Lake of Stars. The sight was so exquisite that she nearly called it to Kerry's attention but she held back, reluctant to let him know that she found real beauty here. No sense supplying him with extra ammunition for the day when she would lock the place up and leave.

84

6

The Last Resort

Hannah checked her watch and studied the warped floor where generations of overshoes and workboots had scuffed the varnish. It was a cool morning, washed and fresh, and she had plenty of time to pick the final traces of Babe's fur from the sleeves of her red cashmere suit before Dennis Windsor rushed up the steps of the granite courthouse. Through the long narrow windows Hannah could see him nervously adjust his tie before he reached for the door.

"Had a breakfast meeting. Sorry. But everything's all set. I filed the will yesterday and the other papers are right here." He tapped his briefcase.

"I have to talk to you, Dennis," she began, quickly matching Windsor's hurried pace down the central corridor. Her pumps were more than a little battered after Saturday's tour of the resort in the rain, but they had stretched enough to be fairly comfortable.

"This will be pretty simple," Windsor assured her over his shoulder. "We'll be out of here in time for lunch. We can talk, then."

"I think we should talk now," Hannah said, reaching for his arm before they entered the courtroom.

"Look, I'm sorry about missing the memorial service," he paused in the doorway. "I've been up to my rear end in litigation, and then yesterday Dad got in a lather because he couldn't get to Hal's funeral. They had to call me out to Northern Lights to calm him down."

"You should have brought your father to Hal's service," Hannah suggested. "They were such good friends."

"Drop it, okay?" He led her to a seat inside the room. "The funeral's over, my dad got over missing it, I got on with my golf game. Now, let's get this over with, too, all right?"

This did not seem like the same man she'd had dinner with on Saturday night. If he seemed a bit nervous, Hannah decided, his abrupt manner was his court persona, or the result of having been delayed. Windsor quickly consulted with two women in the front of the courtroom and caused both to blush and giggle. On his way back to Hannah he stopped to greet a group of lawyers who welcomed him into their circle with hearty grins.

"There's another couple ahead of us, but that'll give us time to go over some details." Windsor took a seat next to her and placed a proprietary arm around the back of her chair. He explained that the two women he'd spoken to were the court reporter and the register in probate.

Just then the register loudly cleared her throat. Everyone stood as Judge Twichell entered the courtroom.

"Good Morning."

In his threadbare black robe, the judge appeared stern and thin-lipped. Only a few strands of hair stretched over a mostly-bald pate that, for some odd reason, Hannah's imagination insisted on topping with a rakish fishing cap.

Windsor busily rustled through the contents of his briefcase and removed the file labeled *Larkin, Harold A.*

"Sign these," he whispered, closing the briefcase for Hannah to use as a desk. "This is the Petition for Waiver of Notice, Order for Hearing on Waiver, Proof of Heirship, and Petition for Administration which we'll be filing with the Court."

"We need to discuss this," Hannah said softly, not wanting to intrude upon the legal action currently taking place in the front of the room.

Windsor had filled blank spaces on the forms with Hannah's name and address, the name and address of Uncle Hal and himself as personal representative. He pulled a Montblanc pen from his shirt pocket with a flourish.

"It's just as we agreed upon Saturday, Hannah," he replied. She took the pen and as soon as she signed the forms he slid them back into the file.

Dan Kerry had shown her how to light the gas in Aldebaran, and then left without saying anything more about her uncle's estate. But she'd slept poorly last night. Once, she imagined, she heard the howling of wolves. Then she heard a thump and scratching sounds against the porch (a bear?) and invited Babe to sleep in bed with her. The dog welcomed the chance to curl up at her side until dawn. Hannah had slept with a number of men in her lifetime but never a dog.

If she were appointed P. R. she might have to endure a few more days—and nights—at the lake. But after what Kerry said, the investment of time might well be worth the effort. True, she had no idea of the responsibilities she might have to assume as P. R., but her mother did handle her father's estate and God knows, Lily Larkin wasn't a legal whiz.

The other couple left the court room and Windsor escorted Hannah to the front table. He would be irritated if she changed her mind. It was time to fish or cut bait, as Ginger would say.

The register handed the file to Judge Twichell.

"The Larkin matter, Your Honor."

Dennis Windsor faced the judge. He was the epitome of confidence, Hannah thought. Almost movie star handsome. Almost a little too polished for a time-worn courtroom in Cedar Springs, Wisconsin.

"Your Honor, I'm here representing Hannah Swann in the Harold Larkin Estate, and appearances today are Hannah Swann personally, and by Dennis Windsor, her attorney. I don't know of any other appearances."

The judge surveyed the courtroom and asked, "Are there any other appearances in the Larkin matter?"

No one responded, so Judge Twichell nodded at Windsor, who proceeded.

"I would like to have Hannah Swann sworn to testify at this time."

The register motioned Hannah toward her desk, where Hannah raised her right hand. Placing her hand on the Bible always made her nervous. Swearing to tell the truth seemed like such a colossal promise. Beads of perspiration on her upper lip tasted salty.

Windsor continued, "Your Honor, I have a Waiver of Notice from the petitioner who, we believe, is the only person interested in this matter."

Windsor handed the Waiver to the register. She glanced at it and gave it to the judge.

"Please state your name and address for the Court," Windsor asked Hannah. She had to clear her throat before she answered. Then Windsor asked, "Did Harold A. Larkin, age seventy-four years, die on May 6, 1998?"

"Yes."

"And, at that time, was Harold A. Larkin domiciled in Lakeland County, Wisconsin, with a post office address of Rural Route Two, Star Lake Road, Antler, Wisconsin, 54561?"

"Yes. He owned and operated the Star Lake Saloon and Housekeeping Cottages at that address."

"And what is your relationship to the decedent?" Windsor said.

"I am his niece."

"Was the decedent survived by a spouse?"

"No, he was not."

"Did the decedent have any children?"

"No."

"Did the decedent have brothers or sisters?"

"Yes, a brother, my father. Fred Larkin. He's deceased, too."

"And did your father have any other children besides yourself?"

"No, I was his only child."

"Thank you, Ms. Swann." Windsor handed the Proof of Heirship form to the register and she gave that over to the judge as well.

Hannah found a Kleenex in her jacket pocket. Her nose always ran when she was nervous.

"Did the decedent leave a will dated August 19, 1993?"

Hannah wasn't sure of the exact date, but it was August something and the year was right. "Yes, he did."

"The original will is now in the possession of the Court, is that correct?"

"Yes. I've been informed that it is."

"And do you request the Court to appoint Dennis Windsor as personal representative, as provided by Harold Larkin's will?"

Hannah had worried the tissue in her fist into a tight, damp wad. Uncle Hal had not made that explicit request, and there was no way she could swear under oath that he had. She took a deep breath.

"Your Honor, I need to ask a question."

In her peripheral vision Windsor's head, bent over his papers, jerked up quickly.

"My uncle appointed George Windsor as his personal representative, not Dennis Windsor. I want to make that clear because I'm under oath to tell the truth, and I don't want to swear to something that isn't exactly correct."

"Thank you, Ms. Swann," Judge Twichell seemed amused.

"And I want to explain that I agreed to let Dennis take his father's place because at first I was convinced that would simplify things. But that was before and now I've been wondering, is it too late, would it be all right? Do I have to agree . . ."

She was inanely chattering, flustered. Judge Twichell gently interrupted.

"You needn't agree to anything that causes you discomfort, Ms. Swann. What do you have in mind?"

"Well, *me*. I thought it might be possible to be, to act as Uncle Hal's personal representative, myself."

"Your Honor, I . . ."

Windsor attempted to catch Hannah's eye and speak with the judge at the same time. No one seemed to be paying attention to him.

"That sounds like a logical request to the Court, Ms. Swann."

Hannah thought she saw the hint of a twinkle in Judge Twichell's eye and in that moment she knew why the judge looked familiar: *Homer Twichell, 50" musky, released.* Now he turned to the lawyer and brusquely snapped, "Mr. Windsor?"

The lawyer's face was grim.

"Your Honor, with all due respect to Mrs. Swann's concern for the integrity of the will and the obvious affection she feels for her uncle and his memory, I do wish to emphasize that we did reach prior agreement on my representation as P. R., and . . ."

"She changed her mind," Judge Twichell retorted. "Women do that, you know." He cleared his throat.

Hannah heard the register and the reporter chuckle at the judge's response, but Windsor nervously drummed the table with his pen.

"Then I move admission of the Will of Harold A. Larkin and that Hannah Swann be appointed without bond," Windsor's clipped words barely disguised his indignation.

"Granted," Judge Twichell said, and Hannah was done.

When she rejoined Windsor, he was scratching his name off the forms and scribbling in *Hannah Swann* with a tight little smile.

"I hope you know what you're doing," he said as they walked toward the parking lot. "I'll bet one of the tree-huggers at Hal's funeral put you up to this."

"You're wrong, Dennis," Hannah said.

Kerry hadn't mentioned it at Hal's memorial service; it was *much* later in the day.

"You were going to let me take care of everything. Didn't want to get your hands dirty, wanted to go home right away. So, what happened, Hannah? Why'd you change your mind?"

They were beside Hannah's Toyota now, and Windsor still seethed.

"I had some time to think, that's all," she said. "We can keep in touch by phone or e-mail or fax, and I can always run up here if I need to. Besides, you told me you expect everything to be settled expeditiously."

"I did say that, didn't I." Windsor's response was abrupt and controlled.

"Look, I don't know why you're so upset; this isn't a personal thing." Hannah extended her hand in an attempt to ease the blow to his ego. "I'll still be retaining your services as my attorney. I haven't changed my mind about that."

"Of course," Denny replied with a lukewarm handshake. "I'll be happy to work with you."

He said nothing more about lunch.

Hannah had not told Tyler about showering at Dan Kerry's after her watery debacle on Monday. Tuesday noon, however, she tried giving Tyler a quick call to describe her courtroom coup. It was a brief conversation—she was on her way to a meeting at the Antler Bank.

"I'm trying to work things out, that's all," she explained as she drove. "It's more complicated than I thought."

"I know you, Cheeks. And I hear you back-pedaling in spite of the static . . ."

"Tyler, if you really loved me, you wouldn't tease me right now."

"Hey, the semester's winding down, my paper's ready for the EPA meeting and I'm going to have some free time. I miss you. That's all. I don't want to argue or start a fight, I just want you back where you belong."

Her heart was as full as it could be then, because he seemed so forlorn.

Early Tuesday morning, unable to sleep and anxious about her eventual appearance in court, Hannah had stepped out onto the porch of Aldebaran to watch the sun rise over the lake. Fractured by the brisk northwest wind, the water reflected the sky and seemed to mirror the forecast of her new day.

When she got out of bed early Wednesday morning, Hannah again took her coffee out onto the screened porch of the cottage. The mug steamed in the damp chill. Star Lake glistened like smooth glass except for the Vs of soft ripples behind a party of otters who slipped into the water at the edge of the lily pads and swam out toward the small island north of the cottage.

A bent-twig rocking chair with a broken seat and a couple metal folding chairs furnished Aldebaran's sloping porch. She sipped coffee and rocked for a while, hoping she wouldn't fall through or get her butt stuck where the woven twigs had ruptured.

Apparently the resort had been operating in the red for quite some time.

"We gave your uncle every chance," the president of the Antler Bank had told her Tuesday afternoon. "All it took was a few bad seasons, and then he got behind. You can let three years of unpaid taxes go by before you get in trouble, but if you miss a mortgage payment, well, that's the beginning of the end. I'm sorry. Hal knew that. There's probably a letter from us on that big desk of his out at the lake, showing where he defaulted. We told him our hands were tied. We hated to foreclose but, banking rules, regulators . . ."

"You foreclosed on his mortgage?" Hannah was astonished. No wonder Hal had a fatal heart attack! Look at the stress he'd had to face!

"His insurance hadn't been paid for a while, either. So the whole amount was called due last June. That's the story, Ms. Swann. We had to call in the entire amount instead of just asking for the payments."

"How much did he owe you when he died?"

"I'll have to check his file to be sure, but I believe it was in the neighborhood of ninety thousand. He put some down last week, maybe twelve, thirteen."

The summer deposits, Hannah swallowed hard. "Ninety thousand dollars? He still owed ninety thousand?" She could barely breathe.

"That's the mortgage itself," the banker explained. "With a year's interest added, at nine percent per year, that comes to—that's eighty-one hundred dollars more. And his back taxes. If I recall, he owed around forty-five hundred a year for two years—that's another nine thousand. Plus the attorney fees to service the mortgage."

"Which attorney was that," Hannah asked, even though she suspected that she knew.

"Dennis Windsor is on the board of directors here at the bank," the president replied. "We use Mr. Windsor for all our legal matters."

Only an hour ago she had left Windsor in Cedar Springs and he *knew* she was going to the bank. He had sent her there, in fact. "Stop by the State Bank of Antler, check on Hal's balances, set up an account for the estate," he'd advised. Nothing about a foreclosed mortgage or back taxes.

"So, what do I do?" Hannah asked the banker with a quiver in her voice.

"Well, I'd advise you to ask your lawyer that," he replied, cautiously. "It's not for me to say. The bank brought a judgment against Hal last summer ordering him to pay up or we'll have to sell the property to pay the loan."

"The whole amount?" Hannah attempted to sort it out.

"The whole amount. Except that, as the resort was also Hal's home, he was given eighteen months to redeem the property from the effects of the judgment. Provided that he could, of course. Your lawyer could tell you this just as well as I, but if we're not paid in full at the end of the eighteen months, then the sheriff forces our lien and it's sold on the courthouse steps."

"And the eighteen months is up, when?"

"December thirty-first. The end of this calendar year.

All set to get down to business," Ginger announced Wednesday when she arrived, mid-morning. She reminded Hannah of a frisky orange ladybug.

Hannah was working at the big rolltop desk in the kitchen, sorting through a cigar box filled with accounts payable. "You'd better sit down," she warned Ginger. "This isn't good news."

She explained Windsor's subterfuge, and the banker's startling revelation. She also explained the deposits for the summer reservations that Hal apparently put toward the mortgage last week.

"I don't know what to say," Ginger responded, shaking her head.

"I know George, that's Denny's dad, pretty good. He bailed us out once or twice when Hal couldn't make his payments. But Hal never said a word, not to any of us, about being foreclosed on. I bet even Dan doesn't know."

"After I left the bank I drove back to Cedar Springs, where Hal moved his checking account," Hannah continued.

"And?"

"There wasn't much left in his balance. Then this morning I started going through the desk and found this cigar box. My uncle may have endeared himself to his guests, Ginger, but he owes everybody under the sun. Here are the papers the banker told me I'd find, plus bills for gas, electricity, telephone, you name it. They add up to over four thousand dollars more."

Ginger paged through the papers and sighed. "Kind of makes you want to throw up your hands, doesn't it?" she said sympathetically.

"What are we going to do? I don't even know where to begin to sort out this mess!"

"Well, that's a start right there, Honey," Ginger said. She gave Hannah a firm hug. "You said *we*, 'What are *we* going to do.' You know you can count on me to do all I can to help. I know you can count on Dan, too."

If I want to, Hannah thought.

"I suppose there's no way we can get out of doing an inventory, is there?" She tried to laugh so she wouldn't cry.

"Taking inventory in this joint is going to be about as much fun as trying to stuff a wet noodle up a wildcat's ass," Ginger agreed. "But we don't have a choice, Honey. Tell you what, let's each of us have a cup of strong coffee and then we'll get this rickety show on the road."

They began by listing the battered red Ford pickup and the ancient snowmobile parked inside the shed that also housed a riding lawn-mower and dented canoe. From there they went up to Hal's apartment where, room by room, they planned to note each item of household furniture, dishes, and linens.

It was four o'clock by the time they got around to looking at Hal's collection of books in the living room.

"Did you see the telescope?" Ginger asked.

"What telescope," Hannah asked. She couldn't even feign mild enthusiasm anymore.

"Miriam used it to look at the stars. It's here in this coat closet. Got one of those three-legged stands and even works. Hal set it up out on the sleeping porch and tried to show me how to use it, but I could never get the hang of what I was looking for. Once he told me I was seeing the rings of Saturn."

"We'd better list that under antiques," Hannah said. "Or miscellaneous. Are you ready to call it a day?"

"I'm so glad to hear you say that," Ginger sat down on the sofa with a grunt and loosened the laces on her high-top athletic shoes. "This miscellaneous old antique would sure appreciate a nice cold beer. Why don't you get one for yourself, too."

Gus Schultz arrived the next evening not long after Ginger went home, just as twilight was settling in. Hannah was sitting out on the pier with Babe, watching the loons and the sky as it underwent its ethereal transition from day to night. Soon the North Star would be visible. Little spring peepers sang shrilly from the marshes. The evening exchange of loon music was beginning its eerie circle from lake to distant lake.

At first Schultz seemed unconcerned about real estate matters. He sat next to her on the pier, made small talk about the weather and asked if she'd been fishing yet. (Fishing! Why would she want to go fishing?) After ten minutes of chit-chat he turned to look back toward the resort and made throat-clearing sounds. The sun was setting and the broken clouds against the darkening sky were burnished gold.

"I came up with some numbers for you," he said, and gave Hannah a suggested asking price of $145,000. But she was to understand that was just a ballpark figure and was not related to a formal appraisal of the estate.

It was enough, Hannah admitted, to probably break even once she paid off all of Hal's bills.

But Schultz was quick to add, "That's if you spruce the place up. Get those damaged cabins fixed. Remodel some. Get your business up and running. A sizable investment in time and money on your part, I would imagine. So you can take that figure with a few grains of salt."

He paused, dug a fat cigar out of his jacket pocket, took his time unwrapping the cellophane, then bit off a segment of the tip which he spat in the lake.

"Of course, you can divide it up, too. Sell it off in separate parcels. We're looking at a little more money that way and a whole lot less work."

Hannah tried to imagine the integrity of what she'd come to know as the Star Lake resort broken into individual parts.

"If anybody wants them," Schultz continued. "Or if you wanted to sell just for the land, or the land plus the Saloon—and I'm thinking of the bar as a business here, not just a building—we're talking maybe fifteen empty lots after some cleanup and landscaping. That'd bring you maybe $200,000 or $250,000 tops, with almost no investment at all."

It took a minute or two for Schultz to get his cigar lit, three wooden matches and a lot of huffs and puffing. A convenient tactic, Hannah knew, providing time for her to mull over his figures. Two hundred thousand would be a significant amount, even minus bills currently owed, to compensate for spending the summer up here.

"Or," he said with a barely disguised smile, blowing a satisfying ring of smoke into the evening breeze, "I got an even better deal I think you'll go for. I can give you a *guaranteed buyer* for the land already this week. A buyer who might go ahead and clear it all off but he'll pay you $250,000, cash right away. Slick as a whistle. That's *cash money*, right in your pocket, right now!"

Hannah didn't know what to say to this unexpected announcement. A guaranteed buyer? Immediately?

Schultz was smiling broadly now. "Say the word and you can get out of here tomorrow, day after that, happy as a clam. It's up to you, Mrs. Swann. Ask your lawyer what he thinks about it, if you're looking for advice."

It was dark by the time Schultz left, and overhead the North Star was visible at the end of the Little Dipper's handle.

Living in the red is the name of the game up here, Honey," Ginger told Hannah over fried chicken and a bottle of Chablis on Friday night. The two of them were sitting on the porch of the Saloon, exhausted after completing their inventory of the business—fixtures, furniture, every last item they could find that was connected to the resort.

"I'm afraid the only way out of this misery is to sell the place," Hannah confessed. "I mentioned that to Kerry last Sunday. He was less than thrilled with the idea."

Ginger replied with a knowing smile, "Dan told me that before Hal's memorial service, but I hoped and prayed Star Lake would start to grow on you."

Hannah had to laugh. "Well, that was before I knew how hopeless the situation was. Now I'm even more convinced that selling's the answer. Schultz made me an offer that's almost too good to refuse. It's *so* good, in fact, that it smells a little fishy."

"Coming from Gus Schultz, it probably stinks," Ginger remarked.

"But if I can't pay back the deposits and take care of the outstanding bills, I may end up having to keep the resort open this summer."

"Why not?" Ginger asked simply. "The way you're whining, it sounds like you're being condemned to summer on death row."

Hannah didn't want to argue with Ginger; she didn't want to go through the same litany of excuses she'd given Kerry.

"I do have another life—I have a summer school class to teach in Madison, a script deadline staring me in the face—and, let's face it, I'm not cut out for this. I've never run a business! But most of all, I don't want to spend my summer way up here. I'm sorry . . ."

"Well, I'll grant you, it's not easy, running a resort," Ginger said, pouring out the last of the wine. "And financially it's not all that rewarding, either. You got proof of that in Hal's cigar box. Everybody up here bets on the come, hopes for a good season that'll wipe them out of debt."

Hannah massaged her throbbing forehead.

"I feel for you, Honey, I truly do." Ginger shoved her chair back and lit a cigarette. "It is a good life, don't get me wrong. But it's not all play and no work. Running a bar, keeping a business this size going, catering to the public, you got to be a plumber, carpenter, electrician, chief cook and bottle washer plus the complaint department, all rolled into one. All you need is an off-season to throw the whole kit 'n caboodle out of whack. This here's a good example."

"Don't tell me how hard it is, Ginger!" Hannah pleaded with a feeble laugh, "I'm already convinced it's impossible!"

Ginger finished her wine, tipping the glass up to get the last drop. "You don't want to hear the labor pains, you just want to see the baby. Well, a long time ago I gave up asking why things happen the way they do." She crushed her cigarette on her plate, then got up to sit on the glider and rested her feet on the chair.

"Honey, we used up most of the last couple of days taking note of every single goddamned flyspeck on this property. Did you ever think this might be a timely opportunity to take an inventory of your life? Let's see—you must be in your late forties and you've been married a couple a times, am I right?"

"I definitely won't get married again," Hannah said, not caring to share the details of her life story. "Although there is a man, sort of, right now, and he's very important to me. My daughter's in Madison too, and my house, and my daughter's cat who lives with me, and my work. I'm not ready to give all that up."

"Oh, well," Ginger pretended to take offense, "I'm not going to ask what a *sort of man* is, and if I was you, I sure wouldn't think of taking a chance on doing something new and different with my life . . ." She raised one eyebrow in mock-disbelief.

Hannah bristled at her implication.

"I didn't say my life was perfect, Ginger. It's not perfect, but it's . . . comfortable. Predictable. I have this routine, with my work, with what I do."

Ginger softened and patted the seat next to her, encouraging Hannah to sit in the glider.

"Honey, I'm sure your uncle didn't mean to cause you any grief."

Hannah joined her.

"Then what *did* he mean, Ginger? I'm not angry anymore, I'm just numb. I've thought and thought about it and I can't come up with a logical answer. There are close friends of Hal's, you or Kerry for example, that it would have made more sense for him to delegate with the guardianship of this place."

Ginger didn't seem to have a ready answer, either. "Could be maybe you're the daughter he always wanted. Or Miriam did. Who knows."

"And if he was as clever as you say he was," Hannah continued, "how could he let this get so out of hand? I don't know anything about estate planning, but Hal must have realized his health wasn't all that great."

"I found nitroglycerin patches in the kitchen cupboard today," Ginger confessed. "A full box. Never opened. Prescription was filled only a couple weeks ago."

"So he wasn't using one . . ."

"The day he died?" Ginger said. "Doesn't look that way. I thought he had a heart problem, but I didn't know he was doctoring for it."

They fell silent and watched as a bank of clouds took on the hue of the sunset and reflected a rosy glow.

"You eventually find satisfactions in this kind of life, too," Ginger said finally, her voice slower now, and softer. "You look forward to seeing the folks who come back year after year. You know you can relax with them and they get to be more like friends than they are customers."

Ginger reached down to pet Babe, who delivered a well-chewed hambone, then climbed up and sat between the women, rested her head on Hannah's lap and emitted a deep dog-sigh.

"There's going to be a lot of folks awful sorry to learn about Hal, because everybody loved him. Hal was a big reason for the repeat business here at Star Lake, let me tell you."

"Kerry said that, too," Hannah admitted, caressing the sleeping dog.

"And now, we have to contend with this dirty business with the mine. Dan said he showed you where they went ahead and drilled the core samples. Ingold's been telling everybody they won't do any more damage than a great big gravel pit would. They got as much chance of that as a fart in a whirlwind. *Where the hell are the hell raisers anymore, that's what I want to know.*"

Hannah gently moved the dog off her lap and got up to clear the table. She pretended she did not see the tears in Ginger's eyes.

7

Keep Dancing

"So I'm showing the guy around," Ginger said after a tour with the official appraiser, "and where does Mother Nature call him? Pollux, of course. That teeter-totter toilet. Even out on the porch I hear him holler 'Ooops' when he sits down!"

Hannah relayed Ginger's telling of the mishap to Tyler when she called him Friday night to say she'd be driving home tomorrow. She was still wearing Kerry's flannel shirt. Despite her disdain for the fishing guide, she was reluctant to give up the shirt's lived-in softness, the comforting warmth and the faded reds and blues of its muted plaid.

All week she hoped Kerry would stop by and lecture her again about selling the place. She wanted to reveal that *she* was handling her uncle's estate, after all. She also wondered if he knew about the foreclosure of Hal's mortgage and craved a convincing pep talk to quell her relentless despair. But Kerry was booked solid, Ginger told her. The opening of fishing season was his busiest time of the year.

Finally, Saturday, on the long drive back to the city, Hannah had plenty of time to ponder her peculiar inheritance. The hard truth was, she couldn't really regain her former self until she raised

$16,000. The summer deposits had to be refunded and reservations expunged before she could stay in Madison. That had to happen even before she could return Gus Schultz's insistent calls.

It felt so good to be home again! Although she had only been gone seven days, it seemed like a *much* longer time. During Hannah's absence her lawn had been mowed. Ratso had been fed and his litterbox was clean, so Chloe had obviously touched base. The cat meowed mournfully and would not leave her alone.

"Poor neglected Ratso," she crooned as she untangled his matted gray fur and felt him purr. His devotion bordered on nuisance, always had.

Sunday's *Wisconsin State Journal* carried a brief item under "State News" mentioning Saturday's protest march from the Tamarack Town Hall to the site of the proposed Ingold mine. Hannah felt strange, reading about people she'd recently met and a situation that now had personal impact. Walt Thoren claimed seventy-five demonstrators trespassed on Ingold's land Saturday and twenty were going to camp there overnight. Ingold's local manager, Axel Graves, had spent the day in meetings with construction engineers and while he was "saddened by the fact that some of the protesters had decided to break the law," he was also pleased to announce that crews would be moving onto the site on Monday to clear a path for an even more secure safety fence.

Ginger had told Hannah she planned to take Babe back to her apartment after the march because, "I'm not going to get all stove up, sleeping on the ground. All that just to make a point that's like a pimple on a gnat's ass, in the scheme of things."

If the result of the effort and planning that went into their protest was only this tiny paragraph in the Madison paper, Ginger's "pimple" wasn't far off the mark. Kerry couldn't say he hadn't been warned, Hannah recalled, her face growing warm with remembrance of her cruelly candid comments.

She missed Babe. She had given some thought to bringing the dog along but Babe wasn't a city dog, and Ratso would never allow Babe to inhabit the house where he so arrogantly ran the show.

Y̲ou want to do what?" her banker said on Monday when she explained her situation. "Frankly, you'd be better off looking for financing up there where your property's located. I'd move up north for the summer while I had the chance!"

With each calculation, Hannah was more convinced that she might as well hand the place over to Ingold, get the cash and get it over with. She tried to explain this to Tyler when he phoned as usual on Monday morning, but he wanted to talk about getting together, not her tortured reasoning about whether or not to sell.

By Tuesday the script for the Wilcox video remained untouched. She had yet to give up her summer school commitment. Everything was focused on the undeniable fact that unless she came up with a reasonable solution to her financial dilemma *quick,* she would be driving back up to Antler again at the end of the week.

Tyler insisted on meeting for lunch on the lakeside terrace of the student union. He had claimed a table in the shade, but it looked as though he'd already finished eating when she joined him.

"I got here early," he explained.

Something wasn't quite right. Hannah sensed warning flags fluttering in the periphery.

Occasionally, after spending a weekend with his wife, Tyler would be contrite and analytical, confess a need to pull back and gain some perspective. Then he would close the office door, pull her to him and begin to fondle her breasts and kiss her neck, mumbling, "It's so hard to keep from touching you."

"So, what's new?" Hannah asked cheerfully. She pulled a metal chair across the flagstones and sat down. It was still there, she noticed grimly, that liquid-honey need she had for his touch, his approbation.

"Not much, semester hassles, the usual academic bullshit. If this next federal grant comes through, I don't want to see another student."

Hannah was watching him closely for any signs of slippage. No, he seemed like the same old Tyler she knew and loved.

"It's good to see you again, Sweetcheeks," Tyler smiled. His voice was silky, seductive, and he held her glance with a lascivious gaze.

"Good to see you, too," Hannah responded, touching his foot with hers under the table and grinning in return. She was wearing sandals with jeans and a T-shirt, and if they hadn't been surrounded by students she'd have run her bare feet up along the inside of his thigh.

"Rode my bike today," he said, "first time this spring."

"My bike needs a tune-up," she said, "and so do I. This morning I tried to run for the first time in over a week, and I can really feel it in my knees."

They both knew they were just killing time.

"I missed you," he said softly, leaning over the table.

"I missed you, too," she mouthed, so no one could hear. "I spent a lot of time thinking about you."

Okay, that was a lie. She'd spent most of her time worrying about her uncle's resort and what to do about it.

"Sometimes I sat alone in my office, just waiting. Waiting and hoping," Tyler said, "for the phone to ring." Hannah knew he was making conversation so it wouldn't appear they'd met only momentarily before running off together. They always tried to be circumspect, it was such a fucking game. A fucking *game*.

Tyler's bike was parked in a rack at the end of Park Street. Knowing his habits, she had locked hers there as well, and they pedaled down the lakeshore path, out to Picnic Point.

They didn't take the trail to the end of the peninsula, but turned left and eventually emerged near a hidden gate where they dismounted and hid their bikes behind a thick hedge of wild grapevines.

Hannah was excited by his urgency, the way he pulled her into the woods and almost lost his footing on the narrow, rocky path that wound through the underbrush. When they reached the hidden cove beside the lake, he leaned against a tree, laughing and exhausted. Then he pressed her toward him, both of their bodies damp with sweat.

"Hannah," he kissed the breath of her name from his mouth into her own. "My Sweetcheeks," he said, thrusting his hands under the waistband of her jeans to squeeze her buttocks and rub himself against her thigh. He pulled her T-shirt up to lick and nibble each breast. Yes, she loved this foreplay, the exquisite torture of waiting, ecstasy building, the tension more perilous to endure.

When she finally came she was twisted against a cluster of tree roots with Tyler's head between her legs. It had been luxuriant and glorious. His beard was soft upon the tender skin of her inner thighs and he nuzzled her there, running his tongue up to encircle her navel. She rested with his head on her belly until her heartbeat slowed and her breathing returned to normal. Then he unzipped his pants, brought her hand there and whispered, "Do me, now."

She was not unaccustomed to this, but it seemed automatic and mechanical today. She wanted to wait a while longer.

"Was that all right?"

"Ummmmm," Tyler murmured, his eyes closed.

"Are you hallucinating?"

"Umm hmmm,"

"What do you see?"

"Colors, flashing colors. Moving across a purple sky."

His flashing-purple-sky dream. Then it was okay.

"Come here," Tyler beckoned sleepily, and Hannah crawled up to curl in his arms.

"This is so beautiful," he said. "I wish it would last forever."

"You mean *forever* forever," Hannah asked, "or just for the afternoon-forever?"

"Silly Cheeks," he said, kissing the top of her head.

"You haven't told me a thing about your Marriage Enhancement experience. Was it *enhanced*, or what?"

"About as much as you'd expect, pop-psychology claptrap."

"Like . . . ?"

"'Say something nice about your partner to at least one other person today. Then tell your partner what you said.' Bullshit like that."

He yawned, stretched.

"That's all?"

"Oh—the last night we were supposed to share sexual fantasies."

"With everybody?"

"No, Cheeks," Tyler chuckled softly and rumpled her hair, "just our partner. I told Dawn about strawberries and cream."

"That one's not very exotic . . ."

"I didn't want to scare her."

"Was she interested?"

"She likes strawberries."

Hannah was ready to leave. She didn't want to hear any more.

"Wait, give me your sunglasses," Tyler said with a grin. "I showed this to Dawn one night. It really cracked her up."

His jeans were still down around his knees, so he knelt and placed her sunglasses over his penis as if it were a nose.

"Looks like Fidel Castro to me," Hannah said.

How could she get mad at someone who could be so open and playful, qualities she desperately needed in her life.

"Was Dawn's sexual fantasy to make love with Castro?" Hannah joked, retrieving her sunglasses. She wiped them on her shirt.

"She wants to take a cruise."

"What?" Hannah sat back, laughing. "A cruise? No wonder your marriage is in trouble!"

Tyler wasn't joking. He was pulling himself together and buckling his belt.

"She's in Chicago today. Has to get her passport lined up. We're sailing through the Panama Canal to Alaska."

"But that'll take weeks!" Hannah was incredulous.

"All of July and part of August. This therapist she's been seeing is going, along with some other Marriage Enhancers. Bunch of dildos. But Dawn's grandmother left her quite a bit of cash and there were a couple openings left. I've arranged to meet with Alaskan Eco-systems. Take some business deductions. That's why I was so anxious to have you back."

"I can't believe this," she said, shaking her head.

"I still love you, Hannah," Tyler said tenderly. He ran his hand along her jaw and tenderly caressed her neck. "I'll always love you, nothing has changed. Nothing *will* change."

"I don't want it to change; I don't want anything to change . . ."

Riding her bike home, she thought about the times she imagined Tyler giving up his marriage for her.

"I love my wife, but I love you, too," he always said. "I know it's not fair of me, but that's what I want. Stupidly, I suppose, but irrevocably. Without any room for negotiation." And Hannah said that suited her just fine.

The paradox was, if he gave up Dawn that would prove, it would seem, that his love for her must be truly boundless and powerful. So whenever he told Hannah that he couldn't leave Dawn, she agreed, knowing she honestly would not be able to love a man who would allow himself to be manipulated like that. A paradox and an attraction: the loyalty he felt for his wife was one of the reasons Hannah loved him.

Their relationship was savage and exhilarating and hurtful and dangerous and comforting and even playful in its own idiosyncratic way.

And even boring.

No, not boring. Predictability can be reassuring. I've lived in this house for seven years and I'm happy, she told herself. My work is satisfying, too; that's how I want my life to be. I've earned the right to be complacent.

Hannah parked her bike in the garage, locked it, and sat down on the back steps.

She meant it when she told Tyler she didn't want anything to change. She sure as hell didn't want to go all the way back up to Star Lake and live in solitary confinement. No intellectual stimulation, no plays or opera, no symphony—not even a movie theater, just a shelf of dusty videos for rent at the IGA. Where would she get her hair cut? Have her nails done? Buy her clothes?

Ratso was clawing at the back door, trying to get closer to her. Hannah couldn't let him outside, he'd go straight for the backyard neighbor's garden. If that old grump spotted him she'd call the Humane Society again and claim Hannah wasn't adhering to Madison's leash law on cats.

Next door Mrs. Glenn screamed at her kids. Mrs. Glenn was

honored in January as Madison's Mother of the Year. Obviously the nominating committee had never heard her achieve a supersonic pitch as piercing as the sirens that wailed down University Avenue. Yes, it was noisy, living in the city. But she had grown accustomed to the city noises. They were even *comforting,* in a way.

"I have what I need. My life is full and I don't want anything to change," she vowed, aloud. "I'm content right here where I know my routine by heart and the pulse of the city masks the sound of my arteries hardening . . . shut up, Ratso! I want to think!"

Hannah reached back to pound the door with her fist. The cat stopped scratching.

"I *am* happy, goddammit! I can't afford to take chances, anymore; is that so terrible? I'm too old to deal with places I don't know, people I don't have anything in common with." She chuckled, ruefully. "And I used to think I'd become one of those independent women of a certain age who toured Europe with only a backpack and hairy legs jammed into a pair of hiking boots! What a laugh."

But Hannah was not laughing.

"This has become my safe place, my safe haven in the middle of my life. If this is all there is, then so what? Is that so bad? Did you ask yourself that, Uncle Hal, when you knew you were dying?" She looked up at the sky, "Did you say, 'Is that all there is?' like Peggy Lee, '*If that's all there is, my friend, then let's keep dancing . . .*'"

Ratso's insistent scratching caused her to yell at the cat a second time.

"Shut up, Ratso! For God's sake, let me alone!"

Like Mrs. Glenn.

She cracked the door so Ratso could slip outdoors. Tail high in the air, he proudly headed for the fence that protected the backyard neighbor's garden.

Hannah kept an eye on him as he scratched around in the bed of brussels sprouts. He squatted to use it as his litterbox, then came back to her as pleased as could be and rubbed against her legs.

Together, they went in the house. Hannah opened a can of

water-packed tuna for Ratso and fixed a cup of herbal tea for herself. Then she calmly picked up the phone and dialed her daughter.

"Chloe? Hi, it's Mom. Could you and Eric come over for dinner tonight? We need to talk. I've got a plan."

2

Oh, you who read some song that I have sung—
What know you of the soul from whence it sprung?

Ella Wheeler Wilcox

8

Gone Fishing

Two boats had left the pier at sunrise; the third boat (and Sirius, the third occupied cottage) was still quiet. Chloe and Eric had worked until after midnight repairing the two windstorm-damaged cottages, Castor and Pollux, and Hannah would let them sleep.

The porch of the Saloon was a pleasant place to experience Sunday morning serenity, a brief hiatus from the exhausting chaos that now commandeered Hannah's life. A week ago she'd brought the Wilcox file along back to Star Lake because—it was ridiculous—in addition to everything else she had to come up with a quick concept for the overdue BWP video.

Hannah scribbled a reference to Ella Wheeler Wilcox's pensive morning thoughts: *Before night something beautiful will happen to change everything.* The poet assured herself of this daily and it frequently came true, so Wilcox claimed.

According to the biography on Hannah's lap, the woman was "a vivid, vulgar personality and a sub-literary talent . . . not a minor poet, but a bad major one." A classic BWP with a scandalous reputation: After the publication of her *Poems of Passion* in 1884 (still a virgin at thirty-three) Wilcox married a Milwaukee silver merchant, bleached her hair, practiced yoga, and photographed Tunesian prostitutes. She communicated via Ouija board with her husband after his death and began harp lessons at sixty-three. Three years later she presented a dance recital, "The Dance of the Adoration of the Lilies," arrayed in Grecian robes, embracing a huge bouquet of yellow flowers.

"Hello there."

It was Mr. Evansville. Hannah found it was easier to keep track of her guests if she privately referred to them in terms of their home town. Mr. Staniszewski, from Evansville, told her yesterday that he and his wife rented Sirius every year.

"Don't stop what you're doing." The meek little man timidly opened the screen door which didn't squeak anymore because Eric had replaced the rusty spring. Babe rose from her place at Hannah's side and padded over, tail wagging, to sniff Evansville's outstretched hand, determined he was harmless, then returned to Hannah and lay down again.

"I'm just enjoying my coffee," Hannah said. "Aren't you going fishing?"

"Yeah, you bet, but the wife's frying up some sausage and eggs. You can work up an appetite, fishing!"

"Is there a limit to how many you're allowed to catch?" Hannah asked. A pathetic attempt at small talk, but she needed practice to survive the summer.

"Sure, you betcha. There's your perch, bluegills, sunfish, and crappies and them, I think it's around fifty per day. With your northerns it's more like five. And walleyes, that's five, too. Bass, it depends on the size and the time of the year—right now it's too early for bass yet. Muskies, well them's another story."

"Another fish story," Hannah said, trying to shut him up.

"Yeah, them muskellunge, they do make for good fish stories. Keep your ears open, you'll get your fill of 'em. D'you hear about the guy from Chicago who went to the wildlife zoo down by Minocqua last summer? They got this tank with a bunch of muskies, see, and, cripes! He reaches in and tries to pet one. They say he actually did touch a musky the first time but his buddy wasn't looking so then he tries again and wouldn't you know he gets two of his fingers chomped off!"

Hannah mentally filed the account.

"He sued the zoo, of course," Evansville said, disgusted. "They oughta put up signs that say 'Don't Pet the Muskies, for Cripe's Sake.'"

His storytelling came to a halt when he caught sight of a boat slowly heading toward their pier.

"When the wife and I heard that Mr. Larkin passed on we felt so bad. And then we worried that the place might close and all . . ."

Hannah wondered if Kerry had prompted this. The sentiment sounded awfully familiar.

"We been coming up to Star Lake since 1962. Brought the boy along, until he got his own farm. Comes up with his own kids now, after they put up their second crop of hay. The wife and I farm for them that week, we don't mind. It ain't easy to hire somebody to milk a hundred head of cows anymore."

"I'm sure it isn't," Hannah replied, guessing that would be true.

"Well," he said, opening the door. "You got better things to do than gab with me."

Babe rose, stretched, and ran outside to greet the man climbing out of the boat.

"Mr. Kerry!" Evansville called warmly, "I'll be darned."

Good thing his flannel shirt was in the wash or she'd be wearing it this morning.

"Stan," Kerry gave him a friendly salute as he made his way up to the porch. He wore a red windbreaker over jeans and a white T-shirt, and seemed annoyingly cheerful, Hannah thought. It had been weeks since she'd seen him — the day of Hal's funeral, her watery debacle. Suddenly she felt very nervous in his presence.

"How they biting?" Evansville asked.

"Not bad," Kerry told him as he joined Hannah on the porch. "Fellow I took out yesterday caught a couple of nine-pound walleyes."

Hannah went into the kitchen for another mug of coffee and

heard Evansville whistle. "A humdinger for supper and a wallhanger to boot. Cripes sake, Dan, tell you what. One of these days I want you to teach me a thing or two about fishing!"

Hannah handed Kerry his coffee.

"After all the years you've put in on these lakes, Stan, you can show me a thing or two, yourself."

"Yah, the wife, there's the fisherman in the family," Mr. Evansville nodded to Hannah, his hand still on the edge of the screen door. "She pulls one in right after the other, walleyes, northerns, you name it. I tell her, 'Gladdy, you know when to yank and when to tease.'"

"That's what it's all about, Stan," Kerry agreed.

"Now this young lady, she was asking me some questions about fishing just a little while ago and you're the one should be answering her," Evansville offered.

Wasn't he ever going to leave? His eggs must be cold by now.

"Is that right?" Kerry gave Hannah an engaging smile that nearly scared her out of her seat on the glider. "Matter of fact, I came over to ask if she'd like to go fishing."

"You got a Sunday free, so early in the season?" Evansville enjoyed this banter. "Cripes, what's the matter? Word getting around you lost your touch."

"The fellow who caught the walleyes booked me for today," Kerry explained, "but his wife says he's too hung over this morning. So I thought maybe Hannah could do a little fishing before the season got real busy."

She was stunned by his offer. A short chat over coffee was acceptable, but she didn't want to spend a whole day with the guy. Since her appearance in court she had looked forward to telling Kerry about that experience. But the thought of being alone with him—even for only an hour or two—made Hannah distinctly uncomfortable.

"Sorry, it's my turn to hold down the fort, today."

Mr. Evansville, still lurking in the doorway was ready with a solution.

"Tell you what," he said, moving back inside, "you go right ahead and take the day off. Bar opens at noon, don't it? By golly, the wife and I know the routine probably better than you do," he chuckled. "You look like you need a break."

With that, Mr. Evansville stepped out through the screen door and stood looking back in at them, hands in his pants pockets, beaming. The little man was really getting on her nerves.

"What do you say, Hannah?" The fishing guide seemed amused by her indecision.

"Dan'll treat you right, don't you worry."

She planned to go grocery shopping with Chloe this afternoon, she explained. Ginger had the day off but Eric was going to tend the bar.

"Okay then," Kerry said, standing as if to leave. Babe jumped up, too.

"Wait," Hannah suggested, "Maybe . . . maybe just for just a little while."

She couldn't see any diplomatic way out of it. And here was her opportunity to explain that she had returned for the summer because of the financial squeeze Hal had put her in, not because Kerry had convinced her it was the right thing to do.

Kerry retraced the ill-fated route Hannah had taken a few weeks ago, across Star Lake, through the culvert, over Sundog to the Lost Arrow River. Hannah had changed into a T-shirt and shorts, glad of the chance to absorb some sun. This time she watched for his house in the bay near the inlet but the foliage had leafed out so much in the intervening time that a fieldstone chimney rising through dark green pine boughs was the only clue to its presence.

"We had rain while you were gone," he said. "The water's up since you sheared that pin."

The comfortable upholstered seats swiveled, and the interior of the streamlined boat was carpeted in dark blue. She asked him about the instruments and he demonstrated one that measured depth and fish location. His guide business must be pretty lucrative, Hannah decided; the boat was more high-tech than she'd imagined.

As the banks of the river narrowed, Kerry turned off the big motor and tilted it so its blades rode high in the water. Then he started a tiny motor in the bow of the boat, one that ran quietly by comparison.

Birch catkins arched over the rippling water to create a graceful fairyland tunnel that nineteenth-century wood nymphs might well have inhabited, Hannah noted wryly. The river no longer appeared dark and ominous. Bright green ferns unfurled and spilled over one another in dense, undulating gardens of delicate fronds. The skeleton of the deer had been (thankfully) submerged.

Sickle Moon was as big as Star Lake but shaped like an irregular crescent. Kerry aimed the boat toward a weedy patch of water half-way down the southern shore, cut the motor and reeled out the anchor.

"You know how to cast?"

"Cast?" she said. "Of course." Her fishing experience had never moved beyond the cane poles her grandfather had given her, but she'd watch Kerry for a while and then fake it.

He selected a rod from a supply in the bottom of his boat and handed it over. Just her luck to get the line hopelessly tangled or catch a hook in his ear, she thought, so she handled it tentatively.

"What kind of bait do you want to use?" he asked.

"You're the expert, you tell me. Are we fishing for muskies?"

Kerry laughed. "Not while the walleyes are biting."

"Why do they call them walleyes?"

"Their eyes are white and they bulge out in a peculiar way. You'll see when you catch one."

"Sure I will," Hannah repeated, skeptically.

"Trust me, you'll catch a walleye."

Kerry attached a jig to the end of Hannah's line. It looked like a florescent pink and white minnow with deadly three-pronged hooks dangling from the front and back.

"Location is everything, this time of year. Walleyes are about done spawning, but we had a late ice-out so the water's still cold. We want to find the warmest part of the lake, like this shallow weedbed that holds the heat."

Hannah had to look away as Kerry attached a leech to one of the hooks.

"You ever fish for walleyes?"

"Never." Might as well be truthful about that.

"Well, we're going to jig this weedbed." Kerry cast his own jig into the weeds and gently jerked the line back, reeling the line in as he did so. "Like this. It's lift, fall. Lift, fall."

"Doesn't look that hard," Hannah said.

"The lift is the attraction, the fall is the trigger. It's always the same, lift, fall. Lift, fall. But try to do it slowly. And don't expect a big tug on the end of your line. In spring the bite'll be softer, more like a little tap. Give the fish five or ten seconds before you set the hook."

Hannah waited until he did this the third time and then attempted to cast. She stood and swung the rod over her shoulder and aimed it out into the weedbed, but nothing happened. The neon minnow still hung from the tip of her pole. Thank God the leech hadn't fallen down the neck of her shirt!

"You have to press down on the catch," Kerry explained softly, trying to conceal a smile. He stood close behind her, his arm circling her shoulder. His hand covered hers as he showed her how to cast. She tried, again and again, to mimic his smooth technique and hoped the rapid thud of her heart was apparent only to her. Finally, success.

"You're on your own," Kerry said, moving away, and Hannah realized she was blushing.

It *was* rather pleasant, the comforting lap of the water against the boat, the birds trilling from the edge of the forest on the shore, the warmth of the pale spring sun. Hannah wondered if that was part of the attraction of fishing: the calm feeling, a sedation, almost, induced by the soft rocking motion, the silence.

"We had a bet you weren't coming back," Kerry said after a while.

"Who did?"

"Ginger and I. We bet a steak dinner."

"Who won?"

"Ginger."

"Woman's intuition."

"I had a suspicion your heart wasn't in it. Still don't."

"You haven't seen me in action," she argued. "I've been scrubbing floors, painting kitchens, handing out life preservers, selling fishing licenses, scraping grease . . ."

"I could be wrong."

"I even climbed up on the roof of the Saloon to fix the TV antenna. And last night I helped Ginger in the bar and fried hamburgers and baked frozen pizzas until two o'clock. All last week my daughter and her boyfriend and Ginger and I worked our butts off. You may have noticed we got most of the cottages in shape so we could be open for Memorial Day, just like Hal promised. . . ."

"Slow down, "Kerry warned, "I said I could be wrong . . ." He seemed amused.

"But I wanted to be sure to tell you," she began, "I mean, I'm not . . ." She took a deep breath. "It's not because of anything you said. Like that night you showed me the core samples and told me to get involved. That's not why I'm here."

Kerry's expression was unchanged. He cast his line, reeled it in, then cast again.

"I had to come back because Uncle Hal dropped a disaster in my lap. Everything's a terrible mess. Ginger probably filled you in."

Hannah noticed the leech was missing from the jig, and Kerry replaced it while she averted her eyes.

"Ginger did say you stood up to Windsor in front of Judge Twichell. I have to give you credit for that," Kerry said.

"I hope it wasn't a mistake," she admitted. "Denny was a lot more upset than I thought he'd be. And our financial situation is in total disarray, I'm sure that's no surprise. There's a big I.O.U. to Denny's father, and then the foreclosure and everything."

"Hal never said a word to anyone."

"According to the bank, it happened last summer. Hal missed a payment. He was behind in his taxes, too. The banker said their hands were tied."

Hannah cast her line out into the water once again.

"We should talk about that one of these days, you and I. If Hal had told me he was in a bind, I'd have helped him out with a payment or two."

Kerry fished in silence for a long time, preoccupied. Hannah did the same.

"I thought maybe your boyfriend had other plans for the summer and that's why you agreed to come back," Kerry said.

"Who said anything about a *boyfriend*?"

"Male intuition."

"Or Ginger's big mouth." Hannah checked her bait. Still there. "Did you haul me all the way out here to pick a fight?"

"Who's picking a fight?"

"Look, I would appreciate a little consideration, if you don't mind. I never fished like this before in my life and I have a gazillion things I could be doing instead of this. . . ."

She felt a need to break the uneasy silence that fell between them. "I used to go fishing with Grandpa Larkin."

"He ever mention Hal?"

"Only once, when I asked."

"What did he say?"

"That when Hal went away, he and Grandma cried. My family's deep, dark secret. I always wondered what happened."

"I can tell you, if you want to know."

"He told you?"

"Yes, he did."

"He told you about that, but not about his mortgage being foreclosed?"

"Looks like it."

She sensed a tiny nibble on her line, but she jerked the lure out of the water and nothing was there. She cast again.

"There's something else you should be aware of," Hannah offered, "unless Ginger already spilled the beans: I've got until the end of this year to come up with about ninety grand or Star Lake Saloon and Housekeeping Cottages belongs to the Antler Bank."

That nibble was there again, it definitely was.

"If you get in real trouble," Kerry offered, "I mean, if there's a serious chance you're going to lose the resort, I hope you'll tell me. With a little maneuvering I think I could pay them off and you could refinance the mortgage somewhere else."

She didn't know what to say. Then, "Oh! Oh, my God! Now what do I do? Oh my God! C'mon! Dan, you've got to help me! Help!"

Something heavy and very alive was tugging back when Hannah tried to reel it in. All attempts to conceal her excitement were abandoned as she whooped with delight.

"Easy now, don't let it get away," Kerry warned. He put down his own rod and talked her through it.

After fifteen minutes of alternating frustration and exhilaration, Hannah saw the glistening fish leap out of the water. She could feel the fish battling her line, frantic in its fight.

"That's a beauty, Hannah. I knew you'd catch a walleye."

She was sweating like crazy. Her hair was falling in her eyes but she couldn't release her grip on the fishing rod to brush her bangs away or push her sunglasses back from the tip of her nose.

When the fish was worn out and so was she, Kerry reached out with a net to bring the flipping walleye into the boat. Hannah fell back into her seat, wiped the sweat from her face and watched him detach the hook from the fish's mouth. The fish made a choking noise. Hannah squirmed.

"Nineteen inches. Not bad for your first," he said, measuring the fish for her. "We can have it for lunch, if you're hungry."

It had been hours since they'd left the resort, and Hannah was ravenous.

A shore lunch was part of the deluxe fishing package, Kerry explained. He pulled up the anchor, started the motor and took her to an island near the far tip of Lake Sickle Moon where he tied the boat to an overhanging cedar bough and helped her ashore.

A group of charred stones were overlaid with pine logs and blackened branches. Kerry started a fire in the circle and brought a small insulated cooler and other supplies from the boat.

Hannah sat on a low, wide stump and sipped a can of soda while he filleted the walleye with a razor-sharp knife. The fire was burning steadily by then, so Kerry placed a long-handled cast-iron frying pan on the fire, threw in a slab of butter and fried the onions he'd sliced. Then he added chunks of potatoes, turning them frequently with a spatula until they were brown and crisp. A can of beans was opened and set to heat among the coals. He coated the walleye fillets with an egg wash and bread crumbs and sautéed them in butter in another long-handled skillet.

She thought she'd never smelled anything so enticing in her life.

"You're sitting on the table," Kerry said, shooing her away.

He spread a plaid tablecloth over the stump, set a couple small logs on end on either side, placed napkins and silverware on the top, and then produced a bottle of wine.

"Do you treat all your clients this way?" Hannah wanted to know. "I'm beginning to understand why you're so booked."

"Usually we eat standing up and share a six-pack of beer," he admitted with an embarrassed grin.

She sat on one of the logs, waiting while he sliced a loaf of home-made rye. Then he served the fish and fried potatoes and beans on white china. He poured the wine into long-stemmed goblets.

"To Hannah Swann, Walleye Wrangler!"

"I'll bet you say that to all your clients."

"Only those who catch walleyes," Kerry said.

The meal was delicious.

"Did you and Uncle Hal ever do this?"

"We were usually too busy for a busman's holiday."

Hannah realized she was shoveling food into her mouth and, between bites, asked Kerry why he'd chosen to live in the north-woods. He told her it was because of Hal.

Inquiry into his personal life might spoil the buoyant spirit the afternoon had regained, so Hannah held back. Just then Kerry pointed to a bald eagle soaring above the lake. It swooped down with only the tiniest splash to capture a fish in its talons and fly away.

"Cripes," Hannah said, and they both laughed.

"Are there really bears around here?" she asked. "I've been thinking about exploring that trail that leads into the woods behind Aldebaran."

"Last week somebody spotted two adults and three cubs on top of the culvert between Sundog and Star. But the black bears in these woods are pretty shy. Take Babe along."

Kerry folded his napkin and set it next to his plate, "Speaking of Star Lake, you might want to be getting back. It's four o'clock."

Hannah had lost track of time.

He was silent again, as they headed across Sundog toward the resort.

"What's new with Ingold," she asked when they passed the area close to the mine site.

"A master's hearing is coming up in a couple weeks. The state's appointed a hearing examiner—it's usually some bureaucrat who's appointed to listen to the testimony and then report back to the court. Ingold's lining up pro-mine supporters, and we're trying to muster all the voices we can to speak for our side."

"I hope you're not planning another rally," Hannah cautioned, then wished she had bitten her tongue. "I mean—I've lived in Madison for a long time, and I've seen every kind of protest demonstration imaginable. Today people have to be shocked. That's the only way you'll grab their attention."

"We're planning a canoe flotilla protest."

"Exactly," Hannah replied, unable to stop herself. "That's exactly what I mean. It's so sixties! Chloe and Eric, my daughter and her boyfriend—I'm sure they'll get involved because they're into things like that. They thrive on it, in fact. And if you're lucky, the state papers might give you another measly paragraph like they did about your demonstration a couple weeks ago. But, I'm sorry, for the most part people will tune it out. They've heard it all before—anti-abortion, anti-war, or anti-fur coats, nobody really cares."

Kerry didn't comment. Hannah figured she'd soured the day with her tiresome harangue. Well, too bad.

"So you get branded a 'tree-hugger' by Dennis Windsor and you tweak Ingold's ass. So what good does that do?" Hannah shrugged.

They were close enough now to read the sign on the front of the lodge: Beer Bait Food Boats Games. If the sign was going to remain in place, it needed a touch-up.

Kerry cut the motor, as Hannah added, thinking aloud, "I just remembered something else I was going to do today. The little star signs Miriam made need repairing. The upholstery tacks or whatever she used to represent the stars are falling off."

"Falling stars," Kerry replied solemnly. "I hope you make a wish."

"This isn't my life's dream," she apologized. "I guess I've made that pretty clear, haven't I?"

She reached out to grab the pier and prepared to climb out of the boat.

"Look," Hannah said, turning to Kerry, "of course I'd like to have Ingold out of here. And it was very nice of you to take me fishing. I'm sorry if I don't seem grateful, because I am. Thank you. I really had a good time."

Kerry nodded.

"And you mentioned some financial help with the mortgage, just before I caught the fish. There's no way I could ever accept that, but I do appreciate your offer."

Hannah climbed up on the pier.

"See you later," Kerry said, leaving Hannah without a clue as to what "later" might mean. She knew it could be one week or two, depending on the weather or whatever affected the scheduling of his clients.

"It was fun . . ." she said, and held out her hand, but the boat began slipping back from the pier, "and the lunch was great," she added, but Kerry was already looking away. Babe was at her side greeting her with licks and wiggles as if she'd been gone for a month.

Hannah found Eric tending bar. He said he'd relieved Mr. Evansville a couple hours ago and Chloe had just gone into town for groceries. Eric also said that Mr. Evansville told him a couple men had been asking for her earlier: Dennis Windsor and Axel Graves, Ingold's manager.

"And the guy who hired the fishing guide for today called," Eric added. "He was mad as hell. Wanted to know why his reservation had been canceled."

The messages intrigued Hannah, but things seemed to be under control and a yearning for a contemplative walk appealed to her more than ever, even though last night she'd distinctly heard someone tell Ginger they took twelve bears out of the American Legion Forest on the other side of Sundog last fall and "One old sow dressed out at four hundred pounds."

"Babe?"

She told Eric she was going to explore the woods and would be back by the time Chloe returned.

Since her first day's inspection of the property she had been eyeing the path behind Aldebaran. It reminded her of paths through Grandpa's woods. She tucked her journal into a backpack and set off with the dog.

Her eyes took a while to adjust to the darkness in the forest. The air was quiet and damp but the mosquitoes weren't too bad. Green moss sprung from tree trunks and rotting logs. A spicy smell: decaying leaves and toadstools, wet bark, rose from the moist footing where the sun came through to warm it in dancing patterns. Babe ran ahead to sniff the narrow trail through dense underbrush and Hannah sang softly in case any bears happened to be nearby.

As she suspected, there were Jack-in-the-pulpits in the shadows. Hannah found star flowers, too, and wild calla lilies, blue flags, yellow violets, and bunchberries. She selected specimens of each to take back for her wildflower press and placed them for safekeeping between the pages of her journal.

Babe made a wide circle around her and returned, panting softly. The low, tangled undergrowth was thick and difficult to negotiate gracefully. If Hannah meandered far from the path, it would be slow going in case she had to run.

Nevertheless, a high knoll to the left of the path looked inviting.

She could see a wide boulder upon the knoll that would provide a good spot to rest and meditate while surveying the surrounding scene and absorbing woodland inspiration.

Low brush and small fir trees cluttered the forest floor. Damp humus was spongy underfoot. Hannah and Babe had to fight their way around clusters of branches, and thick vines hindering their progress had to be lifted and pushed aside. If a bear happened to be within a mile's radius it would surely have picked up Hannah's heavy breathing by now. It had been weeks since she'd had a morning run; she was getting seriously out of shape.

Hannah wanted to put Dan Kerry out of her mind. Yes, he couldn't have been nicer, but just as he suspected her "heart wasn't in it" living at Star Lake, she did not quite trust his motives.

Sure, the man was attractive, she couldn't deny that. Not in a macho, two-day beard, musclebound sort of way, but still, she felt a tug. A definite tug. And that's why, as charitable and kind as his offer of financial help might be, she'd have to turn it down no matter what happened. There were too many opportunities for misunderstandings and implications.

A sure way to cancel thoughts of Kerry was to consider Tyler Cole. She cleared sticks and rubble from the top of the flat boulder to sit cross-legged and write in her journal. *Got to be like Gladdy . . . know "when to yank and when to tease."*

She let her head fall over toward one shoulder and rolled it around her neck, closing her eyes, relaxing in the dense shade beneath the canopy of green. Babe was already snoring next to her, on the broad rock.

I need a warm body to hold in the night and someone who loves the sleep in my eyes to kiss me awake at dawn, she wrote.

Whoa, where did that come from? She was supposed to cancel Kerry with thoughts of Tyler, whom she'd spoken to only a few times since her arrival at Star Lake because of his EPA meeting in Washington. Each time he called she had been in a rush to get away and get on with unfinished tasks.

This is not like me, to be satisfied with only the small pieces of each day that you dole out in hidden places. Your response continues to be, "love me and be content, Hannah, this is all I can give you right now but I do love you, isn't that enough?"

Hannah stroked Babe's sleek fur and found the dog alert, watchful. Then the dog growled, low in her throat as if she'd heard something! Don't let it be a bear!

Afterward, Hannah wondered why Babe hadn't barked. If Babe had barked, the sky would have fallen. But the dog simply watched and listened, as Hannah did, picking up voices from the direction in which they had originally been headed. Someone who had gone into the woods ahead of them, and was now coming back.

Hannah slid back to rest her stomach on the boulder and peered through the pine boughs for a better view. Two men advanced along the path: Dennis Windsor and another man—Axel Graves? They had been told at the Saloon that she was gone for the day.

Their conversation was hard to make out from that distance, but Graves clearly seemed agitated. The path was too narrow for them to walk side-by-side, and every so often Graves paused to turn around and face Windsor, gesturing angrily. She caught, "slip out of your hands," and "smarter than you think," which made her face burn with recognition. When they were almost opposite the boulder, the two men hesitated.

"You know she passed out flyers in Buck's that first day she came into town," Windsor explained. "She plays dumb, but that cunt is crafty as hell."

No kidding, she said under her breath. You don't have any idea how crafty I am, you stupid son of a bitch.

Then Hannah clearly heard Windsor promise, "I'll do my best to convince her." And Graves said he'd better, because "We can always hire another lawyer to look after our interests. One who keeps his promises."

Hannah and Babe waited until the men had gone, and then they waited another half-hour. Night was closing in by the time they made their way out of the woods. Hannah had forgotten all about bears. The human threats to her world were infinitely more evil.

128

Chloe and Eric were just about to go looking for her. She told them she'd fallen asleep.

Later, Hannah tried to call Kerry, to tell him what she had seen and heard from Windsor and Graves. But he wasn't home and she got his answering machine. Shy and flustered, she hung up without saying a word.

9

Full Moon

According to the almanac, June's full moon was known variously as the Rose Moon, the Strawberry Moon, or (serendipitously, in the month of June/moon/spoon) the Honey Moon. As far as Hannah was concerned, the approach of that event and the completion of the long first week of their summer season was significant: thus far they'd remained free of complete lunacy. Hannah prayed that the silvery beams of celestial harmony would continue to reign.

Monday the kids had insisted on perpetuating one of Hal's favorite traditions: the weekly Potluck Supper. Chloe hemmed yellow and white checked fabric to make tablecloths for each dinette set on the porch of the Saloon. Eric grilled vegetarian kabobs to accompany the bratwurst. Guests supplied baked beans, potato salad, sauerkraut, Jell-O with marshmallows, and Ginger brought fresh strawberry pies from the Antler IGA.

A reporter from the *Antler Advocate* became an unwitting dinner guest. The woman admitted she had never interviewed a real writer before, but wanted to know more about Hannah. Despite some trepidation Hannah hoped the free publicity would pay off in the long run.

The traditional Tuesday fishing contest was won by Gladys Sta-niszewski with a twenty-pound northern pike that had everybody blinking. That was the day Hannah shut herself in Hal's study, pushed his as-yet-unsorted things over to one side of the room and worked on the Wilcox project. By the next night, Wednesday, she was ready to fax the final BWP script and Thursday afternoon Joe Mickelson called to say Ella Wheeler Wilcox would achieve BWP video immortality.

The *Antler Advocate* arrived in Thursday's mail with a photo of Hannah and Babe on the front page. "New owner of Star Lake Resort," the caption read, and the article made Hannah squirm. In a small town a fuss could be made from something as simple as a reporter's unwitting claim that you were "one of Wisconsin's most remarkable poets."

Hannah read the article to Tyler when he called later that day, but all he cared about was how her photo looked and what was that about "going fishing"?

"I've had very little time for that," she said quickly. "And the bears I've heard so much about have been making themselves scarce."

"So are my students, thank God. My grant came through so next fall I can spend more time on research."

Hannah told him, "Six women were signed up for my summer school class when I pulled out."

"There must be plenty of Bad Women Poets who haven't been videotaped yet, Cheeks. Your future isn't in teaching or running a resort; it's in documenting deplorable poetesses," Tyler teased.

"Thanks for your encouragement," Hannah replied, imagining his sly grin.

"By the way, while I was out east, Dawn picked up our tickets for the cruise. Our stateroom has a king-sized bed."

Hannah tried to imagine making love with him in a king-sized bed that rocked with the undulating rhythm of Pacific waves.

"Dawn and I talk about you more now. Since we went on the retreat she isn't so detached."

"Is she better in bed?" Hannah asked, boldly.

"Yes."

All right, there it was, she had to ask. "What do you say when you talk about me?"

"She knows that I love you."

"Bet that goes over big."

"Dawn's cool, it's okay. She knows I love her, too."

"Tyler, you are living in some kind of weird dream world. There's no way this can last."

Hannah was tempted to add that she was no longer sure she wanted it to last.

"I did tell her that we've never really had sex . . ."

"You told her what?"

"That we've never really had sex. We haven't you know; there hasn't been actual penetration."

Hannah's anger boiled over suddenly and sizzled. "What do you call what we've been doing for the last three years if it's not 'having sex'? And I seem to recall a time or two, or three or four, when Uncle Wiggily managed to finagle his way somewhere or other that felt like penetration to me!"

"Calm down, Cheeks, okay? If Dawn's definition of sex involves a wholesale conjunction of penis and vagina, then we haven't had penetration. She's satisfied with that."

"Tyler, I'm really tired . . ." she began, but he interrupted.

"I knew this rustic detour wouldn't be easy for you, but there must be compensations, especially for a writer. Has Ginger come up with more of her quirky epithets?"

Hannah wasn't in the mood for that, and told him so.

"What are you waiting for, Hannah? Take the money and run, for Christ's sake. Come back to me, where you belong."

"I've never really left Madison, Tyler; my house is still there. This place isn't my home."

"You know what I mean, Cheeks. It's one thing to hide out in the sticks for the summer, but it's insane to get carried away with a losing venture."

"Must be my midlife crisis acting up. Or menopause," she tried to joke.

"You're still a lovely woman," Tyler said. "Midlife, my ass."

"No, my ass," Hannah replied, "I'm the one with the sweet cheeks, remember?"

Then, hastily, she glanced over her shoulder. No, no one was eavesdropping. The jukebox and laughter in the bar only aggravated her miserable mood.

Although she missed Aldebaran's quaint intimacy, living above the Saloon had not been as noisy as Hannah had feared. Sure, it was only the first week of business, but the Saloon seemed to function primarily as a gathering place. Beer was served, but nobody got drunk. Ginger said that wasn't unusual—she'd never had to break up a single fight in all her years of tending bar. Next week they'd see more customers but they shouldn't anticipate any problems.

Only three cottages were occupied right now. Three couples, six guests in all. Tomorrow night all the cottages would be filled. Even Castor and Pollux were booked and there were no signs of storm damage—thanks to Eric's carpentry skills. Hannah wondered how her little crew would manage with sixteen guests. It would be a good test of their teamwork and preparation.

When Hannah spoke to the kids about giving her a hand up north for a few weeks, she hoped they'd agree to the exchange of time and effort for the minimal salary she was able to offer. She warned them about the futility of the financial situation and of Ingold's threatened encroachment, but that only strengthened their conviction to pitch in and help.

"I can't believe you never told me your uncle had a resort," Chloe complained.

Hannah reiterated what she had learned about Hal from her family and from his funeral. Eric, excited by the prospect of moving into the heart of the Ingold protest, was restless and eager to get involved.

"My first concern, and yours, too, will be to keep the resort open through the summer," Hannah explained. "We need the income. We can't afford to close it down."

"What are you going to do about the mine?" Chloe wanted to know.

"A group of people are working to defeat it, but I don't plan on joining in. I don't have time and I don't expect that you will, either, once you see how much work there is ahead of us. The protest isn't having much of an effect, anyway. It's kind of a grassroots thing; they're not getting much publicity."

"Maybe not in the regular press," Eric offered, "but I've been following Ingold's progress in some of my newsletters. There's a master's hearing pretty soon."

"Will you have enough work to keep us busy until the hearing?" Chloe wouldn't drop the subject.

"I think there's enough work to keep you busy for the whole summer," Hannah told her, truthfully, "but whether or not you want to hang around, that's completely up to you."

A few days later all three of them plus Ratso moved in to Hal's apartment above the Saloon. Eric and Chloe cleared out part of the closed-off section and set up their own living space with selected bedsteads, dressers, and a mattress from castaway junk stored in vacant rooms. They shared Hannah's bathroom and kitchen.

Ratso wandered everywhere, made himself at home wherever Babe wasn't and hissed and spit whenever the dog came near.

Chloe and Eric immediately drew up an ambitious list of repairs and renovations. Hannah had to remind them, "Our budget is severely limited."

Ginger backed her up. "Forget about fixing up the Saloon for now, it's been good enough for the last few summers at least. You just get those roofs and boats patched so nothing leaks, then have enough fresh bait and beer around and get the Evinrudes tuned. Folks are going to think they died and went to heaven, they won't even recognize the place."

But Chloe's enthusiasm was heartening, Hannah conceded. And Eric proved to be an excellent troubleshooter. He was capable of fixing anything from electrical wiring to tipsy toilets. Before the summer was out he was determined to uncover the fieldstone fireplace in the Saloon so it could roar with a welcoming blaze on days that dawned like Friday.

By Friday the full moon was waxing and a cold wind out of the north carried weather damp and raw.

Hannah felt sorry for guests who would be leaving early tomorrow. With this cold gray day they'd linger in the Saloon all morning and Ginger would serve a lot of hot coffee while they played cards. But spring weather in the northwoods could be capricious, so the wet wind might blow over by afternoon.

She left at ten to meet with Dennis Windsor and review the formal appraisal of the estate with him. Glad to get out of jeans and a sweatshirt, under her raincoat she wore a short, soft yellow linen tailored skirt and matching blazer, with a creamy silk blouse and pale hose. Maybe a bit chic for Antler, but when you have your picture on the front page of the local rag you must live up to your celebrity, she reasoned. Besides, the day was dismal, and the yellow linen gave her spirits a welcome lift.

She had tried to reach Kerry all week, without any luck, so there had been no opportunity to inform him about the Windsor/Graves conversation she'd overheard in the woods. Ginger tried inviting him to the Monday night potluck to meet the kids, but he'd been at a meeting out of town. Seeing Windsor and Graves together on the property was definitely bad news, Ginger ventured, and Hannah should "show them where the bear shit in the buckwheat," one of these days.

The urgency of that matter was on her mind, driving into town. Wind gusts swept her Toyota and rain splashed the windshield faster than her wipers could clear it. The rotten weather was reminiscent of the first time she found her bumbling way to the resort on Star Lake Road, and the memory of that afternoon and her own blind innocence, made her shudder.

Dennis Windsor greeted Hannah with cordiality. There was no

sign of his earlier pique over her insistence on being more closely involved with Hal's estate or the cruel remarks he had made about her
on the woodland path. In fact, she decided, Windsor was making a
real effort to lay on the charm.

He brought Hal's file out of his desk and began to shift assorted
papers.

"How're you doing out there, by the way? The *Advocate* says
you're having a swell time. Of course, the paper only knows what
you tell them." He smiled, ruefully. "Back when we first met—how
long ago was that now, couple of weeks? You couldn't wait to hightail
it back to Mad Town. What happened to change your mind?"

"We met five weeks ago. It's a beautiful place." Hannah was reluctant to reveal more than necessary. She even adjusted her skirt,
tried to cover her knees.

"Well, it is a beautiful spot," Windsor agreed with effusive
warmth. "But I'd advise you not to let yourself be seduced by what
it's like up here in summer. There's too much risk involved in attempting to operate that kind of venture. You've got better things to
do with your life."

Windsor clasped his hands on top of the papers on his desk.

"Gus Schultz says he can get you a reliable cash offer right away
that'll clean up Hal's debt and leave you a nice little nest egg for your
troubles. You'd be a smart gal to go for it, Hannah. You won't find
anything better by yourself."

"Considering the foreclosure, you may be correct," Hannah said,
immediately diving to the heart of the matter.

Windsor lost his hearty smile, avoided her eyes and shuffled
more papers.

"I was going to tell you about that, after . . . after we got into this
paperwork," Windsor admitted. "No sense throwing all the bad
news at you all at once."

"You mean there's more?"

"Only that, according to the figures I've reviewed, your resort has
never been what you'd call a money-making concern. And for the

good of the estate, and your own as well, with your lack of experience in this sort of thing . . . I mean, running a business of this kind, well, it's quite a gamble, Hannah. I doubt you'll survive, even with all the effort you and your family are putting into it. Fact is, there's a strong probability you'll go even further into debt. As your attorney, I feel that I should alert you to that."

Hannah uncrossed her legs, then crossed them again. Windsor noticed.

"We pulled things together as fast as we could." Hannah explained. "We're fully booked for this month, and pretty well filled for the rest of the summer.

Windsor started to sort various pages again, silent now.

"Here's a bill for the newspaper publication of the notice. Can you write a check from the estate account?"

Hannah pulled the estate checkbook from her purse while he busied himself with the Estate Inventory and Appraisal. He insisted on going over every item, individually. The value of the real estate was considerably less than Schultz's initial estimate.

"I'll be honest with you," Windsor said. "Compared to the regular appraiser, Gus was a little generous with his estimate. Selling as a going concern, that is. But Gus told me he was anticipating some remodeling and fix-up—I guess that wasn't completed when the estate's appraiser was out there. And Gus didn't have access to Hal's business records, either."

"Dennis, I've decided to stay a while," Hannah informed him, "at least until fall. But I'd like to talk to your father. If he remembers what Hal said about me when he wrote his will, it might help me decide what to do when the summer season's over."

"Out of the question," Windsor replied. "Dad has his good days and his better ones, but even on his better days his memory is fairly shot. Won't speak to me, sometimes. Contacting him would cause nothing but confusion on his part and a great deal of frustration on yours and mine. Guaranteed waste of your time."

She couldn't hold back any longer about his visit to the resort.

"Eric said you and Mr. Graves stopped in, last Sunday."

Windsor was ready for that. He leaned back in his chair and assumed a gesture of deep concentration before he explained.

"I'm sure you've heard that Ingold is thinking about doing some mining in the area, it isn't any big secret. This week's *Advocate* has an article about the upcoming master's hearing, which you must've caught. Flattering picture of you, by the way." He glanced down at her legs again and smiled.

You moron, Hannah thought, but she said, "The paper says the mine will be a boost to the local economy."

"Oh, no doubt about that. No doubt at all. They'll be adding at least sixty or seventy new employees to their payroll. And the mine will probably pay at least three or four million dollars in local taxes once the ore body begins to move. That's nothing to sneeze at up here. We need the jobs."

"So why is there so much opposition?" Hannah asked, hoping her question sounded as virtuous as she intended.

"I don't know that there's so much opposition," Windsor replied with unctuous concern, "just the usual troublemakers." He raised an eyebrow, "Some of them friends of yours, by the way."

This was the same man who'd told Graves (right in front of her!) that she had been distributing anti-mine flyers the day she arrived. He seemed to read her thoughts, and continued.

"I feel I should tell you, there's tremendous resentment about newcomers trying to tell us what to do. A majority of the folks here think the mine will be a real boon. Increased jobs and tax revenue will make the Town of Tamarack and the whole of Lakeland County attractive for other kinds of industry. In ten years or so, after the mine runs its course, Ingold will restore the site back to its original condition, or even better. Everybody wins."

"Are you telling me I shouldn't be worried about my land?"

Hannah wished Kerry could be eavesdropping right now. Her land. That was a new concept, one she would need more time to consider.

"Is that why Mr. Graves came out to Star Lake with you, to alleviate my concerns?"

"Just what concerns do you have, Hannah?" Windsor wanted to know. He placed his elbows on his desk and looked over at her with eyes that were heavy-lidded and solemn. "What are you worried about?"

"Noise, water quality. The value of my property. Or what happens if my business falls off."

"Nothing's going to happen to your business, if you stay out of the dispute," Windsor warned a shade too quickly. Then, more patiently, and with another ingratiating smile he explained, "If you choose not to sell, the Ingold mine could actually be good for your resort. Think about the possibility of long-term renters, mining engineers or geologists. A more up-scale clientele."

And no room for Mrs. Staniszewski from Evansville, Hannah sighed, a woman who knew "when to yank and when to tease."

"But there's an even better option, a way the mine could alleviate your mortgage difficulties," Windsor leaned back in his leather chair, "I want to take you to Lofty Pines for lunch today so you can see our country club. I have to confess I also took the liberty of asking Axel Graves to meet us there. He manages Ingold's Star Lake operation, as you probably know. I suppose I should wait for him to tell you himself but I'm aware that he has a strong interest in purchasing the resort."

"No kidding," Hannah replied guilelessly, returning Windsor's grin with a wide-eyed smile of her own. That had to be the same cash sale Gus Schultz had guaranteed if she sold right away, "as is." Ingold didn't want her property for its scenic value or to control more geography; Graves was too eager. She didn't fall off the turnip truck yesterday, as Ginger frequently claimed.

She needed to talk to Kerry.

The pines surrounding the dark log and smoked glass clubhouse were, indeed, lofty, and Graves's sincere but dour demeanor contributed to the personification of his unfortunate name. "Hannah Swann, our remarkable poet," he said when Windsor introduced her, and that was one of two amusing remarks Graves managed to crack. He was about her age, Hannah guessed, and blandly handsome with blonde, almost-white hair. Most of the conversation revolved around life in the northwoods. He was new here, too, having arrived only a couple months before. When the mine actively assumed its operation he would be moving his wife and small daughters from Arizona to a new home he was constructing on a waterfront lot near Cedar Springs.

"I have some concern about the schools," he said, "but the wholesomeness of this area appeals to me. My wife is planning a great room to encompass her looms."

Hannah couldn't wait to tell Ginger about encompassing Mrs. Graves's looms, and now she definitely had to find Kerry. But she made a detour on her way back to stop at the bank in Cedar Springs for the contents of Hal's safety deposit box: a sheaf of handwritten poems (Miriam's), a woman's wedding ring, an envelope with a tiny lock of hair, and the original deed to the resort, dated June 5, 1945.

Then, outside Antler she made a quick stop at the funeral home to pick up Hal's ashes and thanked Charlie Jenkins for reminding her. "I wouldn't have forgotten," she assured him, "I just haven't been in town."

"That's all right, Hal's never been any trouble to me," Mr. Jenkins replied.

As it turned out, Kerry was on the front porch discussing the upcoming canoe flotilla with Chloe and Eric when she returned.

"Mom," Chloe welcomed her, "look who's here! We met Dan at a rally down in Madison months ago. Imagine finding him on our front porch! Eric and I couldn't believe it."

Kerry wore torn, faded jeans with a paint-stained T-shirt and needed a shave. He was repairing Miriam's star signs. The boards had a fresh coat of varnish and most of the brass tacks had been replaced.

"You're exactly the person I need to talk to," Hannah told Kerry in a rush, "I just had lunch with Windsor and Graves. There's something funny going on. . . ."

Hannah paused, thrown off by the voices she heard in the Saloon.

"Just a minute," Hannah told Kerry. "Don't go anywhere. I'll be right back."

"I've been saying to your friend here that you've been busier than a one-armed paper hanger," Ginger was standing behind the bar. "But you got the place open by Decoration Day like you promised you would."

Tyler was leaning over the bar, grinning into a beer.

"What are you doing here?" Hannah asked, unable to contain her irritation. "You didn't say anything about driving up when you called last night."

Tyler greeted her with an enthusiastic embrace. "I brought a bear hug for my Sweetcheeks," he whispered. "I decided this morning, if I didn't take advantage of this free weekend I probably won't see you until the end of the summer."

Hannah wanted to ask how he'd managed to get away, but she couldn't inquire about his wife in front of Ginger. Chloe would have a caustic remark to make after he left, too; Chloe had never approved.

"Well, my life is full of surprises," she said, smiling, meeting Ginger's skeptical gaze. Who cared where Dawn was. Or what Chloe or Ginger might think. Kerry would have to wait for a few minutes, because Tyler was here right now.

"How long have you been waiting for me? Has anyone shown you around? Would you like to see the place?"

"About half an hour. And of course I want to see more!" Tyler laughed. "Ginger's been entertaining me with tales of the good old days."

Hannah would have to explain Tyler to Ginger, if she didn't already suspect. Hell, she'd know.

"I can show you the cottages we've been working on. They'll be empty until tomorrow," she said to Tyler, leading him toward the stairs. She was afraid to ask if he needed a room for the night. "If it weren't such a miserable day I'd give you a boat ride through the lakes, but you can see Star Lake pretty well from the sleeping porch."

They emerged from the wide staircase and into Hal's apartment, where she led him out onto the porch. He embraced her even more warmly and reached into her raincoat to unbutton her blouse. Hannah made him stop. The wind was too cold, for one thing. And Kerry and the kids were just below.

"I can't get over seeing you here," Tyler admitted. "It's so unlike you, Cheeks."

"Ginger must've told you we've been fixing it up. . . ."

"Ginger's quite a character, all right. But I wouldn't give you two cents for that surly handyman on the front porch with the kids."

Hannah did her best to ignore Tyler's remarks. They were colored by his desire to have her move back, she knew, and the miserable weather. If he hung around here long enough he'd probably appreciate the latent potential of the place. He was a scientist, after all; he dealt with endangered things.

And today, more than ever, Hannah was convinced Star Lake Saloon and Housekeeping Cottages was an endangered relic.

She wondered if Kerry was still waiting for her, downstairs.

"You aren't driving back right away, are you?"

"No, I'm ensconced at the Yank 'Em Inn. Lucky to get a room."

"This back door leads right to the parking lot," Hannah suggested.

"I thought you'd never get the picture," Tyler said, patting her softly on the sweet cheeks that he adored.

10

Unfamiliar Landscapes

Hannah found herself making excuses. For the quaintness of the resort. For Chloe's brusque behavior, for Ginger's lack of sophistication, for not being there when he arrived, for everything, really. If she'd had any idea that she would be spending the afternoon with Tyler Cole she'd have taken a Valium and done a few affirmations—both practices she had abandoned since settling into her northwoods routine.

She imagined the resort must appear pretty primitive to Tyler, as it had to her, just over a month ago. Driving into Antler beside him now, Hannah was chattering like a monkey on speed.

"When we come back," she said, "I'll show you where Ingold plans to dig their open pit mine. And if we have time and it isn't raining anymore, I'll take you on a sunset cruise of the Celestial Chain."

She'd have to juggle his visit with the exodus of this week's guests and the influx of the next, but that could be arranged, anything could be accommodated, and if he'd like, she could get reservations at Lofty Pines for dinner later tonight; she wanted to show him the country club, the thirty-six-hole golf course, the posh lifestyle that affluent summer people—and some year-round inhabitants—enjoyed.

In fact, Tyler's presence unnerved her. He seemed so L. L. Bean, so out of place in his neatly pressed khakis and new hiking boots. What had he expected, rough terrain?

She even apologized for the Yank 'Em Inn, although it was a perfectly nice small town motel, clean enough and adequate.

"This has got to be better than the floor of my office or out on Picnic Point," Tyler remarked with a grin.

The motel manager was standing in the shelter of the office doorway smoking a cigar in the rain as Hannah exited Tyler's car and scurried into the last of the single row of rooms. Fodder for the local gossip mill, she realized. Remarkable poet, indeed.

Tyler flopped on the bed and pulled her down, too. She burrowed her face into his shoulder, and welcomed the satisfying scent of him.

"I'm so glad you're here," she whispered, "I think I'm starved for affection. It's been over three weeks . . ."

"Twenty-four days," he murmured. "Oh, Cheeks, you feel so good!"

Tyler covered her face with kisses, pulled off her raincoat and helped her fall back. He slipped the beige pumps from her feet, then he began to remove her pantyhose. The process was agonizingly slow. Goddamned pantyhose!

It was not the simplest outfit for him to remove. If she'd had advance notice, Hannah thought idly, she'd have worn a garter belt and stockings.

"I love you, Tyler," she whispered, smiling up at him as her skirt slid to the floor next to her pantyhose, raincoat, and shoes. It was one of her compulsions, to remind Tyler how much she cared so he would return the endearment. If Tyler happened to say "I love you," without Hannah saying it first, she prized those three little extemporaneous words with shameless delight.

Another thing she enjoyed about Tyler: he appreciated the nuances of foreplay. The erotic stimulus was often a helpful, if not absolutely necessary, part of their love-making. She hadn't referred to Uncle Wiggily as his wonderwand for a long while, although early in their relationship that's how she'd thought of it—not because it performed wondrous things but because she found herself wondering if it would perform or not.

That's why, when she was finally unclothed except for her silk blouse and he lay next to her, fondling and caressing and reacquainting himself with her body, she unzipped his khakis, and was surprised to see his penis projecting straight and tall, throbbing like a romance novel's proverbial love-muscle.

"Uncle Wiggily missed me," Hannah murmured, fondling the evidence in her palm.

"He wants Nurse Jane Fuzzy Wuzzy," Tyler whispered, turning so he could rub it against her inner thighs. "Phone sex is nothing, compared to the real thing."

"This is the real thing," Hannah said, amazed that he was so firm this time. Was his hard-on due to one of the new medications for erectile dysfunction? Or was it something as simple as meeting in a motel room—she should have tried the tawdry motel-angle earlier.

"I've missed you, too, Cheeks," Tyler said, and he quickly slid off his hiking boots and his pants. "And I've missed these." He folded back her creamy silk blouse and took one of her breasts, then the other, in his mouth to circle the sensitive nipple with his tongue.

He was nuzzling her belly, clutching her buttocks in his palms and working his way down as he often did, but she was ready for him to shove into her.

"I need it," she told him urgently, and reached for him with her hands. "I need you inside me right now!"

"Not yet," he said softly. "Wait a little bit. I'm not ready."

"Well, it feels like you are, and I can't wait," she moaned, squirming so her legs wrapped around his back.

He felt enormous. It had been so long since she'd actually had a man like that, and the tantalizing, slippery friction was almost more than she could bear. If there were something like a gentle rape, this was what it would be like, she thought.

Tyler's passion was unusually intense. Could this be the same man, the same unreliable wonderwand she had labored over for the past three years? He was biting her lower lip, his breath hot and merging with her own desperate gasps. Her nipples tightened, responding to his expert touch.

Hannah groaned. The bud of a glorious climax trembled, spread and pulsed like a blossoming chrysanthemum between her legs. Hannah abandoned herself to the rush of ecstasy as it bloomed.

Then Tyler shuddered and she felt him come, too, shoving even more deeply within, convulsing repeatedly as he climaxed.

"Oh, my god, that was fantastic," Hannah murmured when she was able to speak. "That was the best ever, that was . . ."

Her breathing slowed, finally, and her heartbeat. She drowsily opened her eyes.

That was weird.

There was a fragrance now recognizable in the darkened room, more intense than Tyler's usual cologne. She could hear what almost sounded like someone else's labored breathing.

In the dim light Hannah was mortified to make out a figure standing in the bathroom doorway. Was she hallucinating?

She reached for her glasses on the table next to the bed.

Dawn!

"Jesus!" Hannah mumbled, wresting herself away from Tyler's clutch and letting his penis flop, limp, upon the mattress.

"What the fuck is this?" Hannah cried in disbelief. She stumbled out of bed and reached for the raincoat still in a damp heap. She clutched it to her chest.

"You son of a bitch!" she raged. With her right hand, she threw one of the L. L. Bean boots at Tyler and struck his forehead.

"And you!" She turned on Dawn, "Are you crazy?"

Dawn, her bulging breasts encased in the lacy bra of a black teddy, skittered across the carpet like a nervous mouse, to crouch next to Tyler who had taken refuge on the floor. Together they peered over the mattress at Hannah, who flung Tyler's other boot at them, but it hit the lamp, which shattered with a loud crash.

"Jesus Christ!" Hannah seethed, "I can't believe I'm so fucking stupid!"

She grabbed whatever she could, to hurl at them: her shoes, the ice bucket, glasses, anything that wasn't bolted down. The desk chair.

They watched dully as Hannah, in a mad fury, tore up the room.

"Idiot!" she muttered to herself, "You stupid ass!"

Hannah swept her raincoat around her and tied the belt. The couple seemed frozen in a ridiculous, penitent tableau. The straps of Dawn's black lace teddy had slipped down her shoulders to reveal the secret of her cleavage: duct tape pasted beneath her breasts drew them together.

"Dawn has always liked you," Tyler said calmly, holding his forehead with one hand and reaching imploringly toward Hannah with the other, across the rumpled sheets.

"I'm not some goddamn rent-a-pussy," she spat, picking up her skirt. She stuffed it under her coat.

"Can't believe . . ." she seethed, "Fucked up . . ." She pushed the pantyhose in her raincoat pocket. "Brainless . . . !"

"This was an assignment, Hannah, we dreamed it up during our Enhancement weekend," Dawn said brightly.

"I'm outta here," Hannah hissed. "You two are sick."

"Tyler says you read him stories like this in *Penthouse*," Dawn was whimpering. "You have such a strong spirit, Hannah," she whimpered, "I've always admired you. I want to be more like you. I've written poems."

"Shove them up your ass," Hannah said icily. "Or your husband's. Come to think of it, that's one cock-teasing trick I never tried on him."

Barefoot. She had entered the motel impeccably dressed and emerged barefoot, flushed, disheveled, with nothing beneath her raincoat but a very wrinkled silk blouse.

News of her illicit rendezvous would be all over town fairly soon, Hannah imagined. She paused to find her sunglasses in her purse. The rain had left puddles everywhere, and she splashed through them, oblivious, eager to escape the scene she had just slammed a door upon.

At Buck's she punched the number of the Saloon into the pay phone but her hands were shaking so hard she had to try a second time. "Please, let Eric answer," she implored, but Dan Kerry's friendly "Star Lake Saloon" responded. And when Hannah said quickly, "I can't explain but can you pick me up at Buck's right now?" all he said was, "I'm on my way."

She was still trembling in the restroom, where she sat on the toilet and sobbed without even bothering to line the toilet seat with paper first. Face in her hands, Hannah rocked back and forth. Anguish overwhelmed her like nausea, and she felt that she might be sick.

Someone rattled the doorknob.

"I'll just be a minute," Hannah called.

Concerned that patrons might wonder what was taking her so long, Hannah rinsed her face, then washed herself with wet paper towels and soap from the dispenser to remove as much of Tyler as possible, under the circumstances. She pulled on her crumpled linen skirt and re-entered the dark bar with a brave if somewhat uncertain smile.

Hannah had a beer and swallowed a Valium. Buck may have wondered why she appeared distracted and wasn't wearing shoes, but he inquired about the fishing out at Star Lake and commented on the weather, as any circumspect bartender would.

She was grateful, too, that Kerry arrived quickly. The only question he asked was "Do you want me to drive around for a while?"

Hannah wasn't ready to face Chloe and Ginger. She certainly wasn't ready to face Kerry, either, but short of walking back to Star Lake by herself, barefoot, there didn't seem to be another choice.

Babe had come along for the ride. The dog sat between them while Kerry drove. Hannah barely noticed where they went except that the roads led, vaguely, in the right direction.

At least she had been right about the changeable weather. The wet winds had blown over and by late afternoon the sun was beginning to shine through departing clouds.

"If you don't feel like talking, that's all right," Kerry said. Hannah stared out at the rough wilderness landscape. They drove through tamarack swamps and stands of dense pine, but all Hannah saw were Tyler and Dawn on their knees beside the bed, peering back over at her like humbled, disobedient children. It was so unbelievably preposterous that she couldn't even cry any more. And she felt shamefully disgraced by the memory of the orgasm that had shaken her thoroughly. She pulled the belt of her raincoat tighter and hoped it didn't show.

"Where are we," she asked after half an hour had passed.

"There's the town hall, for the Town of Tamarack." Kerry pointed to a little white building that looked as if it had served as a one room school many years before. "The original village of Star Lake stood here once. That's Victor Redhawk's store and gas pump. It's about all that's left of the original village." He stopped in front of a historical marker.

"According to this, there were eighty-four houses. What happened?"

"Some were moved when the logging operation ended, some burned down, others were turned into something else."

"Two billion feet of pine timber logged off?" Hannah was reading. "They must have taken out every tree within miles."

He pulled away from the sign and back onto the road.

"Miriam's buried in the old Star Lake cemetery. Want to see?"

Hannah sighed. "Why not?"

"Hal told me Larkin Logging and Lumber was one of the jobbers who cut this over. Your family, Hannah, was partly responsible for the harvest of the old growth timber."

Hannah was mildly interested. "Is that why he settled here, do you think?"

"That plus the fact that your Star Lake Saloon was one of the lumber company's buildings."

Kerry pointed out a couple of grassy ruts that led into the woods from the road near an isolated cemetery.

"That logging road leads to your place. You'll find lots of trails like that through the woods if you know where to look. Somebody drove in here recently. See the tracks?"

"Who uses these trails?"

"Kids with ATVs, mostly. But this one's on your property. Tell Eric to make some 'No Trespassing' signs."

"Larkin Logging and Lumber," Hannah mused. "My grandpa and his father were involved with that."

"Most of the residents moved away from here after the Star Lake mill closed. Then, Hal said, your lodge was turned into a hunting lodge for wealthy Chicago hunters. After that it was a little summer resort. Years later, of course, it ended up in his hands."

"Maybe he felt guilty about our connection to the old-growth timber," Hannah suggested. "You sure know a lot more about my family history than I do."

She remembered that Kerry also knew Hal's reason for leaving home, but this wasn't the time to ask about that.

"Maybe Hal walked that trail through the woods to Miriam's grave. Can we stop there for a minute?"

Kerry parked the Blazer next to the gate. He let Babe out, to wander around.

Hannah climbed out of the Blazer, too, and breathed deeply of the fresh, pine-scented air. The rain-wet grass felt therapeutic beneath her bare feet.

The Larkin plot was easy to find: a polished red granite tombstone held Miriam's dates of birth and death, "Beloved wife of Harold A. Larkin," and beside it there was a smaller stone, carved in the shape of a lamb. The inscription read:

Infant daughter
October 10, 1949
"Above dark clouds, everlasting light"

Hannah recognized the line from Miriam's poem.

"I know it's none of my business," Kerry said when she found her way back, "but if you want to talk about what happened to your shoes, it's okay."

He sat on the bumper of the Blazer and handed her a clean handkerchief.

"Did you ever play Uncle Wiggily with your kids?" Hannah asked, realizing too late that he hadn't yet mentioned his children.

"Uncle Wiggily?"

"He had rheumatism," she explained, sitting next to him. "His full name was Uncle Wiggily Longears, and he lived with Nurse Jane Fuzzy Wuzzy. She was a muskrat, I think. There were Uncle Wiggily books, and a children's game . . ."

"I seem to remember a Pipsissewa," Kerry said patiently.

"Right."

"Did I say something just now that made you think of Uncle Wiggily?"

"My friend from Madison. The guy who showed up today."

Kerry nodded, "He's Uncle Wiggily?"

"That's what I called him, sometimes. Uncle Wiggily."

"I can't imagine why," Kerry said with a deadpan expression.

"It doesn't really matter," she replied. "I'm sorry I brought it up. In more ways than one. It's just hard . . . oh, shit."

Hannah tried to laugh at the absurdity of it all, and as she did, tears mingled with the gulps of her dismal attempt at laughter. She blew her nose.

Trust. She had a fleeting concern about trust—would he keep this to himself? But after what she had been through, she reasoned, there wasn't much farther she could fall.

So she began to explain more about Tyler, and, eventually, about Dawn. It was a long story. Kerry refrained from asking questions, didn't show any kind of judgmental reaction, only polite concern.

After she finished relating the part about the black lace teddy and the duct tape, only then did she detect the slightest hint of amusement.

Hannah told him, "The whole sorry episode is like a metaphor for my thoroughly fucked-up life. I don't know whether to laugh or cry."

Babe had returned from her scouting tour and stood, panting, at the side of the Blazer. Kerry let the dog in and climbed behind the wheel himself. Hannah went around to the opposite door.

"So, you screwed up, trusting this shit-for-brains biologist," Kerry said as he drove out of the cemetery. "I'm fifty-seven and I never see my kids. Haven't for years and years. We all make mistakes."

This personal confession was a side of Dan Kerry she'd never imagined, and she was sure in the future the unguarded opportunity would be rare.

"Why don't you see them?"

"They're in Boston, now."

"So, what was your mistake?"

"I worked on Wall Street, made a pretty good salary in mergers and acquisitions; good enough so there was some left over after the divorce to let me work at this fishing guide game in a kind of half-assed way."

"And?"

"And my job was consuming my life. Something my wife and kids tried to tell me, but I wouldn't listen. Then one day about ten years ago I checked out a corporation I'd been instrumental in shutting down and there was this man sitting in a half-empty office. I took him for a faithful old employee at first, but then he told me he'd built the place up from nothing."

He drove in silence for a while, cleared his throat, and began again, his voice huskier now.

"There were the usual complications—alcohol, some drugs. My wife took off, took the kids along and went back to live with her family. After a really bad week I decided there had to another way to live. I threw some things in the car and started driving west. The second night I hit Chicago during rush hour and when I got as far as Madison I slowed down. The day after that I headed north. I ran into Hal Larkin in the Wildwood Coffee Shop in Minocqua."

"But what did Uncle Hal say?"

"At first, it was just an invitation to come to Star Lake and rest. Aldebaran, that big cottage, by the way. Then he gave me Thoreau and Emerson. I sat on the porch of that cottage for days, reading. As a kid I was outdoors a lot, and I felt comfortable here. Safe. Nature is a great healer. At least that's true for me. Hal taught me there are more important things in life than making money, I guess."

"You can say that again," Hannah offered, "Star Lake Resort has been operating in the red for a long, long time."

"He never claimed to be a businessman," Kerry said. "We had some good, rip-roaring arguments and I blew off a lot of steam. But, deep down, our basic philosophy of life was pretty much the same. We developed a friendship that grew stronger through the years."

They were back at Star Lake. Kerry pulled in to the parking lot by the lodge.

She had not been able to look into his eyes until now. It seemed to her that the icy blue had melted a bit.

"That's why you shouldn't be so hard on yourself, Hannah. You have your family here with you. You're not all alone. And you can count on Hal's friends being your friends."

Kerry took Hannah's clenched hands in his and held them firmly for a moment, as if to underscore his part in that bond.

She was afraid he would touch her hands to his lips as Dennis Windsor had, but Kerry looked over at her, smiled and squeezed her fist. Babe nudged Kerry's shoulder, eager to get out.

There wasn't much left for her in Madison, that was obvious. Even when Tyler got back from his cruise he could never be there for her again, not after this. Chloe and Eric were planning to go back to the city next week to put their things into storage and sublet Eric's apartment for the summer. Hannah didn't want to teach anymore, and she obviously didn't have to live in Madison to write her video scripts, either. All she had left in the city was her house.

"Just a second," Hannah told Kerry before they walked down the path to the Saloon, "I left something in my car."

She retrieved the box with Hal's ashes from the front seat.

"I met Axel Graves today," Hannah told Kerry. "I had lunch with him and Denny Windsor at Lofty Pines. Graves wants to buy the resort."

"That's not news, is it?" Kerry asked, holding the screen door to the porch open for her.

"No, it wasn't a surprise. But the offer he made was about double the amount Gus Schultz suggested Ingold would offer. Almost half a million dollars."

Ginger whistled. "Holy cow! That's a lot of moola!"

Even though it was now early evening, the bar was empty and Ginger sat on the glider reading a supermarket tabloid. Kerry moved a pillow aside to sit next to Ginger.

"What's your pal Bigfoot up to this week?"

Ginger responded with a playful punch.

If Ginger wondered why Hannah had gone off to Antler with Tyler and returned with Kerry instead, she never indicated her surprise.

"Oh, Honey, is that Hal?" Ginger asked, noticing the small box Hannah held in her lap as she sat back to rock in the wicker rocker.

"We'll have to decide where to put these," Hannah said. "I've been thinking, we can have a private ceremony of our own and scatter the ashes over Miriam's grave. Or over the lake."

"Oh, that would be so nice, Honey," Ginger said, "now that we've got Chloe and Eric with us, too. By the way, they went into town with the others, to the fish fry at the Sportsman's. Best beer-battered cod in Lakeland County. You ought to try it sometime."

"I had some great fish the other day," Hannah replied. "Walleye. Caught by an expert fisherman."

"Fried up by one, too," Ginger's eyes teased. "You're right, even the Sportsman's can't beat that."

"Last Sunday, after you took me fishing," Hannah told Kerry, serious now, "I went for a walk in the woods." She told him about seeing the men and the conversation she'd overheard.

"You told me Ingold wants this land to give them more leverage, more property to control. But it must be more than that. Graves is too anxious to get me out of here."

"Like I said, that's a heckuva lot of moola," Ginger nodded.

"Is there any sign of ore on this property? What do the aerial surveys show?"

"No idea," Kerry admitted. "I don't think Hal ever met Graves and he wouldn't have much to do with Ingold. Or the Department of Natural Resources."

"Except for being against all of 'em," Ginger added.

"Well, that," Kerry agreed. "And the DNR files aren't easy to access—we've requested more information, but . . ."

"No luck," Ginger said.

"I'll let Graves wait until Monday. Then I'll call Denny and say I'm not interested. How gullible do they think I am?"

For a moment she caught Kerry's eye again and had to look away, the disgrace of the afternoon with Tyler and Dawn still much too fresh to repress.

Ginger sighed and placed her head comfortably on Kerry's shoulder. "I'm so glad you decided to stay here and give us folks a hand, Hannah. The kids, too. We need you guys here."

The sun fell below the horizon and the first star shimmered in the night sky as they remained on the porch, comfortable and relaxed in the gentle twilight. Ginger began to snore.

"I forgot to thank you for fixing Miriam's star signs," Hannah whispered to Kerry. "That was so nice of you to do."

"Glad to help out," he replied softly

Ginger stirred. "Miriam told me once she tried to let the starlight heal something deep in her that hurt."

Hannah left them seated on the glider and went out onto the pier where the stars sparkling overhead now seemed close enough to touch.

11

The Canoe Flotilla

During Hannah's third week of business, a pale sadness diluted every sunrise. Her life was beginning to resemble her dismal attempt at watercolors: too many vivid emotions ran together and were muddied with complications. Even the daily repetition of sunshine and mild temperatures felt unforgivable.

She struggled to find a routine as she balanced requests for more towels, minnows, pillows, and coat hangers, beer deliveries and pizza orders, with a brave attempt to decipher Hal's peculiar bookkeeping. "When the beer sign by the porch door was lit, you could tell Hal was here in the kitchen at his desk or pretty close by," Ginger announced.

Monday night after the second official Star Lake Potluck she built a bonfire at the edge of the lake with downed branches and limbs. Then she threw in remnants of poems written for Tyler that he would never see. Ginger declared the bonfire a great addition. Chloe and Eric found it romantic, and lodgers unfolded their plastic lawn chairs around the crackling flames. Mr. Rockford, staying in Cygnus, pulled out a harmonica and played "Polly Wolly Doodle" and other old camp tunes that the group joined in singing. Hannah wished she could relate the cornball merriment to Tyler, who had, ironically, brought it on.

But as much as she might desire some closure to her blue mood, each day Hannah was more irritable and depressed. She missed him. Even the idea of him. Checking in by phone each day, Tyler had provided a lifeline to Madison and the Hannah she used to be.

Saturday would always be their busiest day. Why hadn't she thought of that when she promised Eric she'd take part in the canoe flotilla? Ginger said she'd have to pass, too, claiming again she'd "get all stove up," if she had to paddle that far. But Eric urged Ginger to sit in the middle of the canoe he'd crew with Chloe and hold their protest sign.

"You make it say, 'Shove Your Mine Where the Sun Don't Shine,'" Ginger dared Eric, "and you've got yourself a deal, Mister."

"I'll fix you a special seat so you can lean back like a lady of leisure," Eric promised.

Hannah felt even more forlorn.

If the mine didn't threaten her own lake would she still think it was a bad idea? Governor Dawson claimed it would be an environmentally safe mine, and the arguments for employment opportunities were compelling. In fact, a wide range of opinions among the local residents were growing more volatile. Saturday morning, while the women hurried to finish cleaning the cottages before the flotilla began, Ginger said, "I've got neighbors in town who lived in the apartment next door for seven years and you'd think if anybody had a lick of sense, the Kapkes would. But now when I say good morning to Bud and Betty I got to be careful not to mention the damn mine because they're every bit as much for it as I am against it, and that's just one example of the way the whole town's taking sides. It's a pity. When I hear Axel Graves brag he's going to add fifty long-lasting jobs in Lakeland County I want to tell him go piss in the Mississippi and try to float a boat."

Ginger was tucking fresh sheets onto one of the beds in Aldebaran.

"Those jobs'll be here and gone before you know it. Nine, ten years after the mine opens it'll close and then what?"

"Speaking of floating," Chloe called out to Ginger from the

kitchen, "be sure to use the bathroom before we get in the canoe. Dan said the flotilla's going to last a couple hours at least."

There was a list of responsibilities for each Saturday's cleaning routine: as soon the first cottage was vacated on Saturday morning, the women swooped down on it while Eric inspected boats and refueled motors, gathered garbage for the dumpster, swept and mopped the Saloon, and settled accounts with the guests who were checking out.

Lodgers were expected to wash their own dishes and stack them back inside the metal cabinets, but some pots and pans needed a bit more elbow grease so Chloe took care of that. She also wiped out the refrigerators and threw away leftover food while Hannah volunteered for the dirty work—scouring the toilets, sinks, and showers, then sweeping and mopping the floors. Ginger was in charge of distributing little packages of Ivory soap and checking supplies of toilet paper in each bathroom, replacing clean towels and bath mats after collecting those to be washed, then stripping the beds and remaking them with fresh linens. Hannah would wash sheets and towels later that afternoon while she waited for new guests to arrive.

This was the third Saturday of their cleaning scheme and Cygnus was almost completed when Eric came by for Chloe and Ginger. Wearing one of Hal's battered old straw hats, Eric looked just like one of the local fishermen.

"Go ahead, I'll finish here," Hannah offered. "Be sure to wave!" She tried to sound enthusiastic, "And have a good time!"

Someone had spilled a carton of milk in Cygnus, so Hannah mopped the kitchen floor twice. Then she plopped the mop back in the pail of water and sat on the porch steps of the cottage to wallow in self-pity. With almost everyone gone, she could feel the silence of the woods seep back in through the branches of aspen and fir, as if serenity hovered while the cottages were occupied, waiting like a cautious ghost.

The bottom step of Cygnus's porch was rotting; she must remember to put that on Eric's "Honey-Do" list on the refrigerator door before someone got hurt. Eric was a marvel, cheerful and ready to pitch in whenever there was work to be done. Hannah had to rue-fully admit that he and Chloe were enjoying their northwoods summer more than she had imagined they would. She had never seen either of them so focused and committed. An uninformed observer might presume the young couple was in charge instead of Hannah, their enthusiasm was so lively.

Ratso peeked out from under Sirius's porch, then scampered up onto Hannah's lap where he curled and began to purr. The cat enjoyed the attention from affectionate guests and a chance to hunt and explore outdoors. He scratched in the dirt and pooped wherever he pleased. He also tormented poor Babe by climbing the nearest tree whenever the dog decided to give chase.

No, it wasn't honest to claim she was so locked into tedious resort duties that she could never get away. Only last night Ginger stayed behind while Hannah went along over to Kerry's with the kids to discuss the upcoming master's hearing on the mine permits and today's demonstration. The group welcomed her warmly enough, but after her outspoken carping to Kerry about protests she felt self-conscious participating in a proactive way.

Everyone there had been present at Hal's funeral: Lyle and Lynne, the look-alike bluegrass fiddlers and their eleven year-old son, Leslie. Walt Thoren, the older man who'd read Whitman was actually a dairy farmer, one of the few in Lakeland County. Red-bearded Ben lived in a home he'd built himself on the north shore of Sundog. Victor, the Loon Ranger, had retrieved Hannah during her boating disaster.

Lyle and Lynne ran a retreat center called Forest Temple on the other side of Sickle Moon, with teepees and a campground where New Age seminars were held in creative healing, channeling, and goddess worship. Lynne, Ginger told her, had come up with the name "Celestial Chain" for their chain of lakes and rivers.

The meeting was actually a cookout in Kerry's front yard. Hannah sat at the edge of the conversation, watching Chloe and Eric greet friends they already knew from other rallies. She balanced on her knees a flimsy paper plate with baked beans, charred chicken, and a chunk of watermelon. It could have been anyone's Friday night picnic, but the exchange was more than neighborhood gossip.

Ben announced that rental canoes were arranged for Saturday; a dozen canoes would be hauled by truck to the boat landing in time for the launch.

Walt handed out samples of a flyer that had been distributed around the state: "Join the Citizen's Navy as we float down the Lost Arrow River to the site of the proposed Ingold Mine."

"We're expecting folks from Minnesota, Milwaukee, and Madison," Kerry told them. "Weather forecasters promise a beautiful day, so the turnout should be pretty good."

"What about the press?" Walt wanted to know.

"The news media's been informed," Kerry replied, "but you know how that goes." He glanced over at Hannah, who felt her face glow like a heat lamp. "If we're peaceful and non-violent, nobody gives a damn; if somebody gets arrested, they might bring a camera."

"There'll be families with kids here," Walt added, "so let's remember all we're asking for right now is a chance for a say about what happens in our own backyard. Of course we all hope that Axel Graves will show up at the mine site while we're there . . ."

A chorus of good-natured boos arose at this announcement.

"He'll probably be teeing off at Lofty Pines," someone added. "Or watching back-hoes dig the swimming pool behind that new house of his!"

Eric wanted to know if they were keeping a video record of their activities because he'd brought his camcorder along. This idea was welcomed by the group, so Eric took the camera out of his backpack and began by shooting footage of the gang in Kerry's front yard before the sun was too low in the sky. Leslie, the pale, lanky son of the two blonde fiddlers, followed Eric everywhere as he taped the gathering.

Hannah had not yet finished her meal when Leslie's mother pulled her chair next to hers. Lynne had a Nordic, angular beauty. She was barefoot, wearing a ribbed tank top without a bra, Hannah noted, and a long denim skirt.

"Dan says you want to know more about our work against the mine. I'm really glad to have more women involved in the effort."

Hannah had a mouthful of chicken and her hands were sticky with barbecue sauce, but she nodded and said "Un huh," while Lynne continued, flipping her long blonde hair back behind her ears. Taller than Hannah, Lynne had to lean down to converse with her and the collection of crystals dangling from thin leather strips around her long neck clicked with a sound that reminded Hannah of the gnashing of baby teeth.

"He also said to ask you if you're going to testify."

"Testify?" Hannah had just taken a bite of watermelon but she managed to spit out the word with a couple seeds. "Testify?"

"At the master's hearing. We're each going to speak against the mine. Dan says you might want to say something about the county choosing mining over tourism because the mine will foul up Star Lake for years after it's gone."

"Testify?" Hannah still couldn't swallow. Watermelon juice drooled from the side of her mouth.

"It'll be pretty easy. The hearing's at the gym. At Cedar Springs High School. A whole bunch of protesters are coming in from all over so there'll be at least a hundred or more of us. You should be there!"

"I hadn't thought about that," Hannah said, her appetite suddenly sated.

"I gathered this file of clippings and stuff for you," Lynne offered. "Dan said to give you some background. This pretty much sums up our efforts so far."

"Thanks." Hannah wiped her hands on her jeans, then placed her paper plate on the grass so she could take the file from Lynne. Babe quickly devoured the rest of her chicken and ran off with the watermelon rind.

Hannah wondered if Lynne knew more about her, if Kerry had said anything else, but the young woman was eagerly relating stories of past anti-mining protests including those that had involved Hal Larkin. She was the epitome of the word willowy, Hannah decided;

tall, Scandinavian, with high cheekbones that she, personally, would die for. And blonde.

"I noticed your son shares your musical talents," Hannah commented as they later went inside. Mosquitoes had begun to swarm as darkness settled in.

"Lyle and I are divorced," Lynne said, "but our teepees are next to each other and we still work together. Leslie lives with both of us, and when we travel around the country, he comes along. We home-school Leslie together, too. I hope you'll visit our Forest Temple, Hannah—it's a very spiritual place. This year we're building a sweat lodge."

"That's interesting," Hannah admitted, but she was sweating already.

Now Hannah dug at the corner of the rotting step with her thumb-nail, flicking the debris into the long grass. It was almost one-thirty and she needed some lunch. Cygnus's porch still had to be swept, and beer cans and other recyclables hauled to the recycling bin in the shed. If she didn't shower pretty soon she might turn away the entire flotilla to say nothing of next week's guests.

She stood up from the steps and stretched. Six weeks ago today she drove up to Antler with a migraine and fled Buck's restroom for an emergency box of tampons. Maybe this lingering depression was PMS again. Over the last year her periods had been getting more and more irregular. She never worried about being pregnant.

No, it was too goddamn burlesque; Tyler actually gets it up by himself for the first time in their relationship and she has an ovum, ripe, ready and waiting? Not possible, not in a million years, especially not at her age. She couldn't be pregnant. Her life couldn't get any more complicated, and at her age it would be terribly unfair. She hadn't used birth control in a long time—with Tyler's plumbing problems she had naturally assumed it wouldn't be necessary.

Lately her life had been filled with an incredible amount of stress. Everybody knew stress could upset all your bodily functions.

The flotilla emerged from the culvert and Sundog by the time Hannah was showered and dressed. With Miriam's old telescope on the sleeping porch, she could even bring the mine site on the other side of Star Lake into focus. Hannah tracked the progress of the canoes as they clustered and regrouped. When the leaves were off the trees she bet she could see all the way to Dan Kerry's, on Sundog. Now there was an interesting thought.

She counted about sixty canoes and other sorts of water-related vehicles in the flotilla: men, women, and children with a variety of paddling skills and those with few skills at all who brought up the rear, trailing at some distance, negotiating their own zig-zag line. In one of the early canoes, a voyageur canoe at least twice the size of the others, she counted nine passengers and a banner that read "Farmers Against Mining." That must be Walt Thoren's.

Hannah watched through the telescope until the flotilla circled the northern end of Star Lake and began to approach the resort. She ran down to the pier to wave. Babe followed, and the two of them stood at the water's edge.

Eric's dark green Old Town canoe was situated toward the middle of the group, Ginger royally enthroned in the center with her pumpkin hair frizzed out beneath a sailor cap turned upside-down. To Hannah's surprise, the kids paddled up to the pier to hand her the camcorder so she could videotape them.

Hannah held the camera to one eye, and focused. She had never used one before, and it was interesting to isolate various watercraft and their passengers at such close range. She zoomed in to find Ginger's smiling face before recording, then panned up to frame "Shove Your Mine Where the Sun Don't Shine." A slow zoom back out and the entire canoe was captured. Eric and Chloe smiled and waved, Ginger pumped the sign up and down and Babe barked from the pier as if on cue.

While Eric waited for others to pass so he could manipulate the canoe back toward the pier and get the camera, Hannah focused the viewfinder on other boats and their occupants. There were Ben and his wife, Holly, at each end of a battered aluminum canoe. She thought Lyle, Lynne, and Leslie would be doing their family thing, but Lyle and Victor paddled together with Leslie, and then she found Lynne in the front of a small birchbark canoe propelled by Dan Kerry. Hmm, was this a revelation?

"Mom? The camera?"

Hannah reluctantly stopped shooting and carefully gave it over to Chloe. Kerry and Lynne were past, now, and she couldn't see them very well without the zoom. Maybe if she ran back upstairs she could follow them back to the mine site with the telescope.

"Hold down the fort till I return," Ginger sang over her shoulder. "Shove your mine where the sun don't shine, and I don't mean in the ground . . ."

"Take care," Hannah yelled at their backs. "Don't get wet," but she knew she was already forgotten. When she had a chance, she would ask Ginger about Kerry and Lynne, in an offhand, nonchalant way. As if it didn't matter. Which it didn't, really. Not at all.

By the time the three sunburned paddlers returned to the lodge that night Hannah had checked guests into all but one remaining cottage: two fishermen from Iowa who wouldn't arrive until Sunday afternoon. The idyllic quiet was once again broken by anxious appeals for fishing licenses, ice, cartons of worms, buckets of minnows, beer, and hamburgers.

"It was really fun, Mom," Chloe said as she joined her in the kitchen. "We pulled our canoes up on shore and then we all walked through the woods until we got to the gate where we sat on the ground and Victor's uncle spoke. He's a Chippewa elder and he talked about the sacredness of the water and how the Celestial Flowage eventually goes through Indian territory, ceded territory, where they gather their medicines in the wetlands and grow wild rice and stuff."

"It's all on tape for you," Eric added. "You can check it out tomorrow."

If Saturday was the busiest day of her week, Sunday was becoming Hannah's favorite. Fishermen were eager to get out on the lake and a few took their boats out before dawn. Everyone else slept late. Ginger said she didn't mind taking Sunday off, so Hannah kept the Saloon closed until noon and gave herself permission to read, write, or walk in the woods. It was like a reward after an exhausting race: one more week down, only nineteen more to go.

Saturday's mail brought a videotape of auditions for the Ella Wheeler Wilcox video. The gesture by Joe Mickelson was perfunctory because Hannah would not be involved in the actual production, but she was eager to see the actresses who had tried out for the role of Ella and it was always fascinating to hear her dialog performed.

There were seven auditions on the tape. Joe's note said these were the best of the lot, and could she give him a call early in the week?

Eric's camcorder lay next to her computer in Polaris's living room. Excited by the opportunity to use her new digital system, she scanned the Wilcox audition tape, poured herself another cup of coffee, plugged in Eric's camera and reviewed what she'd missed on Saturday.

She had enjoyed watching Kerry as the genial host Friday night, but on screen he appeared in a new perspective as anti-mining activist and spokesman, isolated from the overall picture of the actual event. This made Hannah vaguely uncomfortable . . . because he placed himself in a position of danger? Because he seemed even more outspoken than she had known him to be? Because this way she could study him carefully, certain that he would not be aware of her scrutiny as she appraised his shrewd blue eyes behind wire-rimmed glasses, the tanned, lean body that looked so good in jeans.

And there was Hannah, gnawing on a chicken leg with barbecue sauce on her nose. She looked fat. Her sweatshirt was bunched up funny and the wind had blown her hair wild on the boat ride over. At her side, Lynne looked stunning. Willowy, all right. Fucking willowy. The scene quickly shifted as the rest of the small crowd smiled at the camera or waved or winked or mugged.

Quick as a flash there were a few frames that Hannah would have missed, if she had blinked. Now the video focused on Walt, seated in the rocking chair where she had napped that rainy day. He was talking about a public relations firm Ingold had hired. Hannah backed up to the outdoor part and ran it forward again in slow motion. She was sure it was not her imagination: she had seen Lynne in Dan Kerry's arms.

Yes! Only a spurt of tape, like a subliminal message. And Lynne's hand reaching out, the words "Les, put that down!"

Reverse, play; reverse, play. She repeated that section again and again. They were in the kitchen, probably didn't even know the boy had picked up the camcorder. She dropped the speed down to see Lynne slip away from Kerry's embrace, frame-by-frame, and lean forward, reaching her slender arm, her sylphlike hand to cover the lens. What did that mean, Hannah wondered, and even more, why did she even care?

Her face and neck blazed as she recalled her feelings of discomfort, the night Kerry drove her to the mine site and showed her where the core samples had been bored. "I'm not going to make a pass at you, Hannah Swann," he'd told her then. How could she have imagined that he might!

Her thoughts wandering, the haphazard organization of flotilla played out on the screen of her computer—the canoes' progress down the Lost Arrow River, a montage of paddles raised in greeting—and then a woman on a tilted pier in front of a log building wearing cut-off jeans and T-shirt, Birkenstocks, no makeup, sunburned, very much at home in that setting. A black dog sat beside her, wagging its tail. Behind them she could read "Beer Bait Food Boats Games."

Hannah Swann, owner and caretaker of the land, custodian of the environment: she had not recognized herself!

Monday morning she called Joe Mickelson to thank him for sending the Wilcox auditions. He wanted to know what Hannah had been up to lately, and could he and his wife get a reservation for a week in August? Hannah checked the spiral notebook. All she had open was Vega, the smallest and least appealing cottage.

Joe was definitely interested, so Hannah mentioned the mining controversy and described the tape of the canoe flotilla she happened to be monitoring one last time while she spoke with him on the phone.

"In fact," she said, remembering Kerry's statement about the media, "there's this master's hearing coming up on June twenty-third, and you really should send a camera crew, Joe. It would make an interesting story—you know, the mining boom that promises to boost the economy of the northwoods versus the risk of the mine's assault on the environment? Apparently it's happening all over the country in areas like this."

"I don't know, Hannah," he was not convinced. "It doesn't sound like much of a story for us."

"I'll tell you what," Hannah bargained with new enthusiasm, "Vega is vacant for the next two weeks, too. I'll donate it for your camera crew, if you'll send one up."

Joe was hesitant, said he'd need to know more about it. She offered to fax him some information right away, grateful to Lynne for the newspaper clippings, at least.

I had, at that time, a *radiant* bloom," the actress said again as Hannah once more reviewed the audition tape. The actress portraying Ella moved slowly toward the camera from behind a wicker basket filled with ferns. She lifted a bouquet of yellow roses from a brocaded armchair, then was gracefully seated and clutched the roses grandly to her generous bosom.

"Early in my career I was referred to as the Poetess of Passion, for my collected *Poems of Passion*. Well-meaning friends suggested the impropriety of an unmarried woman composing such ardent verses, but controversy has always followed me. My dear friend and fellow poet, James Whitcomb Riley, recently asserted that my stylish hairdo and fashionable gowns are 'too frivolous for a genius,' and we have had a modest falling out. But poets are often egoists, including the doddering fool who accused me of pilfering the lines for my poem, 'Solitude' . . . 'Laugh and the world laughs with you; weep and you weep alone,' from the lid of a whiskey barrel, where *he* had written them." Wilcox chuckled softly.

"Luckily, from reincarnated sources and through prenatal causes I was born with unquenchable hope and unfaltering faith in God and guardian spirits. I always expected wonderful things to happen to me. . . ."

Hannah pressed pause and froze the actress, mid-gesture.

"Let me warn you about that, Ella," she told the woman who cradled the yellow bouquet, "you might be right about the laughter and the weeping shit, but you sit around waiting for wonderful things to happen every morning and the world's going to have your ass for lunch."

12

Call of the Wild

Her mother would say Uncle Hal's ashes rested on the coffee table in his apartment for seven weeks gathering dust because Hannah had trouble letting go of things: clothes she'd outgrown, moldy leftovers, unhappy marriages. Borrowed flannel shirts!

If Lily had known about Tyler Cole, she would have added him to the list.

Actually, if she knew what to do with them, Hannah would have been happy to get rid of the ashes because her uncle's tangible presence was a daily reminder of the havoc he'd wrought on her world.

What should have been only mild annoyances made her sulk. It was mid-July and brochures were still mailed out every week in response to requests for lodging. Chloe found out from the Antler Chamber of Commerce ("The Deerest Place on Earth") that the cheapest cottage at Timber Trails went for a healthy $365 a week and it wasn't even on the water. Star Lake's most expensive cottage, Aldebaran, rented for only $300, and Vega, the smallest, was a hundred dollars less than that.

"No wonder we're not making any money!" Hannah raged. "We're not even in the game!"

Raccoons managed to upset the garbage cans at least once a week and a skunk gave birth to a litter of kits beneath Sirius and had to be (carefully!) encouraged to move with Victor Redhawk's help.

In Madison, Hannah had cherished her time alone; now she was at the mercy of strangers all hours of the day and night. Polaris, Hal's apartment, wasn't really hers, it was still Hal's (and Chloe's and Eric's), furnished with Hal's personal effects and a study filled with clutter.

"I'll be so glad when this is all over and we can go home . . ." she began her daily complaint at breakfast but Chloe interrupted.

"Oh, get a grip, Mom!"

"Chloe," Hannah was stunned at her daughter's outburst.

"I mean it, I wish you'd quit whining. I'm sick of listening to you. I like fixing this place up with Eric and making it beautiful again. I like the fact that all of us are working together to make a difference in something big. We're really involved at a very basic level. Can't you see the good in that?"

Hannah continued, swallowing hard, "I've been thinking of talking to George Windsor, Denny's dad, to get a better sense of what Uncle Hal had in mind."

"Then talk to him! What are you waiting for? Geez . . ."

Chloe rushed downstairs to join Eric who was prying off the plywood that covered the fireplace.

Hannah wandered out onto the sleeping porch. She focused Miriam's old telescope across the lake. No sign of anyone at the mine site. The land had not yet been cleared. So far, so good.

She couldn't shake off her daughter's brusque remarks.

All I have to do, she reminded herself, is get through the rest of the summer. The hearing examiner said he'd conclude his consideration of the testimony by October. Ninety more days before they'd know whether Ingold could proceed or the mining permits had been denied. By October the resort would be closed for the season and she wouldn't have to answer to lodgers who complained about the weather (too cold and wet) or mosquitoes (too many), fish that weren't biting and black flies that were.

Joe Mickelson had reviewed her newspaper clippings and agreed to send up a cameraman and audio recordist from the Green Bay affiliate the night before the June twenty-third hearing. They brought a van full of gear: camera, microphones, recording deck, and light kit. But Ginger had to kick them out of the bar at closing time.

When the master's hearing opened, Victor Redhawk placed a sacred eagle feather staff at the front of the gymnasium to "encourage people to speak the truth. There were moccasin tracks on this continent long before Wisconsin became a state," he testified. "Early in my life I canoed these rivers with my grandfather to gather sacred medicines, and these waterways are also home to the eagle, the highest symbol for our people and for all Americans."

Victor's testimony was lively, compared to most of the others who repeated the same old tired lines about environmental degradation versus the local economy. Worried that her hungover crew would nod off during the drone, Hannah kept them supplied with sandwiches and caffeine. The ten-minute segment she edited on her computer didn't seem as compelling as she'd hoped it would be—even spliced with canoe flotilla footage and her own earnest plea before the camera.

After all that effort, Joe devoted only two minutes of his Friday night news summary to the contentious battle being waged on Star Lake, and half of the coverage was devoted to the pro-mining point-of-view. Hannah was annoyed with Joe, but even angrier at herself for being so naïve: of course Wisconsin Public Television would want an impartial account.

She so wanted to impress Kerry and the others but the minimal results were an embarrassment. To her dismay, the irritability and sleeplessness she suffered weren't only due to Joe's lukewarm coverage of Ingold's nefarious threat; that damned footage of Lynne in Kerry's arms bothered her even more. She found herself going back over the scene in slow-motion whenever she sat down at her computer.

Either initial ignorance had been bliss or they were finally getting an overdue dose of reality. One Friday a couple Ginger had never seen before stumbled into the Saloon around midnight in the midst of a drunken brawl that ended with a broken mirror over the bar when an airborne beer bottle missed Ginger's head by inches.

The septic system stopped working and all the toilets backed up. They had the tank pumped on a Sunday afternoon with all the guests watching and the guy with the pumper truck (and a cap that said "We'll take anybody's crap") remarked, "Looks like somebody dumped a couple gallons of bleach down the drains." That was the same week a prankster poured sugar into the old red pickup's gas tank and Eric had to tow the truck into Antler to get it flushed.

Then, as they made the rounds of cottages the following Saturday, Chloe reported that Castor's toaster was missing and it turned out that all the toasters were gone. Annoying mischief and inconvenience, but the cottages had never been locked, only the Saloon was, after hours. Hannah sent Eric into Minocqua to find seven new toasters and she dreaded the eventual discovery of an old-toaster-cache.

Dan Kerry brought Lynne and Leslie over for potluck and fireworks on the Fourth of July, but this was the heart of his most demanding season. Hannah didn't much care if Kerry ever showed up again; she was undergoing an angry-at-happy-couples routine that would have to run its course and she blamed Leslie, the nosy brat, for an inadvertent glimpse of the fishing guide's private life and her sweat-drenched insomnia. When Hannah finally got up at five-thirty, she needed plenty of hot black coffee to open her eyes and felt as groggy as a slug for the rest of the day.

It had been almost seven weeks since the Yank 'Em Inn debacle, as she thought of it. No postcards had arrived from Alaska. She refused to see herself as a helpless victim because she had used Tyler sexually and emotionally every bit as much as he had used her. But with the way her luck was running these days, Hannah lamented, that disastrous episode may have been the final sexual encounter of her life, and that made her feel really old.

"It means you're depressed when you wake up in the middle of the night all the time," Ginger said. "I read about it in *Redbook* down at Bessie's Beauty Shoppe."

They were in the kitchen off the Saloon on a fresh Monday morning following a dreary weekend of fog and rain. She could have told Ginger, I can't sleep because I haven't had my period in over two months.

Instead, Hannah said, "Last night I made a note to have Chloe check the Tamarack Town Hall for old photographs that might include this place. I can enlarge them on my scanner and we can hang them in the Saloon."

Ginger slipped off her shoes to rub her feet. "I should get these darned bunions operated on but it's easier to get bigger shoes. And if you ever get around to clearing out Hal's study you'll come across a whole bunch of pictures of loggers and stuff from the olden days."

Hannah ignored Ginger's reminder of her penchant for procrastination.

"This collection of odds and ends people leave behind," she indicated a corner of the kitchen next to the desk, "What are we supposed to do about an overdue library book, somebody's prescription sunglasses, and a pair of smelly sneakers? I've been trying to wrap this fishing rod to send back by UPS."

"Let's see that," Ginger said. She pulled herself to her feet and padded over heavily in her sweat socks. She was wearing a bright yellow nylon jogging suit today, and the pants made a swishing sound when she walked.

Ginger unwrapped the fishing rod that Hannah had been attempting to tape inside a cardboard hamburger bun carton. "Busted," Ginger scoffed. "Just send it to the landfill, Honey. You'd be amazed at the folderol some folks forget, beach towels, wet swimsuits still hanging on the line. One time somebody forgot their dog. Can you imagine, driving off and forgetting your dog? Those folks were dumber than owl shit, excuse me for saying so, and I was kind of sorry when they showed up again to get it. Babe thought she had a little sister."

"What about the library book?"

"Oh that I suppose you better mail that, but don't expect to get any thanks for your trouble. Another damn fool left his teeth on the bathroom sink. I tell you, there's no limit to stupidity. When's that book due, anyway?"

"Last week," Hannah said, checking inside the cover of the romance paperback. "You mentioned dentures, Ginger, that reminds me; I've been wanting to ask . . ."

"Let me have a look," Ginger said, reaching for the book and paging through. "Those with the purple covers are supposed to be the juiciest."

"Hal's dentures," Hannah was determined to follow through with another puzzle that haunted her midnight musings. But she was interrupted by Babe's agitation and Ginger's shout.

"Jesus Christ On a Cream Colored Cross!"

The rasping roar of a motor shattered the morning silence. Then another, equally loud and menacing, joined in a furious duet.

"Jet skis," Ginger said angrily, stomping out onto the porch in stocking feet.

"Goddamned things. I hate 'em. Fishermen will be having a shit fit, you wait and see."

Like motorcycles on surfboards, the obnoxious machines cut a gash across the water, circled one another and caused anchored boats to rock in their wakes.

"Where'd they come from, anyway?" Ginger asked angrily. "Better not be staying here! Dirty, rotten . . ." Ginger aimed a string of epithets at the jet skiers while Hannah stood frozen in despair. "You're supposed to stay thirty yards from boats and swimmers," Ginger yelled, "State law! I'm calling the sheriff."

Not until the jet skiers aimed at the loon family near the lily pads off the shore of Aldebaran did Hannah run out on the pier to scream at them herself.

The adult loons issued cries of distress and flapped their wings, trying to divert the jet skis from the helpless chicks.

"Watch out for the loons!" Hannah shouted, although she knew the men couldn't hear her above the deafening motors.

The skis carved a wide splash and came in for a second approach.

Hannah yelled and waved at them with both arms above her head, trying to alert them to the presence of the loons.

Then she realized they could see the loons, in fact they were purposely aiming for the birds and sending the parents into frenzied outbursts of frustration to protect their young.

"Bastards!" Hannah yelled, "Stop! Right now! Stop it!"

"What's the matter, lady?" One of the men drew his jet ski up to the end of the pier and paused, abruptly. He was young, tan, tattooed, was pierced with multiple earrings and displayed an array of heavy gold chains on his hairy chest. "You gotta problem?"

"You're the one with the problem. You can't harass wildlife like that, it's against the law. We're reporting you to the sheriff. And the loon ranger, too."

"The loon ranger? What the hell's that?"

"What's the big deal?" the other rider wanted to know.

"Says we shouldn't buzz the birds. Gonna report us to the Loon Ranger and Tonto. Next thing, she'll say we can't use our skis on this lake. Wanna bet?"

When she turned and walked resolutely back to the lodge the men revved their motors behind her back, taunting her.

Ginger had already phoned Victor Redhawk and Sheriff Cooper, but the sheriff said Hannah would have to find her own reasons to ask the men to quit because there was no law against such devices, just an understanding that they were undesirable on Star Lake as on most of the northwoods lakes.

"You better raise hell and I don't mean maybe," Ginger told her that night after the weekly bonfire. She gave her an encouraging pat on the butt, "I'd do it myself, but you might as well get hung for a sheep as a lamb, so go to it."

Hannah thought Eric might have better luck but he was tending bar.

"I'll go with you, Mom," Chloe offered.

Eric had already painted signs that announced "No jet skis allowed," to be posted in several prominent areas around the resort.

175

The men had not participated in the potluck supper, but sat on the steps of Arcturus idly smoking cigarettes and guzzling beer from cans they crushed and tossed into the lake as Hannah approached.

"I realize you weren't given advance notice of our new policy," she said coldly, "but personal watercraft are not welcome here. This is a quiet fishing resort. If you'd like to leave, we'll be glad to give you a full refund."

"No thanks," one of the men retorted. He flipped his cigarette onto the grass in front of Hannah. She ground it out with the toe of her sandal.

"You don't have a choice," Chloe stepped forward and looked the kid straight in the eye. It didn't seem to bother Chloe that she was about the same age. "We own this place and we make the rules. Get out."

Hannah was speechless at Chloe's bold move.

The other man claimed the women had no right to make up rules as they went along. "We're staying," he told them, "and we'll use our skis, too. There's no legal way you can stop us."

That night Hannah lay awake for three hours trying to devise some way to evict the troublemakers. Why would they drive all the way up here from Chicago (if, indeed, they were from Chicago) to bluster and harass everyone?

True to their word, the men remained for two more days. They rode their jet skis through the culvert, across Sundog and up the river into Sickle Moon, boasting to everyone they encountered that they were staying at Hannah Swann's resort. In the meantime the re-tired couples in Castor and Pollux packed up and left, demanding a return of their deposit. They told Chloe they would never have been exposed to such ill treatment if Hal Larkin were still alive.

"He cared about his guests," one woman said as she tucked the check into her pocketbook. "He would never have let this get out of hand. Don't expect us to stay here next summer or ever again."

Finally, on Wednesday night Chloe insisted that Hannah phone Dan Kerry.

"Of course I've seen them. Heard them, too." He sounded angry. "Everybody on the Chain is saying you're letting the place go to hell. What's happening over there?"

"I've tried everything I can think of," Hannah said plaintively. "I don't know what to do, they won't leave, they won't listen."

"Have you consulted your lawyer?"

Hannah reached Dennis Windsor at home, after a brisk goodbye.

"Sounds to me like they're within the law." Windsor seemed indifferent. Maybe even smug. She should not have listened to Kerry's advice or Chloe's, and wondered why she had.

Arcturus was finally vacated Thursday morning. The men appeared at her desk for a refund of their deposit as soon as she turned on the beer sign. Hannah wrote them a check on the spot, more than happy to bid them farewell.

She had no idea they had completely trashed the cottage.

Glass from broken windows was strewn all over the floor among empty beer cans. Chloe drew up a list of missing kitchen utensils that were probably flung toward the bottom of the lake. At least Miriam's star sign was still intact; Kerry had rehung them all, beautifully restored, and Arcturus shone softly from the constellation with the luster of brass tacks. But the gas heater was destroyed, and the toilet had been cracked with a blunt object of some kind. The metal shower, scratched and dented, was still usable. Mattresses were slashed and torn apart, the refrigerator motor was smashed, and to top it off the brand new toaster was gone. Hannah called Sheriff Cooper for the second time that week.

Their Chicago address was fictitious, of course. Insurance covered vandalism after a five-hundred dollar deductible was met, but new guests were scheduled to check into Arcturus the day after next and all the rest of the cottages were booked for the following week, even Vega.

After a mad struggle they met their deadline, just in time. Hannah hoped remaining guests might pitch in and help, but the spirit of community had disintegrated and visitors blamed Hannah for ruining their vacation. Bills added up to more than she'd made in potential income for the week. And she'd thought the outlay for seven toasters was exorbitant!

Hannah took her morning coffee onto the main pier early Sunday. Nailed to the back of each weathered bench out at the end were Eric's "No Jet Skis" signs. Chloe had printed a bunch of stickers with that addendum to paste on the remaining brochures, and Hannah insisted on writing personal letters of apology to all of last week's guests and anyone who might have been offended, including, of course, Dan Kerry.

Right now, the guests who checked in the day before seemed to be fishing. The water, unstirred by the slightest breeze, mirrored the deep green shoreline and overcast sky. Fish fed later than usual, Ginger predicted, on quiet days like this. Boats were clustered down at the south end where something was obviously seduced by the hook and they floated serenely, as if their occupants felt a similar need for silence and seclusion.

The fact was certainly evident: people came here to hide from their real worlds.

"Mom?"

Chloe padded barefoot out onto the wooden pier with Babe.

"Some week, huh?"

Hannah moved aside to give her daughter room to sit beside her, and Babe dropped a soggy tennis ball in her lap.

"I want to go home," Hannah said, flatly.

"I really think this place is doing you more good than you realize," Chloe argued.

"Give me a break . . ."

"You're healthier, for one thing. You look a lot healthier."

"I've gained weight, that doesn't mean I'm healthier. I haven't been exercising, I'm too busy trying to keep this damn place afloat."

"But you've been doing other kinds of neat stuff, Mom—walking in the woods and working on the cottages with the rest of us. We all went swimming together on those really hot days over the Fourth of July. That was fun, wasn't it?"

"I do enjoy being with you, and I love the fresh air," Hannah admitted, softly.

"Look at it this way, Mom—You were stagnating back in Madison. Here you've got a bunch of new friends. You're trying new things." Chloe gave her mother a quick hug. "The TV spot you did about the master's hearing for Joe Mickelson, that was different for you and it was really great!"

"It wasn't great, Chloe; it was awful."

"Well, Dan and Lynne and all the rest of us thought it was fantastic. You got more exposure for our cause than anybody else has, so far. I was really proud of you."

Hannah's eyes began to sting with tears. She blew her nose, then stated, bluntly, "I haven't had my period in over two months."

"That happens, Mom," Chloe assured her. "It's normal to start having irregular periods at your age, isn't it?"

Hannah tossed the rest of the lukewarm coffee into the lake. "I'm not too old to get pregnant."

"I've got news for you: it's called menopause."

Hannah lifted her chin, took a deep breath.

"You can't be pregnant," Chloe put her arm around Hannah again and drew her closer. "This sounds like something I should be confessing to you, not the other way around."

Hannah couldn't repress it any longer. She had to share her concern with Chloe, there wasn't anyone else. Maybe it was at the root of her insomnia, the cause of her depression. It was the first thing that came to mind in those reproachful early hours, the fear of carrying Tyler's child and desperately wanting that not to be so with all of its associated complications.

"If I bought one of those at-home pregnancy kits, the news would be all over Lakeland County."

"Calm down, Mom. Okay, let's just say that you're pregnant, for the sake of argument. Let's explore that, okay?"

"Confidentially . . ." Hannah warned, clasping Chloe's other hand.

"Of course," Chloe assured her. "It wouldn't be the end of the world."

Hannah's pulse picked up and she felt uncomfortably queasy. Her face and neck flushed with heat. Morning sickness! Or strong, black coffee on an empty stomach and plain old fear.

"I'm willing to bet anything that you're starting menopause," her daughter's voice was firm and comforting, "but the last time I looked, there was still a pro-choice bumper sticker on your Toyota."

Chloe removed her arm from the back of the bench. "Are your breasts swollen and sore?"

"No . . ."

"Feeling nauseated?"

"No, not really."

"More tired than usual?"

"Yes, because I can't sleep. I just lie there, sweating. Pools of sweat on my chest. Really!"

"Hot flashes, Mom."

"And ridiculous mood swings. Give me ten minutes and I can go from manic to depressed and back to manic again."

"Call Dr. Burns and make an appointment," Chloe advised. "You said you want to go home. Maybe you would feel better if you went back to Madison for a few days."

"I could use a break," Hannah's voice was shaky.

"Promise me you'll call and make an appointment as soon as you can. Cross your heart."

Hannah obediently crossed her heart. Then she tossed the tennis ball in the lake for Babe, who had been waiting patiently.

Later that day, just after noon, Hannah stopped at the Antler IGA. Chloe had invited Dan, Lynne and Lyle, and Ginger for dinner to celebrate Eric's birthday. Lynne and Lyle would eat vegetarian shish-kabobs with Eric and Chloe, but Hannah wanted steaks for the rest of them: rare, juicy, and charcoal grilled to perfection.

The butcher was still behind the meat case at the IGA, and she asked him to cut three thick ribeyes. He was usually loquacious, but today his banter was limited to "This okay?" when he offered the first steak for her inspection.

"Great," Hannah answered.

Ordinarily the butcher would've joked, "What time are we eating?" or even, "Any fish biting out there?"

Then when she stood in the produce aisle, selecting romaine and bagging six of the reddest tomatoes, she overheard the tail end of a hushed conversation in the next aisle over.

" . . . a regular Rounder. Lets her daughter shack up out there with her boyfriend."

"I'm not surprised, you know what they say . . ."

"Sheriff Cooper's out there all the time."

Even the clerk at the checkout counter merely tallied the cost of the groceries with a dour expression. Then, glancing up quickly to meet Hannah's eyes she added in a whisper, "I don't believe half what I hear."

Hannah gave the clerk a sympathetic smile.

"Goes with the territory," Ginger remarked whenever she passed along some ridiculous rumor she overheard at Bessie's Beauty Shoppe. But Ginger did not specify whether that territory was philosophical or physical. Maybe it didn't matter.

She stopped for gas and a bottle of wine at the liquor store–gas station and encountered Dennis Windsor.

"Hannah," he said, handing the clerk a fifty for a bottle already twisted into a brown paper bag, "how's everything out at the lake?"

"Great! How's your golf game?"

He was wearing a white golf shirt and a pair of blue cotton shorts. With his deep tan these days he looked even more strikingly handsome, and it was hard for Hannah to stir up feelings of deep loathing for the man.

"Too bad about your jet skiers," he said. "I heard the sheriff was out there again. A place can get a bad rep when word gets around that you can't keep things under control. You don't want to lose your liquor license."

It almost sounded like a threat. Hannah resisted the impulse to make a smart retort, even though a little jab wouldn't be remiss, not after the lawyer's self-righteous testimony at the hearing. He'd closed his statement with the assertion that the anti-Ingold faction was asking, "How can we approve of a mining project which will destroy the Celestial Flowage, convert Antler to a ghost town, destroy tourism in Wisconsin, rape the earth and break Indian treaties, when we could march through history arm-in-arm with Chief Seattle, Gandhi, Rachel Carson, and Martin Luther King?"

Windsor held the door open for her as they exited into the parking lot. "You hear about our caravan?" he asked.

"What caravan?"

"The chamber of commerce organized it yesterday. We had over a hundred and fifty cars and dump trucks, end-loaders, heavy construction equipment, and we paraded from here up to Cedar Springs. Took two hours. And Gus Schultz, you remember Gus?"

Hannah nodded; how could she forget Gus.

"When we got to Cedar Springs, Gus presented a letter to Governor Dawson in support of the mine with signatures of more than two hundred Lakeland County residents."

Windsor flashed a tight little smile.

"I'll need to see you one of these days about the progress of Uncle Hal's estate," Hannah reminded him. "By the way, how's your dad?"

Windsor stopped at the door of the Lincoln Navigator he was driving today instead of his silver Porsche.

"Not up to a visit from you, if that's what you're suggesting. You'd only remind him of Hal and upset the old geezer."

Hannah fussed with her handbag and watched in her rearview mirror as Windsor drove away in the direction of Cedar Springs. Then she turned her car around and headed for Northern Lights, the retirement center beyond the other end of town. Dennis's father might enjoy a Sunday afternoon visit; he surely wasn't going to get one from his son.

George Windsor, tiny, shrunken, and bald, was seated in a wheelchair on the broad screened porch of the retirement home that hugged the shore of Little Bearskin Lake.

"Hello," Hannah said emphatically, "I'm Hannah Swann. Hal Larkin's niece."

"Good afternoon," George Windsor said briskly, folding the Sunday paper and extending his hand. It was warm and dry. He spoke in a small but clipped manner that suggested he was in a hurry. "You don't have to shout, everyone shouts around here as if we're all hard of hearing but some of us can hear perfectly well and I know who you are, Miss Hannah Swann, saw your picture in the newspaper. Saw you on TV at that foolishness up at Cedar Springs, too. Hal talked about you back when he was drawing up his Last Will and Testament."

"I wish you could tell me more about my uncle," Hannah said. She was already glad she had come.

"Let that go," he said, indicating the chair she was about to sit in. "Take me back to that brick patio down by the lake. I prefer to visit with clients in privacy and it's a nice day. Let's have a little sunshine."

Hannah took the handles of his wheelchair and maneuvered it through the door and over the ramp to the sidewalk.

"That's better," he said to Hannah as soon as they were free of the building. "Some of my roommates put on a show of being hard of hearing and then they pass along all their eavesdroppings, usually getting everything topsy-turvy."

"Did my uncle tell you that he and I had never met?"

"I don't recall it that way," the old man replied, "but he said he'd grown away from his family, so to speak. You were the one he wanted to entrust his place to, when the time came."

Hannah felt her heart accelerate rapidly, as if she were on the verge of discovering Hal's secret.

"Did he say why?"

"Seems to me it was as simple as, you being the next generation, you might understand why Star Lake was so important. Something like that, I guess."

They reached the paved patio near the water, and Hannah steered the wheelchair over to a picnic table. She took a seat on one of the benches.

"As a kind of surrogate daughter, you mean?"

"I can't say that, no. But I distinctly remember—and my memory's not always up to par these days—I do remember him saying, 'I think Hannah will understand.' We were fishing on Sickle Moon."

She could see that his eyes were searching, investigating every detail of her dress and her demeanor. In that way he was much like his son. "'Hannah will understand' what? Can you tell me how long before his death he mentioned me?"

"Caught a couple nice perch that day. Must have been a Monday," he continued, his arthritic hands fussing with the lap robe over his knees. "I was prone to taking Mondays off whenever I had an opportunity to go fishing. Stayed in the office on Saturdays to cater to folks who worked during the week. My son doesn't carry on that old-fashioned tradition anymore."

"I had an appointment to meet with your son on a Saturday," Hannah said, reluctant to defend him, but it was true.

"He must have made an exception for such a pretty young lady," the old man grinned slyly. "That's one opinion my son and I would find agreement on, but Dennis and I don't always see eye-to-eye," George shook his head. "This mining business, for one thing. I got a look at his damn fool testimony, thanks to that tidbit you did for the TV. I liked that girl with the dead fish, what was her name?"

"Lynne. Lynne Akkerman."

"Right. Lynne. Pretty girl. Good idea, too, dressing up like The Grim Reaper and handing out those dead fish. Made her point, all right."

"They were smoked chubs," Hannah said. "From the IGA."

Lynne was incredible; it wasn't fair that she had to be beautiful, besides. Around Lynne, Hannah felt like a bloated fireplug. Lynne's musical laughter, the way she tossed her long blond hair back from her face, her slender legs (unshaven, Hannah had noticed, but the hair was practically transparent)—Hannah couldn't begin to imitate the determination and resolve Lynne invested in the anti-mine cause. When she compared Lynne's tenacious zeal with her own wish to defeat the mine so she could sell her resort and go home, Hannah felt like a candy-ass and a fraud.

"After I saw that little tidbit you did on television I told my son he was plain stupid, cozying up to the big boys. 'You'll make more enemies than friends,' I told him, but he doesn't listen to me anymore. Not that he ever listened. Doesn't use the sense he was born with, know what I mean?"

"I think I do," Hannah said.

"I don't know where in hell he gets some of his other cockeyed ideas, either. Does he know you're out here, by the way?"

"No. He said you weren't up to having visitors."

"I thought as much. Wondered why you didn't come out sooner. Who told you I drew up Hal's will?"

"Ginger Kovalcik told me. Dennis did too, when we looked at it together."

"Ginger," George said warmly. His eyes took on a merry gleam and he brushed nervously at the top of his bald head.

Hannah wanted to continue the discussion of her uncle, but she said, "Ginger's been a good friend."

"Still dying her hair red, isn't she."

"Sort of. More like orange, though. I think of it as carrot. Or pumpkin."

"Ginger Peaches, I call her. She was a 'looker,' in her day. You call her Ginger Peaches and see what she says. Tell her to get her butt out here."

Hannah was intrigued by his mention of Ginger. But her real concern was the copy of a loan from George Windsor she had found in Hal's cigar box. It was for $25,000. She wondered if he would allow her to renew the note.

George's mind began to wander and she lost him before she could ask. He talked about his early days as a lawyer, Dennis as a little boy, rambling rapidly and almost incoherently switching from subject to subject like an agitated bee flitting from rosebud to dandelion. He addressed Hannah as though she were his dead wife, then his son, then a woman he once loved. "Don't you pester him again," he insisted, angrily. Irrationally. She could not get him back.

Hannah wheeled the old man back onto the porch of Northern Lights and told him good afternoon.

"Come see me again, won't you?" he pleaded with such a childlike request that her heart lurched.

"Of course I will," Hannah promised, shaking his hand and noting the fragile grip.

"You ought to put more on television about this mining business," he said, returning vaguely to the present. "Ask Hal, he's got all kinds of articles and studies. I gave him a batch when they bundled me over here in such a dad-blamed rush. There's charts and figures and such. You've got talent, you could tell the whole country. You could put one of those documentary shows together, couldn't you?"

"It's a great idea, Mr. Windsor," Hannah humored him, "but it's more easily said than done."

"What's stopping you?" He turned angry, his face pinched, purple and demanding. "You're a smart girl! You figure it out!"

She waved goodbye and slipped away as gracefully as she could. Dennis was right, his father was not altogether stable, but she had to find out for herself.

On her way into town she had spotted a narrow patch of wild blueberries growing in the sandy loam along Star Lake Road some distance from the resort. On her way back she slowed and parked on the shoulder. If she could gather a couple pints of wild blueberries she would surprise Eric with a pie for his party. More important, Kerry had remarked to Ginger on the Fourth of July that blueberry pie was his favorite.

Hannah made her way slowly along the edge of the gravel road, gathering berries. Delicate forget-me-nots with bright yellow centers bloomed in low, swampy ground. Where the soil had been disturbed, blueberry bushes were plentiful and the plump berries were easy to pick. Her fingers were soon stained blackish purple like the sweet, juicy fruit in the plastic bag she had emptied of tomatoes. She would have more than enough blueberries for a generous pie to serve with home-made vanilla ice cream.

All kinds of articles and studies, George Windsor said he had given Hal. Charts and figures, Hannah repeated to herself. She might discover something in Hal's files to indicate why Ingold wanted the resort. In a week or two, after her appointment with Dr. Burns in Madison, she'd sort through the numerous piles of papers and boxes she'd pushed aside.

The shot must have come from the woods, but the exact direction was uncertain because the sound of the windshield shattering was almost instantaneous with the impact of the explosive blast.

Hannah ducked, instinctively, and fell to the ground. She crawled part-way underneath the car for protection.

Confused, she touched her left cheek where something stung. Small, hard pieces of glass were embedded there and in her forearm. She tasted warm blood on her fingers when she brought them to her mouth to stifle sobs of fear.

This was not an accident. It was no mistake, Hannah was sure of that. It wasn't hunting season and in the twenty minutes or so that she'd been picking blueberries she had not heard any other shots so it wasn't target practice, either—unless she was the target.

She waited, her heart pumping crazily and her breath making little moist clouds in the gravel dust beneath her nose.

What was happening? How long would she have to wait? Would she be in danger again if she moved? If she sneezed?

Whoever shot at her must have seen her fall and would not know if she had been hit. She would have to lie motionless for a while, wait and see what happened next. Suppose that whoever it was came to see if she was dead? She couldn't wait all day, she had to get back to Star Lake. She had to bake a pie. Make ice cream. Company was coming for dinner . . .

A car raced toward her. Tires skidded on gravel as the brakes were applied.

If it was the person who shot at her she was as good as gone, she realized. She bit her fist and held her breath to stay as still as she possibly could.

"Hannah, for God's Sake . . ."

It was Dan. He carefully pulled her out from beneath her car and knelt beside her, feeling for her pulse.

He removed the bag of crushed blueberries from her grasp with a gentle tug.

"I've got to call Sheriff Cooper again," she said tearfully. "Shit."

13
Ah, Wilderness

Even without opening her eyes Hannah knew she was in the city again and it was garbage day. The collected clink and clatter of yawning maws crawled along the curb. Every time the garbage truck came she felt a twinge of anxiety, a residual fear she had accidentally thrown away a meaningful part of her life that she would eventually regret.

Instead of garbage anxiety, back at Star Lake she'd be experiencing the soft slap of water against boats tied to the pier, their gentle bumps barely stirring her sleep as she, too, rode the lulling waves. Loons would be yodeling, and the light breeze wafting through her bedroom window would carry a complex potpourri of pine pitch, mildew, water lilies, and wistful woodsmoke.

Beneath her short cotton nightgown, a film of perspiration covered her entire body. At Star Lake she would be covered with at least two blankets and gas heaters would be glowing to ease the early morning chill.

This was the time of day unbidden thoughts rose to the surface of her mind like bubbles in cheap champagne.

She missed Ratso. The cat curled up with Chloe and Eric now, handing surveillance of Hannah's bedroom in Polaris entirely over to

Babe. She missed Babe's musky dog smell, the jingle of her tags, the reassuring deep sleep dog-sighs in the night.

At the Cedar Springs hospital where Dan had taken her for examination, Sheriff Cooper admonished Hannah to be extra cautious. "It might of been those jet ski guys you riled up," he suggested. "If I was you I'd lay low and be on the lookout. Kerry and me tramped all around there but didn't find a trace of any shells."

"You made friends up here when you got TV coverage of the hearing, but you made a few enemies too," Dan added, later. Thin praise from him, admittedly, and dearly won. But praise, nevertheless. She clung to that.

Since that afternoon she had deferred memories of the concern evident in Dan's eyes, his tender caress as he brushed the debris from her face and murmured her name. He had released his hold as soon as she assured him she was not badly injured. Pieces of the Toyota's shattered side-view mirror had grazed the side of her cheek and become embedded in her forearm. She would retain a few minor battle scars.

Now Hannah replayed the way he had rushed to her side and gathered her in his embrace. Here, in the safety of her own bedroom, she was free to envision Dan beside her and slipped her hand underneath the nightgown to circle her breasts slowly with the tips of her fingers, softly pinching and caressing her nipples until they responded to the tease of her touch and she could anticipate his kiss, her fingers tangled in his curly hair, pulling his eager mouth to her own.

She would not risk conjuring such dangerous fiction at Star Lake, and she had attempted to deny her feelings once his relationship with Lynne had been inadvertently revealed on videotape. But it was harmless to pretend here, so many miles away.

She parted the moist lips between her thighs and fell back to unfold like slow-motion fireworks that made her gasp as she pushed her body into his and they pulsed together in a primitive rhythm far back in time with the heated urgency of her need (and then again and again, because she didn't like to end on an even number) until she was limp, sweating all over and panting from exertion.

Next door, Mrs. Glenn yelled at her kids to get up. The day would be hot and humid. Through the open window Hannah could smell the rot of overblown roses. Her house had no air conditioning and the fans were still in the attic.

Unable to resist Mrs. Glenn's stern commands, Hannah climbed out of bed and pulled the bedroom curtains aside. The fuchsia peonies bordering the driveway had blossomed, wilted and dried up without her. The garage was in need of a coat of paint. The whole place had a sad neglected look.

Except for that, it seemed good to be home again.

Thanks to getting shot at, the resort had grown noticeably quieter during the past week. Cancellations began arriving as soon as news of the incident was revealed. Reporters who were around town anyway covering Ingold's nervous hiatus, were quick to grab the story: "Hannah Swann, anti-mine activist and owner of the Star Lake Saloon, was injured Sunday, the target of a sniper attack not far from her resort." They said her cottages had suffered damages and she had received additional threats this summer. The free publicity didn't help. Anti-mine activist, that was a new one. What a laugh.

"Looks like Ingold intends to close us down," she confided to Dan and Ginger. She had an idea the mine could take credit for some exaggerated media coverage, too.

"I don't think you were meant to be killed," Dan agreed, "just scared away. It sure looks like a pattern of sabotage. The fight in the bar, the broken mirror, the septic tank. Those jet skiers were probably hired."

"I bet Ingold stole those toasters," Ginger added without cracking a smile.

Hannah took the sheriff's advice and, except for driving back to Madison, left the resort only when accompanied by someone else. She kept close tabs on Babe, then she started worrying about forest fires. Every departing guest underwent her paranoid scrutiny. She flinched at the slightest noise.

So it was good to be home, for many reasons. While her coffee brewed, Hannah bent over to stretch her legs and flex her shoulders.

"You're getting old, Sweetcheeks." She chuckled at the use of Tyler's favorite nickname. She hadn't heard that in a while!

Her good mood was not altogether due to the release she'd just experienced upstairs—it was also Dr. Burns's declaration yesterday that she was, indeed, menopausal.

"That shouldn't be such a surprise to you, Hannah." He seemed perplexed by her relief.

"I've been preoccupied with other things, "she confessed.

He said he'd give her a prescription for hormones to alleviate the hot flashes, "Or you can go cold turkey," he said, "but I usually recommend an estrogen creme for vaginal use, to keep your tissues from drying out."

Dr. Burns had an impish grin.

Moist crotch or not, she was reluctant to say hello to middle-age. Ruefully, she realized, she had been middle-aged for some time—the half-way point occurred years ago, unless life expectancy for women had been increased to ninety-five.

Her serenity lasted only a few minutes. While Hannah lingered over coffee, Chloe telephoned from Star Lake with frantic news: Hearing Examiner Carl Mead was going to issue his decision on the mine much earlier than expected. Instead of waiting until October, Ingold would announce today that their permits had been granted by the state.

The mine would begin construction at once.

Hannah sat down at the kitchen table, sighed and covered her eyes with her hand.

"We're absolutely numb up here, too, Mom," Chloe said quickly. "Everybody's meeting in the Saloon and we're trying to make some plans. How soon can you get back?"

Then, Dan's voice on the phone. She was grateful he couldn't see her face, still flushed with the afterglow of their fantasy lovemaking.

"Hannah, hi. We need a favor, and you're at the right place at the right time. Do you think you can be at DNR headquarters this afternoon? Mead's going to make his announcement at one o'clock. See if you can have a word with the press afterward. Try to shake things up, okay? We're counting on you."

Hannah agreed without a moment to reconsider. After all their work, after all she had gone through, the evidence . . .

"Be careful," he added.

"I've got to go, Mom," Chloe said. "We can talk again, tonight. And try to come back as soon as you can. We need your help!"

Late morning Hannah rode her bike through campus, dodging students sauntering to and from summer school classes. Was Tyler still in Alaska? She didn't really want to know; no time for him today, no time for him ever again. That seemed extraordinarily odd.

A rough cut of the Wilcox video was set up for her viewing at the station. She made a brief, cool appearance at the door of Joe Mickelson's office and told him the initial footage looked okay.

Joe was in the mood to visit. "I couldn't use it all, but I sure liked that segment you did about the mine. Did I ever tell you that? When you move back to Madison I'll give you another assignment, if you're interested in news and public affairs."

"I may be back sooner than I expected," Hannah confessed, and she quickly explained why she was rushed.

"Hey, you know a good fishing guide up there?" Joe asked. Hannah was sliding into her backpack, ready to leave. She took it off again and handed him a card of Dan Kerry's that she carried in her wallet.

"Super. Just to show you my heart's in the right place, I'll send a couple guys down there to cover the DNR for you this afternoon." He was already punching buttons on his phone. "Mine or no mine, it'll be a nice follow-up to your earlier story. You be careful, young lady!"

He'd read news of the shooting.

No time to vent her frustration, no time for lunch.

Hannah rode her bike down State Street to the State Capitol, then around the Square to the state office building where the Department of Natural Resources had its headquarters. She parked her bike near the entrance. How could she could discover where Mead was making his announcement in this maze of government bureaucracy? Even more important, how could she manage to gain admission?

"Hannah Swann. What are you doing here?"

Dennis Windsor had his hand on her shoulder. She recognized his heavy cologne before she heard his voice. Axel Graves and a couple other men were making their way toward the main door.

"I'm here on business, Dennis, personal stuff. Same as you, I suppose."

Hannah fell into step next to Windsor, as if she had been one of his party all along.

"What do you say we meet on campus this afternoon for a beer," Windsor asked her as she slipped onto the elevator, "maybe the Terrace behind the Union? I know how you like being near a lake . . ."

"Ask me in about an hour," she suggested darkly, as though she had no prior knowledge of the hearing examiner's decision.

When they reached the board room where Mead and other DNR officials were waiting, Hannah stood among the press, greeting Joe Mickelson's breathless cameraman and audio engineer sent over from Wisconsin Public Television.

The hearing examiner, Carl Mead, picked up a sheaf of papers and moved to a lectern at a conference table. Flashes flickered, reporters leaned forward, and TV cameras zoomed in.

In summary, Mead said, his 143-page decision granted Ingold permits and approvals to operate an open pit copper mine east of Star Lake. But any party to the proceeding adversely affected by the decision had twenty days to petition the DNR secretary for review and a possible rehearing.

"The record in this proceeding is one of the most expansive ever produced by an administrative agency in the State of Wisconsin," Mead boasted. "Over three hundred individuals filed appearances in the public input portions of the master's hearing and almost fifty experts testified in the contested case phase."

He went on, stressing that Ingold had met its burden of establishing credible evidence.

"The waters of the Celestial Flowage and the ecology of northern Wisconsin are valuable treasures to the people of this state. No one wants to be a party to the despoiling of these resources, but I am convinced that the permits contain adequate controls to ensure a safe and clean operation."

Hannah was stunned, amazed at his words.

After Mead moved aside, Axel Graves took his place. He looked uncomfortable in a sharply creased linen suit and a sunburn that presumably covered more than just his face. (New pool, Hannah remembered.)

"We are extremely pleased with Mr. Mead's decision," Graves nervously tucked his tie inside his coat jacket.

Hannah had to come up with some kind of comment, but what? How to counter Graves's slick propaganda?

"We look forward to establishing a record of responsible environmental stewardship that will ease all the concerns of those who raised questions about the mine during the permitting process." Graves was winding down.

There was a short period for questions and answers between the press and the men at the table in front.

"Excuse me," Hannah said timidly, and then louder, "Mr. Graves? Mr. Mead?"

For courage, she thought of the gang of friends and family at Star Lake who were depending on her to make a splash, and she stepped forward.

"You may not remember me, but I'm one of those who tried to raise some questions at the master's hearing in Cedar Springs," Hannah said.

Mead squinted to see who was speaking and the lights and cameras turned toward Hannah. She felt her face grow warm, hot, hotter. Heat rose from her chest and radiated throughout her upper body in a suffocating rush. What a time to be stricken with a hot flash, Hannah noted ironically, and tried to think of it, instead, as a surge of power.

"I have one final question for you, Mr. Mead. I'd like to know how you can be comfortable making a decision like this."

Axel Graves had his hand on Dennis Windsor's sleeve, holding him back.

"I own a resort on Star Lake," she explained, "on land that my family has been associated with for over a century. We're just across the water from Ingold's proposed open-pit mine. Your decision today could mean the end of a modest haven that has offered solitude to vacationers since the late 1800s."

She had been speaking with her emotions; it was time to zoom in and focus more clearly. She removed her glasses for a moment to wipe a wave of perspiration from her face with a sweep of her wrist.

"We want you to know, Mr. Mead, that we are not going to give up our fight with the issuance of your decision. You can be assured that we'll get an injunction. My friends and family will appeal. We are not about to let Ingold take over our constitutional rights and our democratic system as well as our natural wealth."

She called Chloe that night.

"We saw you on TV, Mom. You were on every channel up here. You were fantastic! I was absolutely floored!"

"Way to go, Hannah," she heard Eric in the background.

"I have an appointment for a haircut on Thursday," Hannah told her daughter, "it was the only opening they had. I can't leave before that."

"Did you see Dr. Burns?"

"I'm fine," Hannah said. "You were right . . ."

"One more thing, Mom," Chloe interrupted. "Grandma's coming."

Hannah's spirits sank even lower. "Tell me this is a joke," she pleaded.

"No joke, Mom. Sorry. Somebody in Little Wolf sent her an

article from the Milwaukee paper that said you were shot. She's all worried and she says won't be satisfied until she sees that you're okay."

"Good God, Chloe, Lily's coming to Star Lake? When?"

"In time for Labor Day. I told her we'd put her up, what else could I do?"

"We'll have to manage," Hannah replied, trying to imagine her mother shooting bar dice with Ginger in the Saloon and chatting with gamey fishermen. Give Lily a day or so and she will soon have had enough.

She awoke Wednesday with her period. Heavy. And cramps. She weeded the perennials, vacuumed, and finally wandered around the mall at Hilldale where she bought a copy of every newspaper she could find that mentioned the Ingold decision. She also found a swimsuit on sale that she would probably never wear but it was meant to cheer her up. Then she drove to the Pharm House to pick up a supply of soy nuts and black cohosh. For the time being, she wanted to fight hot flashes in a "natural" way.

Killing time, Hannah rode her bike out to Picnic Point early that evening. There was no one else out on the rocks at the end of the long finger of land. Across the water the graceful white dome of the State Capitol rose above the landscape of the city and the four lakes on the Yahara River: Mendota, Monona, Kegonsa, Waubesa. What a long time she had lived and loved in this city. She knew it all by heart.

Right now, at least, the resort seemed to be running smoothly. With the lighter load due to a few predictable cancellations she could find time to sort through Uncle Hal's files and discover why Ingold seemed so intent in acquiring the resort. She also needed to look into a plan to resolve the mortgage foreclosure, or think about finally selling the place—if the mine survived their appeal.

At least when she moved back to Madison she would have some guaranteed employment. Goodbye, BWP's—Joe Mickelson thought she had more serious production skills. George Windsor's closing comment still piqued her interest in doing a mining/environmental documentary.

As a matter of fact . . . she could turn cancellations into cash if she got an advance from Joe for a documentary script. Writing was the only thing she really knew how to do, besides teaching poetry. And with fewer guests, she would have more time to research the subject, and write.

It would feel good to have a project in the works again.

It was a way to get back at Ingold on her own.

Suddenly Hannah missed Star Lake terribly.

Friday morning Hannah woke in her Star Lake bedroom, swallowed her daily dose of herbal remedies and checked her reflection in the bathroom mirror for jowls or double chin. There she was, Hannah Swann, middle-aged, menopausal, scarred from her brush with death in the blueberries, her dull, listless hair still badly needing a trim because she'd fled Madison in a rush.

Ginger evidently had some clout at Bessie's Beauty Shoppe and was able to get Hannah an appointment that afternoon. Between the processing, the neutralizing and the cut, Hannah read every dog-eared copy of *People* and *Good Housekeeping* in Bessie's shop.

"It's fine," she croaked, when Bessie said. "There now, doesn't that look better?" Dyed raven black, her hair was teased and lacquered to fit her head like a tightly woven helmet and emitted a terrible odor.

"It'll look more natural after you wash it," Chloe assured her when Hannah came in from the car. Babe growled as if encountering a stranger and sniffed her suspiciously. Ginger, on the porch of the Saloon with a cup of tea, said, "Well, I'll be," and told Hannah she looked like a new woman. "It's a real pick-me-up, isn't it?"

Celestial Summer was meeting at Forest Temple that night. Of course she had to attend. Ginger was tied up with bar traffic because Eric and Chloe were initiating their first-ever Star Lake Saloon Friday Night All-You-Can-Eat Walleye Fish Fry.

She spent a long time in the shower. Wearing Chloe's baseball cap after dark might seem a bit odd, but a scarf Hannah tried tying over her hair in an interesting way made her resemble Aunt Jemima. "You don't look anything like the woman who was on the news Tuesday night, if that's any consolation," Eric quipped when she left the Saloon. That did give her a peculiar peace of mind. She took his van instead of the Toyota and Babe rode along for companionship.

It was raining by the time everyone arrived, so they gathered in the largest teepee. The group had grown since Hannah had first been introduced—now there were summer people, fishermen, hunters, other area resort owners, and families from Antler that Hannah only barely knew.

Leslie met Hannah at the entrance flap and wanted to know why she was wearing Chloe's baseball cap. He threatened to pull it off her head, teasing, and Babe barked crossly.

"I'm traveling incognito," Hannah whispered to the boy after calming the dog. "Somebody tried to kill me," she pointed to the lingering scars on her cheek and her arm, "I have to wear a disguise."

The statement caused Leslie to treat her with new respect. It also encouraged his appointment as her personal bodyguard for the evening, and Hannah could not shake him except to go to the women's privy.

The meeting had been called to discuss the possibility of a "citizen's injunction" in response to the hearing examiner's decision. Divers from the DNR had found two species of freshwater clams near the section of the Lost Arrow River where the water from the mine would be discharged. One of them was a Purple Warty Back, which was on the state's endangered species list. And the other was a Bullhead clam, which was even less common.

Hannah knew something about endangered clams, thanks to Tyler, and realized there might be reason to celebrate.

"The Purple Warty Back clam was found just below the culvert," Dan said, "and after that the divers looked further up river at the entrance to Sundog where they discovered the Bullhead. The DNR's biologists also recently discovered a pygmy snaketail dragonfly near the mine site, a dragonfly so exclusive to the Celestial Flowage that its name isn't even official, yet. And two rare species of fish: the river redhorse and the gilt darter."

"But didn't they already issue an Environmental Impact Statement?" one of the summer people wanted to know.

"That's right," Dan replied, "Their official Environmental Impact Survey was approved over a year ago. At that time we warned the DNR they hadn't been thorough enough. That'll be the basis of our injunction."

Kerry turned further explanation of this matter over to Victor Redhawk, who was drafting the papers.

"I know why the dragonflies and clams are so important," Leslie whispered to Hannah. "They're indicator species. Clams filter the water when they catch their food. That helps us tell what the quality of the water is."

Hannah tried to recall what she had written years ago for Tyler's video on endangered mollusks. Leslie was right. How very odd.

Dan closed the meeting by congratulating Hannah for speaking out and taking such a formidable stand at the DNR press conference on Tuesday.

"Somebody tried to kill her so she's incognito now," Leslie announced importantly when the cheers quieted. "That's why her hair's dyed black, so nobody recognizes her."

Hannah laughed along with the others but decided she could really despise this kid.

Later, after Lynne served tea and carob brownies, the crowd thinned. Hannah had a chance to inform Dan about Tyler's international fame as a malacologist. "I'm not sure I mentioned that," she said, reluctant to remind him of her rather sensational fall from grace.

"I heard about his reputation," he said, wearily. "The biologist Victor talked to, the one who suggested a new Environmental Impact Survey, that was Professor Cole, strange as it may seem. He was here while you were in Madison, so I figured he wasn't looking for you this time."

Dan did not smile when he said it, he just looked very tired. But Hannah was puzzled.

"I suppose he could've been called in by Ingold for consultation on the clams. He does that kind of work."

She thought it peculiar, however, that Tyler might have agreed to work for Ingold without informing her.

You gotta love those kids," Ginger said Saturday night, refilling Hannah's wineglass and pouring another for herself. "Their walleye fry was a winner. Folks seem to enjoy all that get-up-and-go. Seems a shame Eric and Chloe have to leave pretty soon, I don't know how I can bring myself to say so long."

Hannah agreed, "It's been a strange adventure, hasn't it? I'll be honest, I've enjoyed this summer more than I ever thought I would."

"Hah!" Ginger replied, reaching over to pat Hannah's arm, "Don't try to fool with me! I figured it was your change. I remember how I felt."

"And how was that?"

"Like I was too young for Medicare and too old for men to care," Ginger grinned. "Had me all fussed up for a while, but I was wrong. You don't use it, you'll lose it. It's that simple."

Hannah sipped her wine. "By the way, does the name 'Ginger Peaches' ring a bell?"

"Where'd you come up with such damn foolishness," Ginger asked, feigning embarrassment as she lit a cigarette somewhat un-steadily. "Crazy old coot! Horny as a two-peckered billygoat, too."

Ginger and George Windsor? That was too far fetched even for Hannah's creative acumen.

"Oh, I was attracted to your Uncle Hal," Ginger admitted, "but all his life he was faithful to Miriam's memory."

Ginger finished her wine and put her feet on the railing.

"Georgie though, he was something else. Used to sing, I can't cut the mustard anymore, but that's no sin. I can still lick the jar that the mustard came in. And he could, too. I miss that old billygoat like all get-out, wouldn't you know?"

201

14

Dog Days of Summer

Sirius, the dog star, had been rising with the sun for over a month by early August, and people with reservations for Labor Day weekend were calling to ask if the resort would still be open for business.

Things were just fine for the time being, Hannah told them, "I haven't even noticed if they've begun cutting trees over at the mine site."

That excuse lasted a few days before she had to amend it. "I noticed they were cutting some trees, but I haven't seen any bull-dozing." By the second week in August the groans of earth-moving equipment echoed ominously across the water. "They're doing a lit-tle work over there, but nothing that's inconveniencing us." How long would that suffice?

Except for weekends, when the bar was open late and crowds were noisier, she slept on the screened porch above the Saloon. Sunday through Thursday the cot along the south screened wall became an aerie where her dreams were untroubled by woodland rhythms and haunting tremolos of loons. If it rained she pulled the cot away from the screens and went inside, or fastened the canvas roll-down curtains and reveled in sounds of the storm. It was part of her healing process.

Even when the shot came out of the woods to shatter her windshield and splinter her composure, Hannah knew she would not die. She had grown too resilient to kill. Since her return from Madison, she had been trying to focus on the positive elements of her life. No more reviews of sagging muscles or crowsfeet, no "no one will want me anymore, no one will love me."

Resignation, acceptance—whatever the reason, she felt more content. Summer was moving along and she was progressing with her writing. If the cottages were only half-filled, then Hannah negotiated a couple hours to work on her Mine Games documentary proposal. Clearly there was an important story hidden in the boxes of clippings in Hal's study. As George Windsor had promised, she found records of Ingold's research and analysis, but she found no mention of surveys other than those done on Ingold's land.

The growing commotion over at the mine site only increased Hannah's resolve. She intended to get the project organized and convince Joe of its worth. And not only Joe, but potential funding agencies and PBS and anyone else who had the power to squelch it.

With Miriam's telescope, Hannah could observe what looked like a war zone across the lake. Due to clear-cutting there was a pretty good view of the painful gash in the formerly pristine landscape. A chain-link fence had been installed around the entire perimeter, timber had been removed and they had begun scraping the topsoil and hauling it away. A bomb might have been dropped on that bulls-eye, for all the devastation. The *Antler Advocate* said Ingold would begin digging the pit before winter if possible. The first ore shipments were scheduled for the following fall.

When Hannah tried to focus the telescope as far as Dan's place on the other end of Sundog, his house was hidden by foliage. She might have a better chance after some of the maple and birch lost their leaves. The idea intrigued her, to think she could mark his comings and goings, especially when he traveled by water.

Hannah often heard the now-familiar hum of Dan's boat as she lay awake waiting for sunrise. This wasn't unusual, he frequently came by in the hours before dawn to pick up fishermen, and Hannah enjoyed the knowledge that he was right below her porch.

This morning she tracked his progress by telescope. Dan's bow parted a light haze still suspended above the water. The place was dead quiet. If he'd turn off the motor he would easily hear her whisper hello.

In fact, he did turn off the motor. Hannah wondered why he would arrive before five A.M. if not to pick up a client.

"Good morning," she called softly from the sleeping porch.

"Meet me at the back door." His voice was low and conspiratorial in the early hush.

Babe gave a soft "woof" when she recognized Dan's voice.

"What's up?" Hannah asked, puzzled, when he came in.

He smelled like mosquito repellent, hadn't shaved, and he was wearing the old flannel shirt she'd returned with a faded blue T-shirt underneath. The soft plaid almost moved her to tears, she so yearned to feel its comforting touch.

Babe's tail smacked Hannah's legs in rhythmic joy as the dog welcomed Dan. He gave Babe a hug and let her lick his face.

"I've only got a few minutes," he said in the kitchen as Hannah flicked the switch on her coffee maker. "I'm taking some of your folks out for muskies. We'd have had better luck last night, but they want to take their chances when the sun is up."

They sat across from one another at the kitchen table. "I can't believe how fast things are moving over at the mine-site. I've been using Miriam's telescope," Hannah explained.

"Once they heard about our lawsuit, they started stripping away the soil as fast as they could. All we need is a big rainstorm to cause some bad erosion. That'd be a real mess."

He removed a sweat-stained fishing cap, ran a hand through tousled gray curls and yawned. Hannah felt a sudden swell of energy. She was on the verge of sharing her excitement for the Mine Games project, and almost suggested, "If it rains, let's get some footage . . ." but she held back, wishing to wait until the concept was more fully-formed. He had to be impressed. And wide awake.

"Victor's down in Madison with Ben. The hearing before the new judge is looking good. Yesterday the director of the Bureau of Endangered Resources recommended another environmental survey. We might be able to get a temporary restraining order and force Ingold to suspend construction until that's completed."

"Breathing space," Hannah agreed.

"Even so, there are five more permits for mines pending up here right now, waiting to be reviewed, so Governor Dawson's pressuring the DNR to allow Ingold to go ahead."

They drank their coffee while the sky turned slowly from dove gray to amethyst. It's nice, Hannah thought, this private time together as the day is born.

"I've got to leave," he said then, breaking the spell. "Didn't mean to wake you but I'll be out all day and I wanted to bring you up to speed."

"You didn't wake me," she replied, probably too quickly. "I do a lot of thinking, this time of the morning."

Dan noticed the sleeping porch where the door was ajar. Blankets on her cot were flung aside. "You sleep out here?"

"Babe and I both do," she said. Hannah was wearing a pair of Hal's pajamas, and only now remembered to slip on the robe that hung from the doorknob.

"I like to listen to the water. It has a very calming effect."

"You ought to spend a night at Forest Temple," Dan said. "Try sleeping in a teepee. Lynne calls it ethereal."

"You're right, I should," Hannah said with spurious enthusiasm, "ethereal would be . . . different."

She was trying to block the image of Dan lying next to Lynne in a teepee, when he asked, "Any word from Professor Cole?"

"Not for a long time," she replied. "Not since, you know. That day."

She wasn't even comfortable saying Tyler's name.

"Well, we can expect another ruling pretty soon," Dan said as he turned to leave.

"See you later," Hannah suggested with what she hoped was a

light inflection that sounded like a casual "Feel free to stop in any-time" and not, as she found herself wishing, "Oh, please, caress me again like you did when you saw I'd been shot because I think about it all the time and wonder if you ever will."

"By the way," Dan said, "your buddy Mickelson called to schedule a fishing date. You know how booked up I am right now, but I figured this was important to you."

"Joe's a good friend," Hannah nodded.

"We tried to figure something out and the only day that seemed remotely possible was next Sunday. That was fine with him. But I had to make it tentative until I checked with you about a minor conflict."

Hannah was anxious for Joe to get to know Dan; it would be a strong selling point for her documentary if Joe could learn more about the Ingold situation from someone else.

"What's the problem," Hannah asked, apprehensive.

"Lynne and Lyle are scheduled to play at a bluegrass festival in Ann Arbor. I promised I'd keep an eye on Leslie. If you'd take him for me on Sunday, I could spend the day with the Mickelsons."

A whole day with Leslie! And one of her precious Sunday mornings, besides. She groped for an answer, determined to negotiate more from baby-sitting that kid than a mere fishing date for Joe and his wife.

"I want Joe to produce a documentary about our mining problem," Hannah finally confessed. "I got the idea from George Windsor, of all people. And I'd hoped maybe one day, when you weren't so busy, we could toss around a few ideas between the two of us, you and I, because I've been working on a treatment that I really think has some possibilities."

Okay, she'd gone that far, might as well spill the rest.

"So, is there any way you could help me sell it? I mean, convince Joe the idea's a good one? Like, have a discussion about the mine while you're fishing or something?"

Dan shook his head and smiled. "You're not crazy about Leslie, are you?"

Hannah shrugged. She'd already blabbed more than she intended. So much for wowing him with a polished Mine Games proposal; now she sounded like a desperate neophyte.

Dan said he was working nights now, and usually slept late but he had his afternoons fairly free. "I can take a look at my schedule, see if I can shift a few things around. Maybe I'll be able to squeeze in a tour of the mine site for him while he's up here, if you think that'd help."

Hannah was sure it would. Joe needed to see visual possibilities, and the ongoing destruction was a graphic example.

Summer seemed to be coming to a quick and abrupt end. "Feels like fall already," the guests were complaining. Hannah worried that she would have to move in from the sleeping porch or buy an electric blanket.

Due to another cancellation, Hannah was able to switch Joe and Helen Mickelson from tiny Vega to Aldebaran, her nicest cottage. Dan came over on Sunday morning to pick them up. Still pitch dark, the hour was crisp and chilly. Waterlily buds were clenched in tight little white and yellow fists, awaiting the sun, but fog coated the lake as the water was warmer than the air.

"Somebody told us in the bar last night this wasn't a good time of year to fish for muskies," Joe told Dan as he and Helen stepped into the boat.

"They get sore gums now, right?" Dan replied. "I've heard that, too."

Helen wore a down jacket and had tied a scarf around her head. "One guy said muskies lose their teeth in August," Helen explained to Hannah, whose own teeth were chattering in the cold.

"Another old wive's tale," Dan said, "I fish hard every single month of the year up here from ice-out to ice-up, and I can promise you some of the biggest fish are caught in the month of August."

"Well, we're ready," Joe said, clapping poor Helen's back with excitement. "Let's go. See you later, Hannah!"

The boat left the pier, and Hannah and Leslie waved goodbye as the boat dissolved into the mist. Babe seemed to be contemplating an early morning swim, but sniffed the water and trotted back toward shore. At four A.M. the outdoor thermometer barely registered forty degrees and the day stretched ahead for Hannah like an early nightmare.

"Uncle Dan promised you'd make pancakes," Leslie said.

"Don't you want to go back to bed?" Hannah suggested hopefully. "If you don't want to go back to sleep you can read or watch cartoons on TV. I saved some comic books for you that I found in one of the cottages."

"Oh, cool!" Leslie replied, "Lyle and Lynne don't allow me to read comics. And we don't have a TV. The only time I get to watch TV is at Uncle Dan's."

But the idea of hot pancakes with maple syrup began to appeal to Hannah. So she fixed a big breakfast, then lay on her cot to doze while Leslie read. Besides the comic books, she had no idea how to keep an eleven-year-old boy occupied. What he really wanted to do, it turned out later, was play with Eric's camcorder.

"It's okay with me," Eric told Hannah as he mopped the floor of the Saloon, "I showed him how to use it."

So, Sunday morning Hannah and Leslie walked in the woods with Eric's video camera, and the boy was fairly content.

"Aren't you going to wear your hat?" he'd asked. "You know, your disguise, so you don't get shot?"

Hannah wore Chloe's baseball cap, grudgingly glad of Leslie's company. Even if she discounted the threat of bears, she had not hiked alone along the road or ventured into the woods since she'd been used for target practice. Leslie's monologue about the habitat of pileated woodpeckers, a relay of information that Hannah was certain must have been this week's homeschooling lesson, helped ease her tension as they tracked the forest path.

"What do you think I should film, Hannah?" he asked.

"I'll tell you what," she told him, brave enough now to seek some solitude, "Why don't you make a movie."

"I can't make a movie," he argued, "I don't have any actors except you and I don't want to make a movie about you. Unless you get shot again," he suggested slyly. "Then I could make a movie about that. A murder mystery."

"Thanks a lot, Leslie," Hannah had to laugh. "But you've got Babe," she suggested. The Lab scurried ahead of them, busily sniffing the underbrush.

"What good's a dog," Leslie complained, "I can't make a movie about her."

"Sure you can," Hannah said, latching on to the tiniest hint of interest in his voice, "Do you know what 'subjective camera' is?"

"No . . ." his response was guarded.

"It's where the camera sees the world like you do, or, in this case, as a dog does."

"How do you do that?"

"Let's stop here for a minute. What's Babe doing?"

"Smelling stumps and rotten branches and decaying stuff. A bunch of ferns."

"What's she identifying there, do you think?"

"How do I know? Maybe bear tracks. Deer scat. Foxes."

"And what do you think she's thinking?"

This was crucial. If she could get Leslie involved in a creative project, maybe he would let her alone for an hour or more. There was a new tape in the camcorder, worth at least two hours of standard recording time.

"'What's this stinky smell?'"

"Use your imagination, Leslie," Hannah said sternly. "How about, 'Hmmm, must've been a humongous bear that lumbered past here this morning.'"

"Then what?" he asked, suspicious.

"Then you get down at ground level and use the camcorder as if the lens is seeing what Babe's eyes see. Look at the woods from her point of view. And before you press the button, figure out what she's thinking so you can add her dialogue. You'll have to be her 'voice.'

209

Make up an adventure. Pretend Babe is hunting something, add the clues she's finding. And you can shoot her once in a while, too."

"Shoot her?"

"Get her in the picture. But not when you're pretending to be Babe. Does that make sense?"

"I think so," Leslie said with mild excitement, "I should stand up when I'm showing Babe and what she's doing. And then I can get down on my hands and knees to shoot whatever Babe sees, like she's seeing it."

"You got it!"

Hannah headed for her favorite rock where she planned to catch up on her journal and review the final draft of the mining documentary proposal.

"You won't get lost if you keep Babe nearby," she promised. "Meet me back at this spot when you run out of tape."

He was already calling the dog, who was intently investigating a hollow log, and Leslie's movie was underway.

It was after noon by the time Hannah and Leslie returned to the lodge. Chloe served them cheese and tomato sandwiches on the porch of the Saloon. Leslie was a vegetarian, too.

"You want to watch my movie?" The boy was so eager to look at the video he barely touched his lunch.

"Don't you want to show your Uncle Dan first?" Hannah offered, wishing Chloe would back her up. She had already devoted more time to Leslie today than the Mickelsons' fishing date was worth, even with a promised tour of the mine.

"C'mon, Mom," Chloe teased her, "let's watch Leslie's movie."

"It's called *Babe in the Woods,*" Leslie explained to Chloe.

Hannah laughed. "*Babe in the Woods,* how did you come up with a title like that?"

Because that's what it's about, Babe, in the woods," he said, impatiently, eager for their praise. "That's what Uncle Dan used to call you sometimes."

"A 'babe in the woods?'" Hannah asked, incredulous.

"Once I heard him say 'Hannah's just a babe in the woods.'"

Chloe pretended amazement. "Wow, Mom, what do you think about being called a babe in the woods!"

"I think Uncle Dan was right on," she groaned.

Chloe made some popcorn and they slid the tape into the VCR.

"Babe in the Woods" appeared onscreen.

Hannah had designed the titles on her computer, at Leslie's insistence and under his direction.

A Film by Leslie Akkerman
Starring Babe Larkin
Produced by Hannah Swann

Leslie said Hannah should have her name on it because the movie was her idea.

Following the titles, which Leslie read aloud as they came into focus, there was footage of decaying birchbark, a patch of orange hawkweed, mossy tree trunks, rocks, a shaky close-up of a dragonfly. So much zooming back and forth and swift panning around that Hannah quickly felt woozy. Among the panorama of woodsy imagery were an assortment of snorts and snuffles, panting and sniffling. At one point the camera remained fairly still while a thin stream of water shot into the frame. "I held the camcorder with one hand while I peed," Leslie said. "Because Babe was peeing."

Well, she had encouraged him to be creative.

"Hey, Mom, look at that," Chloe said after about twenty minutes. Footage of Babe among a cluster of orange cylinders was followed by close-up footage of the cylinders themselves. It seemed as though Leslie had encroached upon Ingold's mine site, but Hannah knew that was impossible.

"Core samples," Chloe said, "prospecting holes. Where did you take him, Mom?"

"Leslie," Hannah said calmly, "I told you not to go off our property."

"I didn't," he said. "This was right near that rock where you were writing. I can show you."

But there wasn't time. They heard Dan's boat pull up to the dock—he had returned with the Mickelsons.

Joe hadn't caught a thing, but Helen had caught and released a forty-inch musky, and she and Joe were eager to tell Hannah all about their adventure. Helen even had a Polaroid photo of her catch.

"If I take this picture to a taxidermist with Dan's official certification and a statement of how big it really was, they'll make me one that looks identical to it," Helen said. "He said there's a woman who works here that does that sort of thing."

"Ginger," Hannah offered. "Yes, she's done one or two."

Tired and in a hurry to leave, Dan wasn't in the mood to visit. Hannah assured him she and Leslie had a good time and told him to be sure to watch the movie Leslie made. "It's about Babe, Uncle Dan," she could hear the boy explain as the boat left the pier, "about Babe in the woods."

She hoped Dan stayed awake until the core samples came into view. And she hoped he would be able to tell her how they got there, when they were dug, and what to do about them. The orange tubes protruding from the secluded corner of her property hinted of something foreboding. Why would Uncle Hal have consented to core samples being drilled?

Dan came to the Monday night potluck with Lynne. Joe said he had asked them to come. "I hope that's all right. We got along great. Super guy. Really knows his fish." Hannah stayed out of their way. She helped Chloe serve the meal and heard Lynne invite Helen to visit Forest Temple.

"Oh, yeah, them muskies," one of the guests told Hannah later in the Saloon, "They say the definition of musky fishing is hours of boredom separated by seconds of terror."

Desperate to eavesdrop on Dan's discussion with Joe out on the porch, she set a couple of cold beers in front of them, "On the house."

"Hannah Swann, barmaid," Joe said with a smile of welcome. "What'd you think about Hannah Swann, TV Producer? I was pretty impressed with her coverage of your master's hearing. When she moves back to Madison I'm going to hire her to work on the production end of things for a while."

Hannah was sure the reminder of her return to Madison was not going to be well-received by Dan, but to her surprise he said, "Like I said, I'd like to see her do a documentary on wilderness mining before she leaves."

She wasn't ready to spring this idea on Joe quite so boldly, but Dan must know what he was doing.

"Dan offered to get me inside Ingold's property tomorrow," Joe told Hannah. "Might be something we're interested in, actually. How come you never pitched an overview of wilderness mining? Here I thought you had a good story sense and you're missing a great opportunity right in front of your eyes!"

The Mine Games proposal was waiting for the Mickelsons when they checked out Saturday morning.

Hannah explained, "It compares what we're going through up here to the same thing that's happening in other parts of the country. I know funding is tight, but here's the name of a retired attorney who might have some contacts. He suggested this, by the way, and I used some of his research materials so it's worthwhile checking with him."

If he's lucid the day you call, Hannah considered adding.

Early the next week, Axel Graves called a news conference and made an urgent announcement. "The possibility of irreparable harm to wildlife such as the two endangered clams, warrants an injunction that should go into effect now," Graves quoted the Supplemental Environmental Impact Survey ordered by the judge. "The further along we are in our development of the mine, the more rationale there would be for not stopping the project. Thus anything that is going to involve further substantial investment is now under injunction. Although this may result in the loss of anywhere from thirty-five to one hundred jobs, we are fairly confident that an appellate court will overturn this ruling. In the meantime, we will have to halt work on the liner for stockpiling waste, and construction of the rail spur will be immediately curtailed, as well."

That night in much of Wisconsin the evening news carried portions of Graves's statement and a response from Hannah Swann, spokesperson for Celestial Summer, the group filing the injunction against the mine. Ms. Swann was interviewed at her resort on Star Lake, not far from the proposed Ingold site, and she said she was guardedly optimistic. Further commentary regarding the fate of the Purple Warty Back and Bullhead clams was offered by UW–Madison Professor Tyler Cole, noted malacologist and authority on endangered mussels.

Ginger invited everyone remotely connected with the Celestial Summer movement to a party at Star Lake Saloon. Visiting guests were invited too—there were only four cottages filled, anyway, and with television cameramen on the premises everyone knew what was happening.

Chloe and Eric found additional picnic tables. Hannah ordered a roast pig to be brought in for a Spanferkel, and the chef, "Willie B. Bacon," arrived early in the day. His station wagon pulled an enormous cylindrical oven on wheels with the pig roasting slowly inside. To appease the vegetarians, Eric prepared eggplant lasagna and pasta salad with marinated artichokes.

It was easily the biggest picnic Hannah had ever given, and the happiest, the most celebratory, by far.

Late that night, after nearly everyone else had gone home or retired to their cottages well-fed and content, Ginger, Dan, and Hannah relaxed on the porch of the Saloon while Chloe and Eric cleaned the kitchen.

Hannah dragged herself from the glider with a sigh and went inside to take a telephone call.

"Sweetcheeks," Tyler said, "How're you doing?"

"Fine . . ."

"We were both on the news down here. Pretty ironic, isn't it? I guess the injunction must make you happy."

"Yes," Hannah said, still apprehensive, "but it might be only a temporary victory," she added. Chloe and Eric were silent, listening, all ears.

"When do you think you'll be in Madison again?"

"I was just there a couple weeks ago."

"I know. I was in Antler at the same time."

A convenient absence on her part, Hannah thought. She didn't want to see him or his Uncle Wiggily; not in Madison, not in Antler, not anywhere. In fact, she wanted to get off the phone and get back on the porch with Ginger and Dan before they were ready to call it a night.

"I'm not really interested . . ." she began, then remembered his consultation regarding the clams. "You're employed by the enemy, aren't you? Hannah Swann isn't Ingold's favorite person, you must have noticed."

"I'm aware of that," Tyler replied solemnly. "But I have something for you, Cheeks. Something I think you'll find worthy of note."

Her curiosity was mildly kindled.

"First of all, I want you to know that I gave the presence of those goddamned clams considerable leverage in the report I put together for Ingold, probably more than they deserved. And I'm still doing all I can to discourage the mine from going forward."

"I appreciate that, Tyler, I really do," Hannah said, surprised. "But why are you telling me this? Surely that's imprudent on your part."

"What I have for you is even more imprudent," Tyler said. "While I was reviewing Ingold's permit file I had a look at aerial photos from their magnetic wave surveys done in 1973. The photos measured the ore body and its location on your lake."

"Really?" Hannah said, wondering what was coming next.

"I managed to scan some copies of those photos, Hannah, and the statistical analyses . . ."

Damn, he was being exasperating.

"Tyler, I wish you'd just tell me what's the big deal. We've still got company here, and I don't have time for chit-chat. I'm not in the mood to be strung along."

"As far as I can tell, and I studied the information pretty carefully, a rich vein of copper ore extends from the Ingold site right through your Star Lake resort."

"I see," Hannah said after a moment. "Would you mind repeating that?" She motioned to Chloe and Eric who leaned close to hear Tyler repeat his revelation.

"And you said that you made fairly good copies?"

15

That Sinking Feeling

Local reaction to the injunction against Ingold was swift, vocal, and negative. "They're mad as hell at you, Hannah," Ginger warned. "People who wouldn't say shit if they had a mouthful are squawking that you ought to eat it."

Hannah wondered how far she would have to drive to buy her groceries from now on.

"Minocqua would be safe," Ginger suggested. "I'd forget about getting any more pies from the Antler IGA."

Despite the crisp breeze, George Windsor was seated in his wheelchair bundled in Pendleton blankets on the porch of Northern Lights. He spied Hannah the moment she came through the door.

"Ginger Peaches has been telling me I've got to help her keep you out there at the lake. What do you think about that, Miss Hannah Swann?"

Hannah didn't know what to think. Ginger stood up from the wicker armchair next to George as if to leave.

"You sit right back down there, Peaches. You're not going anywhere until I tell you to."

The old man was enjoying himself. Hannah intended to ask him right away about the note—in effect, a second mortgage.

"You're having trouble keeping the place alive and kicking, Peaches says."

"It's not easy . . ." Hannah took his brittle hand and he held on tightly as if he were afraid she would try to get away.

"And you're working to get a TV show off the ground, something against the copper mine. That so?"

"Wilderness mining and environmental risks. It was your idea," Hannah reminded him.

"T'was?" He chuckled, "Must be sharper than I give myself credit for these days."

"Sharp as a tack with twice the prick," Ginger said. George guffawed and released his grip on Hannah, so she was able to sit next to them.

"Mr. Windsor, I need to ask you about the note you hold on the Star Lake property." She could be forcing the issue a bit, but there was his tendency to wander before their conversations were completed.

"Hal asked me about that the day he died. Maybe it was the day before, I'm not too clear on the date but I recollect his call."

"You never told me about that," Ginger said.

Was the old gent imagining things already, or was he still lucid? Hannah exchanged glances with Ginger, who merely raised an eyebrow and shrugged.

"Well, there were questions about that note. And his bequest, as I remember. I'd just been bundled up and sent over here and Hal knew he wasn't well. He was worried about Denny. And something to do with a tombstone."

"Graves?" Ginger suggested.

"Denny and this Graves fellow, they were out at Star Lake. Hal said he was sawing up a tree. They were pestering him to sign a paper of some kind. He told them he wanted to consult his attorney. But Denny said he was Hal's attorney now that I was sent over here, Denny had the will and the paper they wanted Hal to sign was up to snuff."

The women tried to question him further, but that was all they were able to gather.

"Still owes me the ten bucks I took from him in poker. Why'd that son of a bitch have to up and die, goddammit?"

He reminisced more about the good old times, and then he began to sob, mumbling how he missed his old friend. Hannah was uneasy. Ginger rubbed his back through the blanket thrown over his thin shoulders and spoke in tender tones that Hannah never heard her use.

"Georgie, I'm going to go now but I'll be back to see you again on Sunday."

George raised his head, wiped his eyes with the edge of his blanket and spoke in a renewed and confident voice.

"Peaches, you give this girl a hand. Can't you see she's tuckered out, trying to fight that mining company by herself?"

Hannah smiled, and bent to give the old man a hug.

"And Sweetheart," he told her, "if Denny didn't have my power of attorney I'd help you out. I surely would."

Hannah's heart sunk, but she should have suspected: with George's power of attorney, Denny controlled all his father's finances, including the note. As they left the building, Hannah asked Ginger why she hadn't said something about that.

"I didn't know for sure," Ginger admitted. "We're up the creek, aren't we?"

"Almost," Hannah agreed, "but let's not jump overboard just yet."

She had never seen such bloodthirsty mosquitoes. They swept out of the damp shadows like puffs of smoke and swarmed around her head in whining clouds. Deerflies buzzed Babe's head and nipped her back. It was not the best time to be walking in the woods, but Leslie was showing Hannah and Dan the place where he videotaped the prospecting holes.

"It's all that rain," Dan explained. "Ticks have been bad this summer, too. Graves made a fuss in the *Advocate* this week about the 'massive tick infestation' at the mine site, I suppose he figures that'll change our plans for the clambake."

"Are you guys really going to bake clams?" Leslie asked.

"Clambake can just be another name for a picnic," Hannah explained. "We're calling it a clambake because of the endangered clams that are holding up work on the mine."

"At a real clambake you dig a hole in the sand, then wrap clams and corn on the cob and fish in wet seaweed and bury them on hot coals," Dan told him. "Usually on a beach, near the ocean."

"Yuk," Leslie said. "Do you have to eat the seaweed, too?"

"Only the vegetarians," Hannah quipped, and Dan laughed.

The slender, bright orange tubes drilled six hundred feet into the earth were well-hidden by dense forest growth. Dan showed them how easily the location could have been accessed by the logging road he'd pointed out to Hannah earlier that summer, near the Star Lake cemetery.

Hannah consulted Tyler's aerial map with Dan. He pointed out the lodge and the cottages as they appeared from the air. According to the explanation, gleaned from Tyler's accompanying letter, the ore body clearly ran through the resort with a heavy concentration in this area.

"Exactly where we're standing," Dan said. "No doubt about it. And I can assure you it was not Hal's intention to have any prospecting done here."

Leslie wandered through the orange pipes sunk into the forest floor, searching for clues. "The tire tracks don't look real fresh."

Dan said, "These were drilled after Hal died."

"But I was up here right away, I would've heard them," Hannah argued. "You can't bore six hundred feet into the ground without making a lot of noise."

"You'd have heard something, that's for sure," Dan said. "And this many samples aren't driven in an hour or two, it would have taken a couple days. How long were you in Madison, after Hal's memorial service?"

"A week. Just a week," Hannah said.

"That'd do it," Dan said. "The resort wasn't open yet, nobody else was around."

"There's sixteen of them," Leslie said, tallying his count.

"It explains what Dennis and Graves were looking at, when I saw them out here in the woods."

"That was right after you spoiled his plan to execute Hal's estate."

"It was your idea," Hannah reminded Dan.

"He must've had more riding on it than we were aware of," he continued, ignoring Hannah's pointed comment. "We need more information on this before we make a move, but the injunction isn't going to hold them off forever. We can cause Ingold big trouble by proving they dug on private land without permission."

She explained her recent visit with George, and the phone call Hal made to him the day he died. Or maybe the day before.

"I'll be damned," Dan said. "Didn't I warn you Denny Windsor was a dishonest son of a bitch?"

Hannah clasped a smooth orange cylinder in her both hands, then let go and sighed deeply.

"This isn't the only thing he's been dishonest about," she said. "Dennis holds George's second mortgage on this property. I talked to the banker in Antler and he said it would come due the same time as the first, at the end of the year."

Dan's indignation frightened her even more.

"Hannah, if Denny can get the money to pay off the first mortgage—how much did you say that was, ninety thousand? Then he's in the driver's seat. He can take over your resort just like that and force you out. He doesn't have to wait until the end of December!"

She had no idea. "And of course he'd sell it to the mine."

"Right away. And make his ninety thousand back and hundreds of thousands more."

"It's already awkward, working on Uncle Hal's estate with Dennis as Ingold's spokesman. Now that I know he has that kind of power," her voice cracked, "and has probably been conspiring to do me in . . ."

"Are you desperate enough yet to let me help?" Dan asked. "My offer still stands."

"I haven't forgotten," she told him. "I'm grateful for the backup position, but I'm stubborn enough to want to try to handle this myself."

"You must be related to Hal Larkin," Dan muttered.

"I guess I am," she smiled weakly. "In fact, Tuesday I'm meeting with Dennis, to finish up Hal's estate. I want to sit across the desk from him knowing he wants to take us over, that he can, and not let it show."

"I've got a feeling you can handle Denny just fine," Dan embraced her with clumsy one-armed hug that caught her entirely by surprise. "Maybe he'll give himself away and we'll have some ammunition we can use."

She was intrigued by the chance to get the attorney to slip up. She was also intrigued by Dan's hug.

"It'll have to be a great acting job on my part, considering what I know. Or what we suspect."

"You can be, like, a spy, Hannah," Leslie suggested.

"Just what I always wanted," Hannah joked.

"Maybe he was the one who shot at you!"

Leslie concocted an imaginary scenario as they tramped back to Star Lake through the woods. "He hid up in a tree and waited for you to drive past."

"Dennis?" Hannah scoffed, "He probably couldn't hit the broad side of a barn door."

"Well, he missed you, didn't he?" Leslie retorted.

He and Dan had a good laugh, but there was something almost ominous in that suggestion that made Hannah pause.

"Don't take any foolish chances," Dan said, as though reading her scrambled thoughts. "For all our joking around, Windsor might be getting desperate. We know he's playing for pretty high stakes."

Hannah studied the framed paintings of ruffed grouse and wild turkeys in the cool, wood-paneled waiting room, avoiding the careful scrutiny of Windsor's thin-lipped, elderly secretary. She had chosen to wear a new dress; it was a soft pink rayon print with a plunging neckline. There was no point letting the lawyer think she'd gone to seed even with the five pounds she'd gained.

He's probably hoping to take some of the edge off our appointment, Hannah decided, checking the time once more. But her sense of purpose was still strong when he came out from behind the closed door of his inner office and beckoned her inside.

"You're looking well," he said, carefully appraising her appearance as she knew he would.

Although the air-conditioning was a welcome respite from the exceptionally warm August day, Hannah felt a distinctly ominous chill. His face was grim above the starched collar of his white shirt, and the conservative striped tie was softened by a blazer with gold buttons that he carefully arranged across the back of his office chair.

"I'm feeling well, Dennis," Hannah replied. He closed the door behind her.

"I haven't seen you since we ran into each other down in Madison," he said. "Never did get to buy you that beer out on the Union Terrace. But you've been a busy little beaver, haven't you. Seem to be making quite a name for yourself." A smirk accompanied a leisurely sigh, as if he were too tired to provoke her. He seemed relaxed, bemused.

Hannah didn't know how to respond to what she was certain was a passive-aggressive posture.

"Well, I didn't ask for any of that," she replied. "It just happened."

Windsor was held by her glance for just a moment too long and his face grew serious. Hannah felt, in that moment, a glimpse of her victory. Then he nervously began to tap his pen on Hal's file on the top of his desk.

"This summer has been a revelation to me, Hannah. I had you pegged all wrong. You've gone from timid little city-gal to one of our leading outside agitators, and, if you'll forgive my saying so," he looked up and smiled again, "a royal pain in the ass."

"I thought we were going to close my uncle's estate today,"

Hannah shot back, "and I'm hardly an outside agitator, Dennis—I'm living here on Star Lake."

With that out of the way, Windsor opened the file and the actual probate details were pretty straightforward. Dennis, or his secretary, Hannah suspected, had carried out all the necessary chores and the papers were ready to be signed with only brief explanations.

She placed her signature in the designated spaces. Then he placed several copies in a separate file that he handed over to her with a flourish.

"There's just one more thing I want to mention," he said as if it were an afterthought, when Hannah tucked the file next to her purse, "and that's the matter of my father's note. You'd better start making arrangements to take care of it," Dennis warned her. "Word around town says your reservations have fallen off, so I hope you're keeping that payment in the back of your mind."

"Of course," Hannah assured him. This was not the time to plead for mercy.

"You know," he suggested, going back to his earlier, more patronizing persona, "you ought to watch what you say to those reporters who hang around you like lovesick pups. You might think you're saving Star Lake by speaking up against Ingold, but that just advertises the fact that your resort is going under, mine or no mine. People take it to heart."

Hannah knew this was partly true and she found herself in resigned agreement. What could she say?

"Tell you what," he said then with an abrupt about face, "since we didn't have that beer on the Terrace, why don't we have one at Little Bohemia. It's almost happy hour."

The lawyer's grin was disarming. Dan had advised her to be careful, but if Dennis were relaxed and did not see her as a threat she might be given an opportunity to casually quiz him about his last visit with Hal and the questionable prospecting samples.

"We'll take the Porsche," he said, slipping into his blazer.

"Just for happy hour," Hannah said cautiously.

"Just one beer for my fellow Badger, Hannah Swann."

Yes, it was a risk. She heard the sarcasm in his voice and, knowing his affinity for alcohol, realized it wasn't a good idea to leave her car parked on Main Street and ride out to Little Bohemia with him. But she didn't want to throw away any possibility of reasonable negotiations, either.

So she was not at all surprised when they ended up having dinner together at Dillinger's favorite resort. As the evening progressed, Hannah waited and watched for the right moment to inquire about the mortgage, Uncle Hal, and the core samples. It never arose. Dennis never ordered a beer, he preferred martinis. Hannah drank only a single glass of wine. His mood meandered as he talked about his days in law school, his wife, and the expectations that he'd follow in his dad's footsteps as a small-town lawyer. By the time they were ready to leave he was mellow and he could not have been more attentive.

"Hannah, I worry about you, I really do," he said. He took her arm as they crossed the dark parking lot. If he were not such a devious adversary, Hannah decided, she might almost feel sorry for him. Dennis admitted at dinner that he sometimes felt isolated and longed for a big-city practice. His marriage was evidently not the happiest, and she could understand his need and desire for the association of Ingold's prestige.

"I always wanted to drive a Porsche," she told him, smoothly finessing her concern about his ability to drive. He handed her the keys.

"Here's your chance," he said, "I wouldn't do this for just anyone, understand?" He looked at her intently with heavy-lidded eyes.

"I'm really a very good driver," she explained, blithely, "but I seldom have a chance to drive really fast."

Hannah kept talking, before his relaxed warmth would have a chance to fade. She swore she had been in love with his silver Porsche since the first time she laid eyes on it, and after the first wind-whistling mile he apparently began to believe her.

"You know, I had a similar attraction for you," he said, and he placed a damp hand on her right knee. "The first time I laid eyes on you."

Was now the time? Could she carry this off and not give anything away?

"Dennis," she said lightly, ignoring his hand and shifting gears one final time. "I really do appreciate the fine work you did on Hal's estate. I mean, despite all the differences we've had, you know, about the mine and everything."

He was moving his hand down now, and slipped it underneath the hem of her skirt. She wasn't that appreciative. She moved his hand aside and pressed down even harder on the accelerator.

"You've always respected those differences, and I think you know why I've had to take the position that I have," she explained in a matter-of-fact tone.

"You are one sexy broad," Windsor said sleepily, "I like a spunky woman."

"Spunky?" Hannah tried to laugh. Now he was making lazy circles over her dress in the vicinity of her breasts. She could feel her nipples harden to his touch, and willed them not to react. Shit, it was no use.

"C'mon, Dennis," she said, "I'm trying to drive your car! You wouldn't want me to have an accident, would you? How would that look, for God's sake?"

"Then pull over," he suggested. "There's a side road up ahead on the right. I want to talk."

"I've got a feeling you don't really want to talk," Hannah hedged, trying to maintain a playful tone that wouldn't put him completely off.

"No, I really do . . ." Dennis argued. He fingered the deep neckline and slipped his hand deftly inside. "Don't you trust me?"

"Do you think I should?" Hannah said coyly, trying to maneuver a curve during his lascivious advance. She sped past the turnoff he suggested. Antler was only a few more miles ahead.

He slid his hand under her bra and fondled her breasts, nestling his head on her shoulder so he could kiss her neck. The brakes squealed when, at last, she pulled to a stop on Main Street and parked in the space next to her own.

"This isn't a good idea, Dennis," Hannah whispered, removing his hand. His response was to reach for her face and kiss her, long and hard and deep.

"Oh . . ." Hannah said. She hated the way her voice sounded: breathless, as if she'd become aroused. Which she had. Which she was, but she tried not to be. Didn't want to be. This was a big mistake.

"What if someone sees us," she said, trying to push him away.

"It wouldn't be the first time, would it?" His voice in her ear was seductive, menacing. "You've been with other men before. Even married men . . ."

"I don't know what you're talking about," she said with a shaky laugh as an icy chill spilled down her back. She knew now that he would use her in any way he could.

"What's the matter? Afraid it'll hurt your reputation? You haven't wasted your time since you've been here, that's for sure. C'mon, you owe me a little taste of that sweet pussy, too . . ."

His words were slurred and she knew she would have bruises on her arms from his crushing grip.

"You took some guy to the Yank 'Em Inn. And Dan Kerry—everybody knows you two have been getting it on."

Without thinking, Hannah struck him across the face and squirmed away. She reached for the door.

"Your uncle would be ashamed of you, Hannah Swann. I may have had my differences with Hal," Windsor said cynically, rubbing his cheek, "but to his dying day he was a decent man. A decent man."

"Tell me about his dying day," Hannah demanded. "You were there just before he died. And not long afterward, too, isn't that right?"

Her fury was still building. How could she have even thought of trusting this man, letting him touch her as he did? He might have tried to kill her. He might have killed Uncle Hal!

By the light of the streetlamp she could see his astonishment. She may as well have struck him again, for the shock that registered in his face. It lasted only briefly, however, and was replaced by a ruthless grin.

"I expect to see that mortgage paid right on time, you splendid cunt. Pay up or I'll take over and have your ass out of there before you can kiss it goodbye. I've had it with your constant whining. Little prick tease . . ."

There was probably more, but by that time Hannah was in her own car where her hand shook so violently that she had trouble inserting the key in the ignition.

On the drive back to Star Lake she couldn't stop trembling. Dan had been right; this man was dangerous. Now Dennis Windsor would try even harder to sink her, if that were possible. She was so incredibly weary of the effort to keep the place high and dry.

16
The Clambake Incident

Hannah drove down to Minocqua on Thursday with a long grocery list and her mother in the car. Now close to seventy-five, Lily Larkin was as talkative as ever. Since arriving Saturday night for a two week stay, Lily had complained nonstop about being cold.

"You know, if you'd come down to Tampa once in a while you could play bridge and we've got a dinner theater, and we golf at a nice little par-three. We're very civilized. The gals all ask about you. I've got plenty of room. How many times have I told you that?"

"More than enough," Hannah sighed. "And I wish you'd stop saying 'gals.' Nobody says 'gals' anymore except old women who bowl." Hannah shivered with disdain. "And play bridge."

"We go bowling," Lily said, defensively. "They bowl up here, too; there's nothing wrong with bowling. Or bridge, either, for that matter. What's wrong with gals?"

Hannah felt immensely weary.

"Go ahead and say gals if you want to, Mother; it's all right."

"If you're coming down, though, better make it soon," Lily said suddenly. "I might sell the condo and move into a retirement community. Now that Daddy's gone, our condo feels too big. But I haven't made up my mind yet. All those widows at Dolphin Cove—the retirement place—I kind of like to have a man around to talk to. Ginger and I were chatting about that yesterday and she says that's one of the reasons she likes working in the bar, because of the men."

"Mother," Hannah said, "you and Ginger are about as much alike as . . ." she searched in vain for one of Ginger's colorful phrases.

"We get along just fine," Lily told her. "You watch your sharp tongue, Hannah. I don't want to hear any derogatory comments about Ginger. She's a great gal."

"I love Ginger," Hannah said, exasperated. "I only meant that . . ."

It was useless to try and explain. She and Lily had always been on different wave lengths.

The Toggery was next to a real estate office that Hannah passed by in a hurry, giving the snapshots of "Homes and Vacation Property" in the window only a cursory glance. But as Lily tried on one knit outfit after another, Hannah eventually wandered over to pick up a "Northwoods Home Showcase" brochure.

A tall, thin woman with a no-nonsense haircut emerged from an office inside.

"I own this place up on Star Lake," Hannah began, reluctant to commit herself to anything. The realtor, Margie Campbell, invited her to have a seat so they could discuss the situation more comfortably.

Hannah told her she was interested in knowing about other resorts in the area that were for sale, and what they were asking. Then, with only a little prodding, she explained her predicament.

Margie felt the sale of the Star Lake resort—in spite of the mine and the mortgage—could be addressed without a great deal of difficulty. "I'll be happy to come out and give you a free market analysis," she offered, "no strings attached."

Hannah felt encouraged. They agreed upon a meeting for the next afternoon, and she was well on her way back to Antler before she remembered to go back to the Toggery for Lily.

Hannah was not quite as hopeful, however, when Margie came out to Star Lake the following day.

"We sell an awful lot of cottages like this to Illinois buyers," Margie said. "You know how Wisconsin residents are sometimes referred to as 'Cheese Heads?' Well, we call our Illinois buyers 'Cottage Cheese Heads.'"

"Maybe you could suggest a few other alternatives," Hannah replied. "I'd prefer to retain the integrity of the resort."

"Well, right now buyers like to clear the property and put up their own summer homes. If you don't mind compromising a teensy bit there might be solutions out there you haven't even considered. And then there are the mineral rights."

"I sort of thought I'd hold on to those," Hannah hedged.

"Hold on to the mineral rights?" Margie seemed alarmed.

"I don't want Ingold to take over the resort, or to buy the property."

Margie was mystified.

"If I listed with you I'd do two things: I'd specify that the property had to be continued as a resort, and I would refuse to sell the mineral rights."

"Good luck, then," Margie said with a frown. "I don't think I can do much for you because you're really limiting your options."

Hannah saw Margie out the back door to her car. As the realtor was driving away, Mr. Clintonville, staying in Sirius, asked, "When's the bar going to be open?"

"I didn't know it was closed," Hannah said.

She went inside, where she found herself confronted by Chloe, Eric, Lily, Ginger, and Dan.

"What's happening?" Hannah asked, innocently.

The group was silent, but all eyes upon her had a troubled, questioning look.

"Who was that," Chloe wanted to know.

"A realtor from Minocqua," Hannah answered. "I'm not hiding anything, I asked her to come up here and give me an appraisal."

"How much are you asking," Ginger said coldly.

"I haven't listed with her," Hannah threw back, "I just wanted some free advice. What's wrong with that?"

"We're moving back to Madison on Monday," Eric reminded her. "Chloe and I wondered what you were planning because, you know, we've gotten really attached to the place. If it weren't for Chloe's master's thesis, we'd be staying. We'd stay through the winter, even."

That was quite a speech from Eric, who was usually taciturn. He and Dan sat at a table, empty coffee mugs between them.

Over the summer Chloe's hair had grown out and she looked softer now, more feminine. Even vulnerable, Hannah thought. She wanted to hold her daughter and receive some comfort in return. But Chloe was standing with her arm around Lily's waist, as if they were hanging on to one another.

"I'm sorry to lose you kids," Ginger said to Eric and Chloe. "You're like my family, which I don't have much of anymore. And the thought of losing Star Lake Saloon and Housekeeping Cottages, which has been my home base for all these many years, makes this the sorriest day in my life."

"I know what you mean, Ginger," Lily offered, "a person needs to feel like she's welcome."

"We love it here, Mother," Chloe told Hannah with an accusatory tone. "I wish you'd have talked it over with us before calling a realtor. Maybe we could have made other arrangements."

"What kind of arrangements?" Hannah wanted to know. "You don't have any money, the bank is breathing down my neck and so is the mine, not to mention Dennis Windsor. Besides, I haven't signed anything. How many times do I have to remind you of that?"

She was embarrassed by this family squabble in front of Dan. He had no right being present. Ginger must have issued a summons.

"Maybe the rest of us could've bought it from you," Ginger offered. "You never asked."

"It's more complicated than that," Hannah replied. "Dan offered to help, a couple times. But I had to turn him down. There are other issues. I'm in a difficult situation here! I don't have any business acumen, God knows I'm not cut out for this rustic lifestyle, and even though I know we need people around because that's where the money is, I'm sick and tired of mopping up after a bunch of strangers. With you and Eric going back to Madison," Hannah addressed her daughter, "that leaves Ginger and me to clean the cottages ourselves. And that's just one example."

"But if only half the cottages are filled there are only half that many to clean," Chloe retorted sharply.

"I suspect Hannah wants to list the resort now," Dan said calmly, "because of the injunction against the mine. That makes it seem like a more viable business, at the moment. And after all the work you've done here the place looks better than ever."

"No kidding," Ginger said. "It's worth about as much as a pee-hole in the snow."

"Oh Ginger, shut up." Hannah said brusquely, "I've had enough of your sappy platitudes! I can't take any more of your stupid clichés." Then, immediately she was sorry for yelling because Ginger's wrinkled face crumpled as if she had been slapped. "I never promised to keep the resort forever, remember?"

Hannah grabbed a napkin from the bar and blew her nose.

"At this point I'm willing to settle for less money just to get out of debt," she explained as patiently as she could. "The mortgage has to be paid in full by the end of December or we'll lose the place, anyway. If Dennis can buy out the first mortgage we're dead in the water. Then there's the loss of revenue from cancellations; I'd planned on using that to pay bills. My house in Madison is sitting empty, and Chloe and Eric are leaving. And even though Dan has been generous enough to offer financial aid," she glanced at him, "I'm just sick and tired of the whole goddamned mess."

What else did she have to offer, besides the ugly stuff that Dennis said, that she was a disgrace to her uncle's memory, that she was a slut and sleeping with Dan—which everybody would believe if she let him help refinance the mortgage so that was completely out of the question, of course, but she would never ever be able to let Dan know why.

"I'm pulled in so many directions," Hannah admitted, angrily. "I'd hold onto the mineral rights if I could sell it as a resort, just to keep Ingold from mining here. Doesn't that make it better?"

Ginger had enough. She kissed Chloe on the cheek, gave Eric a hug, embraced Lily and announced that she was leaving.

"I'm going to get my bunions operated on, and I'll have to take it easy for a while. Got to get hopping on Helen Mickelson's musky mount, too, so it looks like you'll be cleaning those cottages by yourself, Hannah. I wish you luck."

Ginger let the screen door slam so it smacked, and Babe started barking.

Eric watched the Saloon over the weekend, while Chloe packed their things. Lily stayed in her cottage. Hannah tried to keep out of the way. She cleaned the cottages alone and in silence, skipping over some tasks and lamenting the loss of lighthearted gossip.

Monday morning Hannah watched Eric's van drive out onto Star Lake Road with deep regret. There was so much more she should have said: that she loved them both, that she appreciated their dedication to Star Lake and their spirit and the help they'd so generously given. But things had not improved since the confrontation Friday afternoon. The kids had barely spoken to her and there had been no long and tearful goodbyes, merely, "See you at Thanksgiving, Mom," from Chloe before the doors to the van slammed and they were off. Even Ratso went back to Madison to live with them, so she and Babe were alone, except for Lily, who retired to Vega again after saying goodbye.

"I'm just in the way," she said. "I should go, too."

At least five of the cottages were filled, so Hannah didn't feel completely bereft. There were requests to be attended to, a dog who loved her unconditionally (she was grateful for that), and now it was cool enough at night that she moved into the bedroom, giving up her fight against autumn.

Of course she had known this time would come, when the kids would depart and the resort would have to be sold. Hannah had, in fact, looked forward to it once upon a time. She had even been counting the weeks. Hell, even the days.

You grew to love it here, she warned herself, recalling Chloe's anguished argument.

Remarkably, Lily ventured out of Vega on Monday afternoon to lend a hand in the Saloon. "I've been thinking about what happened and I can fry hamburgers and serve beer," she told Hannah. "I may be an old gal and I'm not Ginger, but I'm not completely helpless, either."

It was the last week in August. Labor Day weekend was approaching. There had been no cancellations, and by Saturday night all the cottages would be filled. Hannah didn't want to think about the insanity she would be facing with or without her mother's assistance.

Nevertheless, Hannah worked like a whirling dervish, spinning between the kitchen and bar, waiting on fishermen, vacationers, attempting to pacify people who had come by boat expecting Eric's beer-battered walleye on Friday night. Lily tried her best but she lacked Ginger's enthusiasm as a bartender and couldn't play bar dice worth a damn. By two o'clock Saturday morning Hannah was dead on her feet.

"Last call," she announced shortly before shooing the remainder of the crowd from the Saloon. Her mother had been sent over to Vega at ten o'clock.

She climbed the stairs to her bedroom and hugged her faithful Babe. "Thank God that's over," she told the dog as she collapsed on the bed. "But we have to start cleaning cottages as soon as the sun comes up."

No one would know if she crawled between the sheets without washing her face, or even putting on pajamas.

"I don't have enough heads to put hats on," she said to Babe, and she missed Ginger's presence more than she could put into words.

You look like you've been rode hard and put away wet," Ginger said when she showed up on crutches unexpectedly, on Labor Day. "If you don't mind my saying it, that is."

Hannah rushed to greet her with a very warm hug of appreciation. She apologized for losing her temper and Ginger told her, "Georgie says you've got to be settled in your own mind about what you do with this place, Hannah. It's not up to any of the rest of us to be judging you for what you decide."

With Ginger back in charge and Lily helping, Hannah was free to attend the Labor Day protest. The clambake rally was organized to coordinate with Ingold's presentation of a new fire truck to the Village of Antler. She hoped her appearance would help her score a few points with Dan, who hadn't shown his face or called during the week of Ginger's absence.

It was a brilliant, sunny late-summer day. She drove to Forest Temple, where the group was gathering to ride into town on a converted school bus. Lynne was giving a tour of the teepee grounds to a man who looked familiar, but it took Hannah a moment to recognize Tyler Cole in that setting. Tall, lean and dark, standing next to Lynne in his khakis and green T-shirt they made an interesting couple.

To his credit, when he greeted her he didn't indicate that his friendship with Hannah was anything more than casual.

"Professor Cole has been showing me the map of the ore body that includes your land, Hannah," Lynne said.

"I asked him to join us this weekend," Dan's voice sounded firmly behind Hannah before she could express her dismay. "Professor Cole has developed a scheme that might help us determine who gave Ingold permission to prospect on your property."

It was crazy, that's what it was, to see Tyler here with her friends. And participating in one of their demonstrations! Hannah couldn't get over it: Dan and Tyler working together in a plot to put down the mine.

"Aren't you going to explain Professor Cole's scheme to me?"
Silence.

"It's not exactly lawful, Hannah," Tyler explained quietly. "The less you know, the better off you'll be in case something goes wrong."

"You'll find out soon enough," Dan said. "When we've got what we need, we'll tell you. Probably tomorrow night."

The Antler Volunteer Firemen had constructed a stage in the street in front of the Fire Department garage. Pennants fluttered and volunteer firemen mingled with the crowd in full fire regalia, their yellow rubber coats and glistening black helmets giving them an official, other-worldly look. Even Dennis Windsor was there in a fireman's outfit, Hannah noted with amusement. He looked rather silly in his fire hat. She could not imagine him climbing a ladder to a burning roof.

After the high school band played several marches, the assembled crowd was treated to the opening of the garage door. The brand new fire truck stood there, red, hot, and sparkling. Sparkling like a diamond in a goat's ass, Hannah could imagine Ginger remarking dryly, and she wished Tyler were near so she could tell him. Where was he, anyway?

Sirens blared. Lights flashed. The band played and the truck emerged from the garage with its siren screaming and all its fancy paraphernalia on display.

Celestial Summer kept a low profile during these festivities. They hid their banners and kept their protest under wraps. But as soon as Mayor Gus Schultz stood on the podium to make his speech of acceptance on behalf of the Antler Volunteer Firemen, an anti-mine activist from Madison who had designed a sandwich board that looked like a warty purple clam shell, sashayed beneath a multi-colored wig, proclaiming himself to be the Purple Warty Back "Clamentine."

Lynne, again costumed in her Grim Reaper outfit, was sweeping through the crowd, distributing dyed-purple clamshells.

One of the firemen, a former miner who'd testified at the master's hearing, approached Hannah and said, ominously, "It's not a good idea to piss off your local volunteer fire department. What if you need us out there one of these days?"

Suddenly the gathering seemed to have swollen to at least double in size, and although Hannah had no idea where they had come from, one faction took control of the celebration and began leading the way to the mine site, singing loudly,

"Come to Star Lake, for our clambake,
See where Ingold wants its mine,
Watch the fish die,
Hear the earth cry,
Meet our Darling Clamentine . . ."

This caused the rest of the festivities to be knocked off balance. The media went where the action was, away from the brand new fire truck presentation that Ingold had engineered.

At the mine site, a place now so ravaged in its recent transformation that it took Hannah's breath away to be this close, the group crowded around the gate. Hannah stood back from the chain-link fence. For a change, she didn't wish to get in front of the television cameras.

A double-wide trailer had been set up as a construction office, and a number of hulking bulldozers, scrapers, and graders stood nearby. The land cleared of trees and other flora looked painfully raw, Hannah thought; silt fences had been constructed around the general area where soil was removed and an earthen berm was partially completed. Thousands of hay bales littered the site, many pressed up against the dirt, to help prevent erosion.

"That's where they're going to pour foundations for the water treatment plant," Leslie said, pointing to an area behind the office where a covey of end-loaders were parked. "And over there's where the settling pond is going to be."

"It's all so . . . so big," Hannah stated, awed to see the massive devastation up close. "I had no idea . . ."

"Some guy told my mom that it was only going to take up the same space that a shopping mall would."

"Makes about as much sense as a shopping mall, out here in the middle of the forest," Hannah added, dryly.

Ginger and Lily had driven over to watch the protest. Lily fluttered with excitement and said this would be something to tell her friends—they'd never believe she took part in a demonstration!

"I could see Hal participating in something like this," she told Hannah. "He was rebellious in high school, too. I wasn't surprised when he took off. Grandpa Larkin was hard on his boys."

Victor climbed over the ten-foot-high chain-link fence and ran around the silent, heavy machinery tapping each bulldozer and dump truck with the sacred eagle feather staff he had brought to the master hearing. He proclaimed the power of the trucks to be subdued and vanquished. A symbolic victory.

"Fred, my husband, wasn't at all like Hal," Lily told Ginger. She was on a kick now, and there would be no shutting her up.

"Can this wait?" Hannah asked, "I want to watch what's going on."

"Hannah worshipped her Grandpa Larkin," Lily explained to Ginger, "thought the world of him, and he felt the same about her. But the truth is, Grandpa Larkin had expectations for Hal that the boy wasn't able to live up to."

"Parents tend to do that," Hannah said flatly, barely able to hide the sarcasm in her voice.

"If it hadn't been for the war, and for Grandpa Larkin's work with the draft board . . ."

"What then?" Ginger wanted to know.

"Grandpa was chairman of the county draft board during the second world war," Hannah told her. That was hardly news.

"Grandpa Larkin said he couldn't order other men's sons to war when his own son was such a coward," Lily said. "He was so ashamed that Hal was a conscientious objector. Mortified, really."

Hannah leaned against the chain-link fence. She felt light-headed and slightly breathless.

"It caused a lot of hurt and heartbreak," Lily was saying.

"Hal was a C. O.?" Hannah said, amazed. It went a long way to explain his estrangement, his need for solitude. His gentle nature that everyone spoke of should have been a clue. He probably did alternative service of some kind before coming here to Star Lake. Dan already knew!

"Hannah," a well-wisher said, "how's it going?"

Joe Mickelson stood beside her. "Kerry told me this would be good, and he was right. It'll add some color. Great visuals."

"Hey, Joe!" Hannah smiled, "Color for what?"

"It's Mine Games! We got funding, Hannah. Anonymous donor. Big bucks! Enough to go ahead. The only thing is, I've got a lot of stuff on my plate right now so you're going to have to be involved Big Time. You'll get paid for it, though. It's a pretty nice grant. I want to talk with you about it later on. Got a check here for you to cover the first part of your work. Should be enough to keep you busy."

Hannah was astounded. So many secrets. Had Ginger been able to squeeze Mine Games money out of George Windsor? She wouldn't put it past her. Maybe he had a secret cache socked away from his son's prying eyes.

It was more than funding for a documentary, though. It was a ploy to keep her involved, she realized.

Beyond the chain-link fence, Victor still ran through clusters of enormous backhoes and earth movers with the eagle feather staff. And now Lynne wandered, wraith-like, over the ravaged landscape. She murmured a death chant, her eyes closed and her skin chalk-white. The cameras ate it up.

Ingold had erected a flagpole on top of a small mountain of rocks and boulders, where an American flag snapped and billowed in the breeze. Hannah had been talking with Joe, so she hadn't seen Leslie shimmy up the flagpole and release the flag from its perch. It dropped downward heavily, where it was caught at the base by Victor and Lynne.

Just at that moment, Sheriff Cooper and his men opened the gate with the assistance of Axel Graves. Lynne, Leslie, and Victor scurried away from the authorities.

"Hannah, catch," Lynne said, appearing suddenly opposite her on the mine-side of the fence. The flag, folded into a clumsy bundle, was thrown over the top of the fence and Hannah reached for it without thinking.

"What do you want me to do with this," she started to say, but heard, instead, "You are under arrest."

"I didn't do anything!" Hannah protested.

The flag was taken from her grasp and her hands were roughly pulled behind her back where she felt the cold snap of handcuffs.

"Dan . . . ?" Hannah pleaded, seeing him approach her with a concerned glance as she was led away to a squad car.

"Take it easy," he whispered softly in her ear and he pressed what felt like cash inside one hand.

"For bail."

It was all so humiliating, and her mother was watching!

She needed to be there, back at the mine, to know what Tyler was going to do, to see what he and Dan had planned! It was her land that was in jeopardy, after all, or was this part of the act? Lynne's flag-toss? What a rotten gimmick, Hannah decided. She felt like those tourists in Rome or Paris who have a gypsy baby thrown at them and they reach for it while pickpockets steal their purse. If somebody throws you a folded-up flag, of course you're not going to let it fall on the ground.

The sheriff's deputy took her up to Cedar Springs in the back of his squad car where she immediately threw up due to fear or carsickness, whatever. Then, at the county jail, despite her remonstrance of innocence, she was charged with theft. She was placed in a holding cell and told she could not be officially charged and would not be able to post bail until the next morning since today was a holiday.

Hannah couldn't get over the irony. Despite her intention to remain apart from any acts of civil disobedience against the mine, she had been roped into becoming its spokesperson. Now, even worse, she had been duped by Ginger, probably, and Dan and Lynne, and Tyler (of all people!) into this arrest. At least her daughter and Eric weren't there to see this happen. But her mother was!

Wait until the gals heard, down in Tampa.

And Joe Mickelson had captured it all on camera.

I believe in the laws of cause and effect, and that each soul must work out its own destiny; that guardian angels of unseen beings in a more advanced state of existence endeavor to aid and help us through this world. . . . Thoughts are things, full of electric force, and they go forth and produce their own kind.

Ella Wheeler Wilcox

17
Mine Games in Progress

September blazed with a glory that Hannah was not prepared for. It slipped in with a whisper on the fading green shoulders of summer. Almost imperceptibly at first, then more boldly, the leaves of the aspen and the birch began to burnish into coins of brilliant gold. Soon the orange and red of the maples, the beech and the oaks, began to flame. Yellow and scarlet and bronze fanned the splendor against the deep green backdrop of pine and cedar.

Visitors still came to Star Lake for a week of fishing, but they also came to witness the changing seasons. The crazy bedlam of summer folded into the patchwork hues of autumn.

On Labor Day, while Ingold officials wrung their hands over the onslaught of demonstrators and busied themselves with Hannah's arrest, Tyler covertly explored the files at Ingold's Antler headquarters. Later, he appeared at Dan Kerry's home with a copy of an agreement that appeared to authorize Ingold to prospect for copper ore on Hal Larkin's land.

The paper was signed by Hal.

"Dated the day he died," Hannah noted when it was shown to her the next morning. Ginger had driven to Cedar Springs with Lily to pick up Hannah and confessed that her removal had been cooked up "because you'd be the first one they'd suspect if Ingold found out somebody rifled their files."

"Some alibi," she snapped at Ginger.

Hannah had barely slept, smelled awful, needed fresh clothes and a shower, and was having a really bad hair day.

Tyler was still at Dan's. That did not thrill her, either.

"I don't believe we've met," Lily said, extending her hand.

"Professor Cole, Mrs. Larkin," Lynne explained to him. "This is Hannah's mother."

And this is a goddamned soap opera, Hannah decided, dropping into the nearest chair. She pretended not to see The Willowy Lynne brush her blond hair back with one long slender hand and slide the other beneath Tyler's arm. They were seated on the sofa and he wore a goofy smile that Hannah did not recognize—perhaps because she'd never spent an *ethereal* night with him in a teepee.

Dan said, "This is not Hal Larkin's signature."

"If he was weak, his handwriting would've been different," Hannah argued. She felt ornery and contentious and just plain cross.

"Sick or not sick," Dan explained patiently, "he always signed his name, 'Harold A. Larkin,' not 'Hal.'"

"Yes he did," Lily offered, timidly.

Ginger nodded. "Liquor license, checking account, credit cards, drivers license, even his fishing license, everything was in 'Harold A.' He never would've signed 'Hal.' Sick or not, that just wasn't like him."

"Okay," Hannah conceded. "So, who forged it?"

"One guess," Dan said.

"Denny Windsor," Ginger cracked smartly, before Hannah could take a breath.

"That way Denny could take the credit for getting something Ingold couldn't get on their own," Lynne offered, helpfully. "It makes sense, doesn't it, Hannah?"

This was obviously being reviewed, step-by-step, as if she were feebleminded.

Hannah described the label, "Harold A. Larkin," written on the file that held her uncle's will, and the other papers she had reviewed during the settling of his estate.

"Wouldn't Dennis have realized that Hal didn't sign his name that way?"

"He forged it before he looked at the will," Dan argued.

"Or he forged it before Hal was dead," Ginger added.

"Or he was careless," Lynne suggested.

"I thought you told me you were with him when he died," Hannah accused Ginger. "When you called me in the first place, you said Hal told you to call."

"That was when he came back from his doctor's appointment. A couple weeks before. 'Get ahold of Hannah in case anything happens,' he said, and I did, just like he asked."

"It might bear some looking into," Dan offered, interrupting, "if we could find out where Denny was when Hal died."

"You're not suggesting that Dennis killed him, are you?"

"I don't think he would go that far," Dan assured Hannah.

"Wouldn't have the heart for it," Ginger said. "Denny doesn't have shit for brains, but he's not a murderer."

Tyler was quiet, and Hannah managed to avoid meeting his gaze whenever she felt it trained on her, which it was when he wasn't dreamily smiling down at Lynne. If this piece of evidence turned out to mean something important, she would be disgustingly indebted to him. She already was, in fact, for the aerial view of her land indicating the vein of ore. In addition, there was his crucial testimony on the Purple Warty Back clam that helped stop the mine's progress, at least temporarily.

Dan and Celestial Summer were ready to charge Dennis Windsor with forgery and the shooting incident and other sabotage, but Hannah stubbornly refused to make a formal accusation. She didn't feel there was enough proof to accuse him of anything substantial, she said.

Besides, her hearing for the clambake arrest was set for early October, a month from now. Those charges weren't a big concern for Celestial Summer, even though they readily admitted responsibility for her "crime." Nevertheless, she would certainly have to pay a fine, and she could still be sentenced. Dennis would seek considerable retribution if she began an action against him now. One night behind bars had already been one night too many and, just in case he *was* involved, she didn't want to incite more vandalism to her property or threats on her life all over again.

"I have to think about this," she pleaded.

They were pushing her too hard. Everything, everyone was.

"She needs a good night's sleep," Lily apologized to the gathering. "My little gal's always cranky when she hasn't had enough rest."

This Mine Games project was your idea. We pushed ahead, got the funding and now it's your baby," Joe informed her. He'd sent her entire master's hearing footage to *Frontline* where they had an unexpected vacant slot available in mid-December. So they'd be fighting the clock and the calendar together to meet a demanding deadline.

Sunday she would drive to Minneapolis, put Lily on a plane back to Tampa then visit Babbit, Minnesota, where, she'd been told, a recently closed taconite mine left behind large waste rock piles with high concentrations of sulfides. Rain turned the sulfides into sulfuric acid and poisonous heavy metals leached out, polluting the Kawishiwi River that flowed through the Boundary Waters Canoe Area, one of the largest wilderness areas in the country. Hannah's contacts had before and after footage of the mine as well as interviews with frustrated sportsmen.

Ingold's plans were probably a drop in the bucket compared with wilderness mining further west. But whether it was for gold or copper or taconite, every scenario Hannah investigated seemed to follow the same depressing format: the mining company formed a subsidiary, bought up a bunch of land for a song, pushed the concept of a boom in the local (usually ailing) economy, the environment be damned. They promised to hire local people but brought along many of their own experienced miners. The community flourished for a few years until the mine was abandoned and the subsidiary went bankrupt. Then everything else went bust.

She planned to bookend Mine Games with examples of the Star Lake model—scenes of the mine site before any land had been cleared, master's hearing testimony pro and con, and, thanks to Eric, videotaped demonstrations for and against the mine. In her summation she wanted a neutral mining expert to review options such as recycling, rather than a dependence on virgin metals, or ideas for substituting fiber optics for copper wire—alternatives that would cause less environmental damage. Closing with something hopeful would help keep the program from being seen as mere liberal propaganda.

Ginger agreed to stay at Star Lake and watch over the place while Hannah was traveling. Their day-to-day routine was diminished, anyway. Reservations had thinned and most of the summer people had gone back home.

"Pretty quiet in town now," Ginger complained. "Not much going on. I've had those rooms above the Wampum Shoppe for about ten years, and nothing gets past me."

Hannah would move some of her things over to Aldebaran. The cottage was vacant for the rest of the season, and she looked forward to using the fireplace. It was a quiet place to write, and her work wouldn't be disturbed. Besides, staying there provided a nice synchrony with her arrival at Star Lake last spring.

During the week Hannah was in Minnesota, the DNR completed its Supplementary Environmental Impact Statement. Tyler's recommendation to use the Purple Warty Back clam for the toxicity tests was ignored, and another species of clam, one that was more tolerant of environmental changes, was substituted in the study, instead.

Quietly, the SEIS was accepted. And almost as quietly, before anyone really realized it, Ingold's mine was back in business—little more than thirty days after Celestial Summer's injunction had been filed.

Her arrival home was accompanied by the grumble of bulldozers and diesel fumes drifting nauseatingly across Star Lake on the crisp edge of a frosty autumn breeze. Almost at once, reporters called for Hannah's impression of the situation. "It seemed like a rather slipshod and lopsided study to me," she told the press after a quick check with Dan for particulars. When TV interviews aired—including one on Wisconsin Public Television—some incorporated footage of Hannah's Labor Day arrest. If Chloe and Eric saw the footage, they did not call Hannah to comment.

Hannah carried her computer and printer over to Aldebaran one morning in mid-September, wincing at the reverberation from dump trucks and earth-moving vehicles across the lake. Construction was proceeding at full steam. Sounds carried so clearly across the water, she could even hear people yelling amid the clamor.

There wouldn't be a telephone in Aldebaran, but that was fine with her. Last night, still in Polaris, she had received a troubling call around midnight. The woman's voice whispered nervously: "I thought you ought to know, my husband was with Denny Windsor and Gus Schultz and all of them other guys earlier. They're trying to scrape enough together to buy you out."

It was the timid clerk from the IGA, married to the butcher. Hannah recognized her voice. Dan's earlier warning, about Denny taking her over, was now perilously real.

Perhaps it was time to take action, Hannah considered. *I'll have your ass out of there before you can kiss it goodbye.* She placed the computer on a table she'd arranged as a workspace in the other Aldebaran bedroom, the one with the too-soft bed. Her hearing was two weeks away.

There was a new seat in the bent twig rocking chair on Aldebaran's porch, thanks to Eric's handiwork. She ran her hand over the smooth twigs and recalled her first morning in that cottage. Nervous about appearing in court, she had sat in that chair and watched the sun rise over Star Lake. There was no indication, then, of the assortment of worries that lay ahead. "I'm more like you than I realized, Uncle Hal," Hannah mused. "If my father tried to pick a fight with me right now, I'd probably turn my back and walk away. I don't blame you for leaving town."

Babe nudged her with a tennis ball. Together they went out on the pier where Hannah idly tossed the ball in the water for Babe to retrieve. The dog couldn't seem to get enough of the game. No matter how far Hannah threw the soggy thing, Babe valiantly dogpaddled and brought it back to present to her on the pier, alert, begging for more. Hannah was careful not to toss it toward the loons, who dove and swam nearby. The chicks were almost indistinguishable from their parents, and they would all be migrating soon.

She wished she could migrate, too. Every annoying burst from Ingold's heavy machinery was a warning that she must not let down her guard. *I'll have your ass out of there before you can kiss it goodbye.* That was after she'd allowed Dennis to fondle her breasts, of course. And kiss her, too. Stupid. Stupid!

"Ginger, do you like to gamble?" Hannah asked later that afternoon. Her suitcase was packed and she was restless. Ginger sat on the glider enjoying a summer-like warmth on the porch of the Saloon that was a gift, this time of the year.

"I been throwing bar dice since I was three years old, Honey, if that's what you're talking about," Ginger replied.

"No, I mean like slot machines. That realtor in Minocqua has some clients looking for a place to open an Indian Casino.

"Here?"

"It's just an idea. They manage bingo halls and gambling casinos for tribes all over the state," Hannah explained, half-heartedly. "They estimate they can fit at least fifty slot machines in the bar."

The squeak issuing from the glider picked up its pace as Ginger pushed it back and forth faster and faster with the toe of a new orthopedic shoe.

"Gambling's a very competitive business," Hannah said firmly, trying to ignore Ginger's irritation. She pulled up a chair.

"Tell me something I don't already know," Ginger replied.

"A casino wouldn't be affected by the mine. That's the only reason I'd even consider it."

That, and Dennis Windsor's underhanded treachery, Hannah noted. Ginger seemed to read her thoughts.

"You want something to bet on, here's something for you: Until he drew his final breath, Hal Larkin never gave up the fight to save this land that he loved so much. Seems to me, he must be getting mighty fidgety up there in Heaven, looking down at his niece. Hell, you're holding *all* the cards we got to play right now, and that's not fair to him or the rest of us!"

"I'm working on it," Hannah mumbled, getting up to leave.

"I guess you don't realize what you got here," Ginger said, quickly. "It might look on the map like you're sitting on copper ore, but what you're really sitting on is a gold mine, that's what I think, and I don't know why you're so blind to it. Most likely because it's not gold you can dig up and spend, or take from somebody else and pocket. Or gamble away on," she added sarcastically.

"It's gold like you see on the birches out there. In summer all the thick green kind of sops up the light but now those changing colors glow and melt together so you can't explain them."

Hannah saw the gold. In this hour of late afternoon the sun was at just the perfect angle to warm the brilliant slash of red maples behind Aldaberan. Black-eyed Susans nodded drowsily along the shoulder of Star Lake Road and clouds of soft blue asters reflected the cerulean sky.

"You sign any papers for a casino, and I'll go on strike, Hannah Swann, this very minute," Ginger scolded. "Seems to me we went over this before. I'd rather the bank close us up tighter than a tick on a dog's belly, and if I quit you'll have to hire some stranger to tend bar or do it yourself. Had a taste of that already, and you didn't take to it much."

Ginger had never spoken to Hannah so roughly. In fact, Hannah had never seen her so distraught.

"It's all just speculation." Standing with her hand on the screen door, Hannah spoke calmly. She wanted to talk over last night's furtive phone call with Dan before telling anybody else about Dennis Windsor's latest scheme.

"Well, you keep that 'speculation' to yourself," Ginger said, rocking even faster. "I don't want to hear about gambling or any other cockeyed crappola. You glue yourself to your computer and get that television show cranked out."

Hannah interrupted, "Who's going to want to fish on Star Lake next June with that racket in the background. There are plenty of other quiet resorts within a thirty-mile radius! And later on, when they start blasting everything all to hell, we'll be reminded every hour of every day of the mess they're making, a mess that might last far longer than our lifetimes. I'm seeing the same thing everywhere I go."

She had got the argument out of her system now, and Ginger's eyes held disappointment instead of indignation.

"I guess I gave you credit for having more gumption," Ginger said, bitterly. "Maybe Hal did, too."

"Give me a break," Hannah pleaded, but Ginger was on a roll.

"Can't turn on the stupid television set but there she is, one channel after another. Can't look at the news without seeing Hannah Swann going blah blah blah, so wrapped up in herself, all goody-goody and self-righteous about the way the mine is pushing everybody around, carrying on at the expense of our wonderful northwoods. And now she tells me she can't see the pony in the pile of horse shit. Ready to give up and let them win over there just because it looks like she lost the first round. "Excuse me, Honey, but you've got your head so far up your ass we're going to have to get you a glass bellybutton to let you see where you're going."

Hannah couldn't believe Ginger's attitude. The two women stared at one another for a long, awkward moment.

"A glass bellybutton?" Hannah sputtered, unable to contain a wild burst of hilarity.

The glider came to a halt and the squeaking ceased.

Ginger put a hand over her mouth to stifle her reaction, but she couldn't help breaking into a laugh.

"I do get carried away, don't I? Surprised you didn't tell me to 'shut up' again like you did when Lily was here."

"Oh, Ginger," Hannah wiped tears from the corners of her eyes, "you are a prize."

She joined Ginger on the glider and they began to rock back and forth together, watching the colors fade as the light began to dim.

"Now, tell me," Ginger patted her leg. "Have you done anything at all about Denny's signature on those prospecting papers? All the shenanigans we went through to grab that stuff from Ingold's files with your Madison boyfriend and getting you sent off to jail, seems a shame not to contact the authorities. Or even call Denny into question. What are you waiting for?"

"Just a minute," Hannah interjected, "in the first place, Professor Cole is *not* my boyfriend. And secondly, we don't have any real proof that Hal's signature was counterfeit."

"All right, let's make us a deal," Ginger squeezed Hannah's arm. "I won't tell you what to do with your choice in men or this property. But when you get back from Colorado, I want you to promise that Denny gets taken to the cleaners."

Hannah sighed. "I know. It's time. I'll see what I can do." She was glad of the truce between them.

"And don't you worry, I'll stay out here at the lake and take care of visitors, tend bar like always, until you get your TV business together."

"That's a deal."

"But I can't help you clean the cottages," Ginger cautioned. "Nothing personal, just too hard on my feet right now to move around like that. The doctor says I got to take it easy.

It was late Saturday morning when Hannah arrived back from Denver. She had driven from the regional airport outside Wausau in drizzling rain, and the resort had undergone a dismal transformation during her absence. There was a woebegone aura about it now. The brilliant color had faded from the landscape and many birch and poplar already divulged haggard limbs. The old buildings looked ramshackled and worthless in the dreary light.

Ginger was in the Saloon tallying up accounts and checking out departing guests. Hannah grabbed a needed cup of coffee and began cleaning cottages. The job took most of the rest of the day, but the menial tasks gave her an opportunity to gather her thoughts. By seven o'clock she wanted nothing more than a hot bath before falling into bed.

Three cottages would be vacant the next week, including Aldebaran, and Ginger had already checked in the rest. Ginger told her that Dan had called and wanted to see her as soon as possible. So she should get her butt over there right away.

"Did he put it like that?" Hannah asked, irritated.

"Not exactly," Ginger admitted with a grin.

"Does it have to be tonight? I'm exhausted . . ."

"Honey, if I was you and a guy as good looking as Dan wanted me to come over to his place I'd drop everything to get there. Including my drawers, if you'll forgive my saying so."

"I won't," Hannah didn't even have the energy to laugh, "drop my drawers, or forgive you."

She arrived at Dan's place with Babe, her hair still wet.

"You look beat," he said as he took her jacket. "Ginger said you were hungry and tired."

He was wearing that same old flannel shirt she loved and faded jeans, spending a lazy Saturday night at home. Apparently alone.

But Hannah's guard was up. Maybe Ginger blabbed about the casino. She could be such a busybody.

"How's the documentary coming along?" Dan asked then with what seemed like real interest, and that threw her off. "Ginger says PBS is going to air it in December."

A fire crackled in the fireplace.

"I'm sending some remarkable footage back to Madison," she volunteered, hesitantly. No sense going into detail, that wasn't why she had been summoned.

The fire felt wonderful. She could feel it beginning to ease her agitation, and yawned. If there was still enough dry wood piled in Aldebaran, she'd build a fire there when she got back. The sound of rain and the warmth of a crackling fire never failed to soothe her. As it had months before in this very place, she recalled with embarrassment.

"My contacts in Denver were really helpful," she called out to Dan in the kitchen. "They said to be sure to tell you hello."

Whenever she mentioned Star Lake she was asked if she knew Dan Kerry. Everyone seemed impressed when she said he was a personal friend. Who knew what they thought after that, but his name opened doors and it wasn't exaggerating to say he was a friend. More or less. Less than more, ah, yes. She'd half-expected to find Lynne here, too.

"What's this all about," she asked as he handed her a bowl of steaming chili on a tray. No sense wasting time, let's get right to the point.

"In a minute," he said, and returned to the kitchen for a bowl of his own.

Dan proved to be as adept at making chili as he was at frying walleye, and while they ate in front of the fire she found herself responding to his questions regarding Mine Games. He made a few suggestions of his own and expressed satisfaction with the direction in which she was headed.

She set the almost-empty chili bowl on the floor for Babe, who licked it greedily and pushed the bowl across the floor with her nose, relishing every last spicy smear.

Hannah ran her fingers through her still-damp hair. She hoped she didn't look as sleepy as she felt.

"What' are you doing about the bank's foreclosure?"

"I guess I could always sell my house, but I hate to give up that connection with Madison. I think one of the reasons I've been able to survive up here is the knowledge that I have that to retreat to, when I need it."

"Still don't want any help from me, I suppose."

Hannah shook her head. "Remember when we found the core samples with Leslie, and you told me Dennis could take over my mortgage?"

"I wasn't far off, was I," Dan said.

256

So that was it, he had called her over here to tell her she was doomed.

"Do you know something I don't?" she asked, choosing to sit cross-legged in front of the fire.

"Tell me what *you've* heard," he replied.

"Well, once he said 'I'll have your ass out of there before you can kiss it goodbye.'" Her face felt hot, but he might think it was from the fire. "And just before I left for Summitville I had a call from the clerk at the IGA."

Hannah coaxed Babe to lay next to her. She told Dan about the hasty message and her concern that Dennis might succeed.

"Why don't you confront him?"

"Does he have the money to do it?" she asked.

"Close," Dan said. "It's still up in the air."

"Who told you?"

"Sources," he said simply.

"I don't know what I can do with Dennis," Hannah replied. "The last time I met with him, when he said that other stuff . . . something happened. It wasn't pleasant."

"I know that, too."

"How could you?"

"Somebody who lives in Antler keeps her window open. It's a *very* small town."

Ginger again. But I'll bet you don't know Dennis assumes we're sleeping together, Hannah thought. If you did, you'd understand that if I accepted your help, Dennis would claim I was "putting out" for profit. Or some dumb thing.

"Since then you've gained an advantage. You have new information," Dan suggested.

"The prospecting papers," Hannah said. "Okay, I'm not thick-headed. You think I should blackmail Dennis into dropping his plans to buy me out."

Dan mused, "That's a possibility."

"Next Tuesday I have my hearing on the clambake charge . . ."

"It doesn't have to be blackmail," Dan reasoned. "You can keep

257

this legal and above board. But it wouldn't hurt to call the District Attorney and send a complaint to the State Bar Association. Raise some questions. Let them take it from there. It's the only ammunition you have, at the moment. Hell, it's the only ammunition *we* have, and you're sure taking your own sweet time."

Dan left to get more wood for the fire.

Hannah knew he was right. But she barely had time to make plane reservations and arrange the details of her travels.

"Chicken shit," she told herself. "You're just plain scared. Get over it."

Babe snuggled closer, snoring comfortably. Hannah liked the woodsy dog-smell. The measured sound of Babe's muffled snores was oddly reassuring. And soporific. She yawned again.

Dan still hadn't returned, so Hannah curled up next to Babe, just for a moment. She placed her head on the dog's glossy fur feeling Babe's chest rise and fall, rise and fall, with each snuffly breath.

When she awoke, the room was in darkness except for glowing embers that twinkled red and snapped like sparkling stars. Babe was still curled in front of her and Hannah's arm was thrown over the sleeping dog. But Hannah was lying on a thick, soft sheepskin with a pillow beneath her head, and she was covered with a heavy quilt.

It took her a moment to realize where she was. Then, when she knew, she was so tired that she didn't even care.

She stretched, and turned over.

Dan was lying beside her, his right arm under her pillow.

"Hannah, don't leave me," he whispered softly and brushed his hand across her cheek. Then he pulled her closer.

The cozy arrangement, the length of her body pressed against his warmth, felt natural and right and good. She rested her head on his chest, beneath his chin. To be held this way, against the soft flannel of his old plaid shirt, it felt so *safe*.

Outside cold rain still drizzled from the eaves.

She hoped she would be able to remember what he had said to

258

her, in the morning. She had a feeling if she were awake it might be important.

For now, though, she was relaxed, comfortable.

Babe stirred and sighed a deep, long, contented dog-sigh.

It could wait, Hannah decided.

And again, she fell asleep.

18
October
Finishing Touches

Hannah stretched. No, she wasn't back at the lodge, so the events of last night must not have been a dream. When was the last time she woke with a smile on her face like this? Or with such an aching back?

"I've got to go," Dan said.

He stood above her in a thin shaft of light from the kitchen, showered, shaved, and wearing a denim jacket. It was still pitch dark outside.

"Got a date over on Plum Lake. No need for you to get up, though. In fact, use my bed if the floor's getting too hard."

Hannah rose to a sitting position and yawned.

He leaned over to sweep the hair back from her eyes, then tenderly cupped her face to kiss her forehead.

"Poor Hannah," he murmured, "you're knocking yourself out. So much to do, and running as fast as you can."

"Is it morning?" she asked, hesitantly.

Did her breath smell awful, she wondered, and covered her mouth.

"Remember, there's more to life than increasing its speed," Dan said tenderly.

"Somebody said that," Hannah's mind was sluggish, still asleep.

"Mahatma Gandhi. Better read your own T-shirt," Dan grinned.

"Oh, right. Gandhi. Uh . . . where's Babe?"

God, what a dumb thing to say. She really knew how to break a mood. *Did you really lie here beside me, beneath this quilt, in front of the fire,* she wanted to know, *Did you say something in the middle of the night that I wanted to remember?* Even more than that, she wanted to hold on to this moment of intimacy. Instead, "Where's Babe?" she said, looking around as if the dog were the single most important matter on her mind.

"Babe's outside," he told her, rising to his feet. "I'll let her back in before I go. Can I get you something?"

He headed toward the kitchen. No more kisses, no "See you later," or even, "It's been fun."

"I could use a toothbrush," Hannah said truthfully.

"There's a new one in the bathroom. And I put out clean towels. Breakfast's ready."

She felt she ought to apologize, but it surely had not been her intention to spend the night, and if it had she wouldn't have chosen to sleep on the floor. Except that—well, what *had* he said? *Hannah, believe me?* No, that wasn't it, but she could still feel the warmth of him beneath her cheek, and hear the steady, comforting, beat of his heart.

Hannah rubbed her eyes.

Dan disappeared into the kitchen so it was safe to smile again.

Babe rushed in smelling of fresh air and autumn leaves. The dog wagged her tail hard and wiggled, prodded Hannah with a cold, wet nose and placed a half-chewed bone at her side.

"Bye," Dan called then, and the back door closed.

So, he wasn't ready to acknowledge what happened last night. Well, that was all right, they didn't need to talk about it but she certainly would be thinking about it for the rest of the day at least and maybe for another month or two.

She and Babe watched the tail lights of the boat trailer behind the Blazer disappear in the woods. The sky was bleached and clear in the east; soon it would be deepen into the rich turquoise of autumn.

261

Sunday morning. What a way for the day to begin.

What would she say to Ginger?

An omelet, bacon, and toast were waiting in the kitchen. Hannah was amazingly hungry. She ate quickly, because Dan's absence gave her an opportunity. It wasn't snooping, exactly, but an excellent and unexpected chance to learn more about this man, who, overnight, had become a lot more interesting.

There were no photographs of Lynne, not even in his bedroom as she had secretly feared. On his nightstand was a copy of *The Atlantic.* She had expected *Field & Stream.* The flannel shirt hung from the doorknob of his closet and she buried her face in it to inhale the familiar scent of him. It was so very strange, she marveled, these feelings awakening that she had thought would lie dormant forever with the changes in her life, her Change-of-Life. Someone she could not even admit to anyone that she cared about, actually cared about her! *Hannah, don't leave me.* That was it! He wanted to hold her, wanted her to stay, not leave, and whether what he'd said meant don't leave him last night or tomorrow it didn't matter, he said it. She was sure he said it, and she pressed the shirt to her face and fell backward onto his bed. He had said to use his bed.

She lay there a while, staring at the ceiling, then over at the windows and the pines until they became more defined in the sunrise.

How often had Lynne awakened in this house, Hannah wondered. How would it be, to watch the seasons change in harmony with the reflections on the lake. To have a place so private, so quiet. So quiet she could fall asleep again.

Ginger rushed from the back door of Polaris as soon as Hannah's car rolled to a stop.

"I thought for sure you'd be back before I closed down last night. You fall asleep?"

"As a matter of fact, I did," Hannah replied briskly.

"Aw, hell, I suppose you did," Ginger said, disappointed. "When it got to be midnight and you still weren't back yet I thought maybe you'd been sidetracked so I had Victor check and see if your car was still at Dan's." She adjusted the waistband of a new pair of jeans. "Did he fix you breakfast like a gentleman or did he go fishing?"

"He went fishing," Hannah said. "But he fixed breakfast anyway."

She flashed Ginger an enigmatic smile, then headed down the path to Aldebaran.

"I've got some letters to write," she explained, over her shoulder.

"They better be about Denny's dirty tricks," Ginger called after her. "I'll take and mail them for you on my way through town. Packers aren't playing 'til tomorrow night so I'm closing this afternoon and going out to Northern Lights. Won't open the bar until three. Getting cantankerous in my old age."

Sunday morning, Hannah's special time of the week. But today, instead of writing poetry, she composed lengthy letters to the District Attorney of Lakeland County and the State Bar Association, stating her concerns about illegal trespass on her property, Dennis Windsor's duplicity, and suspicions regarding the signature attached to Ingold's prospecting papers. "I would prefer that my inquiry be kept anonymous, if possible," she added, and could imagine Dennis's sneer if he, too, knew where she had spent the night.

No, she hadn't "got it on" with Dan, although Hannah would have given anything to relive that playful moment when he kissed her forehead and she stupidly asked about Babe. More than once Hannah found herself looking out over the lake at crisp waves that scuttered across in the direction of Sundog and orange leaves that drifted down to float in matted rafts. Autumn made her melancholy, anyway. She had seen flying wedges of geese and ducks overhead since Labor Day.

Hannah paced the bedroom in Aldebaran where her computer sat on the wobbly table. It was not easy to work one's self into a mood of righteous indignation when you felt weak and soft and pliable, drowsy and relaxed. It was not easy to put aside the comfort she felt, still, surrounded by Dan's embrace.

After Ginger left with the letters, Hannah worried about mailing them before she'd had time to digest what she had so hastily written. But if she waited any longer, she might not feel so bold.

Hannah went for a walk.

Most of the leaves had fallen from the birch and maple, so the landscape of the woods was not dark and foreboding as it had been with the abundance of summer foliage. Shadowy hollows were revealed. Her depth of focus had to adjust to the change. Babe bounded on ahead, ignoring what remained of the trail. The rock on the raised mound seemed much closer, and she sat there to survey the autumn forest with its lack of vegetation. Babe joined her, placed her head on Hannah's lap and closed her eyes.

From the rock, Hannah could see the cluster of core-sample cylinders, no longer concealed by underbrush. She was still a little uneasy over sending the letters off as quickly as she had. The illegality of Dennis's actions was clear in her mind, but she lacked real proof.

Hannah found Ginger sitting next to George's bed, and the frail little man looked even smaller than before. A stroke suffered while she was in Colorado had left him nearly helpless, but Ginger explained that he was able to hear.

"I brought you some bittersweet," Hannah said. She placed the bright orange berried vines on top of his night stand, next to a urinal. She spoke clearly and probably more loudly than necessary. He'd told her to not to yell, at her first visit, and she wondered if his hearing was still as acute.

"I'm sorry I haven't been able to visit you more often," she explained.

There was no indication in his gaze that he recognized who she was.

"Are you sure he can hear me?" she asked Ginger. "Do you think he knows who I am?"

"Here, hold his hand," Ginger placed George's knobby little hand in Hannah's. "He'll give you one squeeze for yes and two for no. Go ahead and try."

"Do you know who I am?" Hannah tried again to make a connection with his vacant gaze.

She could feel his hand twitch. Yes, that was a feeble squeeze. Once. Yes, he knew who she was.

"He does," she told Ginger and then, back to George,

"I've been wanting to tell you how grateful I am for your contribution."

There was no response from George, tucked like a swaddled baby beneath the white bedspread.

"What contribution?" Ginger asked.

Hannah explained that when an anonymous donor came forward with funding for the mining documentary she assumed the donor had been George.

George squeezed her hand twice. Hannah was mystified.

"He said no," she told Ginger.

"Well, big surprise!" Ginger huffed. "How'd you expect George to pull that off with Denny controlling his purse-strings?"

"I didn't think it had to be actual *money*," she said. "Maybe George has some influence with The Sierra Club, or a sportsmen's group. He's the one who said I should do the documentary, he suggested it when I came out to see him in July so I assumed he was involved."

George's expression was still blank, but he squeezed her hand twice more.

"The important thing is the show's moving forward, isn't it?" Ginger said. "Tell him about your trips and all. The places you've been. What you expect to see out at Yellowstone."

Hannah related the structure of Mine Games, explained the other mines out west that she planned to compare and contrast with Ingold's. George's expression never changed.

What Hannah really wanted to ask was if George had any knowledge of the prospecting samples. During her last visit he'd briefly referred to Hal's call.

"Before my uncle died," Hannah began, cautiously, "just before he died, he telephoned you at Northern Lights. Do you remember?"

George indicated that he did.

"And he told you Denny and Axel Graves wanted him to sign some papers."

Yes.

"Were they to give Ingold permission to drill core samples at Star Lake?"

No response.

"The papers that Dennis wanted Hal to sign," Hannah asked again, more slowly, "did Axel Graves and Dennis want Hal to let them test for copper ore on Hal's property?"

Nothing.

Hannah looked questioningly at Ginger. It was as if George's mind had short-circuited again and they'd lost contact.

"Georgie!" Ginger asked sharply, and he blinked. "Wake up. Hannah's asking you something important, so you pay attention!"

She nodded at Hannah. "Go ahead now, ask him again."

"All I want to know is if he thinks Hal would have okayed Ingold's prospecting on Star Lake property."

George squeezed her hand twice.

"No?" Hannah asked, wanting to be certain she got it right.

One squeeze.

"Yes?"

Hannah was confused. "You mean yes, you meant no? That Hal would not have let him go ahead?"

"Oh for Pete's sake," Ginger's patience was wearing thin. "He told you no. No, Hal wouldn't have let them do it. What more do you want? Why don't you go and let us alone."

"I have to ask one more thing," Hannah added quickly, still uncomfortable with the letters Ginger had mailed. "I want to find out if Dennis ever mentioned that Hal agreed."

"You mean you want Georgie to tell you if his son lied to him? You got more balls than I gave you credit for, Honey, asking a helpless soul to rat on his own son. Even I can't imagine doing that."

"Okay, if Denny ever *implied* that Hal agreed. I don't need to know the exact words."

"That's enough," Ginger said. "You're getting me as uptight as a two dollar watch." She pulled herself to her feet and separated their clasped hands.

But before Ginger pulled them apart, George signaled "Yes."

Hannah could read deep sorrow in the old man's rheumy eyes.

"Thank you, George," Hannah said, kissing his cheek, "I know you loved my Uncle Hal. He loved you, too." She blinked away tears, "And so do I."

When Hannah left his room, Ginger was seated on the side of the bed, tenderly caressing his tortured face.

There was a crowd in the lobby waiting for the elevator when Hannah emerged.

Dennis Windsor nodded perfunctorily as she tried to slip past.

"Your father already has a visitor," she said, wishing to preserve the couple's privacy a few moments more.

"Then how about letting me buy you a cup of coffee," he suggested. "Coffee Shop's right down the hall."

Hannah paused, uncertain—letters had just been dropped in the mail that could destroy his career.

"I want to apologize for the misunderstanding. You know, the last time we were together," Dennis said. He steered her by the elbow into a white-tiled room where the addition of flowered curtains made the Coffee Shop only slightly less antiseptic. Booths lined one wall and round tables were scattered around the interior. A couple women with ruffled aprons bustled, serving sandwiches ordered from the blackboard above the counter just inside the door.

"I'll have a cup of coffee, black," he told the waitress, "and bring us each a slice of pie. Pumpkin, if you have it."

"And a cup of tea," Hannah added.

Dennis led her to a booth in the far corner.

"That's better," he said. "I don't like to leave things dangling between us."

An appropriate metaphor, Hannah thought.

"I've been wanting to talk with you, too."

"Oh, yeah?" He seemed interested. "What about?"

The waitress served two slices of pie with white tits of artificial topping, and then returned with the coffee and a metal pot of tea.

After she came back one last time with paper napkins and plastic forks, Hannah continued.

"You know how it is in autumn, when the leaves have fallen and you can see things that were hidden during the summer?"

"Sure," Dennis replied cautiously.

"Well, I was hiking the other day, and I came across something really strange. Orange tube-like things, sticking out of the ground. Brighter orange than this pie," she joked, taking a tentative bite.

Dennis's fork was poised in mid-air as he waited for her to continue.

"How big," he asked. "As tall as you?"

"Taller," she said, taking another bite. "On the northwest corner of my land. I saw some tubes just like them on Ingold's property before they put in the chain-link fence last spring."

"Is that so?" Dennis put his fork back down, his pie untouched, and took a hesitant sip of his coffee. His hand still had a discernible tremor.

"They were core samples," she said, "drilled to check for the presence of ore. Did you know the rock drilled that deep is one-point-eight *billion* years old?"

"No kidding," Dennis said.

"I wondered how they got there on my property. And when."

She was not good at lying; her face always gave her away, but this wasn't so much a lie as it was a change in chronological sequence. Dennis wasn't watching her anyway; he was studiously investigating his pie.

"It's really good," she reassured him, as if he lacked the courage to take a bite. "The thing is," she continued, "last spring when I came up here the first time, you remember, when we met and you took me out to dinner at Little Bohemia and we talked about my inheritance?"

"What about it." His voice definitely lacked enthusiasm.

"I moved out to the lake from the Yank 'Em Inn after the memorial service, and the shock of my uncle's death, the grief . . ." She was pouring it on a little thick. "Well, I went for lots of walks in the woods then. There are logging trails all over the place. I explored nearly every inch of that property with Hal's dog and I never came across a single orange tube like that. I can't figure out why."

Dennis cleared his throat. Would he buy her bluff?

"Well, maybe the tall brush, ferns and leaves and so forth . . ."

"And another thing," Hannah pressed on, as if she hadn't heard, "I have a hard time coming to grips with the fact that my uncle gave his permission to have them drilled."

"I don't know why you're bringing this up now, Hannah," Dennis told her. Then he dug into his slice with determination and carved out a huge bite. "Seems to me that's over and done with." He swallowed the pie quickly and took a generous slurp of coffee.

"Because I wondered if those samples were drilled without my knowledge. When I went back to Madison, after the funeral—but before I returned a week later and then stayed for the summer. During that week I was gone."

"Oh, I doubt that, Hannah," Dennis told her with certainty.

"And I have another idea." She knew she had him, now. "I think someone forged my uncle's signature to make it appear that he gave his consent."

Dennis blinked in amazement as the last of his pie went down with a muffled sputter. "Who told you that?"

"I determined it myself, from a document I had an opportunity to inspect."

"There weren't any copies in Hal's files," Dennis said, much too quickly. Then he wiped his mouth with his napkin as if, Hannah thought, smiling, he could wipe the words away.

"You're right. I didn't find it in Hal's files."

Why hadn't she thought of that? If Hal had signed such a paper, he would surely have kept a copy.

"Nevertheless," she continued, "I have a copy of the permission that Hal was purported to have signed, and when the original of that paper is subpoenaed, handwriting experts will be able to prove the signature is not his."

"Your uncle was sick, you know," Dennis said weakly. "He might have had trouble signing his name."

Sick or not, Hannah knew, he wouldn't have signed "Hal," when he signed everything else "Harold A." But she didn't want to play her entire hand.

Dennis seemed to gather courage from the implied agreement of her silence.

"You might not think I'm the greatest guy in the world, Hannah. And yes, I did go out to Star Lake with Axel to see if we could run some tests on Hal Larkin's land. But when I saw how sick he was, sawing up those trees by himself without any help, I knew he was in trouble and I told Axel we ought to back off. Go slow for a while, anyway. Then I took Axel over to the mine and I went back to give your Uncle Hal a hand."

So far so good, Hannah thought. But he seemed to be grasping for an explanation, now.

"He . . . ah, said he'd had second thoughts and decided to sign right then and there. Then he collapsed. So, you see, it was his signature, after all."

"He collapsed?"

"Signed it, then grabbed at his throat and fell. Heart attack. Of course I felt awful. He was a good friend of my father's and I figured maybe the stress of signing that permission on top of the work he was doing, caused it. I dragged him away from the brush pile and gave him CPR. Then I carried him upstairs to his bed and called 911 for the fire department's emergency medical squad because there wasn't anything else I could do for him at that point in time."

Hannah was astounded. This was not the confession she had anticipated. But it reminded her of another question that might test his veracity.

"When you gave him CPR, did you remove his dentures?"

"Actually, I did," Dennis admitted. "Every year the volunteer fireman get updates in CPR. One of the things they always stress is to remove dentures when we're working on the elderly, especially if the dentures are loose. It's so the victim doesn't choke on them. I took Hal's teeth out and set them on a stump while I gave him CPR.

Then, after I heard later they couldn't revive him, that he died, I thought about his teeth. So I went back out there and found them and put them up by his bed. So *you'd* find them, matter of fact. Charlie Jenkins had already gathered up the body. The back door wasn't locked. It was the same day I met you. I got there and left before you came."

Dennis had recovered his poise. The explanation for Hal's teeth seemed reasonable, she had to admit. No one had said Dennis had been at the resort when the EMS arrived, but that was not unusual; they were part of the volunteer fire department and he was one of them.

"You've got a court appearance coming up next week, haven't you?" Dennis asked, his gaze narrowed.

"Yes, I do," Hannah replied.

"Who's representing you?"

"No one. I didn't steal that flag, and I had no intention of stealing it. I was just an innocent bystander. I'm not guilty. That's all I need to say."

"You're awfully naive, Hannah Swann," Dennis's warning was self-righteous. "Ingold's going to run right over you with that defense. As a fellow Badger, I feel I ought to advise you to hire an attorney."

"Perhaps," she said, measuring her words carefully, "as a fellow Badger, Dennis, you might suggest to Ingold that my charges be dropped. Or eased somewhat."

Dennis was clearly taken aback by her suggestion, and glanced around hastily in case any of the elderly patrons in the Coffee Shop might have heard her make such an outrageous request.

"You don't know what you're suggesting," he said, his voice lowered and filled with disdain. "As a member of the State Bar I'm an officer of the court. I'm going to pretend I didn't hear you say that."

Hannah lowered her voice, too, and kept a smile on her face while she seized his wrist beneath the table and clamped it so tightly she could feel his pulse racing beneath her fingernails that cut into his skin.

"I'll buy the fact that you had nothing against my uncle, Dennis, and maybe you even felt some affection for your father's friend. I'll even buy the CPR story and the explanation about the dentures because it's too far-fetched for someone like you to invent here, right on the spot."

"You're a spunky bitch. I've said that, haven't I?" Dennis chuckled nervously.

"But what I *won't* buy is Uncle Hal's signature on those prospecting papers. Not when you were being pressured to get him to sign by that same powerful corporation that's going to run right over me."

Dennis shook off Hannah's grasp.

"Hal stood to gain a great deal if there was copper under his property. Which there isn't, by the way," he swiftly added, rubbing his wrist. "No, it's too bad, really. That kind of discovery might've given him the kind of windfall he needed to pay off both mortgages and save his ass. You, too, now that his financial troubles are yours. Too bad it didn't pan out. After he signed that prospecting agreement like he did . . ."

Hannah smiled appreciatively, thanked Dennis for the pie and said she had to get back to the lake.

"See you in court," she said.

"Think about what I told you, Hannah. Or you're going to regret it."

"I certainly will think about it," Hannah replied. He was unaware how much he had revealed. She was glad the letters were on their way to seal his doom. Sometimes it paid to be spunky. And when he learned what she had done he'd call her something worse than that.

Despite Windsor's recommendation, Hannah represented herself and was ready to plead not guilty at her hearing the following week. Notwithstanding his earlier, dire prediction, Ingold backed down; the theft charges against her were dropped. Judge Twichell warned her to stay away from the mine site for at least six months, and solemnly quoted Whittier, "Shoot, if you must, this old gray head / But spare your country's flag . . ." before she was free to leave the courtroom. Ginger and other members of Celestial Summer who had come along for moral support rose to follow.

Attorney Windsor would not return Hannah's quizzical glance.

On Monday, November second, Hannah and Ginger were awakened by the wail of a faraway siren and moments later an enormous eruption echoed across the thin skin of ice already lacquering the surface of the lake. A dark and ominous plume of dust hung above the Ingold site.

"I'm glad Hal's dead and gone so he don't have to hear the sound of those bombs," Ginger told Hannah. They stood at the end of the pier, hands jammed in their jacket pockets, and watched the distant shoreline for further signs of destruction.

"Good thing fishing season's over, too," Hannah said. "They're scaring every fish from one end of the chain to the other."

A cold wind blew over the ice and the women cringed as another blast tore the silence. The thunder had continued all morning, interspersed with the continuous complaint of heavy machinery.

A railroad spur from Antler to the mine site had already been completed, and concrete foundations for the administration building, lab, maintenance shop, and water treatment facilities were in readiness, too. This was Ingold's preproduction mining phase, now, moving the overburden, blasting away a shelf of rock to expose the ore body.

Babe, who had been sitting patiently at Hannah's side, suddenly whirled around and raced off the pier to welcome Dan Kerry and Victor Redhawk with a joyous, barking dance.

"We heard you needed a couple of hired hands," Dan called out to them. Hannah was glad the stiff wind could be blamed for the rising color in her cheeks.

"There's so many trucks on Star Lake Road," Victor said as the women joined them, "Ingold's sure not wasting any time. They're moving ahead full steam, over there."

"You guys can stand out here and jaw if you want to," Ginger announced, "but the coffee pot's inside and I need a warm-up. Look, I'm shivering like a dog passing peach pits."

They sat at the kitchen table. Victor again congratulated Hannah on the success of her clambake hearing in front of Judge Twichell. "You should have seen her, Dan, she had Denny Windsor biting his fingernails."

"Wish I could've been there," Dan replied, "but I've got too many things I need to wrap up."

He seemed pensive. Or maybe uncomfortable with her, it occurred to Hannah. She was feeling self-conscious, too.

They had brought their hip boots to pull out the pier, drag the pilings up on shore and haul the boats out of the lake. Victor would check the motors and decide what maintenance had to be done over the winter.

"You going away, now that fishing's over?" Ginger asked Dan.

"Plan to visit my kids," he told her. "It's been a long time since I've seen them, and I can't think, anyway, with that blasting next door."

Hannah had not considered the possibility of Dan's absence. But she had been gone, too—in Montana to get footage of the site near Yellowstone where she'd met with a group working to block the development of the Crown Butte Mine. "It's one of the most unsuitable places imaginable," the spokesman told her as they toured the site above the northeast corner of the National Park.

She'd spent a week in Madison to begin editing Mine Games after that. Maybe she would stay in Madison for all of November and December so she wouldn't have to face the collapse up here. With so much happening, she had pushed the financial situation into a far corner of her mind.

Hannah warmed her hands with the hot coffee mug and studied Dan, Victor, and Ginger, deep in conversation. She felt privileged to share the friendship of these good people, if only tangentially. How much she had grown to trust and appreciate their loyalty. Yet, despite the way she'd appeared in the video of the canoe flotilla, a woman comfortable in her surroundings, she did not really belong in this landscape.

Ginger's face was ruddy from being outdoors and Dan's tan had not faded. He was wearing a heavy, hand-knit sweater today, a heathery navy that made his eyes seem even bluer. The scent of his cologne, so familiar now and associated with that evening, was driving her wild. Although Hannah had not seen him since the night they had slept next to one another, he was never far from her thoughts. She spoke with him by phone when he called to ask if she had written the letters about Denny, and she repeated the information gleaned from the lawyer's revelations at Northern Lights.

Except for asking if she'd fallen asleep, Ginger never asked what had happened when she hadn't come home from Dan's. Maybe she figured it was none of her business (although Hannah doubted that; everything was Ginger Kovalcik's business), or maybe she didn't care. Maybe—and this was a long shot—Ginger resented that Hannah was moving in on Lynne's territory.

Another blast sounded from the mine site, rattling the dishes in the kitchen cupboard.

"If they get any closer we'll have to hunker down," Ginger muttered. But nobody laughed.

Snow mixed with rain fell later that afternoon as the women began to close up the cottages. They started the pre-winter chores with Vega. Sirius would be next, and then Cygnus, if there was time. Tomorrow they'd tackle Arcturus, trashed by the jet-skiers in July but thoroughly redecorated afterward. Castor and Pollux weren't in need of as much as the others in the way of upkeep since Eric and Chloe had done so much maintenance on them in May.

Hal usually shut the resort down with the close of fishing season, Ginger said, but he kept the bar open for locals and snowmobilers all winter, and as long as she was already snug and comfortable living above the Saloon she'd be glad to carry on with that plan, if Hannah agreed. With the trouble they'd had earlier it was a good idea to keep somebody there to discourage funny business, and even bar income would be helpful, considering their financial bind.

Yes, Hannah would have to do something drastic, if she planned to meet the second mortgage deadline by the end of December, but what? She could still hear Dennis Windsor's hot threats in her ear.

The wheels were in motion to destroy his legal career but she would need cold, hard cash to take care of the mortgage. When she let herself think about it, she felt sick.

The screen door on Sirius was almost off its hinges, and Cygnus's roof leaked above the kitchen sink. Vega needed paint.

Working in the littlest cottage with Ginger, Hannah was reminded of the Saturdays they'd cleaned with Chloe. The Silly Sisters, Ginger had tagged the trio. It had been fun, sharing girl-talk and hearty laughs among their tasks.

As if she were reading Hannah's mind, Ginger asked, "You hear from your daughter, lately?"

"No," Hannah replied. "I had a message on my answering machine a couple weeks ago. Chloe's wrapping up her master's thesis."

Hannah hoped to host her family in Madison for Thanksgiving dinner as usual. Lily was coming up from Tampa, too.

"I sure miss those guys," Ginger said again, later. She was folding the blankets from the bed in Cygnus and would take all the bedding to the Laundromat while Hannah was away. "They added the spice of life to this place. Now when you're gone, not just to Montana or California, I mean, but back in Madison for God knows how long, we're a pretty sad sight out here, all by our lonesome, just me and Babe. Even Dan's going to abandon us."

Hannah didn't know how to respond. It wasn't like Ginger to feel sorry for herself, but the resort had been her life for so many years.

As if nothing were wrong, they made a list of the absolute necessities they needed to accomplish before winter set in: strip the beds, mop the floors, drain water pipes and turn off water, pour antifreeze in the toilets and sink traps, turn off gas, empty and scrub out refrigerators, leave refrigerator doors open and unplug them, place mouse poison around. The big things, like the screen door and the roof leak, would go on a list to be considered when there was enough time and money and manpower to do something about them, if they still wanted to. If they could.

"Every Christmas my son asks me to come to Hawaii," Ginger continued. "He'll send me a check, he says, for the airfare. They got a room over their carport that I could have to myself and the weather's always nice and warm. Every Christmas I tell him I'm not ready yet, but this year, well, I don't know. Today, for instance, it's getting so the cold's awfully hard on these old bones."

"Maybe you should give that serious thought," Hannah said, sadly.

"And I can't get used to it being an hour later," Ginger declared as they closed the door on Cygnus and headed back to the Saloon. Three cottages down and only three more to go. Aldebaran would be kept heated, minimally, so the water pipes wouldn't freeze. That way, Ginger said, Hannah could come back whenever she wanted and "make herself feel at home."

"I always dread the loss of daylight savings time," she told Ginger. "When it starts getting dark at four-thirty I go into my winter depression mode. The only way I've found to fight it is by lighting a fire in the fireplace. It must be a primitive thing, fighting off darkness with a fire."

"Relaxing, too, isn't it," Ginger said with a grin and a friendly poke in the ribs. "Tends to make you doze off, so I hear."

That was the old Ginger that she loved. "Speaking of Dan Kerry," Hannah said, opening the Saloon door with a shrug of resignation, "what kind of a relationship does he have with Lynne?" She was trying to be casual about it, as if it didn't matter. No problem. No big deal.

"I suppose you should be asking Dan that," Ginger told her. The lights of the Saloon flickered on. It was damp and cold in there because of the rain and the wind, and Hannah turned up the thermostat so the furnace kicked in with a trembling shudder.

"Oh, come on, Ginger," Hannah argued, "I don't want details, I just want generalities. How do you put it, 'I don't want to hear the labor pains, I just want to see the baby?' Well, I'm not asking to see the baby. Does Lynne have designs on him?"

What sort of language was she speaking, she wondered; *designs?*

"And where *are* Lyle and Lynne these days, I haven't seen them around."

"Oh, they take off every autumn," Ginger called out from the kitchen where Hannah knew she was hanging up her coat on the hook behind the desk. "I'm going upstairs to get washed up," she said when she came back through the swinging doors. "Can you keep an eye on the bar?"

"Take off where?" Hannah asked tenaciously. Now that she'd approached the subject she was not going to let it drop, even if Babe was making a racket out on the porch because she wanted to be let inside.

"Here and there, all over the country. You ever hear of the Windigo?" Ginger asked. "No reason that you would, though, since Chloe's grown up."

"*Windigo?*"

"It's a 'Bigfoot' type monster, here in Wisconsin. Windigo's the Indian name for it. They gave the name to their musical group. Lyle and Lynne, sometimes Leslie, they go to schools and perform. Show slides, play fiddles, sing, tell stories. Environmental stuff. Northwoods history. That's why Leslie's home schooled, because they're traveling all the time."

"What about Forest Temple?"

"Oh, heck, they fold up their teepees and close the campgrounds as soon as school starts. I thought you knew. Maybe you were out west somewheres. They'll be gone until next spring, unless they get back here for Thanksgiving. It depends on where they're at."

Ginger began to climb the stairs to the apartment. Her arthritis must be really bothering her, Ginger's progress was agonizingly slow.

"And Dan?" Hannah asked, getting up to follow her progress, "How does he feel about Lynne?"

"Why, Hannah Swann," Ginger looked back down over her shoulder, "I wonder why you're so interested. Maybe you better ask the man himself."

"Ask me what?"

He and Victor stood in the open doorway of the Saloon. Babe wriggled past and ran to Hannah's side with a woof and a grin.

"Hi there, Silly Baby," Hannah, blushing, bent to give Babe an overly enthusiastic hug.

"I got steaks defrosting," Ginger's voice carried down from the top of the stairs. "You guys, take off your coats. Hannah, get 'em a beer."

"You hungry, Victor?" Dan said, removing his gloves.

Victor replied, "Dan, I'm so darned hungry I could eat a Windigo, even."

Hannah grimaced; they had heard her ask about Lynne.

19

Flurries

The aroma of roasting turkey bathed the house with savory promise. Hannah drizzled it with the baster and slammed the oven door shut with her hip. Two more hours. The meal was coming together.

Lily had flown into Madison the day before. Her mother bustled about in a lavender jog-suit to dab at the dust on Hannah's houseplants and pinch off dead leaves. Then she frowned at the stain around the inside of the powder room toilet bowl and asked for a toilet brush.

Hannah thought of all the toilets she'd scrubbed at Star Lake and bit her tongue.

Eventually, the words of Ella Wheeler Wilcox drifted out of the sunroom. If the video kept Lily quiet for a while, that was a good sign. Since the California trip Hannah had been isolated in an editing suite at the station. Mine Games was on schedule; her life was still anything but. One of these days she'd like to find a few minutes to view the finished BWP tape, herself.

"*I had just purchased a Ouija board of my own,*" the actress playing Ella was declaring, "*And both my friend and I were shaken by a power which beggars description; it was like an electric shock.*"

"Did you know she tried to contact her husband with a Ouija board?" Lily called out to the kitchen.

"*The Board seemed to be a thing alive. It moved with such force that we could not follow it. When the table rested, we read these sentences: 'Brave one, keep up your courage. Love is all there is. I am with you always . . .'*"

Hannah checked the timetable for her day posted on the refrigerator door. Another twenty minutes until she was scheduled to pare and cube the rutabaga. After that she'd peel the potatoes and brown the peanuts for Chloe's pineapple peanut stew. This year she especially wanted to please her daughter.

"Can I help?" Lily asked without taking her eyes from the television screen.

"I've got it under control," Hannah replied curtly. She was already restless from too much caffeine, but sat beside her mother to glance at the TV.

"How long until the kids get here?"

"Not for another hour or so."

"You should've let me treat you all to Thanksgiving dinner at Quivey's Grove," Lily said.

Hannah ignored her mother's repeated complaint. She hoped Chloe wouldn't detect the chicken broth in the orzo dressing inside the turkey; in the past her daughter was known to carry her vegan diet to extremes merely to annoy her.

"I'm getting a kick out of this old gal," Lily said. "Do you know what she just said?"

"I put the words in her mouth, Mother."

"The gals down in Tampa get the Ouija board out every once in awhile. It can be boring, though. Some of those spirits are pretty humorless."

"What do you expect, they're dead!"

"My goodness," Lily scoffed, "I haven't seen many smiles out of you since I've been here. Such a long face, and you're still walking around in the world of the living, so far as I can tell."

The phone in the sunroom was next to the sofa, and Hannah impulsively dialed Ginger at Star Lake.

"Good thing you called when you did," Ginger sang out happily, "I'm just about to skip over to Dan's while we're quiet, here. I'm so hungry I could eat the north end of a turkey waddling south, and Dan's fixing a twenty-four pounder with all the trimmings."

"It's quiet there?"

Hannah could see the empty Saloon, maybe a dusting of snow on the ground and the lake a smooth mirror of ice.

"Dead at the moment, snowing an inch an hour and colder'n a witch's tit. But we've *been* busy," Ginger replied. "Deer season opened last Saturday. Every hunter from here to Chicago's heard about Star Lake and they all want to meet the famous Hannah Swann who's been on TV. You're a big shot with the blaze orange crowd."

"I miss you, Ginger," Hannah said, her voice choking up.

"I don't suppose you could call us over at Dan's, later? Lyle and Lynne and Leslie's going to be there, so it'll be like family. I'll want to talk to Lily, too."

Hannah promised to call back early in the evening.

"You could ask Dan about Denny then," Ginger added. "Grapevine says the state Attorney General's looking into his law practice. Denny's not a happy camper."

Hannah hung up and opened the back door to a blast of cold wind. The thermometer on the garage read twenty-nine degrees. With the leaves off the trees, shriveled remnants of the neighbor's garden were visible.

"Eighty down in Tampa today, the Weather Channel says," Lily reported.

Hannah closed the door against the wind and leaves that had blown into a dusky drift against the steps.

"I wish you'd lighten up, Hannah. You didn't used to be so serious," her mother pointed the remote control at the TV and flicked off the Wilcox video. "When you were a little girl you were quite a happy child."

"I was never 'quite a happy child,' Mother. You must have me confused with someone else."

Ten more minutes until the rutabaga.

"Let me pare that squash, at least," Lily said. "And I can do something about your potatoes. Mix your pie crust. I don't feel right, just sitting. When you were little I'd get up at five in the morning to put in the turkey. Grandpa Larkin never liked having Thanksgiving dinner so late in the day."

"It's not squash, Mother, it's rutabaga."

Her voice was drowned out by the sound of the kitchen faucet which Lily turned full blast to wash her hands.

Hannah had spent only a few days at Star Lake before leaving for California.

"Sure, we got rain," Ginger said when she returned, "more rain than we can handle. Rained every day like a cow pissing on a flat rock and because of it, Ingold's got big trouble. You know those fancy-schmancy erosion controls they made so much of at the master's hearing? The ones that were supposed to hold up to a once-in-twenty-five-year flood? Well, you can see where the mud's draining right into the Lost Arrow River and if I was you, I'd take pictures, lickety-split."

Joe Mickelson had a cameraman at Star Lake the following morning, and they were able to get aerial footage as well as appropriate sentiments of outrage from Celestial Summer, environmentalists, and sportsmen.

Her mother was fussing about not being able to find what she needed in the kitchen and, for once, Hannah did not hurry to help. Let Lily throw Hannah's plans out of whack, everything was out of sync anyway. Back in Madison she felt her shoulders tense with more lists, urgent deadlines, so many decisions. She was not eating right, glad to shed the extra pounds, but her days were plotted hourly, often the night before, and she was having migraines again.

In part, Hannah had orchestrated her cooking chores so she would be freed from the obligation of family happy-talk. After the initial awkwardness of their arrival it was enough to overhear Lily visit with Chloe and Eric while she set four places at the dining room table and arranged a centerpiece of orange gourds and bronze mums. Lily wanted to know what it was about Star Lake they missed most.

Chloe said it was new friends and continuing a family tradition. Eric said he liked the challenge of odd jobs around the place.

Hannah put the potatoes on to boil, then removed the turkey from the roasting pan so she could prepare the gravy. This was ordinarily something she looked forward to but this year her mood was less than festive.

Ginger was missing. And, yes, Dan Kerry.

She had always taken pride in her turkey gravy. Now, as she browned the flour in the roasting pan and added broth to stir the savory liquid, she could not deny the strong pull back toward Star Lake, an attraction as unwavering as the magnetic needle on a compass. It didn't take much imagination to envision Dennis Windsor's smirk as he was handed the deed to the resort. Was Ginger remembering to check the pipes in Aldebaran? Was Babe waiting for her to come back?

Dan's image flashed past repeatedly on footage in the editing suite, and she never tired of hearing his voice or watching him move. She was reluctant to let Joe cut any scenes where Dan appeared.

On screen the colors of the California mine she'd visited were eerily beautiful. Creeks were stained a brilliant red, and dark green water as caustic as battery acid poured from underground caverns.

The script was strong and she had plenty of vivid and powerful visuals like those from Iron Mountain and Crown Butte. "This is going to get you serious recognition," Joe assured her. "Stop wasting your time on those fusty old poets. You've got a job here with me as soon as you're ready."

The possibility was very much on Hannah's mind.

Evenings she tried to catch up in her journal, but there were blank pages intended for descriptions of her travels. She couldn't get beyond silly fragments of poems, meanderings. Reading again the entries that documented their meeting last spring, their growing friendship, and the night in front of the fire, she preferred to reminisce about Dan rather than noting anything of real substance.

In contrast, Tyler's phone calls had been relentless. So, on the Monday before Thanksgiving, a mild autumn day with a temperature in the mid-50s, Hannah returned to Indian Lake. The hill where they once made love, so lush and green in spring and summer, stood in sharp relief against the bleached sky.

Her Toyota, alone in the parking lot, rocked in the wind. She saw his car approach and her heart beat faster not out of passion, but from dread.

"I wanted to be alone with you, the last time we were together," he told her, taking her hand, "but it was clumsy, with your mother and all the rest."

Clumsy barely described it. She still had no idea why he had become involved with Celestial Summer. As they headed for the trail to the hilltop she commented, "It's one thing for Ingold to ask you to serve as their consultant, but why would you want to threaten your reputation by ransacking their files?"

"Very simple," Tyler trudged up the trail at her heels. "It's *very* simple."

Hannah continued climbing, but he caught her arm and pulled her backward so she fell clumsily into his arms.

"Hannah, we need to talk about what happened."

She wrenched out of his grasp and started back up the rocky path. "That was almost six months ago," she told him over her shoulder, "I've tried to put it out of my mind."

"I'm still sick about it, Cheeks. I have to tell you, from my heart, how sorry I am. Dawn was sorry, too."

There was an embarrassing, desperate throb in his voice.

Hannah reached the crest of the hill and went inside the little chapel. The scent of mildew was thick in the shadowy chill.

"My marriage is finished," Tyler explained quietly behind her.

"It's an amicable split, but I'm the one filing for divorce. Dawn is moving to California."

He stood in the doorway, obliterating the light, but a feeble glow from the small window illuminated the altar, the Madonna, the crucifix, undisturbed. She touched the spiral notebook, curled by dampness and tied to a pencil. It held signatures that evidenced their visit nearly three and a half years before.

"I loved you once, Tyler, but I don't anymore. So I hope this isn't about asking me to marry you or anything like that."

She turned to face him. "It's hard to be so painfully blunt after all you've done to help us at Star Lake, but I have to be truthful."

"You have no idea," Tyler said. He made no move to come closer.

"No idea, what?" She was impatient.

"What I did to help you and your friends fight Ingold."

It was a tactic to leave her hanging, she knew, so she finally asked, "What *did* you do, Tyler?" She was beginning to feel claustrophobic in the stuffy little chapel.

"I planted the Purple Warty Back clams in the Lost Arrow River. Those endangered Purple Warty Backs. I threw in a Bullhead, too, a foolish risk because that species of mollusk wouldn't normally be found up there and they're even less common. I can't believe no one caught on."

Hannah was stunned. She reached toward the rock wall to quell her dizziness.

"You want the mine stopped, don't you?" Tyler asked, simply.

"Not that way," her voice was weak, "not illegally!"

"After what happened at the motel—I had to make it up to you. And when I looked at Ingold's samples I was fairly confident that I could encourage an Environmental Impact dispute. There wasn't enough evidence to close Ingold down without the clams. You needed to buy some time. I thought I could give you that, at least."

"This is unbelievable, Tyler."

If he hadn't smiled so hopefully, perhaps she would not have been so exasperated, Hannah decided later.

"Now that Dawn's out of the picture, you probably think we

should finally get together." He smiled, apologetically. "I owe you that, too."

The sour, breathless chapel was unbearable. She had to get out of there.

"But I've met someone else," he confessed. "Someone . . ."

"Willowy?" Hannah offered.

"What?"

"Willowy, I said. Someone *willowy*, goddammit!"

She read recognition in his eyes and there was only a slight pause before Hannah lunged. She pushed him backward, escaped the damp rock walls, then nearly tripped as she ran down the path toward the foot of the hill.

"We're even now, Tyler," she said when he caught up with her at the door to her car. "You don't owe me a thing."

"I have your shoes," he said, "and your jacket." He brought a plastic bag out of his car.

But she backed her car away, shifted into first and tore out of the park.

Can I give you a hand?"

That was Eric, always ready to help. She had not been watching the time.

Thanksgiving dinner was served with mixed feelings and little appetite on Hannah's part. Midway through the meal she realized that Chloe was actually having a second helping of turkey and ladling more gravy over her mashed potatoes.

When the buzzer rang, Hannah went into the kitchen to remove the pumpkin pie from the lower oven. Lily followed, carrying the untouched bowl of peanut stew.

"Have you noticed?" Lily's voice was low and conspiratorial.

"Noticed what, Mother."

"Chloe."

"She looks fine. Beautiful. Radiant, just as you said. The ring isn't in her nose, or the diamond stud, either. I noticed that."

"Oh Hannah, for goodness sake."

"What, Mother?" Hannah set the pumpkin pie aside, then opened the door to the upper oven and removed the mincemeat pie. "What *about* Chloe?"

"She didn't drink her wine. She ate turkey and gravy and all that talk about getting her major food groups, weren't you listening? Now she says no caffeine. I got up to come out here for the coffee, and she asked for de-caf."

"So?" Hannah was weary of this facetious attempt at fullness and light. "I gave up long ago trying to figure out my daughter's whims."

Throughout the entire meal she hadn't stopped thinking of Dan and the group sharing their holiday dinner together at his home. She wanted to report Tyler's confession about the endangered clams. She wanted to find out if Dan knew about Tyler and Lynne!

Holiday dinners were always vaguely depressing, anyway. It wasn't just the countertops piled with dirty dishes; the entire event never lived up to her expectations. Now her mother was whipping cream and prattling on about Chloe's appearance and eating habits. This was not unusual nor unexpected; Lily maintained that Hannah had been too lenient with the girl and attributed it to "that Communist Dr. Spock" whom she held responsible for her granddaughter's tattoo and nose ring.

"All right, if you're not going to ask her then I will," Lily said.

"Ask her what," Hannah mumbled.

"If she's pregnant."

"Oh, Mother!" Hannah burned her hand on the edge of the pie tin. "Are you out of your mind?"

"It all adds up. You're probably not up on the latest and I can't blame you because you've always been self-centered." Lily's voice had assumed an all-too-familiar self-righteous tone that Hannah despised. Yes, she *did* know the symptoms of pregnancy, hadn't she watched for them, herself, only a matter of months ago?

"I'm not listening to another word, Mother."

Hannah pulled a chair over to the cupboard so she could reach the dessert plates.

"Well, if you're not going to ask her, then I will."

Hannah handed the plates down to Lily, who blew on them to remove the dust.

"Don't you think I'd know if my own daughter was going to have a baby? And besides," she added, "even if she were, it wouldn't be up to us to ask; we should wait until she's ready to tell us."

"Humph," Lily sniffed. "That's what she should have done, waited. Until she was *married,* if you ask *me.*"

Lily rinsed the dessert plates and stacked them on the counter. "Not that she had the best role model in you, Hannah, but at least you got married as soon as you could. We gave you a nice wedding and a big reception . . ."

"Times have changed," Hannah interrupted.

"Decent moral values haven't changed," Lily continued. "It's not that I have anything against Eric, he's a fine young man. But if he's worth our Chloe, then he'll insist on getting married. It's the decent thing to do."

Hannah grabbed her mother by the arm and pulled her into the stairway that led down to the basement where there was less chance they'd be overheard.

"Mother, you're building this up into something crazy. What if Chloe *isn't* pregnant and it's all your imagination? Think how you could damage your relationship with her, and with Eric, too, if you insist on bringing it up."

Lily, chastened, looked at Hannah for a long moment. "Maybe I'm too quick to jump to conclusions."

"Of course you are," Hannah assured her with all the confidence she could feign. "Now, you go back in the living room where they're waiting for coffee and I'll be there in a minute with both of these pies."

Hannah leaned back against the door frame and took a deep breath. The day was taking forever. Snow sifted like grains of rice against the kitchen windows. She wished she could call Dan and get it over with, but she would have to wait another hour; Ginger hadn't said what time they were eating and she didn't want to interrupt their meal.

Soothing piano music in the background began to calm her, momentarily. Still hugging the door, Hannah heard Lily's voice raise above the CD to ask if Chloe and Eric had seen the Ella Wheeler Wilcox video—which, of course, they had not.

"You should see her tell about when she used the Ouija board," Lily said. "Didn't you used to have one, Chloe?"

"Oh, please, Mother . . ." Hannah moaned to the empty kitchen. She knew what her mother was up to and shook her head in resignation. Lily would see that her question was answered, one way or another, before the day was over.

Hannah served the pie and insisted on doing the dishes although Eric offered to help. She preferred to tidy up, she said (mocking Lily for her own entertainment) while the others played with the Ouija board.

"I'm going to walk to the park and back," she said when the dishwasher was loaded.

The kids were seated in chairs facing one another, the Ouija board on their knees, hands resting tentatively on the planchette. "Watch this, Mom," Chloe said, excited, "it's going so fast we can't keep track of the letters."

"Ask if I should stay in Madison," Hannah remarked, only half-joking. She began to button her coat.

"We already did," Eric replied.

"What did it say?"

"It said you should," Chloe told her.

Hannah was rummaging on the top shelf of the coat closet for her other mitten. She had decided to wear an unmatched pair, when Chloe told her, bitterly, "You know, Mom, if it's such a tough question, if you have the slightest desire to spend the rest of your life in Madison, go right ahead."

"What are you talking about?"

"You never seem to be able to make up your mind! Stay here, go there!"

"Chloe . . ." Eric warned, moving the Ouija board from his lap.

"Go ahead and join all the rest of the hangers-on, the PhDs

who're driving cabs and academic wannabes that stay on the fringes and teach extension courses and pretend they're doing something meaningful."

"What brought this on?" Hannah shot her daughter a startled glance. "I don't intend to become a hanger-on, Chloe." She tried to sound calm and reasonable while wondering what had generated this outburst. "As a matter of fact, I've been asked to work full-time in public television."

Chloe's eyes were glistening with tears.

"I like the mother I had up at Star Lake better than the mother I have down here," she admitted tearfully. "That one laughed and had time for the rest of us. She was more relaxed and a whole lot happier, too, in spite of the problems we had. You've been back here for how long? A month? I've been calling and calling and every time you say you're too busy to talk to me."

"That's not true," Hannah replied firmly, yet she knew that it was.

"I've had something to tell you that's important," Chloe said, pausing a moment to blow her nose. She stood next to Eric, whose arms were circled protectively around her waist.

"See what I told you?" Lily's silent grimace said to Hannah.

"Mother . . ." Hannah warned her, "Please stay out of this."

"Eric and I are leaving Madison as soon as I'm through school in December," Chloe said, sniffling. "We want to open an inn, or a bed and breakfast someplace. Up north. Some place like Star Lake."

"Are you getting married?" Hannah asked casually, as if she didn't really care, as if were an inconsequential matter.

"Yes," Chloe said. "At Christmas, if we can arrange it."

She felt a need to slap back with something hurtful. "Your grandmother says you're pregnant."

Chloe looked over at Lily, who was uncharacteristically silent.

"Grandma's right."

Chloe gazed at her grandmother with a glistening smile that disappeared when she turned back to Hannah.

Hannah's voice was high, tremulous. "Isn't that wonderful, Mother?"

Lily couldn't respond; she was digging inside her sleeve for a handkerchief to dab at her tears.

"Honey, I'm so happy for you," Hannah enveloped her daughter, and then Eric, in a warm hug. Lily was hugging Chloe and Eric, too.

Eric interrupted the awkward scene. He said they wished to be married at Star Lake if the resort wasn't sold by then, and if Hannah agreed.

"We want all our friends to be there," Chloe said, wiping her eyes. "It feels like home to us."

"Let's call Ginger right now," Hannah suggested. "For the first time in her life, Ginger will be speechless!"

"I know," Chloe wore a forgiving smile. "It happened up at Star Lake. I thought I was pregnant when we left at Labor Day, but I didn't know for sure until after we got back."

A loud cacophony of voices and music blended in the background when Ginger picked up the telephone. Hannah could imagine the scene in Dan's log home, with the warm walls gleaming and the crackle of the fireplace, Babe wagging her tail, snow cloaking the pines outside Dan's bedroom window.

"Chloe's here," Hannah said, "with an important announcement."

Hannah listened to her daughter give Ginger her news about the baby and the upcoming wedding with a joyful exuberance missing earlier. Then Chloe spoke with Lynne and asked if she and Lyle would play for their wedding.

Hannah waited to talk with Dan, but when Chloe hung up she said, "Everybody says hello. They're all going cross-country skiing."

Hannah could still hear the laughter and music in the background. Suddenly, she felt completely alienated from Star Lake. And bereft.

Still in her winter coat, she fell back onto the sofa and covered her eyes. Then she took off her mittens, found a linty Kleenex in her pocket and blew her nose.

Chloe asked what was wrong. Hannah admitted, "It's everything. I've tried every avenue, counted every penny, and I can't avoid the fact that we're going to lose the place to Dennis Windsor in only a month."

"Oh, Mom . . ." Chloe sat beside her and held her close.

"Sure, I made quite a bit from Mine Games," Hannah admitted, "because whoever underwrote it specified that I be extremely well compensated for my efforts. But even with that I've only been able to set aside nine thousand dollars."

Lily said, "What's keeping you from selling this big house? Why can't you let go of it, for goodness sake? That would help you out."

"I'm not convinced I should give this house up for . . . for that."

"What would help you decide? A sign from God? The Ouija board?" Lily was regaining her stride. "If you knew you wouldn't lose the resort because it was paid off, then how would it look to you?"

"It's a moot question, Mother," Hannah responded irritably.

"I've got eight thousand to put toward it," Eric offered, "and I know Chlo's got five or six."

"Twenty-two thousand," Hannah said bitterly, "that's a long way from what we need."

"About this wedding, "Lily said, "I hope I'm invited."

"Of course, Grandma," Chloe said, surprised. "We're planning on it!"

"There's something else I want to talk over with all of you. Take off your coat, Hannah, you'll get overheated and catch your death."

"If it's about the baby, Mother . . ." Hannah warned her.

"It's not about the baby. It's about Tampa. I don't want to go into Dolphin Cove."

"This is hardly the time to discuss your condo situation," Hannah said. "Can't that wait until later?"

"Hannah, I've got something to say and I'm going to say it, so you just keep your mouth shut for a change."

"Honest to God, is the question of Dolphin Cove something we have to deliberate this very minute?"

"Hannah, I said take off your coat and sit back down. The Ouija board says you're supposed to go back to Star Lake. Chloe wasn't telling you the truth."

Lily's cheeks were flushed with excitement. Hannah didn't want her mother to have a heart attack on Thanksgiving.

"When I came up to Star Lake this fall I saw something I liked, and that was family. I miss that down in Tampa. Oh, sure, my friends are nice and all that, but they don't take the place of flesh and blood. I saw you, Hannah, working with Chloe and laughing and having fun, and my heart was so full it almost burst. Your friend Ginger, she was as nice as could be. Seems to me I could rock out on the front porch up there just as well as I could rock on the front porch of Dolphin Cove."

"Grandma Larkin," Chloe said, "what are you suggesting?"

"And up there I'll have a great-grandbaby to rock to sleep," Lily was still addressing Hannah. Now she turned to Chloe and smiled, "If you'll let me."

"Mother . . ." Hannah, alarmed, spoke sharply. "It's *not* your kind of place! This is ridiculous."

"If you're trying to tell me that I'm a demented old woman, think again," Lily warned. "Hal lost his heart to Star Lake and I could see the rest of you love it there, too. I always felt bad that Hal didn't have a chance to share in Grandpa Larkin's estate. Daddy made quite a bit of money, when he sold Larkin Lumber Company. I put some of it away, and it's kept me going for quite awhile. Dolphin Cove has already been given a fifty thousand dollar down-payment so I can move in there the first of the year."

"Mother, you're not making sense," Hannah remarked. She slid her winter coat back on.

"*What I'm saying*, Hannah, if you'd only *shut up and listen*," Lily told her, "is this: Go ahead and keep this house if you want to. I'm going to ask for my money back from Dolphin Cove. I want to give it to the kids. If they put that together with some of my proceeds from the condo, they can pay off the resort's mortgage."

Chloe and Eric looked at one another in disbelief.

"What's the catch," Hannah said, flatly. She knew Lily must have a plan.

"I have only one little bitty stipulation. That you let me live there, too."

"Shit," Hannah said under her breath.

Lily beamed. "I thought you'd be surprised, but I can't tell if you're happy or not!"

Chloe said, "It would get us out of trouble, wouldn't it, Mom?"

Hannah merely shook her head in disbelief.

Then Eric said, "We could all be partners, Hannah, and be a real part of Star Lake, together."

Her brain was whirling. Leave it to Lily to meddle with her life.

"The resort might be meaningless, because of the mine, Mother. I don't want you to make a poor investment."

"Let's get this straight," Lily said. "When I decide to do something, I don't have to go through a lot of hemming and hawing, unlike some people I know."

Hannah collapsed on the sofa and unbuttoned her coat. She tossed the mismatched mittens up in the air. There was still the second mortgage, but that could be handled if they could pay off the first entirely.

Chloe and Eric were dancing around the room, and Lily grinned like she'd swallowed a whole truckload of canaries.

So, the Ouija board said she should go back to Star Lake? She needed to contact the Spirit who gave this message to Ella: *Brave one, keep up your courage. Love is all there is.*

20
Winter Storm Warning

"You wouldn't believe how much snow there is up here, Mom," Chloe said when she called from Star Lake the week after Thanksgiving. "It's up to the windowsills in Aldebaran and they're already ice fishing on the lake." Then she added, "Ginger wants to be a bridesmaid," and Hannah couldn't tell if Chloe's tongue was in her cheek or not.

Ginger got on the phone to share her astonishment at the amazing turn of events. "Denny was on the verge of making his move but poor Georgie's at the Cedar Springs hospital with another stroke and wouldn't you know, last Sunday I ran into Denny there. Of course he's as full of shit as a Christmas goose. After he left one of the nurses said his wife kicked him out so he's sleeping at his office. I figured that put the kibosh on his buying us out for the time being, but *Bless Your Mom* for coming through, Hannah! We're partying up here like you wouldn't believe. Lyle and Lynne, the Redhawks, Walt, Ben, the whole gang. Even Leslie. The only ones we need for a full house are you and Lily!"

Ginger had to speak up to be heard above the festivities in the background, and Hannah admitted, "It's still pretty unbelievable."

"Could of knocked Denny down with a feather, I'll bet," Ginger continued, still excited.

Hannah reminded her of the investigations she had set in motion with the District Attorney and State Bar Association. "I hope the extra stress and his father's illness don't push Dennis over the edge."

"Don't you dare go soft on us," Ginger retorted. "It serves Denny right to get in hot water. Oh, somebody else wants to say hello."

Dan's voice on the other end of the line made Hannah wince.

"Hannah," he said, and she could hear the warmth in his smile. "We're having an early Christmas!"

"Sounds that way," she said, faintly. Damn! She hated that merely hearing his voice could get her so unstrung.

"You said you wanted to take care of the mortgage yourself, and you were as good as your word."

"It's not exactly what I had in mind," she confessed, "but my life has been anything but predictable since last spring."

"When are we going to see you again?"

"The documentary's wrapped up, but I can't get away just yet. I guess maybe Chloe's wedding," she told him. "They haven't set a date . . ."

"I hope it's sooner than that," Dan said affectionately. And he handed the phone back to her daughter.

That was before she had seen the finished version of Mine Games. And that's why she was on the road right now. The documentary had been completed two weeks ago, but Joe had not been able to do a run-through and critique with her until yesterday. Helen's musky mount prowled fiercely on the wall above his desk, Hannah noted; Ginger had done a nice job.

During the closing footage Hannah watched the credits roll. Her own name appeared several times, but she wanted to be sure that acknowledgments were made for assistance and archival footage from Minnesota, Colorado, Montana, and California, and the various environmental groups that had given her so much help. After the predictable announcement that "Funding for this program was provided by the Corporation for Public Broadcasting," she was stunned to hear the announcer intone, "Additional funds were provided by Daniel Kerry."

"What in the hell is *this* all about?" she accused Joe.

"What's *what?*" he responded, warily.

"This 'additional funding' crap."

Joe laughed. "Kerry said that might bother you. He wanted to keep it quiet altogether, but I said you deserved to know."

She let it drop then, but anger and resentment continued to build overnight as she recalled Dan's initial reception of her idea for the documentary back in July. She remembered the time he spent alone with Joe in August, the tour of the mine site he'd arranged, the questions he'd asked of her as the project progressed and his interest in her travels.

Her pride had not allowed his assistance when he wanted to help refinance the mortgage. Yet his backing kept the resort open and running until the end of the fishing season, after all.

By morning she was sleepless and agitated, tempted to phone at two A.M. to give Dan a piece of her mind. But she lay awake and was up before sunrise to pack her things.

Mine Games was scheduled to air nationally on *Frontline* that evening. Chloe and Eric were back in Madison and planned to watch with her. Hannah left a message saying she was unexpectedly called out of town. Then she phoned Ginger to alert her of her arrival. As soon as she could get her things together and close up the house, she hit the road.

Now, no kidding, she had to pee.

Damn coffee. Her bladder pressed against the zipper of her jeans like a swelling water balloon. She shifted her seatbelt.

Near Westfield, Hannah stopped at a cafe beside the highway.

"Where you headed," the cashier inquired as she paid for a Hershey bar.

"Antler," Hannah said.

"Hope you get there before the storm hits. We're overdue for a big one."

Back on the highway, she tuned in the radio and heard a Winter

Storm Warning for freezing rain changing to snow in the southern part of the state; between eight and twelve inches in the north, with blowing and drifting.

She had never met a Wisconsinite who wasn't titillated by the threat of bad weather. The sky was heavy with sagging clouds. An early cold snap had caused even the Madison lakes to freeze over by Thanksgiving. If the first blizzard of the season struck right now, the idea of sleeping in Aldebaren with snow swirling around seemed rather picturesque. So far all she had encountered were bare fields, a bleak landscape, and a somber day.

Wind began to whistle around the car and drops of moisture collected on the windshield. A few miles up the road she met county trucks spreading salt and sand on a thin crust of ice that was freezing on the highway.

By the time she reached Wausau, the storm had become the kind that meant serious business. Sheets of snow, blown by winds out of the west, whipped across the countryside. Traffic slowed almost to a stop. Her hands cramped from her death-grip on the steering wheel and her eyes burned from staring into the whiteout. The prudent thing would be to get a motel room in Minocqua and watch Mine Games by herself. It was already later than her estimated time of arrival. She dug her cell phone from her purse, but as she expected, there was no signal.

Hannah resolutely kept going. The tires on the snow had a muffled sound, almost a soft squeak.

For ten miles or so she was able to depend upon a pair of red tail lights behind a truck. She would follow those lights off the edge of the world and gratefully, she thought. But the truck parked in front of a roadside bar near Tomahawk.

She followed a faint track for another hour, and the day grew steadily darker. Mesmerized by the motion of moving into the snow she felt as if she were hurtling headlong into a milky void.

Where *was* everyone? Probably sitting around the kitchen table talking about the damned fools who'd venture out in such a storm.

At last, Antler. The deer family near the Yank 'Em Inn was up to its haunches in drifts. She stopped at the liquor store/bait shop for gas, and picked up a couple bottles of wine. Within the hour the entire town would know Hannah was back.

Star Lake Road was even more difficult to follow than the state highway had been. The car skidded whenever she accelerated, and slithered dangerously around every curve. It was early evening now. Twice she had to stop to brush a crust of ice from her headlights and tail lights, and chip away at her windshield where wiper blades got stuck.

The last few miles she slid off the road, or what she thought was the road, more than once and had to rock the car to back out of the ruts she'd made. Apparently plows had abandoned this area to concentrate on the main highway.

When she saw "This is it!" and "Thank Your Lucky Stars," she thanked her stars and guardian angels and Uncle Hal and whoever else had ridden along.

Welcoming barks and yips greeted her appearance as soon as she opened the car door. Babe knocked her into a snowdrift, then covered her face in wet kisses and whipped her legs with an enthusiastic tail.

Dan pulled her to her feet.

"Do you have any idea how worried we've been," he asked, his voice as sharp as the December wind.

"Cut her some slack, Dan," Ginger was there, bundled in a down jacket. "It's almost time for the show!"

Then Hannah saw Leslie and wondered where Lynne was.

She was hustled inside the Saloon only half an hour before *Frontline* aired.

The rest of Celestial Summer had planned on gathering to celebrate the documentary and Hannah's achievement, but the weather canceled their plans and the potluck as well. Ginger heated two frozen pizzas and turned up the TV in the deserted Saloon.

Mine Games was broadcast with wind howling ominously around the fieldstone chimney. Hannah opened the wine. This was the first time she had seen the program in its entirety knowing that

300

Dan had manipulated her actions. The sense of joyous exhilaration she'd anticipated over its telecast was dulled by a sense of having been deceived. And television was so ephemeral—you worked for months on a project and then it was over so quickly.

Her shoulders throbbed from the tension of the drive but she still was not able to relax. Even the knowledge that the resort had been salvaged from financial ruin gave her little satisfaction at the moment.

As the final credits hit the screen, the telephone rang. Ginger missed Dan's name as it rolled across the screen. Hannah followed her into the kitchen to take Chloe's call.

"It's going to open a lot of eyes, Mom! You really did a terrific job."

"Good work, Hannah," her mother said when the phone rang again, right away. "I see by the Weather Channel you're having an old-fashioned blizzard! Wish I could be there to enjoy it with you! Next year, I will be, won't I? Tell Ginger hello for me."

Just before the lights flickered and went off, Hannah heard from Dennis Windsor who said he'd been drinking to her success.

"He said more that wasn't very pleasant," Hannah told Dan afterward, "I'd overstepped my bounds, still needed to learn my lesson. Whatever. We were cut off."

Ginger had set a Coleman lantern on the bar. "Might be a couple days before we get power again. My fingers were crossed all the time your show was on."

"What do we do now?" Leslie asked. He'd told Hannah he was staying with Dan until Christmas, when Lyle and Lynne came back from a Windigo trip through the southwest.

"Now we decide who's going to sleep *where*," Ginger replied. "Unless you guys want to fire up Hal's old Arctic Cat and ski your way back across the lake."

"Uncle Dan?" Leslie's eyes lit up.

"Oh, hush, Leslie," Ginger admonished, "that old snowmobile hasn't been started in so long I don't think it's got a spark left in it. Besides, if you think I'm going to let the two of you head out into this whirlwind and leave Hannah and me all alone, you're crazy as a couple of coots."

"There's a day-bed in Hal's study," Hannah offered.

"I turned on the heater in Aldebaran as soon as I knew you were coming," Ginger added.

Leslie had another idea: he wanted to sleep on the sleeping porch above the Saloon. Hannah said absolutely not.

"You're no fun," he argued, "I've got a mummy bag in Uncle Dan's truck, I've done wilderness camping! If I get cold, I can always come inside and sleep on the floor. Besides, your cot's still on the porch. If I put on a ski mask to cover my face and zip up my mummy bag, I'm good down to twenty below. Tell her, Uncle Dan!"

Dan admitted that Leslie would not freeze to death, so Hannah conceded, albeit reluctantly. Leslie went out to the Blazer with Babe and a flashlight to get his sleeping bag.

"Well, I'm heading over to Aldebaran," Dan said. He grabbed his coat.

Hannah added quickly, "And I'll take Hal's study."

"When are you going to stop calling this place 'Hal's,'" Ginger said, brusquely. "It's yours, has been since he died and now it is more than ever, plain and simple. Why can't you just open up your arms and . . ."

"I don't know anyone who can ruffle Ginger's feathers like you, Hannah," Dan laughed.

Ginger was struggling for the right word.

"Why can't I *embrace* it?" Hannah offered.

"That's why you're the writer and I tend bar," Ginger chuckled. "Even if you didn't want to *embrace* it in the first place, you earned the right to do it now."

"Good to have you back," Dan said with a grin. He zipped up his jacket and extended a hand to Hannah. "Great job. Congratulations."

"I'm glad you approve," Hannah said archly.

They could hear Leslie stomp his boots on the porch. When he entered the Saloon he had snow up to his knees. Babe burst in behind him, covered with a white veil that she shook off, vigorously.

"You guys should see it out there," Leslie said. He dropped his sleeping bag on the floor. "It's snowing so hard I almost couldn't find the Blazer. Hannah, your car's going to be all covered up by morning."

Dan told Leslie, "Sweet dreams, buddy."

"Wait," Hannah said sharply, as Dan began to leave, "We need to talk."

Ginger and Leslie were making their way upstairs with the lantern.

"Follow me over to Aldebaran. I'll light a fire."

Was he kidding? Hannah's face grew warm with mild rage. Sure, a fire would quell her indignation and put her to sleep. How could he treat the memory of the night they spent together so boorishly?

"I didn't bring any boots," she said, as if that excuse would keep him here.

"Use Ginger's. There, by the door. She won't mind."

He was holding out her jacket, so she slid into it without further argument.

"What were you thinking of, coming up here in December without a pair of boots?" Dan's lips were close to her ear, and she shivered. "Did you bring a cap?"

Ginger's old knit cap was shoved down over her head. There was no way she could rest until she'd questioned his "anonymous" funding, so she trudged after him.

Hannah tried to match her steps to his deep tracks as he plowed on ahead with an unopened bottle of wine in one gloved hand, a flashlight in the other. The snow was above her knees, and she had trouble keeping her balance. Babe, struggling to get through by leaping, couldn't keep up, and Hannah could hear the dog panting hard above the echoing wind and snow sifting through the pines.

The steps of Aldebaran were drifted over. Dan had to pull the screen door out through a deep white crescent sculpted against the door.

"I thought I was in good shape!" Hannah apologized, puffing.

Immediately, she pulled off Ginger's cap, kicked off the boots and brushed the snow from her jeans.

"Now I'm worried about finding my way back," she said, wringing her hands to get them warm.

Dan's deep sigh of resignation was answer enough, but he added, "It's not a matter of life and death right now, Hannah. Try and relax, okay?"

She half-expected him to add, "I'm not going to make a pass at you . . ."

Hannah lit an oil lamp, found a corkscrew, and flopped down on the sofa while he started a fire.

"To Mine Games," Dan said a few minutes later as he clinked his juice glass against Hannah's and toasted her success. "I talked to Joe."

"Guess what's bothering me," Hannah inquired, testily. There was more, if she had the nerve to ask. "Why did you do it?"

"You were too proud to let me help you out."

"It wasn't just pride; I was trying to save your reputation."

"My reputation, huh?"

"Dennis said everybody knew you and I were sleeping together. I figured that if I let you help me with the mortgage then all of Antler would be sure that we *were*."

"Sounds like Denny." He grinned. "I don't suppose he meant sleeping together on the floor, though. Really sleeping."

"I wish you'd be serious," Hannah exclaimed. "Don't you see, I feel like I've been duped! I was so excited, thinking somebody believed in me and in what I was doing. . . ."

"Somebody did," he said simply. "But that's not the only reason you're feeling down. What else is it, Hannah?"

She took a deep breath, sipped her wine and finally tried to explain the melancholy that came with the completion of the documentary. The closure of an exhausting project. The settlement with the bank. Chloe's impending marriage.

"I know in my heart I should be encouraged by all the possibilities ahead, but right now all I can see are the hard work and expense of the wedding. And then, a baby! And, my God, my mother moving up here. Of course I'll have to be here, too, if she is—Lily can't be Chloe's responsibility, especially not with a new baby."

"Still don't want to live up here full-time, I guess."

"I don't think so . . ."

She waited, finished her wine, then studied the flickering glow of the flames on his face. He removed his glasses and when he leaned over to place them on a nearby chair, she added, "I want to know about Lynne."

There. A question that had dogged her for months, caused sleepless nights and curbed her fantasies when she wished to let her dreams about him take flight.

"What about Lynne?"

"Are you . . ."

"Am I what?"

He was enjoying this.

"I'm too tired to come up with a snappy rejoinder," she said.

"Lynne and I have been friends for years. She and Lyle opened Forest Temple maybe six, seven years ago. They never were married, by the way—Lynne might have told you they were divorced, but that's for public consumption. They're every bit as committed to one another as they ever have been. You'll have to ask Lynne, if you want to know more. She doesn't conceal her emotions, she's a very loving and generous and natural woman."

"And very beautiful." Hannah couldn't help it, "Willowy."

"There are all kinds of beauty," Dan said. "You're beautiful, too, when you're not being such a bitch-on-wheels."

He traced a finger softly along the edge of her jaw, and she didn't know what to say.

"My turn," he told her, returning to his wine. "What's up with Uncle Wiggily?"

"Uncle Wiggily?" she smiled ruefully. "He's out of the picture. Except—don't laugh—he's quite taken with Lynne."

"She mentioned that," he said soberly. "She says he does a remarkable impersonation of Fidel Castro."

305

"Did she actually say *remarkable?*" Hannah asked, trying not to laugh.

"Remarkable. Or *unusual.* Maybe she said *incredible.* Something like that."

"*Idiotic* is more like it. Poor Lynne," she laughed. "Oh, and by the way . . ."

She told Dan about the endangered clams Tyler planted.

"What some men won't do for love," he teased.

Her mood lightening, now, she poured another glass of wine for each of them, and he threw a chunk of wood on the crackling fire.

She wondered, idly, if there could be any better way to hide out during a blizzard than tucked inside a cozy old log cabin with this man.

"The first day I arrived here I found Uncle Hal's teeth on the nightstand next to his bed. I thought maybe he and Ginger were making love when he had a heart attack, and then afterward she dragged his body back over to his bed and forgot about his dentures. I was really an imbecile, wasn't I?"

Dan nodded. "I never thought you'd stay on. None of us did."

"A real *babe in the woods.*"

"Well . . ."

"So, what did I do to change your mind? There must've been an epiphany or you wouldn't have invested in my documentary."

"I don't know that it was any one thing. Just kind of became accustomed to having you around. Sure, you were a pain in the ass sometimes, but you could be pretty funny, too."

"Not always intentionally," she sighed.

"I didn't want you to leave."

There was a long pause before she admitted, "I heard you tell me that once. You said, 'Don't leave me, Hannah.'"

"That was intended as a subliminal message. You were supposed to think you were dreaming."

"I'm a very light sleeper," she said.

21

Dark December Morning

Babe was growling, a low, rumbling demand. Only on the edge of sleep, Hannah rose on one elbow. Next to her Dan slept soundly. She pulled the blankets up to her chin and nestled back into the spoon of his warmth where his arm had encircled her all night.

While snowy winds buffeted Aldebaran, they sat before the fireplace until the flames quieted to embers. Lamplight smoothed all the dark corners of the cottage with soft shadows. Lazy, relaxed, they shared slow kisses and a comfortable embrace that seemed to melt past and present.

Later they retired to the bedroom that had been Hannah's, where they made love languidly and with exquisite ease because there was no reason to hurry it along; this snowbound night could run into another and another and they were oblivious to time. His touch was gentle, with none of the furtive haste she had learned to anticipate.

Hannah tried to ignore Babe's persistent warning. It was too cold in the cottage to get out of bed. If the dog had to pee she'd have to wait until morning or pee on the floor, tough luck. Hannah snuggled against the curve of Dan's body and he responded by pressing her even closer.

But still, the ominous growl. This was not a signal Babe usually made—then she would nudge Hannah with her cold, wet nose and whimper. This agitation was different. Something was wrong.

Hannah draped a blanket over her shoulders and tiptoed to the front door where Babe crouched. Still-glowing coals in the fireplace revealed the hackles on the dog's back stiffly raised.

"What's the matter, Baby?" Hannah asked gently, listening for the sound of wind swirling around the eaves. But the wind had died down. She shivered in the frigid room.

Ginger's boots were near the door where Hannah had left them hours before. Balancing on one bare foot and then the other, she put them on.

"It's nothing," she reassured Babe and patted the dog's head, "C'mon, let's go back to sleep . . ."

But the dog barked urgently.

Hannah opened the door to the porch.

The fresh snowfall glowed, luminescent, as though lit from beneath with ethereal luster. The overcast sky was creamy. The entire landscape was visible and eerily still.

"What's up?" Dan was at her side, getting dressed.

"I'm not sure . . ."

The muffled hum of a motor from the shore of the lake sent snow swirling into loose clouds. A bright light. Another.

"Snowmobile," Dan said. "What the hell . . ."

Babe charged, heading for the shadowed bulk of the Saloon where a flashlight's beam bobbed near the porch. Then the light moved away from the building, toward the idling snowmobile.

Leslie's voice.

Shouting.

Hannah dropped the blanket, shed Ginger's boots, slipped into her jeans, then yanked the boots on again. By the time she pulled on her jacket, Dan and Babe were halfway to the lodge.

Still unzipped, she plunged through deep drifts.

A moment later she was thrown backward by the blast.

There was no pandemonium afterward, only the crash of breaking glass and the clunk of tumbling logs. Even Babe's barking ceased, and the sound of the snowmobile rushing away was sucked up in the void.

Hannah scrambled to her feet, a scream caught in her throat.

"Dan!" she shouted, "Ginger!"

Babe was at her side immediately, tugging on her sleeve.

"Careful . . ." Dan warned.

The spectral, otherworldly scene revealed the porch of the Saloon: a pile of rubble in front of the building.

"Leslie!" she hollered, stumbling toward the ruined structure, and then heard him answer, "I'm okay . . ."

Babe barked.

Ginger called her name, and Hannah gulped grateful tears. Everyone was alive.

Dan and Hannah reached the remains of the porch—logs had been tossed every which way and the French doors were knocked in, but the force of the blast seemed to have been mostly repelled by the sturdy structure.

Ginger stood beside them and asked, "Who in the hell caused this goddamned ruckus? And where are my overshoes?"

Hannah reached for Ginger. She was shaking uncontrollably

"It's only the porch," Dan reported, inspecting the damage more closely.

"They wanted more than just the porch," Hannah protested, "and Leslie was sleeping out there . . ."

"I saw lights, Uncle Dan," Leslie declared, "but it was just one guy. He tried to get inside so I yelled, 'What do you want? We're closed . . .' And he hollered something about Hannah. So I ran, I mean I hopped . . ."

"He hopped inside and woke me up, didn't even get outa that sleeping bag," Ginger said. She had a quilt pulled over her night-gown. "I grabbed Hal's old galoshes and we got out the back door just in time. Damn fool could've blown us to smithereens and back!"

In the distance, the red flicker of the snowmobile was obscured by a ghostly swirl.

"Hey, it's only three o'clock," Leslie announced. "My watch glows in the dark."

"Well, I'm up for the day!" Ginger declared.

Dan said he was going to use the phone in his truck to call the sheriff. "Go back to the cabin. I'll join you in a few minutes."

The women went back to Aldabaran where Hannah, still trembling, fixed mugs of hot chocolate and gave thanks for the reliable gas stove. Dan returned and said the sheriff wouldn't be able to get through until the snowplows did.

"I called Victor and Eric and Chloe, too," he added. "Where's Leslie?"

"We thought he was with you," Ginger answered. "Don't tell me he went back inside the lodge . . ."

Then they heard a pop and sputter. Again, the same spitting, coughing sound. Dan opened the door—the noise was coming from the shed.

The motor caught, and Leslie emerged riding on Hal's old Arctic Cat. He eased over the drifts to Aldebaran and yelled, "C'mon, Uncle Dan! We can catch that guy!"

"Let's go," Dan said, "Hang on!" He climbed onto the old snowmobile behind Leslie and they headed for the wide expanse of the lake where tracks led off in the distance.

"Hal probably showed the kid how to start it," Ginger mused, watching them disappear into the winter night. "Hal liked to tinker and you know how Leslie always likes to tag along."

About an hour before dawn, the women heard the welcome scrape of the county snowplow before it came into view. A parade of vehicles tagged behind—an ambulance, the sheriff's car, the new fire truck, several pickups and SUVs. Ginger fussed with Aldebaran's percolator and made sure everyone had a hot cup of coffee.

"They set off an explosive device, all right," Sheriff Cooper exclaimed, "but it didn't detonate completely. Looks like the timer might've got screwed up or something."

"Screwed up is right," Ginger told Hannah. "That had to be Denny Windsor."

"Whoever it was wanted to get rid of me once and for all," Hannah replied, still shivering with a mixture of astonishment and dismay.

"All the more reason," Ginger acknowledged. "Denny's reached the end of his rope and he's hanging himself with it."

The fire chief pronounced the lodge structurally safe after a complete inspection. The fieldstone fireplace would need some shoring up but except for that and a few shattered windows, most of the damage occurred to the porch, now a clutter of logs, broken tables, and upended chairs. The old glider jutted out of one corner, a tangled wreck.

"Can't hold a wedding here in a couple weeks, that's for darn sure," Ginger lamented.

Morning sun on the fresh snow created a brilliance so blinding that the lone snowmobile approaching from Sundog was lost in the glare.

"We got him," Leslie shouted, "We got him! He almost froze to death!"

Leslie sputtered the old Arctic Cat to a stop at Aldebaran where Hannah ordered him to go inside the cottage and get warm by the fire. His nose was running and his cheeks were chapped with cold.

"But I can't! I've got to tell the sheriff!"

"Tell us first," Ginger urged, "Real fast."

"Victor met us out on Sundog. We went upriver and found the guy near Sickle Moon. He crashed into the old railroad piling that sticks up there. Everybody knows where it is. You have to stay away from it because the ice doesn't freeze solid there. Anyway, he was halfway in the water and half out. His snowmobile's okay but his leg might be broke."

"Broken," Hannah said, "not broke."

"And maybe one of his arms is broke, even. They're bringing him back here."

"Who was it, for Pete's sake?" Ginger asked, but Leslie rattled on, overexcited.

"Uncle Dan wanted to beat him up even more. Victor had to stop him. You guys should've been there! Hey, here they come . . ."

Two snowmobiles approached from the lake and skidded up the bank where Sheriff Cooper waited. A slumped figure in a silver snowmobile suit was helped to the ambulance.

"Wait! Dan, tell them to wait," Hannah called, struggling through the snow as the doors to the ambulance were being closed.

She had one last message for Dennis Windsor, a few choice words of her own. Come to think of it, a selection of Ginger's spicier epithets would not be terribly out of line.

22
Synchrony

Hannah was wearing Dan's flannel shirt again. She sat on the pier with Babe—a big dog now although still a pup in spirit—and watched the loon chicks ride placidly past on their mother's back. Hard to believe an entire year had gone by since her boating odyssey after Uncle Hal's memorial service.

Babe was shedding a heavy winter undercoat. Hannah brushed the dog until Babe had enough of her grooming, slid into the water slick as a seal and left her covered with fur. Hannah knew she was procrastinating, putting off an inevitable task.

How her life had changed, she reflected, since she drove up to Antler almost a year ago. After much soul-searching she had given up her house in Madison, put her belongings in storage, and moved in with Dan. It was getting late now and he would be looking for her.

She had to admit that her involvement in the mining controversy had been personally satisfying: the mine's progress had been halted. Axel Graves was not pleased with criminal charges Hannah filed for prospecting on private property without permission. Ingold was unhappy with Dennis Windsor's subterfuge; Windsor's law license had been suspended and he awaited a criminal trial.

No one assumed Ingold's hiatus would last forever and other mining companies remained active threats in northern Wisconsin. But Hannah's documentary had given new life to environmental issues in the state and reawakened interest in preservation of wilderness resources nationwide. She was now researching a documentary proposal for *Frontline* on the effect of gambling casinos on Indian tribes.

She had seen star flowers blossoming in the woods this afternoon, wild calla lilies, yellow violets, and bunch berries. Fishing season would open in a couple days and the mailbox overflowed with requests for cottages and rooms.

After their wedding at Lofty Pines, Eric and Chloe spent January through March directing repairs to the lodge. A new porch was constructed and the logs were stained to match the aged patina of the original. The Saloon, closed since the blast, had been restored to its original glory along with the adjacent dining room and fieldstone fireplace. Ginger and Dan agreed that Hal would have been pleased with the renovations. Future plans included a sandy swimming beach and Starlake Inn, designed by Eric and built by local craftsman, that would be set back from the lake with a wide view of the Celestial Chain. The resort, still welcoming fishermen, would become a four-season retreat offering educational tours, workshops, and seminars on environmental issues. Chloe told friends, "Our dining room will feature regional entrees with wild rice, cranberries, cherries, maple syrup, and artisanal cheeses and wines."

There was a baby girl upstairs in the lodge, now: Hannah's granddaughter, Miriam Larkin, was born in April. She slept in a nursery where Hal's bedroom used to be.

George Windsor died during the winter, never recovering from his second stroke.

Ginger and Lily bought a small home together on Lake Sickle Moon and because it was Friday, Hannah knew the women would soon be heading out for the Friday night fish fry at the Sportsman's Club.

She climbed into the boat at her side and Babe followed, sitting in the bow. Hannah wanted to row for a while on the silky surface and soak up the silence.

Birch trees and maples were budding. A soft haze of green rose over the forest behind the lodge. Nature was renewing itself and Hannah was well aware of what she must do to achieve the final step in her own renewal

Babe was silent as Hannah rowed, and only the sound of the oars in the water, the squeak of the oarlocks, disturbed the solitude. When they reached the place near where the mine would have stood, Hannah finally saw a bear. A female black bear with two cubs stood on the bank and gazed solemnly back at them.

Hannah turned the boat around and rowed back into the middle of Star Lake. There she and Babe remained until the ripples folded out and quieted and tranquility grew as darkness fell. The night was like velvet, with no refracted glow to interfere with the dazzling stars.

"I will name a star after you as you asked, Uncle Hal," Hannah promised. "The North Star, the one I can always find without any trouble, right there at the end of the Little Dipper's handle. *Polaris.* The star that never seems to move, the guiding star, the dependable one."

Hal's ashes were in the small box at her feet.

"Thank you, Uncle Hal, for guiding me here."

Starlight reflected in the water where Hannah scattered his ashes.

Phosphorous in the bones turned the lake white all around her and Babe until it glowed like the Milky Way.

Curt Leviant
Ladies and Gentlemen, The Original Music of the Hebrew Alphabet *and*
    Weekend in Mustara: *Two Novellas*

David Milofsky
A Friend of Kissinger: A Novel

Lesléa Newman
A Letter to Harvey Milk: Short Stories

Ladette Randolph
This Is Not the Tropics: Stories

Sara Rath
The Star Lake Saloon and Housekeeping Cottages: A Novel

Mordecai Roshwald
Level 7

Lewis Weinstein
The Heretic: A Novel